Wild West Exodus
The Jesse James Archives

Abundant Riches

Craig Gallant

Zmok Books

To my wife, Karen, without whom none of this would have been possible.

Zmok Books is an imprint of Winged Hussar Publishing, LLC
1525 Hulse Road Unit 1
Point Pleasant, NJ 08742

www.WingedHussarPublishing.com
Twitter: WingHusPubLLC

www.Wildwestexodus.com

Cover by Michael Nigro

ISBN: 978-0-9889532-9-1
EPCN: 2014902352

I would again like to thank Romeo and everyone at Outlaw Miniatures for giving me this opportunity; Vincent and Brandon from Winged Hussar for making this book as pretty as it can be; Pete, for his yeoman's work as alpha reader; Karen and Rhys for putting up with my often confusing and always grueling work schedule; and Russ and Raef for forcing me to jump into the podcasting pond. And finally, all of the listeners of The D6 Generation, without whom most of these other people would not even know who I am - CG

Something Wicked is Coming

Blood drenches the sands of the Wild West as the promise of a new age dies, screaming its last breathe into an uncaring night. An ancient evil has arisen in the western territories, calling countless people with a siren song of technology and promises of power and glory the likes of which the world has never known. Forces move into the deserts, some answering the call, others desperate to destroy the evil before it can end all life on Earth.

Legions of reanimated dead rise to serve the greatest scientific minds of the age, while the native tribes of the plains, now united in desperate self-defense, conjure the powers of the Great Spirit to twist their very flesh into ferocious combat forms to match the terrible new technologies. The armies of the victorious Union rumble into these territories heedless of the destruction they may cause in pursuit of their own purposes, while the legendary outlaws of the old west, now armed with stolen weapons and equipment of their own, seek to carve their names into the tortured flesh of the age.Amidst all this conflict, the long-suffering Lawmen, outgunned and undermanned, stand alone, fighting to protect the innocent men and women caught in the middle . . . or so it appears.

Within these pages you will find information on wild skirmishes and desperate battles in this alternative Wild West world, now ravaged with futuristic weapons and technology. Choose the methodical Enlightened, the savage Warrior Nation, the brutal Union, the deceitful Outlaws, or the enigmatic Lawmen, and lead them into the Wild West to earn your glory.

As you struggle across the deserts and mountains, through the forests and cities of the wildest frontier in history, a hidden power will whisper in your ear at every move. Will your spirit be strong enough to prevail, or will the insidious forces of the Dark Council eventually bend you to their will? Be prepared, for truly, something wicked is coming!

Learn more about the world of the Jesse James Chronicles at:

www.wildwestexodus.com

Prologue

Shadows stretched over the northern plains as the sun sank into the west. Gently rolling hills swept away to the south, fading to a dull brown in the distance. Lush grass and full trees dominated this border region; a last bastion of quiet, serene greenery. As far as the eye could see, all was at peace.

As darkness settled in, a spray of sparkling lights sprang up across the plains, echoing the stars appearing overhead. Guttering campfires stretched for nearly a mile in every direction. Iron Hawk settled into the grass and eased one hand, palm flat, behind him. Unseen in the growing shadows, a band of Warrior Nation scouts lowered themselves to the ground.

The large force of easterners had moved into Warrior Nation territory several days ago. Armed, they rode a mismatched variety of loud, loathsome vehicles that defiled the land with their foul vapors. Dispatched by the united chiefs of the Warrior Nation, Iron Hawk had stalked into the prairie with his most experienced fighters, shadowing these outsiders as a larger war party followed along behind. The invaders spread across the plains in disorderly camps each night, easy to spot and track. When Iron Hawk's scouts caught up to them, they were settled around a shallow dale, many camping in a series of limestone caves beneath the hills.

There was no real pattern to the mongrel exodus. They had violated the territory of the People, fleeing from the south east. Moving at a slow crawl, they had advanced across the plains in an arch that brought them gradually back around toward the south. Behind them they left a foul trail of discarded equipment, empty containers, and shallow graves.

Iron Hawk touched the medallion at his neck. The stylized bird of prey had been painstakingly carved from a plate of Union armor; its chain had once held a plain gold band and had been snapped from the neck of the armor's previous owner. The rough feel of the iron on his fingers always served to remind the war leader of the new world that had risen up to overtake his people. The men spread across the plains ahead had violated an immutable law of that new world. He had been sent to see that they were punished.

Iron Hawk looked back into the lengthening shadows. He could just make out the shapes of his scouting party crouching in the darkness. He nodded to himself and then made a quick series of gestures. Each warrior raised two fingers in silent acknowledgment and settled deeper into the grass. The sun was nearly gone now, the western sky washed with warm, muted colors that did little to illuminate the dell below.

The war leader lowered his head and began a low, sonorous chant. He felt the power of the Great Spirit rising from the earth, answering his call. Although he had not yet mastered the ability to surrender his body to the shapes of his spirit guides, he had inherited vast reserves of power from his father, the renowned medicine man, White Tree. His father and an entire scouting party had disappeared over a year ago, and Iron Hawk knew in his soul that he would never see him again. He had been eager, ever since, for every opportunity for vengeance.

The shaman stood as the colors and shadows around him began to swirl together, answering his call. Like a massive, impenetrable cloak, the powers of the Earth rose up to conceal him from the eyes of his enemies. He looked back to his warriors, each seeing with clear eyes through the illusion, and nodded once. With calm, measured steps he strode toward the haphazard encampment of his enemies.

The sentries posted by the invaders were nothing to fear. The scent of their unwashed bodies carried for hundreds of paces downwind, further tainted with the acrid trace of tobacco and the sour smell of alcohol. The inescapable stench of their unnatural energy hung over everything. Iron Hawk was certain that, even without the power of the Great Spirit, he could have walked through the camp unnoticed.

The shaman paced among the enemy, his dark gaze passing unseen over the invaders. These poor apparitions radiated wary, brutalized exhaustion. They clung to their ragged belongings as if the horrible conditions of the encampment were a paradise they feared could be stripped away at any moment. The warrior snorted softly in contempt.

Even shadowing the enormous mob for days, he was not fully prepared him for the number of dispossessed. There were thousands, most dressed in tattered rags, their feet bare; their bodies shrunken by starvation. As darkness descended, most of the men were lying down upon the grass without any sense of order, merely falling asleep where they had come to rest. Here or there the massive shadows of vehicles loomed over him, most unarmed and unarmored; rusting wrecks, their twinkling crimson lights dim and dying. Men stood atop some, watching everyone who passed with a suspicious glare, ill-kept weapons clutched in shaking hands.

Moving through the camp, he caught bits and pieces of conversation in their harsh, alien tongue. They crouched in fear; pathetic, flickering fires all the comfort they could claim. Most were silent. Those that spoke did so in dull, stunned tones. Iron Hawk was passingly familiar with the language of his foes, and the conversations all seemed to revolve around a deep sense of betrayal and disappointment.

A sense of disbelief made them numb to their current state and to the world around them. It was as if the changes that had wracked the world for a generation had finally, in their darkest moment, been made manifest. Their reality consisted of their immediate, pathetic surroundings; huddled around ramshackle vehicles in the middle of hostile territory, watching each man that passed as if the whole, shifting world were their enemy.

Iron Hawk shook his head as he passed among them. The trucks likely contained what food and supplies that remained to these outcasts, and yet he was not surprised to see that no unified organization had been made for their defense. Each mob acted on its own, huddled around a decrepit vehicle, or glaring jealously at the vehicles of others. It became more and more apparent that this was not a single army, or even a single united mob. It was, rather, countless smaller bodies of tired, frightened wretches determined to hold their own against the wider world. There was no unity or trust here among his enemies.

Rather than take heart from their obvious weakness, he found it sad.

Iron Hawk moved through the camp, making his way toward the sunken valley at its center. As he came upon the lip of the depression, he wrapped the concealing shadows more closely around himself, peering down into the dell. A series of caves were visible around the bottom of the small valley. Some were no larger than a rabbit warren, but others could hold entire parties of the enemy. More of the defiling vehicles were parked all along the floor of the dell. These seemed to be in better repair and included several heavily armored monsters bristling with weaponry. Scattered among the larger machines were over a hundred of the smaller, horse-sized contraptions capable of carrying men gliding over the ground like low-flying birds.

There was more organization here than with the rest of the rabble above: the leaders of this ragtag band must be camped within. He wanted to get as close as he could, to learn more about these men, before unleashing the full might of the Warrior Nation with the rising sun. His chest reverberated with a low hum, and the shadows grew even darker around him. A ring of more alert sentries watched the valley, but hidden by the power of the Great Spirit, he stalked right through them.

As Iron Hawk moved further into the hollow, he saw that tattered sheets of rough fabric had been hung across the mouths of the largest caves. Dancing firelight or the muted, crimson-edged illumination of their foul lanterns flickered weakly around the edges. One of the curtains sheltering a cave nearby was suddenly pulled back. Light washed out into the clearing as a man emerged, a rifle held in one hand. With his free hand he pulled the cloth shut behind him, killing the wash of light.

The shaman stopped, trusting to his spectral cloak, and the man walked past, oblivious. He found himself wondering at the man's story. Iron Hawk shrugged. It mattered little. Soon enough, they would all be dead. He eased his way closer to the cave mouth and settled in the shadows of a rocky fracture, craning his head toward the opening.

"—left the place standin' at all!" An angry voice muttered from the cave.

"Well, I blame that fast trick he's been ridin' with since the breakout; you want to know what I think. Ain't no way she was a normal nurse, no how." Another voice, bitter but resigned. Both spoke in soft, conspiratorial tones.

"Loveless? She's a bitch Union spy an' you can take that to the bank." The first voice, speaking again, quavered with barely-suppressed emotion. "How else would she have gotten out of there alive? That burg was a nest of whores' sons, and deserved to be burned out after everythin' they done! Weren't gonna be nothin' but pure justice, plain an' simple!"

"Henderson had it right, an' that's true enough." A third voice now, stoking the fires of resentment in the other two. There was an edge to this one that set Iron Hawk's skin crawling. "Burn a place like that to the ground, you send a message that the damned blue-bellies'll get loud an' clear!"

"Shut yer, mouth!" The second voice spoke. "You want 'im to gut us an' leave us behind fer the savages to pick over? Jesse done made up his mind, and it's over. That woman might o' got in his head, might o' turned him around, but that don't matter none now. We been duckin' and runnin' through Injun territory like we was the ones that got whooped, an' that's Gospel." Someone spat. "But Jesse hears you bad mouthin' that Rebel angel or second guessin' his call? We're gonna be staked out fer the scorpions faster'n you can say Billy Yank."

"Ain't no scorpions out there, Galen." The first voice again. "Not in all that grass."

Iron Hawk heard the sharp rip of another spit, then a grunt. "Then snakes, 'r gophers, 'r whatever in the name o' Hades it is up here eats folks that're staked out – It don't' matter none, Colton, fer the sake 'o the Lord! Just hobble yer lip, will ya?"

"I was just sayin'," that angry voice, Colton, again. "We shoulda burnt down that town when we had the chance. Hell. We'd a been better off stayin' in Robbers Roosts for all the boodle we're comin' outta this little adventure with."

Iron Hawk eased away from the cave and scanned the bottom of the dell. There were others, and he could hear the low mutterings of other conversations. Most of the caverns connected farther back beneath the hills. He doubted that the men hiding within them had taken the time to investigate, however. They probably thought they were safe talking about each other as long as they were huddled within different mouths. The warrior smirked. If this Jesse was the bad medicine these cowards were making him out to be, he hoped he was listening. Watching easterners kill each other was always good sport.

He spotted a larger cavern nearby, several strips of cloth obscuring the light within. Iron Hawk slid down next to the opening and settled in to listen once again.

"—would have wanted someone to come after me, that's for sure." This voice carried no anger or resentment. It was calm and relaxed; louder than the other voices. There was no fear of being overheard here. Iron Hawk was sure that would change before long.

"Nah, I get it. And if my brother was being held by those rat bastards, I would have gone in all guns a-blazin' too." There was a crunch and hiss as someone stirred a large fire. When this voice continued, it was pitched lower than before. "Just not sure I would have wanted to be dragged in myself, is all. We could have stayed back with General Mosby and been none the worse for wear. We lost a lot of good men goin' in there."

The first voice muttered grudging agreement. "We did. But Frank James seems like a good man. Captain Ingram says Jesse needs him, if we're gonna be able to turn any of this around."

"He seems like a good man, right enough." Another voice spoke. "But is he better than any of the men who fell fetching him out? Better than Shady Joe, or Johnny Fu, or any of the other guys we lost?"

"You best keep words like that to yourself, Cord." All of the voices around the fire quieted down. "Don't you be in any doubt: Frank's more important to him than any of us he picked up along the way. You know he's been on the shoot since long before Captain Ingram offered up our services. Only safe place to be when he's like that, seems to me, is behind him or beside him, and that's a fact."

"I'm just sayin'," continued Cord in a softer voice. "Something to keep in mind, as touching on the man's loyalties, is all."

"And your loyalties wouldn't lie with your own brother?" This voice was edged with contempt.

"I ain't got a brother." There was a sullen tone to the second voice now. "And I'm not sure I would have traded a bunch of good men for him if I did."

"Well, if he was *your* brother, he wouldn't have been worth trading good men for in the first place." The contemptuous voice deepened. "If you're so concerned, go back to Cali. It's just about three thousand miles that way, is all. Now shut your trap. I'm trying to enjoy the fire."

Iron Hawk ignored the muttered response as he pivoted on his heel to survey the bowl around him. The man with the rifle had not yet returned. Whether he was heading out to water the grass or to relieve a sentry, someone would be coming back toward the caves soon. He passed several of the larger vehicles as he moved toward another cave. He summoned the Great Spirit's energy, his hands warm as the familiar sensation of ghostly knife handles filled them. But he held the burning fire in check, the radiance of the spirit power the merest aquamarine lightning skittering around his fists and deep within his eyes.

A man surged out of the cave he was approaching, and Iron Hawk lurched back into the deepest shadows, hiding behind an armored brute on metal wheels. The man was careless with the hanging fabric and left it askew as he stomped into the central clearing.

"I don't wanna talk about it no more!" The man gestured behind him, one hand filled with a vicious-looking fighting knife. It was a comment that made no sense to Iron Hawk until another man rushed out into the night after him.

The second man's voice was hushed but urgent as he grabbed the first's arm. "Well, you gotta talk about it some more. He was our brother!"

Iron Hawk looked more closely. He could just make out the family resemblance between the two men in the light from the cavern. The first man spun around to confront his older brother, knife glittering as he spread his hands wide in a dismissive gesture.

The older man ignored the gesture. "He weren't our brother when Jesse did for him. They changed 'im in that Union camp, an' that thing in that building? That weren't Johnny." There was pleading in the man's eyes, and Iron Hawk could tell that it did not sit easily there. "C'mon, Bobbie. I heard what both you and Jesse said. It weren't John. John was gone."

The younger man shook his head, the knife quivering. "An' Jesse couldn't o' saved 'im? He saved Frank, though, din't he. An' that woman from KC." It was a statement, not a question, and the older man shrank from it.

"Bobbie, there weren't none of John left to rescue, you told me yourself. He was like one o' Carpathian's monsters, only worse! Ya'll din't have no choice!"

The younger man, Bobbie, grabbed the other by the shoulder. "Cole, he was our brother, an' we left 'im to die in a hole like an animal, put down by Jesse *damned* James!"

Iron Hawk did not hear the response, whatever it might have been. As soon as he heard that name his heart surged in his chest and he lurched backward, fetching up against the iron tire.

Jesse James? The man was known by all the Warrior Nation as an avatar of the darkest powers that had come to grip the land. Those unnatural arms of his, monstrous creations of the vile outsider, marked him as a demon of the first order.

If this band was running at the command of Jesse James, then a tribute truly worth of White Tree was near at hand. In the morning, the Warrior Nation would claim a major victory against the darkness and remove the blight of this infamous monster from the sun's sight.

Iron Hawk rose and moved back toward the gently-sloping wall of the vale. When he turned, however, the man with the rifle was there.

"Hey, who—" The sentry tried to bring the weapon up across his body to defend himself. He took in a lungful of cool night air, preparing to sound the alarm.

The shaman did not hesitate. His eyes flared with a burning hatred. His empty hand floated up and past the startled sentry's face, sliding around his jaw and head, grabbing a filthy hank of hair at the base of the man's neck. The white man's eyes went wide.

Iron Hawk pulled with all his might as he brought the other hand, a sliver of burning azure shadow appearing in a reversed, knife-fighter's hold, up and across. The phantom blade dripped with blue flame as the warrior's eyes ignited in an answering surge of power.

The outlaw twisted around, his head yanked in a disorienting spin. He clutched the rifle more tightly to his chest, helpless. As the man's face came back around, pulled by the native warrior's off hand, the burning blade slid across his throat, opening his veins and spraying a fan of burgundy into the grass at their feet. The blue flames flickered into darkness, reflecting once in the depths of the dying man's eyes as he stared, disbelieving, into the face of his killer.

Iron Hawk lowered the body to the grass and glanced around to be sure the scuffle had not been heard. There were no shouts of alarm, only the muffled voices of the two men still arguing over their brother's fate.

With a grim smile, Iron Hawk sneered down at the quivering body. The first blow in retribution for his father's death had been dealt, and with the rising sun, countless more would follow. His father's spirit would rise upon their cries of pain and despair, with the howls of one truly worthy of such sacrifice the last and loudest of all. He made his way casually back up the slope. The other war leaders needed to know who led this tattered army of derelicts.

It was a new world, with new laws and new punishments. And Jesse James, the man whose very body defied the Great Spirit, the wretch who symbolized everything the Warrior Nation fought against, must die.

Chapter 1

Jesse James looked into the depths of the fire and let his mind wander. The landscape that stretched out before his mind's eye was bleak and empty. Nearby, his brother Frank lay curled beneath a heavy blanket. His brother was in rough shape after his ordeal in the prison camp near Andersonville. He was alive though, and he was free. Jesse's face twisted into a vague snarl. For, although he had succeeded in breaking Frank out of Camp Lincoln, nothing much had gone according to plan since then.

Loading up the enormous ore-haulers with the quickest of the prisoners, they had struck north, deeper into Union territory, just as he had planned. Charging up behind them had been an army of prisoners who had not made it onto the massive wagons, but had stolen transportation from the town of Andersonville itself. Jesse knew that once the prisoners had passed through, there could not have been a hand cart left behind. The best he could tell, nearly half of the ten thousand prisoners had joined them as they all fled north and west, visions of a glorious free society alight in their minds.

But the ore-haulers were energy hogs, they sucked down the RJ at a prodigious rate; and most of the wagons freed from Andersonville were rusted out rattle-traps. They had been shedding dead vehicles behind them like a Union cur sheds fleas. The enormous wagons from the Union train, traveling cross-country, had been so slow that only the weakest or worst injured prisoners had been unable to keep up, even after they had been reduced to walking along beside the towering behemoths.

The Union had wasted no time in chasing after the pathetic band, either. Outriders had begun to harry the ragged tail of their scattered column only days out of Camp Lincoln. They lost men every day, traveling under both sun and moon to maintain as much distance as they could from the main force of their pursuers. What food they had taken with them quickly ran low. Their fuel began to run out. First one ore-hauler had to be abandoned, then another; what fuel remained was divvied up among the other vehicles.

As each day ground them down and pushed them onward, Jesse's glorious dreams faded like a washed out photograph. More and more of the freed prisoners were vanishing, losing themselves in the countryside, their faith in Jesse's vision failing. He held no anger toward the men who left, having felt the urge more than once himself as they continued on their way. He would be damned if he was going to let the Union taint this victory like they had soiled so much in his life already.

They had been forced to abandon the last ore-hauler on the banks of the Mississippi. None of them could figure out how to ferry the huge wagons across the mighty river. That had been a blessing in disguise, really, as their company had been able to pick up speed almost immediately. Those who could not keep up were encouraged to scatter and hope for the best.

The Union had been preparing to meet the escaping column in the borderlands leading into the Contested Territory. Jesse knew that, and so, at the last minute, under cover of darkness, he had forced his group to turn directly north, heading straight up into the plains: Warrior Nation lands. It had worked, and it had been days now since any Union forces had been sighted.

Now, Jesse just had to hope he could stay away from the savages long enough to loop back down south into the Contested Territories, and home. His stomach was an aching void, and he knew the sorry souls following him could only feel worse. There might even be a chance to think about establishing that town that had haunted his dreams immediately after the prison break, if God was kind.

If God was not kind, they would all end up scalped, or worse, before they ever saw civilization again.

He reached out with one metal arm and stirred the dying embers of the fire, breathing yellow life into the sullen crimson glow within the charred pile of wood. If ever there was a time to strike out on his own, to make his impression in the world, this was it. The Union was still wrapped up in the east, most of its strength spent against the Warrior Nation. But those creatures of that mad doctor from Camp Lincoln would still be out there, and they seemed like they could well be more than a match for

Carpathian and his disgusting menagerie. If he could only bring President Lee around, breathe some life into the old coward, there might be hope for the Confederate Rebellion yet.

Camp Lincoln. His lip curled with disgust as he settled back on his haunches. The man had been twenty years in his grave, and still the very thought of the vile monster filled Jesse's mouth with acid. No one man had every surpassed Emperor Lincoln as the symbol of everything that was wrong and evil and despicable about the Union, and even death had not unseated him in this regard.

Jesse looked across the fire to where Lucinda Loveless sat, legs curled beneath her. She was wearing mismatched men's clothing in place of the tattered nurse's uniform that she had been left with after her ordeal in the foul camp laboratory. The ragged clothing served to enhance her beauty, somehow, rather than diminish it. Every time he looked at her like this, however, his mind threw the memory of a green-eyed dancehall girl back at him. Misty's red, weeping eyes stared accusingly down through the intervening months, causing him to look away from Lucinda with a guilty jerk of his head.

In front of her, on a soft white cloth, were all of the parts to her two over-sized derringers. The RJ-1027 power packs had been removed while she cleaned and serviced the weapons, sitting off to the side and pulsing like tiny ruby hearts. Nothing could have differentiated Lucy more from any other woman than the calm, contented look on her sweet face as she took care of her lethal weapons. The woman's flawless features were at peace as she reassembled one of the pistols, unaware of Jesse's gaze.

He shook his head. What was he doing, mooning over this woman? He knew now that she was a servant of the Union. He knew she had lied to him, allowed him to believe things that were not true. But for the first time in his life, such things did not seem to matter. And if they did not matter, then why bother the ghost of an abandoned dancing girl? The thought of leaving Lucy behind had never crossed his mind. Besides, she had left with him, right? How could she carry one shred of loyalty for the Union after what they had all seen at Camp Lincoln? After what that monster, Tumblety, had very nearly done to her?

Jesse knew that no one in the Union army cared a whit for Lucinda. She was a pawn to be moved around the board and sacrificed at the proper moment. Yet, somehow he knew, even now, that a part of her still clung to her loyalty to the Union. In a way, that loyalty was even attractive. But it was going to cause them trouble if things did not shake out the way he hoped.

"Sir, a group of freed prisoners is outside. They want to speak to you about the food." The voice was hoarse and soft. Jesse had to shake off his thoughts and drag his eyes up to the stoop-shouldered man standing over him.

"What?"

The man stood up a little straighter and forged onward despite the vague animosity in the outlaw chief's tone. "There's a group of prisoners asking to see you."

Jesse's eyes narrowed. He did not know him, but the man was obviously one of the less-damaged prisoners they had pulled from the ruins of Camp Lincoln. As they had journeyed north, he had paid less and less attention to the ragged mob that trailed along behind him. He knew that men such as this, healthier and stronger than their fellows, had risen to lead small groups of fellow escapees. They were starting to act like savage tribes, each man ruling his shabby little empire like an Injun chief.

Many of the men from the prison had been near dead of starvation, and Jesse honestly had no idea where they were getting whatever food they did have. Things were desperate for everyone, and he knew that every day saw several pass away. Those that left friends or kin behind were covered with a loose layer of earth. The friendless and the weak were left sprawled where they fell. Each day more and more were left where they dropped.

What did this man, or his little gang, want from him? Jesse surged to his feet and toward the cave mouth. Lucinda looked up from her work with hooded eyes, but schooled her features to a calm passivity and looked back down. Frank, under his blankets, snorted and sat up, glaring blearily around. By that time, Jesse was gone.

The floor of his little valley was crowded with vehicles. The sun was just rising in the east, the sky stippled with the first rays of dawn. Standing near one of the Union Rolling Thunder assault wagons was a ragged group of men struggling to maintain eye contact with the outlaw leader. Jesse felt his old anger rising. He always hated men who could not look him in the eye.

"What d'you lot want?" He snapped, sneering as he watched them cringe.

One of the men, crushing a soft gray cap in his hands, stepped forward. "Mr. James, sir, we was just hopin' . . . well, there's folks starvin' up yonder, and—"
Jesse stopped the speech with one raised metal hand. "You think we ain't all hankerin' after somethin' we can cram down our gullets?"

The man pulled up short, still struggling to maintain eye contact. "Well, sir, we followed you out of the prison, an' we thought—"

"You thought I was goin' to hold yer hands an' lead you to the Promised Land, did you?" The contempt in his voice was like a lash, snapping down on the shoulders of the cringing men before him.

"Well, you said we were gonna be gettin' a fresh start." Now even their leader was looking at the dirt. "But we're starvin'—"

Jesse stomped toward the man, taking his tattered lapels in both hard, metallic hands. "I ain't your momma, coffee boiler! It ain't my lookout to keep you and yours fed and clothed." He pushed the man back into his friends and a sullen anger kindled in their dull eyes. Jesse could not have cared less.

"Didn't we just lick the Union for ya'll at Camp Lincoln?" He demanded. The men nodded slowly.

"Did we free every last mother's son trapped inside?" His teeth ground together between each word. The resentment in the former prisoners' eyes started to give way to fear. They nodded silently.

"An' now, just when we're on the verge o' somethin' great here, you lot are whinin' about food!" Jesse's mechanical hand lashed down to his holster and he drew one of his sleek, custom-made Hyper-velocity pistols. He leveled it at the spokesman of the scruffy crew.

"Say, what if I shoot you, an' let the rest o' them animals eat yer carcass?"

A thin flap over another nearby cave was torn aside by a strong-looking young man, his sharp, rodent-like face twisted with anger. The man lashed out with a long pistol, gesturing toward the huddled prisoners. "You lot back off!" He stepped in front of Jesse, empty hand splayed out before him as if the cowed men had been an angry mob ready to surge. "Ain't you got no sense? We gotta get back down outta the grasslands to get food, you idjits! An' it ain't Jesse's job ta feed ya!"

"We're starvin'!" One of the men in the back of the group barked. The newcomer laughed.

"Damn straight yer starvin', you dumb knuck! You're too stupid to live! There's food up yonder, ya'll were just too slow to grab it! An' now you want Jesse to step in and keep the weakest fed? Why for? What good you gonna be when time comes for gun play?"

The disdain in the man's voice was even harsher than Jesse's. The prisoners cringed before him, their hands half raised as if fearing a beating. Another man in a trim mustache stepped out of the cave. He bore a close resemblance to the first, and moved toward him, his own hand raised.

"Robert, settle down. They're just hungry, is all." He made a soft gesture, his face relaxed, his eyes pleading. "There ain't no need to draw on 'em."

Jesse slid his own weapon back into its holster and nodded, taking a deep breath of the cool morning air. He had known his patience was wearing thin, but to lose his cool like this in front of the men who had followed him out of hell, that was no way for a leader to behave. "No, Robert, Charlie's right. We ain't got nothin' to feed these bummers, but we don't need to get all out of sorts our own selves neither."

The newcomer nodded. "Just send 'em back up to the rest. They'll stand or fall on their own, up there."
Robert looked at his brother as he holstered his pistol. "I might be a hothead, Charlie, but that's cold."

His brother shrugged, and Jesse nodded. The outlaw chief hooked one metal thumb behind his gun belt. "True all the same, though. We ain't runnin' no charity kitchen." He turned back to the huddled men. "You lot, you either gotta get yer own food, or make your peace. We ain't got space fer shirkers no more. Until we get back down south, it's every man for hisself. There's food up yonder with the others. You want it? You take it."

The men muttered among themselves for a moment, hope dying in their eyes. As Jesse and the two brothers continued to stare at them in silence, the men began to back away. Some shook their heads, some muttered under their breaths. Jesse noted that some of them had tightened their hands into fists; preparing for the confrontation they knew must come if they were going to eat.

As the small clump of prisoners moved up the slope, Jesse turned to the two men and smiled. "Well, boys, you sure do know how to make an entrance."

"Yeah," the younger man stood up straighter with a smile. "We're reg'lar dancehall swells."

Jesse's eyes darkened for a moment before returning a shadow of the younger man's smile and patting him on the back. "You sure are. Can't wait to see your name up in lights, Robert." He turned to the older brother. The man's face pensive. "You care to jump onto the boards with your brother, Charlie? The two of you could put on a show, call yourselves the Ford Brothers?"

Charlie shook his head. "That's always been more Robert's inclination. I'm more in the way of just wantin' folks to leave me alone." Even now, he seemed uneasy.

Jesse smiled grimly at that, even though he was not entirely sure the elder brother was joking.

"Seriously, Jesse," Robert Ford hooked his thumbs behind his gun belt and rocked back on his heels.

"If any good's to come from all of this, we're gonna need to keep the hale folks healthy."

"We're behind you one hun'erd percent, Jesse, but Robert's right. Even if we had the food to feed those folks, they ain't no real army."

A strong contralto voice emerged from one of the larger cave and Lucinda stepped into the brightening day.

"You won't have any army, soon, if you tell them to fight each other over the food that's left."

Jesse looked a little sheepish and raised both hands to ward off further criticism. "Now, Lucy, you know how things sit! Those folks ran out of Andersonville with us, an' that was all well an' good. An' we outpaced the Union boys sent to chase after us, an' that was swell. But we only got so much food, an' only a few of the prisoners were smart enough to grab what they could."

He tilted his head and raised one hand higher as she started to speak, hands balled on hips. "I know this ain't the best, but it's all we can do fer now. I need my men in fightin' trim, an' that ain't negotiable. We don't know when we're next gonna have a fight, an' we gotta be ready. We're in Warrior Nation territory, an' last time I was here, they weren't none too friendly. We gotta turn around soon. There'll be more food south. Until then, though, we only got what we got, an' we gotta be smart with that."

"Men are dying every day." Her voice was flat, her eyes bleak. "Every day we spend up here, more of them die."

Jesse nodded. "An' that's a shame. It really is. But we're headin' down again, and when we get there, there'll be more food for them that hung on."

Lucy shook her head, her full lips pursed in frustration. "Never mind. I'm going to go up and see what I can do. Cole and his brothers are ready for you inside with that Confederate officer and the odd stick in black, the one from the Butcher of Lawrence?"

Jesse shook his head. "I wish you wouldn't call Colonel Quantrill that, Lucy. An' Henderson is a good man. He's been a big help. Without him, we wouldn't a gotten into Camp Lincoln." Jesse softened his voice, his eyes asking her for patience. "We wouldn't a gotten you an' Frank out without him."

She shook her head again, however, and moved to follow the prisoners. "The man's a butcher, like his boss. Nevertheless, they're waiting for you."

Jesse watched Lucinda walk up the hill and out into the wider camp. "Boys, that woman drives me to madness on a daily basis."

The Fords both nodded but said nothing. Jesse stared up to where she had disappeared over the rise, and then shook his head. "Well, fellas, we gotta figure our next move." He led them back into the cave.

*****

Cole Younger lounged beside a small camp table he had set up. A map sat there, weighed down at the corners by several power cartridges and a small knife. It showed the region that was coming to be known as the Contested Territories, where Carpathian, the Warrior Nation, and the Union continued to clash, turning the land into a tortured, poisoned wasteland.

Cole stood on the other side of the table, his arms folded. To either side of him were his surviving brothers, Bob and Jim. Bob, of course, had one of his huge fighting knives held negligently in one hand, a whetstone in the other. Near them stood Captain Ingram, his cavalry hat spinning slowly atop one long finger. Standing across from them with his legs spread, his hands clasped behind his back, was the slouched figure of Allen Henderson, former adjutant of Jesse and Frank's old commander during the War of Northern Aggression, William Quantrill.

Henderson looked up as Jesse entered with the Ford brothers flanking him. The gaunt figure nodded quickly, shards of reflected fire glinting in his thick spectacles, as he tapped the map with one long finger.

"As I've been saying, we need to strike while we have the force and the Union's on their back foot, Jesse." His voice was cold, his eyes indifferent.

Jesse looked down at the map. Henderson was tapping the region between the Union and the Contested Territories. The outlaw chief could just read the names of several towns straddling the border. He shook his head.

"Hitting those towns don't make much sense. They might not be Confederate sympathizers, but that sure ain't Union territory, neither. Those folks're just tryin' to make a livin'. You want to hit some juicy towns, we gotta move further east, past the Big River." He pulled at his chin with one metal hand. "But I ain't sure we wanna spend this little army here hittin' one-horse towns. I'm still thinkin' we might want to head west, set up shop for ourselves, somewhere away from all this trouble."

One corner of Ingram's mouth turned down, and the Californian shook his head slightly. "I've gotta say, Jesse, this ain't really the hoedown my men and me signed up for. We're looking to pick up some treasure, maybe stick it to the Union. We're not really in the burg-building business, and it's getting harder and harder to keep my men in line."

Henderson nodded. "How many men do you think you have, Jesse?" He picked the knife up and started to flip it between the fingers of one hand. The map, freed from the knife's weight, curled up at the corner. "How many rode out of Andersonville with us, five thousand? O' those, how many are left? How many can fight today, if they had to?"

Jesse shrugged stiffly. "That don' matter if we ain't gonna fight today. Most o' those men'll stand with us when the time comes. You saw Camp Lincoln. You know what they did there. Ain't no man can call himself a man would go through that, come out the other side, and not give his last breath to burn down the bastards that done it to him."

The outlaw boss shot a sidelong look at the Younger brothers, all of whom were staring at Henderson with blank faces.

Henderson looked from Jesse to the Youngers, and then to the Fords. He forced a smile onto his face and gave the hand holding the knife a casual flip of dismissal. "'Course, Jesse. I just thought, striking along the border, you'd keep both President Johnson AND President Lee guessin'."

That was enough to twist Jesse's mouth into a bitter snarl. "PRESIDENT Lee my old granny's behind. If it weren't for Lee an' his pack of ole biddies, we wouldn't be hidin' up here now."

Ingram's thin lips stretched into a predatory smile. Henderson nodded, his own smile tightening. "Exactly. Hit these towns, towns whose loyalties waver, and neither will know where you stand. It will be the perfect way to keep Lee off balance until you're ready to overthrow him."

Cole raised his hands in a quick warding gesture. "Whoa! What's this talk of overthrowin', eh?" He looked at Jesse. "We're still lookin' at goin' west, right? Where there ain't nobody that'd need overthrowin'?"

Jesse was staring into Henderson's foggy lenses, but he nodded. "I think that's the way to go. We'll head south, cut through the territories, an' see what we shall see. If we find us a juicy Union target, we hit it. Otherwise, we find us some food, look to those that need our help, and see which way the wind thinks to blow us."

Robert Ford coughed. "We never got too far south, Jesse. There's folks down along the gulf I know, feel more'r less the way you do."

Bob Younger laughed. "Yeah, more'r less, 'cept that little bit about the black folks an' all."

Ford glared at him. "An' when they hear Jesse talkin' about how things are, an' how they gotta be, most folks've come around, no?"

Bob shrugged coldly, pointing at Jesse with the knife. "The folks he talked to, sure."

Cole put a hand on his brother's arm. "Bobbie, now ain't the time."

Jesse looked questioningly at the Youngers. Bob's face was cold, Cole's concerned, and Jim's usually dapper face looked torn. There was only one thing that could be pulling them apart like this. Jesse sighed.

"I know there ain't nothin' I can say to bring John back, Bob. Your brother's dead, an' that's that." Jesse tried to speak in even tones. He still felt the edge of guilt, but he also knew there had been no other choice. Cole agreed, primarily because Frank had corroborated the story, had seen the thing that had once been John Younger, and had known there was nothing of the young man left in that hulking, mindless brute. Cole's brothers, however, were harder to convince, even though Bob had seen the beast for himself. Hell, Bob had been there when the beast attacked them. Whether he wanted to admit it or not, he *knew* what Jesse had had to do.

"I know the story, Jesse." Bob nodded. "An' I know Cole backs it." He looked right into Jesse's eyes without flinching. "But I ain't ready to let it go yet. We went in, we lost a lot of good men, an' we pulled Frank and that Loveless woman out." He nodded to Frank. "I'm glad we got Frank. He's been a friend o' my brothers' for longer'n I can say, an' he's a man I can hold with. But you left MY brother behind, Jesse. No matter the story, that's the fact. It's not somethin' we can't wink at."

Jesse nodded. "Yeah, we left John behind, Bob, because he was dead before we ever got there. What that Union doctor left behind din't have nothin' of John in it. I put a monster out of its misery, an' I did a passed friend a kindness." Jesse stood up taller, metal thumbs behind pistols, and looked straight back at Bob. "It was what needed doin', an' I did it. You gotta be able to drop that an' leave it behind, 'r we're gonna have trouble neither of us wants."

"He's gonna drop it, Jesse, never mind." Jim tried to pull his brother back but Bob shrugged off his grip.

Frank stepped up then, still pale and haggard from his ordeal. He grabbed Bob Younger by the shoulder and pushed his hollow-eyed face into the younger man's.

"You saw him, Bob. That weren't John. He was a goner the minute they dragged him out of his cell."

Bob looked at Frank for a moment longer, nodded slowly, and then looked at Jesse over his shoulder. "I'm goin' walkin'."

Jesse nodded and watched him go. Then he turned back to the rest of the men. "So, any other objections? We head south, find those croakers been followin' us some food, and see what we can see, once our bellies are full?"

"Whatever your lady love prefers, Jesse." Henderson reached down and pulled the map from beneath the cylinders. He rolled it up with quick, easy motions, a cold smile on his face.

Jesse stared at the skeletal figure in the dusty black for a moment before speaking. "It's what I prefer, Allen." He walked toward the man, his own face cold. "You been with us long enough, you best never make the mistake of assumin' I don't do my own thinkin'. You got that?"

Henderson's expression never changed. "Oh, I got it, Jesse. Never fear."

"Jesse knows what he's doing, Mr. Henderson. You should believe that if nothing else."

The men turned to watch Loveless sweep gracefully past the fabric blind and into the cave. "Jesse knows that power grows from a free people, united behind a common cause, regardless of color or creed. Your plan to attack innocent civilians will do nothing but damage his cause, and the cause of the Rebellion." She moved to stand behind the outlaw chief. "Like Jesse's said, true power doesn't come from gold, or fear, or even the barrel of a gun." She turned a little to grin at Jesse. "Although I have to say I'm not sure I believe that last one completely."

Jesse watched the woman with admiration. He did not remember saying half of those things, and he was not sure he believed them entirely himself. He knew that the men around him gave him power – more power than he had ever wielded before – and he knew that, if used correctly, they would open up a future for him that he could never achieve on his own. What exactly that future might be, he could not yet say. The grueling journey north had been trying, and the attraction of civil leadership had waned with each punishing step. He found a certain amount of reassurance in the thought that his natural talents were leading him to battle, rather than becoming a burgermeister.

The trail before him might lead all the way to a resurrected south, and maybe even beyond. With the strongest and orneriest former prisoners, outlaws, and bushwhackers behind him, he knew he had the beginning of the Union's defeat within his grasp. What was he supposed to do now, return to the territories? Throw a barn-raising? Take up his old feud with Billy the Kid, and scrabble in the dust for a few gold coins and a mention in the local paper?

"We're headin' south, like I said." Jesse nodded to Lucy. "As we go, we keep our eyes open. We take what we need, we lick at any blue-bellies we find along the way, and we look for our main chance. Maybe we make contact with folks in the Rebellion that might not agree with Lee and his grannies."

Henderson's smile slipped just a bit as he noted the resolve in Jesse's eyes, then he shrugged and slipped the map into a small leather case beneath his flowing coat.

"Of course, Jesse."

Jesse smiled and gave the tall man a stiff shot in the arm. "We'll burn some buildings down yet, don't you worry. We just need to –"

A shout from outside the cave brought Jesse up short and he stepped to the mouth to look out. Several of his men ran past. Bob Younger was jogging back toward them, his face bleak. He held up one hand slick with blood.

Cole muttered something and stepped forward but Bob shook his head. "It ain't mine. Dustin Fletcher had the last watch. He's over yonder, past that Thunder."

Jesse began to walk in that direction, Frank following slowly along behind, the rest of his party rushing to keep up. Bob Younger fell into step beside him.

Jesse's words were clipped. "He dead?"

Bob nodded. "Throat slit; all the way back to his spine."

Jesse felt a cold itch down his back. "Cold steel?" He knew the answer, but had to ask.

"Not likely." Bob was breathing heavily, trying to keep up. "The edges were all charred, and there weren't nearly as much blood as there shoulda been. I think you'll recognize it when you see it."

Jesse nodded as he turned around the large vehicle and stopped to stare down at one of his men, a blaster rifle discarded beside him. The man's eyes were wide, staring blankly up into the bright blue sky. The wound gaped sickeningly, and Jesse saw that Bob had been right. Only a small stream of blood was leaking out of the dark slit. The edges were black, small branches of char reaching out like the roots of a vine.

Behind Jesse, Lucinda came up short. One look at the body was enough for her to confirm the suspicions of the others.

"Warrior Nation." The woman's voice was cold. The men all looked from her back down to the terrible wound, the flesh scorched with the furious energy of the Great Spirit.

They had been found.

Chapter 2

Jesse was halfway up the hill, legs pumping furiously and pistols clutched in metal fists, when the screaming began. Barreling up over the lip of the small valley, he was nearly pushed back down by the flood of emaciated prisoners charging toward him. Behind them, columns of smoke rose in the distance. As the terrified mob flowed past, meaning emerged from their panicked noise.

"Savages!"

There was no coordinated resistance. Most of the folks were still in shock from their ordeal in Camp Lincoln and the subsequent retreat through the wilderness. Faced with the full fury of a Warrior Nation assault, their courage had abandoned them. Jesse knew there were only moments to turn the tide before even his seasoned fighters caught the panic and turned tail.

Jesse turned to his posse. "Cole, you and your brothers head out and try to stiffen up the Andersonville boys as close to the front as you can. I'm goin' to have some of the heavy stuff come up behind you. If you can't stop the Injuns short of the vehicles, we're lost."

Cole nodded and jerked his head toward the rising smoke. Jim followed his older brother directly, but Bob gave Jesse one last, dark look before running after.

"Henderson, you go back down and rally some of the boys that've been workin' with the Union armor. See if you can't get those Thunders up and runnin'. That oughta give the savages somethin' to worry about. Ingram, rally up your Rangers and see if you can't set up some firin' positions to fall back on, up here on this lip." Jesse was still moving toward the front, pushing through the frightened men that flowed past. Only the Fords and Lucy were still with him.

"Lucy," Jesse shouted over his shoulder. The roar and echo of the terrified mob was surging around them. "Head south and try to stop this stampede the best you can!"

She nodded. "I had Will Shaft and his Exodusters collect the food wagons down that way. There should be some order there!" She spun around and moved with the flow, away from the onrushing combat.

One terrified man, eyes white with thoughtless panic, tried to push Jesse down in his flight. The outlaw boss had had enough. He cracked the man in the throat with one cold, iron forearm. As the ragged prisoner halted, coughing around his bruised gullet, Jesse brought his knee up into the man's crotch. He dropped like a stone, curled around his pain, all terror forgotten.

"Alright!" He turned his head toward the Fords. "Enough o' this! There ain't no way any of us're makin' it out if these bummers start runnin' down the fighters! I need you two to keep 'em outta the valley while Henderson and Ingram rally the boys an' get the vehicles movin'!"

Charlie nodded, pulling his massive weapon from its sheath. A custom shotgun, barrel sawn-down to a menacing snub-nosed bore, the thing demanded respect, and Charlie knew how to use it. Robert, however, hesitated.

"Jesse, I think I oughta stay with you." He nodded toward the sounds of slaughter and screaming to the north. "It's gettin' hairy out there, an' I'd rather you din't wade into it with no one to watch yer back."

Jesse almost laughed, but stopped himself. "Kid, where I'm goin', ain't no bodyguardin' gonna help." He held up one articulated fist, the lethal beauty of the Hyper-velocity pistol shining in the risen sun. "When you get into the heat of it, only thing that can keep a man alive is himself an' his luck." The familiar grin flashed in the hat brim's shadow. "An' if there's one thing I got in spades, Robert, it's faith in myself an' a heap o' luck!"

Robert Ford nodded and Jesse moved away, shoving a path through the thinning crowd of terrified prisoners. As he pushed his way toward the fighting, he could hear the Fords behind him, shouting for the attention of the mob. Several sharp gunshots sounded, and the tenor of the screams changed again as the flood of panicked men split like a river, flowing to the east and west around the shallow valley.

Jesse moved through the churned ruins of the camp, stepping over discarded clothing, boxes and bags of God knew what. He moved quickly past the bodies of those who had been trampled by their friends. Ahead he could hear the crack of RJ gunshots, detonations as munitions exploded, and the shouts of his men forming up a decent defensive line under the direction of the Younger boys. With each step that Jesse took, the lyrical chanting and harsh war cries of the savages grew louder.

The line of contact was clear as he moved up. At first, he was surprised there were not more dead prisoners scattered about. A line of outlaws and rebels hunkered down behind hasty fortifications built around the rusted-out bodies of the worst Ironhide wagons they had taken from Andersonville. Many had been overturned to provide better cover. Men were crouched down behind them, taking careful shots with rifles and pistols into a massive swirling wall of bodies that pushed ever-closer.

The surging wall consisted of more Warrior Nation savages than he had ever seen in one place before, spinning and dancing through an undisciplined mob of prisoners who had been too stunned or too stupid to run. These men clutched ancient, makeshift weapons; they stumbled around, slashing blindly or firing wild shots, trying to stagger back toward the line Cole and his brothers had been building around the abandoned vehicles.

Jesse dismissed the tangled free-for-all, more concerned with what might be hidden on the other side. He could see flares of blue spirit energy on the warriors' primitive weapons as they slaughtered the prisoners, but there were none of the nightmare man-beasts dancing among them. The strongest warriors, he knew, would be coming up behind. There was also no sign of the twisted horses the natives rode into battle. With a mob the size of this one, they had to be out there somewhere.

"What's happenin'?" Jesse shouted to be heard over the clamor of battle. Cole Younger leaned down with his rifle braced across the back of an old flat-bed wagon, taking careful aim on the press of bodies that crawled ever closer. He held up a hand, settling behind the sight of his short weapon. The thing barked, spitting crimson-edged smoke out toward the line, and then he stood up.

"The braves're all tied up with the prisoners who din't run." He gestured toward the fighting with his chin. "But those sad bastards ain't gonna last long." He grinned.

"We'll be dancin' soon enough."

Jesse scowled and shook his head. "We don't wanna be dancin' here, Cole. We wanna be savin' our strength for the damned blue-bellies." He scanned the line of combat. It was rushing forward now, the last of the prisoners disappearing beneath the wave of doeskin and tanned flesh. Behind the furious line of attackers he could see looming shadows: the true horrors of the Warrior Nation, held back for this final assault.

"We gotta hold 'em off long enough fer Henderson to get up here with the armor. Give 'em a taste o' the ole' Union Thunder. That oughta give 'em pause." Jesse took careful aim with one pistol and dropped a war leader with a tall crest of hair and feathers wagging over his head.

"I'm not sure that's gonna work." Frank, gasping for breath and pale as death, came stumping up beside Jesse, his long rifle, Sophie, clutched in white knuckles. That massive gun had been wrapped in a pack on the back of Jesse's 'Horse for months. He had never been happier for following one of his strange impulses.

Jesse took a shot, watched another savage fall, and then turned to his brother. "What?"

Frank sighted along his rifle, pointing with bladed hand down the barrel. "Those things comin' up? Their some kinda beast we ain't seen before. An' they're nearly big as the Thunders."

Jesse peered through the smoke and rising dust. He could see massive shifting shadows shuffling behind the Warrior line, but could not tell if they were shapeshifters or something worse.

He shrugged. "Well, that's what we got. We take our chances, play the hand we been dealt, an' maybe the draw falls our way."

A deafening roar behind them announced the arrival of the first of the Union armored wagons. The thing was a wall of studded iron, its main cannon sitting in a squat turret that crouched behind a sweeping cowcatcher. It rolled up beside the Ironhide Jesse and his men crouched behind and unleashed a blast of ruby light that ravaged across the field which cut down a swath of natives in the distance.

A heartened cheer rose up all along Jesse's line, redoubling as two more Rolling Thunders came up to rest beside the first. These added their hellish roars to the battle, and soon the Warrior Nation advance was crumbling, falling back across piles of discarded equipment and dead prisoners. The rotating Gatling cannons nestled beneath each turret spat torrents of red fire into the fleeing warriors. Jesse's teeth flashed in a vicious grin. He leapt atop the broken-down vehicle in front of him, sending blasts of crimson energy into the sky.

"Yeah! You rock-worshipin' heathens!"

From the back of the wagon, Jesse got his first good look at the beasts moving up behind the savages' front line. Five enormous monsters, still strolling forward, were splitting the retreating natives into tight streams between them. Their eyes glowed the haunting blue of spirit energy, and an enormous rack of edged antlers swept out from each beast's head, swaying with their shambling gait.

"Well jumped up . . ." Jesse's mouth hung open. The things were at least twice the height of a Rolling Thunder, the ground shaking with each step. As he watched, their pace quickened, thick legs rising and falling faster and faster, and soon they were charging across the churned field. Their plate-sized hooves crushed bodies or sent them spinning up into the air behind them.

"Fire! For the love of –" Jesse screamed, lashing down with one pistol to stab it at the oncoming beasts.

The three Rolling Thunders spat crimson flame at the creatures, the grass before them flattening with the concussion of their blasts. The victorious shouts of the tattered army staggered into silence as the ruby bolts glanced off the surging mounds of muscle and matted fur, blasting into the dirt or scattering up into the sky. One of the animals was struck squarely, the bolt caving in its shoulder and erupting out its back in a geyser of blood and entrails. It staggered as its forelegs collapsed, bellowing as it sank slowly onto its side. The rest, however, did not slow in their ponderous charge.

"Get ba—" Jesse started to shout, jumping off the wagon. His duster was flying behind him like a cape, legs churning the air, when one of the enormous beasts struck the vehicle a glancing blow with one bone-spurred shoulder before crashing into a Rolling Thunder with a deafening clangor.

The rusted wagon cartwheeled away from the impact, crushing several fighters and scattering the rest. The monster's gargantuan antlers caught the Rolling Thunder beneath the turret and tangled with the ironwork of its cowcatcher. With a furious roar, the thing twisted the thick muscles of its neck and sent the vehicle crashing onto its side.

The other animals slammed into the Thunders, silencing their guns. One reared up onto its hind legs and brought the heavy weight of its fore-hooves crashing down, caving in the sloping front armor and pushing the weighty vehicle backward in the grass.

Jesse came rolling up to his feet and glanced around. More and more of his steady hands were rushing toward the front, but most had stopped as the giant, twisted elk made their appearance. He looked back at the mountain of fur and flesh that continued to pound at the overturned wagon, snorting blue-tinged steam.

Gritting his teeth, Jesse clapped his two pistols together, thumbed the switches beneath each barrel, and aimed them at the thing's lashing head. Ribbons of crimson energy reached out from each pistol, tying them together and glowing with a fierce light before he pulled the triggers and sent a single wave of destructive, roiling flame up at the beast. The fireball struck the monster in the head and detonated, sending blood, bone, and curves of antler splashing out in every direction. The beast's body shivered convulsively as it collapsed into the dirt.

The men around him cheered as the beast fell and began to fire into the surviving elk, even though their standard blasters seemed to be having little effect. Jesse took two steps back, surveying the battle around him, and came to a grim decision just as Frank shouted at him.

"They're comin' again!" Frank's voice was muffled by the battle-din. He pointed to the north. The outlaw chief looked back to see the Warrior Nation rallying behind their beasts, once more working themselves up to charge, chanting and waving their weapons in the air.

"Skedaddle, boys!" Jesse started to wave at the men around him, gesturing back toward the valley. "We need to get outta here, get around behind the camp. Go!"

The men tried to follow his direction, firing as they moved backward, but the surviving great elk, turning from the twisted wrecks of the Thunders, snorted fiercely and began to stomp toward the nearest clusters of men, their muscles bunching for another charge. In moments, the most capable fighters his crew could boat were fleeing, running back toward their encampment and the remaining Union armor.

Jesse grabbed Frank by the back of his vest and pulled him away. Cole and his brothers were falling back as well, shooting as they went. The assaulting savages pushed forward in a wave, engulfing the abandoned vehicles and screeching their unholy challenges to the sky. The outlaws and escaped prisoners moved back in good order, though. Jesse was certain that if they could take up positions around the caves with the last few Thunders, and Loveless and Shaft could rally the prisoners capable of fighting, they would be able to hold back the warriors and their twisted beasts indefinitely.

The blast, when it came, took the entire motley army by surprise. A howling like a thousand desert storms fell upon them, the crackling of heat lightning snapping beneath. Sheets of silvery-blue energy came sleeting in from either side, riddling retreating fighters and blasting them off their feet. Jesse had never heard anything like the hellish noises that accompanied this fresh attack. His head whipped around, looking for the source.

Low-slung wagons had been pushed into position along the encampment's flanks while the fighting had distracted the shabby mob. Most seemed to hold antique Gatling cannons, but the savages manning them were chanting and swaying to their own music rather than crouching behind the weapons like a traditional crew. From the spinning barrels of the guns blazed not the grey smoke of black-powder weapons, or the crimson-tinged fury of RJ-1027, but the clear blue fury of the natives' spirit energy.

Jesse shielded his eyes from the glittering brightness as the firing continued. Somehow, he knew, the warriors were channeling their Great Spirit's force through the old cannons, focusing and aiming it like gunfire. The streams of blue bolts blasted men from their feet, sent huge, sparkling geysers up into the sky, and churned the disciplined retreat into a full rout.

For a moment, the fleeing men staggered to a halt as three more Rolling Thunder wagons came up over the lip of the valley, their own Gatling cannons lashing with red flame back at the Warrior Nation platforms. The reprieve was short lived, however, as other platforms, hidden by a dip in the hills, were pushed into place.

These new carts each held massive cannon, their ancient brass barrels darkened and pitted with age. Again, the crews danced and chanted. This time Jesse watched the entire process. Deep within the shadows of each cannon's mouth a blue ghostlight began to form, pulsing with the rhythm of its crews' chant. The glow burned brighter and brighter as phantom lightning began to play along the barrel, crawling from the muzzle and melding with the ancient metal. When the crews' dance reached a frenetic peak, energy tore from the mouth of each weapon with the wrath of a devastating lightning strike. The blasts struck the emerging Union wagons with a thunder crash.

Each vehicle was rocked back on its massive iron wheels. The armor held under the onslaught, but molten steel dripped into the burning grass and smoke began to pour from the vision slits of each wagon. The munitions in one vehicle detonated in the heat and the entire thing disappeared in an eruption of twisted metal and burning fuel.

Jesse looked down at his pistols in helpless rage. There was no way he could range in on these new weapons. There was no way he could close the distance in the face of their power. Beside him, Frank was taking slow, methodical shots at the weapon crews. Each time Sophie barked her sharp report, a warrior was thrown into the smoldering grass. No matter how many he took down, however, it was not enough, as others came to take the place of the fallen.

Jesse's army was paralyzed by the incoming fire and the approaching wave of beasts and warriors. From behind, he saw a small group come up out of the valley, Lucinda and Will Shaft in their midst. The agent's eyes were haunted as she rushed to Jesse, her head shaking.

"Their cavalry was waiting to the south." The anger burning in her eyes was a match for his own. "Ingram's Rangers charged in and saw the braves off, but they took heavy casualties. The runners didn't have a prayer."

Jesse shook his head. "I'm not sure any of us have a prayer, darlin'." He holstered one pistol and bent down to pick up a discarded blaster rifle. "But they sure are gonna know they been kissed."

"Jesse!" Frank's voice was sharp.

The outlaw boss looked quickly to where his brother was pointing. The crews of the strange spirit weapons were silent, watching the huddled remnants of the refugee mob with dark, hooded eyes.

"Well, why don't that make me feel any better . . . " Jesse murmured. He turned around again to where the mass of the Warrior Nation was still approaching, although with a slow, terrible pace now. The warriors in front of the mob were clearly eager to get to grips with their enemy, but something held them back.

All along the rolling hills, the savages began to close in on Jesse's exhausted, ragged force. At a glance, the outlaw would have sworn he had less than a few hundred fighting men left. He did not know how many might still be in the valley, nor what vehicles might remain. But he did not think it was going to matter, as the natives in their thousands stalked in for the kill.

A large warrior with glowing azure eyes emerged from the press of bodies moving toward Jesse. The man was at least a head taller, his muscles bulging beneath ceremonial armor of bone and leather. He held a long slashing blade low, the entire length of the weapon glowing with blue energy and dripping sparks of force into the grass.

With his free hand the warrior pointed to Jesse with an animal snarl on his smooth face.

Jesse stepped forward with a slight nod. He grinned at the approaching warrior and then casually raised his pistol and shot the man in the head. The body fell heavily backward into the torn mud. Jesse looked down at his hand in uneasy admiration. The arms had been giving him so much trouble lately, it was almost a surprise to have them answer the call so readily.

A howl arose from the surrounding warriors and they crouched down at the sharp blast of the pistol.

"Ya'll ain't gonna fool me into some dancehall show, you savages!" Jesse barked out, and the natives slowed their advance. "You got plenty of bodies, you're gonna take me down eventually." He grinned even wider and spat into the grass at his feet. "But I reckon I can take twenty, maybe thirty of ya'll with me afore you do. So, if those folks wantin' to die'll step forward, I say let's start this little dance, no?"

Both of his pistols were drawn, held casually to either side. Behind him, Frank, the Younger brothers, and Loveless stepped up to stand with him. Will Shaft and his two dark friends stood warily by the lip of the canyon. The Fords, nearby, were the only people moving on the plain as they paced carefully toward their boss.

The warriors watched the outlaw with blank, glowing eyes, their mouths a uniform snarl of rage. Every muscle tensed for a final charge.

"*Wotaka!*" The voice was strong but fluid, like the water of a slow but powerful river.

"*Eenahzee Keezay.*" The wall of braves parted and a man stepped gracefully through. He was younger than Jesse might have expected, but his body was thick with muscle and he walked with the grace of a giant cat. The man's hands were empty, held wide in a gesture of pacification. His eyes were dark and cold, with just the slightest azure flame burning within their depths. He was wearing elaborate ceremonial armor beneath a beaded vest. Around his throat flashed a silver chain holding some sort of strange bird-shaped medallion. He stared at Jesse with a deep loathing.

"I am Maza Chaydan, leader of this band. You are the outcast known as Jesse James?" The man's voice was still soft, but there was a contempt in it that almost convinced Jesse to charge him then and there and damn the consequences.

Instead, he merely nodded.

Maza Chaydan nodded in turn. "Then I commend your ghost to the Great Spirit, demon. And I cleanse the world of your poison."

Without further warning, the savage war leader barked a thunderous chant, his hands flying up in a rapid series of gestures. Bolts of cerulean lightning leapt from his fingers, crashing down around Jesse and slapping him into the churned earth. There was a buzzing in his ears that he tried to shake out as he leapt back to his feet, his clothing steaming and his trembling arms sparking.

"Why, you ten bit savage bastard." Jesse's hands still clenched his Hyper-velocity blasters, and he slashed them both up at the snarling brave. Dual streams of crimson fire lashed out at the undefended target, and Jesse snarled in frustration as half his shots sailed wide, his left arm twitching aside.

Jesse's eyes widened as the savage, a grim smile playing about his thin lips, brought one hand up in a warding gesture. A shimmering curve of blue energy intercepted the barrage of ruby bolts and sent them streaking up into the clear sky.

The outlaw chief's brows came down, his eyes hardened, and he muttered, "Alright then, dog-boy. Let's dance." He jerked his entire body to the right, then dove to the left, sprinting around the brave, his custom pistols stabbing out and crimson bolts flashing between them, only to bounce away over the silent, gaping crowd.

Outlaws, rebels, and savages all watched the cataclysmic battle as legendary outlaw boss and mystical Warrior Nation shaman clashed across the muddy earth. Bolts of nature's own lightning crashed down upon Jesse like a lash of fire, while his answering attacks were turned aside by Maza Chaydan's glowing shield of flickering, ghostly blades that shimmered into and out of existence at need.

Jesse's mouth was twisted in desperate hatred now. His clothing was scorched, his arms slow and clumsy, and yet he had not managed to land a single bolt on his proud foe. With a grunt of effort Jesse brought both of his pistols together and stroked the small buttons that would combine their power cells. He laughed with grim triumph as he brought the twinned weapons to bear on the shaman, a wispy red power-bridge forming between them.

Before Jesse could launch the most devastating attack, the brave dove toward him, rolling on one shoulder and standing quickly within the outlaw chief's defenses. His left hand swung wide, a glowing blade appearing in his clenched fist and burying itself in Jesse's thigh.

The enormous wave of crimson fire billowed up into the air as Jesse collapsed to one knee with a furious cry. He punched out with one fist, still filled with a custom pistol, and drove the savage's hand away from his wounded leg. Maza Chaydan danced away before he could do more, however, and the outlaw chief was left panting in impotent fury, looking up at the calm face of his enemy. What he saw there, however, gave him cold pause.

The powerful young medicine man gestured toward the outlaw chief's battered Stetson. "You bear a token from our people." One hand gracefully rose to indicate something hanging from the back of Jesse's hat. The outlaw was discomfited to see tears of frustrated rage standing out in the war leader's glittering eyes. Jesse grasped the hat and looked at the leather thong fastened around its base. Geronimo's feather hung there, limp and forgotten. The thing had flapped along behind him throughout his adventures in the south.

Jesse sucked in gasping breaths of air, looking up at the war leader standing before him, and nodded again. "It was given to me by Chief Geronimo." He tried to grin through his confusion and exhaustion. "He seemed impressed."

The war leader's eyes turned hard. "Do not speak the name of Goyahkla in this place again. Do you know the significance of the token you hold in your cursed hands?"

Jesse looked down at the feather. It was pretty ratty. He had dragged it through hell and back, it seemed, since that day the Injuns had handed it to him and let him walk away. He shook his head, pushing himself back to his feet. "It's an owl feather. They gave it to me and let me go."

Maza Chaydan nodded again. "It is an owl feather. I do not know why Goyahkla released you, but with this feather, it was not as a friend, nor for you to return to our lands with a ragged band of wastrels at your heels."

The men behind Jesse bristled at that, but he quieted them with a raised hand, never taking his eyes off the Injun. "Well, they weren't talkin' much after I got it."

The war leader raised his voice so that all of the men and women nearby, rebels, outlaws, and natives, could hear him. "Jesse James bears a token of the People. An *osniko wiyaka* rests in his hands."

As he said the words, a hushed murmur rose up among the surrounding warriors.

Maza Chaydan turned back to Jesse. "You must leave the lands of the People at once. And you must not return. The *osniko wiyaka* is not the badge of a friend, nor will it save you again."

Relief warred with disbelief in Jesse's chest as he struggled to bring his breathing under control. "Hold on one cotton pickin' second," he holstered a pistol and raised a hand. "You killed all these folks, and now you're just gonna let us go?"

Maza Chaydan shrugged. "We knew nothing of the *osniko wiyaka*. Had you been killed before we realized it, it would merely have been the wishes of the Great Spirit. But once I recognized the token for what it is, I had no choice."

Jesse sneered. "An' if I shoot you right now?" The free pistol rose to point directly at the tall warrior.

Again, the man shrugged. "If you try to kill me now, there will be no saving you or your people. Every last one will be killed, dying in excruciating pain before your despairing eyes. And only then, when your mind is broken and your body wracked with agony, when every hope and dream you ever held dear has been stolen from you and scattered to the wind, will we throw you down into the dust." Maza Chaydan straightened, hands on hips, and looked down his proud nose at the outlaw chief. "The intentions of Goyahkla, whatever they may be, will have been thwarted by your own stupidity."

The pistol dropped slightly at this, and Jesse's grin slipped to match it. He nodded slowly, his shoulders slumping in exhaustion, and he looked down at one treacherous, gun-filled hand. "Okay, sounds fair."

Maza Chaydan folded his arms before his broad chest. "You will leave the land of the People now."

Jesse looked down at the wreckage and scattered bodies that covered the ground. The smell was already starting to remind him of Payson; reason enough to leave as quickly as possible. "What about our gear?"

The warrior gave a casual flip of his hand. "You may take with you whatever you can carry. Your dead we will see to. You will not be allowed to stay long enough to care for them."

Jesse took a step back and turned to his brother. "South?"

Frank nodded. "As fast as we can."

Jesse scanned the faces around him. Even Henderson, watching from the rim of the valley, nodded.

The outlaw turned back to face the war leader. "We'll take yer offer and head south."

The shaman's head dipped once, but he said nothing.

Jesse looked into the dark eyes for a minute longer before giving his own sharp nod. "Alright then."

The remaining Ironhide wagons and Iron Horses were more than enough to transport the survivors of the attack back into the Contested Territories, escorted by three remaining Rolling Thunder armored wagons. Of the thousands of escaped prisoners, outlaws, and rebel Rangers who had fled Andersonville onto Warrior Nation land, only a few hundred emerged.

Chapter 3

Colonel George Armstrong Custer made sure never to miss the sun rising over the rolling hills to the east. From the high stone watchtower of Fort Frederick, pushed up against the very roots of the western mountains, the sunrise was always beautiful. Unless the savages were attacking that day, of course. Then there were more important things to focus on than the splendor of the morning.

Custer rested his hands against the warm metal guard rail of the tower's outer walkway. Far below, the main gates of the squat fortress were closed to potential infiltrators, despite the apparent emptiness of the land all around. Sentries walked their rounds in squad strength, and an entire troop of his newly-reestablished 7th Cavalry Regiment was somewhere out there, riding the circuit set the day they had arrived, over a month ago.

Custer took in a deep lungful of the fresh mountain air and braced himself for another unpleasant day. Aside from the natural unhappiness of any cavalry officer tasked with the defense of a fixed position, Custer had even greater burdens to bear. Fort Frederick, named after one of General Grant's slaughtered sons, had been purpose-built, here in the middle of God's country, but far from anything remotely resembling the important events of the modern age, to house extensive laboratories and storage facilities for the Union's greatest scientific minds.

The cavalry colonel found those minds to be the most onerous burden of his new, seemingly prestigious, posting. It galled him, every day, to know that he owed the worst of their ill-feathered flock for the meteoric upturn in his professional fate. He cursed the ironic luck that had turned his first full military command in nearly a decade into a prison of the soul.

When Doctor Tumblety had tempted him with the chance to command a mysterious post out west, he had balked. He knew in his heart how much a debt of such magnitude, owed to a creature of such foul character, would weigh upon his conscience. Yet, before being sent to Camp

Lincoln, his career had languished in the doldrums of mediocrity for more years than he cared to think.

Of course, that offer was made before the colonel or his patron even realized that just such a post already existed, and that it had already been staffed by none other than Tumblety's chief rival for the War Department's attention, affection, and coin: Nikola Tesla. In the harsh light of reality, Custer was not the only one to find their new posting less than he had hoped.

"Sir." His adjutant, Lieutenant Willa Shaw, broke into his thoughts. Her cavalry boots cracked smartly on the stone floor as she stopped behind him.

Custer looked around, hands still on the railing. He quirked one eyebrow in inquiry.

"Mister Tesla is making ready to open those crates from Washington, sir." The young woman coughed. "You wanted to be notified?"

Custer gave a slow nod, cast one last look out over the rolling hills, and turned from the view. He settled his battered hat over his curly hair and moved around the walkway, back into the tower. The heels of his adjutant's riding boots clicked along on the stone behind him. Even after all these years, he still found it difficult to reconcile himself with serving beside women. Even a woman as competent as Shaw.

He entered a wide room designed to keep watch over all possible approaches toward Fort Frederick. A large seat, almost like a throne, had been built in the middle of the chamber for the officer of the watch. Wide windows of thick, bubbled glass gave a slightly distorted view of the hills below. It all seemed modern and invincible; an appearance he would have more faith in had he not known that, during an overwhelming attack last year, with the fort barely completed, the commander of the watch had been plucked from that very chair, thrown through the window, and fell screaming to his death in the courtyard far below.

The tower was now named Carter's Keep, although the men still called it the high seat. Or the launching pad, if they were feeling spirited.

Fort Frederick had very nearly been abandoned after that attack. General Grant, however, had refused to abandon the fortress to the savages. The Warrior Nation had torn up the fortress's Heavy Rail spur line after the attack. The relief columns sent to retake the fort had stretched for miles, guarding enormous pack wagons built specifically for the purpose. They had travelled for months through hostile territory, fighting a running battle all the way.

But that had been over a year ago. Now, Fort Frederick was one of the most well-defended strongholds of the Republic, even if few in the Republic knew it existed. Given how strange most of the communication with Washington had been since his arrival, Colonel Custer was not entirely sure even President Johnson knew about the place. Grant did, that was for sure. He watched over everything that happened here like an eagle from afar.

The spiral stairs leading down from Carter's Keep were steep, opening out into cramped firing positions every half-turn. The place reflected the very latest in defensive engineering. Custer's mouth twisted in a slight, bitter sneer that curled his mustache back from his lip. He wondered if Captain Carter had thought the same thing, before the twisted half-man, half-bird savage had yanked him from his chair and tossed him through the window.

The courtyard at the base of the tower was extensive, but the massive pack wagons, their RJ engines cold and dark, dominated the space. The heavy iron gates had been rebuilt and reinforced since the attack. Heavy cannons were interspersed with Gatling positions all along the parapet of the thick outer wall. The local natives were now aware of the weapons' maximum range, always stopping to taunt their crews from just out of reach. Custer had been forced to assign an officer to watch over each battery, lest they be in danger of wasting their precious power cells. Here, trapped at the ass-end of the longest land-supply line the Union had ever tried to maintain, there was no room for waste.

The heavy metal doors into the squat fortress itself were open, the unmistakable burning smell of RJ-1027 thick in the air. The recharge stalls for the Regiment's nearly one thousand Iron Horses and Locust support vehicles were dug into the walls of a long bunker sunk into the bedrock beneath the fortress. The bunker was wide enough for five 'Horses to ride abreast during deployment, which made for quite a sight when a troop was heading out or returning from a patrol. Twenty ranks roaring out was a brave show of force; but it was nearly as disconcerting when they disappeared into the surrounding hills almost at once.

Custer continued to move deeper into the fortress, waving a cursory salute at troopers and soldiers that snapped to attention as he stormed past. If Tesla was opening the damned crates, they better still be isolated in Deep Storage D, where the colonel had put them. Grant's pet scientist had a way of making free with orders, and the thought of whatever monsters might be contained in those coffin-like crates made Custer's blood run chill after the things he had seen at Camp Lincoln.

"Are they still in the same storage room?" Custer snapped the question over his shoulder without slowing down. Shaw, skip-stepping to keep up, responded in a level voice.

"Yessir. D, sir." The answer echoed away down the wide corridor.

"Well, let's hope he doesn't smell up the room the way that damned sawbones soils his area, eh?" Custer's muttered question did not call for a response, so Shaw merely nodded in the semi-darkness.

Down several wide flights of stairs, the dressed stone walls gave way to carved bedrock. The bones of the mountains had been hollowed out to make way for the Union's greatest minds and stockpiles of their inventions. Banded wooden doors came up and receded into the shadows on either side as they stalked down the narrower hall. Most of these massive chambers were empty, waiting to be filled with mechanical marvels from Washington, stores from the border forts, or the products of the advanced manufactories being planned for deeper underground.

Each set of doors was labeled with a double letter painted in hurried splashes. They stopped at two messy 'D's dashed across one set. The doors were partly ajar, a dusky light spilling out in a wedge over the packed earth of the floor and slashing up the opposite wall in a ruddy bar. Low, muttering voices could be heard from within. Without waiting to listen, Custer rapped twice and pushed the door wide.

The room was large, more than fifty feet to a side, with low, vaulted ceilings looming overhead. Several piles of large crates bearing stenciled military-style labels stood near the center of the room. Three men stood over a box that had been set close to the door. Illumination was provided by RJ-powered wall sconces, but two stand-alone electric lamps of Tesla's own design had been set up to provide further lighting near the crate.

In the shadowed recesses of the large room were tables of equipment that the colonel could not identify. Coils of metal rose toward the low ceiling while twists and loops of glass and rubber connected a collection of boiling containers in tangled snarls. Throughout the confusing mess were an array of black boxes attached with wires and coils of tubing.

"Mr. Tesla." Custer's voice rang out in the stone room. "I believe I asked you to inform me before you began to access your new cargo?" The colonel forced his voice to remain calm. Tesla had never quite recovered from his weeks of hiding in these very tunnels after the savages sacked the fortress above.

The youngest man in the group, standing beside the box and wedging an iron crowbar beneath the lid, shrugged. "Is that Shaw there beside you?"

Custer looked at his adjutant, who gave a shrug of her own, and then back down to the scientist many were claiming would be the Savior of the Republic. "Yes."

"Well, then somehow, word got to you." The man tilted his smooth, mustachioed face up into the light with an unkind smile. "And so any further effort I spent on the task would have been wasted, would it not?"

Custer stared into the snide face for a moment, fighting the urge to slap it. When he had tamped down his reaction, he sniffed slightly and nodded to the box. "You have not yet opened one?"

Tesla shook his head and bent back to his task. "I have not. The boys back at the Pipetown Works in Washington were most diligent in their application of nails and hammers."

Shaw cleared her throat, glanced at Custer to make sure it was okay for her to speak, and then continued at a nod from her superior. "Should we have more troopers here, just in case something goes wrong, Mr. Tesla?"

"We should be perfectly safe, Lieutenant Shaw. I had not intended to activate the unit at any rate. We are merely inspecting today." The two older men, wearing long, thin white coats identical to Tesla's, cast quick glances up at the colonel and his assistant, and then looked just as quickly away.

Custer grunted softly and gestured for them to continue. The three men soon had the box open. One of the assistants carried the heavy pine lid away, dropping it behind them with a startling crash, and the men leaned down into the box. The colonel, almost against his own wishes, moved forward to look inside. He was relieved when the ruddy light revealed only metal, rubber, and sawdust; no flesh was in evidence.

Tesla pushed the wood chips away from the metal shape. It shared the basic form of a man: two arms, two legs, and a boxy shape sitting on its trunk where a head would be. It was gigantic, however; easily twice the size of an average trooper. It reminded the colonel of the metal marshals deployed into the territories to bolster the lawmen still willing to clash with the vicious criminal caste. Those machines were sleek, with a smooth, rounded look that softened their alien appearance. The manikin shape in the box was crude by comparison. Armored plates were bolted directly to the hulking chassis, giving it a heavy, threatening appearance. Each arm ended not in a hand, but rather in the bulk of a large Gatling blaster. They were clearly a more advanced version of the UR-10s that had guarded Camp Lincoln.

Tesla and his men tried to get their arms beneath the robot to leverage it into a sitting position. They grunted and strained for several minutes, coming at it from several different directions, but it refused to budge. The scientist shot a quick look over his shoulder at Custer, watching with an amused sneer, then reached into the box, around the back of the thing's neck, and flipped a switch.

"Hey!" The colonel's weapon was out of the holster moments before the metal man in the crate sat up, shedding wood chips in a dull cascade.

"Immediate Operational Parameters?" The voice was an unpleasant, insectile buzz emanating from a crude grate beneath its cyclopean eye.

Tesla, with another look at Custer, snapped, "Inspection protocols only." His hand was held toward the colonel as if trying to pacify him while he spoke.

The automaton was still for a moment and then buzzed. "Acknowledged. Inspection protocols." As it spoke, it stood up, rising to an imposing height.

The robot towered over the men in the room, intimidating in its silent, heavy stillness.

Custer whistled softly. "Mr. Tesla, I think you got yourself a winner here."

The younger man nodded slightly. "If we can manufacture them at a quick enough pace, pretty soon there will be no need for conventional soldiers."

Shaw snorted at that, and Custer rocked back on his heels, hands hooked into his belt. "You're serious? You think these tin soldiers are going to replace real fighting men?"

Tesla shook his head quickly. "No, of course not! Nothing will replace the initiative and skill of the modern soldier." He waved a hand dismissively. "Well, not right now, at any rate. However, these automatons will be more than equal to the task of holding a line or standing a post. They will bolster our numbers in the face of growing threats until we can produce something better."

"Growing threats?" Custer paced around the metal man. "We seem to be holding our own well enough for the time being."

Tesla shook his head. "We are holding our own against the savages, somewhat. And through the efforts of the UR-30 Enforcers, the lawmen are holding their own against the lawless ruffians who stalk the Territories. You must remember that Carpathian's forces will not suffer from the vagaries of time and entropy like the rest of us. With each man and woman that falls on the frontier, his armies potentially grow. His prospective strength is no less than every person living, and who ever lived, in the western territories, under the worst case scenario."

Custer shook his head. It was sometimes hard to understand the little man behind his thick accent. "Those walking corpses aren't worth much, if you ask me."

Tesla looked back at the colonel. "As a single soldier? No, you're right. But imagine one hundred of them coming at you at once. Or a thousand? Or ten thousand? The reports I've seen talk about Carpathian's influence stretching throughout the west. Should he suddenly decide to turn every man, woman, and child in those towns and villages into one of his stumbling soldiers, how many do you think he could field?"

The young scientist settled his back against one of the crate stacks, arms folded, and shook his head. "No, colonel. We will need something to help us meet those numbers when he finally decides to make his move. We cannot hope to do that with standard soldiers alone. The race is on for the future of our world, and we can only hope that we win. Because trust me, you do not want to live in a world of Doctor Carpathian's imagining."

Custer nodded. He had fought the animations while serving down in the territories, and he had no doubts the little European was speaking the truth. "So the race is on, between his corpse soldiers and your metal ones?"

"Well, it is a little more complicated than that." Tesla gestured toward the back of the room where his equipment was bubbling away. "The race is between dead flesh powered by RJ-1027, and metal powered by electricity." He shrugged. "I'm afraid my advances with all things electric are not progressing as quickly as I would like. For now, I am using the devil's blood nearly as much as my nemesis. But I have no doubt a breakthrough is near at hand!"

Custer shook his head, but did not seem to be paying too close attention. "Where's Tumblety fit into this race of yours?"

He grimaced with distaste. "I try not to pay too close attention to that fraudulent butcher, truth be told, colonel."

One of the older men snorted, his eyes flashing in the crimson lighting. "The man's a dangerous quacksalver, not fit to inhabit the same facility as Mr. Tesla!"

The colonel smiled at that. "Really? I would've thought you scientific types would stick together. Especially out here on the edge of civilization, surrounded by us straight-laced military men – I mean personnel." He shot a quick look at Shaw, but she was staring at the assistant who had spoken.

Tesla shook his head. "Dr. Tumblety is following a line of inquiry that posits that the human body, through augmentation and artificial enhancement, can be a match for the animations of the Romanian fiend. The things he is doing crash through the limits of sane scientific inquiry and break every convention of civilized research. We each have our supporters back in Washington, I assure you, but I would rather put my faith in good old fashioned iron and technical innovation, rather than the twisted gothic romance stories fashionable with the wealthy ladies of leisure."

Custer nodded again with a frown. "Can't say I blame you, if it comes to that. Are there any other little inventions you'll be springing on us, just so I can keep an eye out?"

Tesla straightened, a boyish grin on his face. "Oh, I'm following countless avenues of research that have been most promising, colonel! The soldier robots should be ready to stand posts in the next few days at most, and I have several prototypes of larger, assault-oriented automata on the way. But they are honestly the least of my concerns now, their development all but complete. We will be designing and creating construction facilities for them down the hall when I've perfected the design, but for now, I am focusing on a whole new area of research."

The young man gestured for the officers to accompany him deeper into the room. The shadows were darker toward the rear, and the constant babbling of the boiling liquids made for a disconcerting, sibilant backdrop. Tesla's excitement drove his voice into louder, higher octaves, and it was not difficult to hear him.

"You see, I was able to isolate several wavelengths of light while studying the raw RJ-1027 we have been able to obtain from our operations in the west." He was rubbing his hands together gleefully. "The light seems to ebb and flow in a standard RJ generator, yes?"
Custer and Shaw nodded.

"Well, many of us assumed this was an indication of the instability of the material itself. We have yet to create the refined substance ourselves, and are forced to rely on raids into the territories and the open market for our supplies." He gestured to one of the glass containers holding a roiling red substance pulsing like a human heart. "But as it turns out, the light does not ebb and flow due to any inherent instability, but rather the very nature of the element itself! You see, apparently, it exists both within AND without our space/time completely!"

Custer looked into the excited face of the young scientist with an utter lack of understanding. "Space time? What's space time?"

Tesla shook his head in frustration. "No, not 'space time', space AND time! RJ-1027 somehow fluctuates between the here and now, and some other place and time!"

Shaw snorted slightly, and Custer cocked his curly head to one side. "I'm fairly certain you've lost us both, Mr. Tesla."

Tesla's shoulders sagged. "Never mind. Suffice it to say that, manipulating this property, I am toying with an invention that will allow a person to travel from one place to another without having to move through the space between."

Both officers were now staring blankly. Tesla took a deep breath and forged ahead. "If you take one of these gauntlets," he pulled a white sheet from a table and revealed several ancient-looking metal gloves. Each was shimmering slightly with a red glow as if reflecting a bloody sunset. "With a little more work, you will be able to point at a person with one of these and pull them toward you. They will cease to exist where they are and appear before you."

Shaw barked a cruel laugh. "I've seen that done a hundred times in dancehalls and barker's tents across the country, sir! There's nothing new about that!"

Custer nodded. "What you are describing is a fairly common trick, Mr. Tesla."

Tesla balled his fists in irritation and tilted his head toward the ceiling above. When he looked back at the officers, his eyes were flat and cold. "Someday your forces will be able to jump across the battlefield to come to grips with the enemy without having to cross through their fields of fire. Injured will be evacuated without risk. Someday, walls, moats, and even mountains will be as nothing as you assault the enemy." He tilted toward them both, his dark eyes flashing from one to the other. "And when that day comes, I want you to remember that it was in this dank cave that you first heard the idea."

Custer put his hands up to calm to the scientist down. "I'm sure you're right, Mr. Tesla. I'm sure. They look right impressive and no mistake."

"The wealth of the world will be ours one day, colonel, because of science. There will be nothing we do not know, nothing we cannot do, and it will all come to us through the investigation of the world around us and our own powers of creation."

The colonel took a step back, nodding. "I have no doubt." He turned with a casual tap of his finger to the brim of his hat. "Shaw, you're with me."

"Yessir." The young woman hurried to catch up.

Over his shoulder, Custer called out. "Mr. Tesla, I have to meet with Dr. Tumblety now. I'm planning a foray into the surrounding territory in the next month or so to teach the savages a sharp lesson. I would be greatly obliged if as many of your metal soldiers as possible would be ready to take the field with us as you think prudent."

As the colonel walked from the room he could hear the eagerness in the scientist's voice. "I will do that, colonel! And thank you for this chance to prove the efficacy of my work!"

"Shaw, I swear." Custer muttered under his breath as they moved deeper beneath Fort Frederick. "I'm going to go barking mad by the time they get us out of here."

*****

The lowest levels beneath Fort Frederick were damp and poorly lit. As Custer and Shaw moved down the final corridor, their footsteps echoing hollowly around them, the two officers found themselves closing ranks without conscious thought.

Custer shook his head and turned to his young adjutant. "I hate these visits, Shaw. You weren't at Camp Lincoln, but God, if you'd of seen what sorts of things he did there . . . The man's no surgeon. He's a butcher, and a madman." The colonel knew he was babbling, but could not help himself. He had been able to keep ahead of Tumblety's demand for test subjects, barely, with the captured savages his outriders occasionally dragged back to Fort Frederick. He had refused to provide the poor, innocent victims that had kept the maniac's more violent rampages in check. So far, there had been no serious repercussions, but the Colonel knew that time would come.

Shaw nodded as they marched down the hall but said nothing. As disquieting as it surely was for the colonel to visit Doctor Tumblety's dungeons, she found it more disturbing by far.

A scream bubbled up from ahead of them, drowning the fading sounds of their footsteps and opening a ringing cacophony as echoing screams bounced back all around, filling the narrow hallway. Dazed, directionless moaning and animal growls rose up as if in answer to the squeals of pain. Shaw started to take more careful notice of the doors that passed to either side. Most of the windows were barred.

The scream faded into quiet sobbing, and then silence. Custer and Shaw shared a dark look as they stopped in front of a pair of doors set into the rough wall at the end of the hallway. The colonel frowned, Shaw cocked one eyebrow, and Custer turned to knock.

"Doctor, we've come to inspect your work." The colonel pushed the door open without waiting for a reply. Whether his mind had actually banished all memory of Camp Lincoln, or it had only been a moment's lapse, he would spend the rest of his life wishing he had allowed Tumblety time to cover up his current subject.

What was left of a once-proud native was fastened to a slab of shiny metal by leather straps slick with blood. The savage's hands had been removed at the forearm, his legs removed just above the knee. Wires connected the stumps to various metallic items on the table that rattled or scratched as the man's body flailed against its bonds.

Custer was chivalrous enough to hope the subject had been a man. The flesh of the subject's chest had been stripped down to the meat-enclosed ribcage, the bones flashing wetly in the dim, crimson light. The skin had been pulled down like a blanket and was draped, glistening, over the lower abdomen and upper thighs.

The face had also been stripped of several layers of flesh. Lumps of meat floated in various glass containers on a smaller cart, noxious fumes adding to the slaughterhouse stench. Custer saw long, ivory teeth or claws projecting from some of the lumps, lank hair or fur floated around still others. The doctor was working over the pool of blood that had once been the unfortunate victim's eye socket, a pale orb rotating wildly within the crimson fluid. Two strong orderlies, their white aprons splashed with blood, held the wretched creature down.

The self-styled Doctor Tumblety looked up from his work and smiled as he saw Colonel Custer. Beneath the stained apron, the doctor wore a ridiculous costume based upon some fanciful notion of a military uniform. The smile vanished, however, when Lieutenant Shaw walked into view.

"The woman must leave at once, colonel. I do not allow members of the distaff sex to be present while I work." His face, behind the ludicrously elaborate mustache, had hardened into a mask of barely-contained fury. "Their energy is disruptive to the process and distracting to my assistants."

Custer had expected something like this. He had seen for himself the man's downright allergy to women, but he had not expected him to be quite so direct and insulting. He felt his own anger rising in defense of his adjutant.

"Doctor, I'm afraid I'm not going to be able to let you –
"

The doctor held up one hand, dripping with blood, and stopped the colonel in his tracks. "I thought we had an understanding, colonel. Further, I was informed by General Grant himself that my work would receive every possible assistance from the command staff of Fort Frederick. Was that assurance somehow in error?" The haughty manner and exaggerated upper-class accent were horribly incongruous with the blood-drenched apron and gore-encrusted hands.

When Custer failed to respond, Tumblety leaned forward. "I'm afraid I did not hear your response, colonel. I would hate to think that I had made an error in selecting my chosen champion. Am I not to receive every possible assistance with my work?"

Custer nodded. The blunt reminder of Tumblety's patronage, and the man's legendary caprice, stung deeply. The anger was still there, but the damned charlatan was right. He waved Shaw back toward the door without turning around. "Go get a drink, Lieutenant. God knows I wish I could join you."

"Sir." The colonel could hear the anger and resentment in the young woman's voice, but she pivoted on one heel and snapped out, closing the door with dull finality behind her.

The moment the door closed, the doctor completely relaxed. His shoulders sagged, his face thawed, and a smile emerged from beneath the mustache. "Thank you, Colonel. I do find the presence of a woman can be so distressing when conducting serious work, don't you?"

Custer shook his head and forced himself to approach the shining table. One assistant moved away to give him a better view. "Lieutenant Shaw is an exemplary officer. Women have been serving beside men for years now, ever since the casualty lists of the war became unsustainable. I guess we just got used to it."

Tumblety nodded. "Indeed, Colonel. The ability of the human mind to adapt to even the most uncomfortable, outrageous situations has always fascinated me. I intend, when time permits, to look deeper into the phenomenon. Perhaps publish a paper on my findings." He waved one crimson-stained hand over the body before them. "But, happily, there is one hardship, I think, that may soon cease to vex us. With my current line of research, our difficulties with recruitment and retention may soon be a thing of the past!"

The body on the table between them shuddered with continued, moaning sobs. Tumblety rolled his eyes and gestured for one of his assistants to wheel the table further into the shadows of the long, low room.

"Honestly, colonel, life can often be quite lonely here on the edge of scientific advancement." His face was curled into a cartoonish mask of sadness. "So few understand the inevitable benefits of my work. For instance, sir, are you aware of the revitalizing blessings of RJ-1027?"

Custer nodded. "There aren't many fighting men today that don't notice we tend to last longer than those who aren't." He grimaced. "Those of us who aren't burned down, of course."

"Of course!" The doctor wagged a finger in the colonel's direction. "And yet, almost no research is being conducted upon this phenomenon! In Zeus's name, sir, we do not even truly understand what RJ-1027 is, entirely!"

"No, I'm aware." Custer's sour tone was lost on the doctor. Most non-military government workers failed to understand the inherent weakness in depending upon the enemy for their only true source of power. The world had been turned upside down by Carpathian's appearance; more than most people realized.

"Exactly." Tumblety nodded. "Thankfully, there are those in Washington who want nothing more than to understand this fascinating world around us and how it can be bent more to our will. By the time I am done here, Colonel Custer, that Romanian charlatan will have no hold over us. His legions of the stumbling dead will hold no terror for a people who have mastered the human body itself."

Custer nodded, eager only to escape. But the doctor continued.

"I was just telling the Secretary of War himself before coming out here, sir. The secret is within us, and we only need to open our eyes to see it!" The man's smile was ghastly. "He agreed wholeheartedly." He made a shooing gesturing with one hand, his face twisted in dismissal. "Let Tesla run around lighting fires and making metal men. The true victory will be here, sir, in this lab, with these all-too human creatures, in elevating them to godhead!"

One orderly stopped to spit on the floor, his eyes glowing with reflected lamplight in the shadows. "Tesla's not fit to polish your medals, sir."

A low moan escaped from the shape on the table, as the doctor glowed in the praise of his minion. He looked to the colonel with sad eyes. "I apologize, colonel." He shrugged. "Sometimes my subjects are less focused upon the work than I would like."

Custer watched the masked attendant pull the mutilated body deeper into the shadows. He nodded vaguely.

"I can . . . imagine, doctor." He shook his head and cleared his throat. "Washington would like to know what kind of progress you are making, and if you require any further supplies."

"You are in communication with Washington?" This seemed to perk the doctor up again, his smile wider than ever.

Custer found himself retreating into the stiff parade rest stance of his rocky time at the Academy. "The latest supply run included a command-grade vocal reiterator suite. If there is anything you require from the War Office or the White House, we are in constant communication as of last evening."

Tumblety dried his hands on a dirty cloth and tossed it onto another table. "Excellent! That will be ideal when I have reached the next phase of my research. Currently, however, I believe I have everything I need . . . That is, as long as you intend to follow General Grant's orders to provide me with my pick of all prisoners taken?"

Custer could not stop his eyes from flicking back into the shadows. The wretch back there moaned softly. He swallowed and clenched his hands tighter behind his back.

"Those are my orders, doctor. I intend to follow them."

"Excellent!" Tumblety came to stand beside the colonel and rested one hand on his shoulder. It was everything Custer could do not to flinch away. "And tell me, Colonel, when might we be finding another opportunity to acquire further prisoners? I am nearly finished with this latest batch, but the next phase will require many more."

There was nothing Custer wanted more at that moment than to escape from this fusty, dark, foul-smelling room. He took a deep breath through his mouth. "I'm inclined to launch a punitive expedition against the local savages in the next couple of weeks, doctor. They are initiating most of their attacks from a nearby village. We will have a strong enough force to ensure overwhelming victory." He swallowed sharply. "There should be plenty of prisoners."

"Excellent!" Tumblety repeated. "And women too, I expect? Then I will await this glorious day."

"Washington is hoping you will have some of your experiments advanced enough to provide the strike force with samples, so they can be evaluated in the field?"

Custer kept his eyes focused on the middle distance.

"Absolutely!" The foul man sounded like a child on the morning of his birthday. "I have some excellent examples prepared!"

"Well and good, doctor." The colonel nodded sharply and stood to attention. "With your permission, I have a great deal that requires my attention."

"Of course, colonel. I will continue with my work here." Tumblety turned, gesturing into the shadows for his assistants to draw the whimpering subject back into the light. As Custer pushed the door open, however, the doctor called back to him. "Colonel, where is this savage village? Is it close?"

Custer nodded without turning around. "Not far. On a small tributary a few miles away. Little Big Horn, the Injuns call it."

Chapter 4

Lucinda held the tin cup of diluted coffee tightly to her chest, absorbing as much of the warmth as she could. Most of the men in the camp could not even claim this much to nurse along, and so she tried not to let the fresh disappointment of each sip affect her. The fires were mere piled embers this late at night, and most of the army was rolling up into their blankets and bedrolls to get what sleep they could. She envied them.

Jesse's ragtag army of survivors, once outlaws, rebel guerillas, or former prisoners, still had faith in the man that led them. Lucinda was not so sure.

"I'm telling you, Jesse," Henderson began again. "You're fighting a two-front war, and you need to use every weapon at your disposal!" The gaunt, black-clad man jabbed the fire with a long stick. "I know you've been shyin' away from it, but that includes the power of fear."

Around the central fire, Jesse and his closest friends and advisors were talking deep into the night. They had been running through the same arguments for the better part of two weeks with no real shift in the battle lines. Stumbling upon a major border trail had brought it all to a head. Frank and Lucinda were adamantly opposed to attacking the border towns, while Jim and Bob Younger, still bitter at John's loss, did not share their restraint. Caught in the middle, either through lack of interest or conviction, Captain Ingram, Will Shaft, the Ford Brothers, and a few of the more prominent prisoners sat back, watching things unfold. As for Cole Younger, he was keeping his own council, for now.

Lucinda's fiercest competition for Jesse's ear was the mysterious Allen Henderson. An advisor and assistant to a man Jesse very nearly worshiped, William Quantrill, Henderson carried far more weight than she thought he should have. The influence he had over Jesse was maddening. So far, Frank and Lucinda had been able to balance the late-night arguments, but eventually Henderson was going to catch

Jesse's ear. She had nightmares imagining what sorts of chaos that would cause.

"Ain't the common man's doin', anythin' that happened to us." Frank's voice had been a raw shadow of his old booming tones since being pulled from the hellish laboratory at Camp Lincoln. Somehow, though, the soft words carried even greater weight.

Jesse, gazing down at his arms as if lost in thought, nodded slightly. "Frank talks a lot of sense."

"Well, I can sympathize with your emotional reaction, Jesse." Henderson's voice resonated with reason. "But we're talking about a much larger picture than any of ya'll are focused on presently. You know what we would have done in the old days: the border region has to burn. We have to send a message. Not only to our foes, but, even more importantly, to those who might side with us, should their consciences fall in the right direction."

Lucinda shook her head. There was no way she could let this man coax Jesse down this path. Despite her own freshly-ambiguous feelings toward her lords and masters, she could not let Jesse take his frustration and rage out on the innocents of the border lands, no matter their allegiance.

"Jesse, just think before you do anything rash." She poured every tone and nuance from a lifetime of training in deceit and performance into her voice, infusing it with pure, naked conviction. "Think about your next move. If you kill women and children in their homes . . . That's no easy thing to walk back from. You need to keep that firmly in mind. Whether you want to carve out your own place or you're looking to go around Lee and his cronies and see the south rise again, you don't want that kind of stain on your story."

"It's no stain if they're the very people keeping the south down!" Henderson's poise slipped as his eyes, eclipsed behind their thick lenses, glared at her over the fire. "The Union army does not feed itself, it doesn't give itself orders, it doesn't spontaneously create soldiers from the ribs of the ones that have gone before. The Union army exists on the backs and at the tacit complicity of the people. And that includes those border towns supporting Johnson and his cabal."

"Not the women and children, Henderson." Frank spoke again, taking up the thread. Considering his run-in with the Union at Camp Lincoln, his opinion could not help but carry weight. "Most of the men and all of the women and children of those towns deserve a hell of a lot better from the world than they got. And that means the Union army as much as it means us. The last thing they need is us comin' at 'em from one side, while Grant's grindin' over 'em from the other."

The Youngers maintained their silence, but they watched everything through hooded eyes. Bob, in particular, was staring at Jesse, one of his broad-bladed fighting knives glittering in his hand as he oiled it.

A hard edge had entered Jesse's eyes at Henderson's, and Lucinda knew there was still hope.

"Well, this is a new world, Henderson." Jesse was still staring into the fire, but Lucinda could see, as Frank relaxed and the Youngers tensed up, that everyone had felt the change. "I don't believe we'll be doin' ourselves any favors, hittin' towns that we ain't sure are standin' with Grant."

That was too much for Bob Younger, who surged to his feet, pointing with the gleaming knife at the outlaw boss. "You got a lot of nerve talkin' about favors, James! Your brother walked out of Camp Lincoln! Ours died there, no matter the why's and wherefores. The Youngers owe those blue-bellied bastards, Jesse, and we mean to make 'em pay!"

Cole sat unmoving. In the old days, he would have reined his hot-tempered brother in with a clever joke or a biting observation. But like all of them, he had changed. He had been far less vocal in his opinions and much less prone to laughter since they had emerged from the prison camp. The fact that he let Bob's comment stand was telling, and Lucinda feared again for the civilians that lay in their path.

Jesse, however, was unmoved by either of the Youngers' speech or silence. He stared into Bob's eyes and spoke in slow, even tones. "John Younger followed me of his own free will. He was followin' me when he was taken. The man who . . . did that, to John, will pay. You have my word on that. But these towns ahead of us now? They ain't never heard of Andersonville, or Camp Lincoln. Killin' 'em for that wouldn't make no more sense than killin' 'em fer the cold weather."

"We also need to think about food." Lucinda pushed forward. "It will be much easier to buy supplies from friendly towns than it will from hostiles. And when you burn your first border town, Jesse, every other town right down to the Gulf will be your enemy."

"You don't do business with the enemy, missy!" Henderson scoffed. "You take what you want. Hell, we got enough food, now that the Injuns separated the wheat from the chaff. We ain't heard no whinin' about it since we headed south!"

Lucinda stared at the old rebel and shook her head, then turned back to Jesse. "The decision has to be yours, Jesse. There's no one else to make it. But if rising to true power and influence, either back in the Territories or down south is your goal, please think about the reputation you'll carry with you if you leave a trail of dead women and children in your wake."

For a moment, the only sound was the soft popping of the fire. When Jesse spoke, he was still staring into the embers. "I'm hearin' everyone's words, an' I ain't made up my mind yet. We'll come up on the first border town in the next couple of days: Moberly, if I've figured our position right. I ain't never been there, so I don't know much about it."

He looked up, first at Lucy, then at Frank, then to Henderson. "I say we leave it up to them. If I walk into Moberly an' I see Union flags flyin' in the town square, 'r any soldiers, 'r any other sign o' twisted loyalties, we'll take up this conversation again." His dark eyes settled on the Youngers. "But if they ain't got no truck with the Union, 'r if they're hidin' the stars 'n bars in their hearts, then we ain't gonna do nuthin' but maybe trade fer some beef 'n whiskey an' be on our way. Is that clear as moonshine fer you boys?"

The Youngers all nodded, their eyes ranging from flat to hostile. After a moment, Jesse nodded in return and rose to his feet. "Well, that's just rosy. Happy to hear it." He turned toward the nearest supply wagon, its RJ engine glowing softly. "I'm gonna saw some logs. I'll talk to ya'll in the mornin'."

The group around the fire sat for several moments in silence and then drifted off to their own blankets. Lucinda was the last to move away, pushing the glowing embers around in the heart of the fire until they muted to a dull, glowing orange.

Henderson, settled back against the wheel of one of their remaining Rolling Thunders, watched her through lenses that reflected that light back in crimson gleams. They nodded to each other, faces cold and still. Loveless turned without a word and went to find her own bedroll.

*****

There was nothing to set Moberly apart from any other border town in the war-torn region the big bugs on all sides had taken to calling the Contested Territories. There were twenty or so buildings huddled around the intersection of two major trails. The side streets were little more than packed dirt paths branching off between the rickety structures. Farmland was visible off to the east, small herds of cattle milling in the middle distance. Off south, a low range of hills probably promised silver to any fool willing to put in the back-breaking work. That promise was what most likely kept this little scrub-town alive.

The buildings Jesse could see, as he and his small gang rumbled into town, sported an intriguing mix of RJ generators. He saw both the heavy-framed Union models and the more elegant Carpathian jobs, but neither seemed more prevalent than the other. Clearly, Moberly was a town that had not yet taken sides between the Union or the European. That was good for Jesse and his battered crew, anyway. Not that it meant that his people would be welcome, but at least this little burg was not already taking up with an enemy.

Jesse's eyes tightened behind the rose-colored goggles. Although they had not come down for Grant or Carpathian, that did not mean they might not take up the Union cause against any sons of the south who happened to ride on in.

The outlaw boss raised one metallic fist and the riders with him slowed. The Iron Horses dropped into an idling rumble and glided to a stop in the middle of the packed dirt trail. The Ford brothers scanned the scrub brush to either side. They had hardly left him a moment's peace once they had taken up their self-appointed roles as his protectors. The much larger, dark-skinned man at the back of their little group sat his 'Horse impassively, looking straight ahead with calm, dark eyes. A bandana hid the lower portions of his face, while a tight hood was draped over his head. A strange bulge pressed against the fabric on one side.

Jesse smiled at Marcus Cunningham. They had found Cunningham in one of the deepest, darkest pits in Fort Lincoln. Due in no small part to his strange deformity, he had been a favorite subject of Tumblety's. The big black man had never ridden with the Confederacy; he had been much too young. The mad doctor must have requested his presence, special. One thing was for sure: Camp Lincoln had been no safe place for a man of Marcus's skin tone.

Lucy had been dead-set against it when he told her he was bringing the big black man, but Jesse had been unyielding. He had thought about having Will Shaft join him, but the young man's rebel gear might confuse the issue Jesse was trying to establish. Riding into a border town with a man whose skin was as black as pitch was very likely to cause trouble no matter what flag they flew behind their eyes. Lucy was right about that. If Jesse could not get a bunch of hayseeds in a no-account border town like Moberly to see his new vision, there would be little reason to continue south.

Within the frame of his trimmed beard, Jesse's mouth quirked in a crooked smile. His arms had not twitched once on him since riding out of camp, almost as if they approved of this mission. Besides, he was in the mood to bust some heads, and if there were a few folks in town that would take exception to a black man riding with white folks, well, then, so be it. Jesse knew something about forging a reputation. Making a public display of violence on behalf of a dark-skinned friend would set just the right tone for what had to come after.

Jesse nodded to the big man, who nodded back without a change in his expression. Marcus Cunningham was no man's fool. He knew why he had been chosen to ride into Moberly, and he did not care.

Marcus was the son of escaped slaves. His parents, having crossed the Mississippi looking for a fresh start, had been captured by a Warrior Nation raiding party. His father was killed by the warriors, but his mother, large with child, had been spared and brought into the small tribal village, adopted as one of their own. Marcus had been given his father's name, but he had been raised by the Warrior Nation.

While still a boy, he had been eager to follow the path of the warrior, but had lacked the patience and the serenity to follow the slow pace set by the medicine men. Something had gone wrong, resulting in the misshapen crest of bone that emerged from the side of his head, hidden by the cowl. That horn had landed Marcus in Camp Lincoln, and Jesse knew he was sensitive about it. The big man saw the horn as, not only the cause of his most recent suffering, but also as a reminder of his failure as a boy. He had been known to kill men just for looking at it.

He had just the temperament Jesse wanted for this little detour.

"Looks like the joint's dyin' a slow death, Jesse." Robert Ford spat into the dust. "Not sure they're gonna be any good for much of anythin', you ask me."

Jesse's grin widened as he turned back to survey the cluster of buildings. "Nonsense, Robert. Everythin's good for somethin'. Worse comes to worst, this little burg'll make a great bad example."

The four men brought their mounts back up to a growling roar and rumbled into Moberly in a cloud of dust. The streets were nearly empty. Only a few folks stood around, gaping as the outlaws rode in. A couple of horse shaped blackhoofs, cast iron frames showing no great artistry, were standing still as statues a few buildings down. A large, battered passenger wagon was parked a little ways down the street, probably stopped for supplies and food on a regular passage along the major trail.

Jesse tipped his hat to a pair of ladies standing in front of a row of businesses that shared a boardwalk and wooden sunshade. The women stared as the four vehicles growled past, moving toward a low, two-story corner structure. A sign hanging kitty-corner to the street announced this to be The Pavilion saloon and eatery. Jesse's first thought was that it was a rather grandiose title for the unassuming little shack. His second, as three scowling men emerged blinking into the sunlight, was *here we go*.

Jesse brought his 'Horse around in a tight turn, nose-in toward the saloon's porch. There were only two recharge pads there, and he settled down on the closest. Cunningham brought his machine rumbling up onto the other, and the Ford brothers settled for grounding theirs in the dirt to either side. Jesse pulled his goggles down off his face and nodded to the three men standing there.

"Howdy, folks!" The outlaw's voice boomed with easy confidence. White teeth flashed in a predatory grin.

The lead man on the porch gave him a grudging nod while his companions stared coldly at the big black man in the strange headgear.

Jesse took clear note of the men staring at Marcus and his grin disappeared. He looked down without a care, pulling the makings of a quirley from a pouch in his front pocket. Casually, he began to roll up a cigarillo. His eyes remained focused on his blurring hands as he shrugged and muttered, "You boys havin' a problem?"

The two men jerked and looked back over to the outlaw chief. The lead man, a healthy gut pushing at his fancy vest, put his hands on his hips. The right hand settled in close to the silvered grip of a custom blaster.

"Folks round these parts don' want no trouble." He jerked his head toward Marcus. "But we ain't likely to cower down when it shows up at our door, neither." The men behind him nodded.

Jesse tossed the quirley into his mouth and caught it with pursed lips, lighting it with a match he swiped across the palm of one hand. He grinned, and smoke began to rise from the corners of his mouth. "Marcus?" He tilted his head in the direction of the big black man. "He don't mean no trouble. You mean trouble, Marcus?"

The large body was completely still, the eyes glittering in the shadow of the hood. "Nossir, Jesse. I don't mean trouble."

Jesse flicked the match in a smoky arc out into the street. "You see?" He folded his mechanical arms across his broad chest. "Marcus don't mean no trouble. I don't mean no trouble. I KNOW these boys don't mean no trouble, do you boys?"

The Fords shook their heads, but their eyes were cold and flat. Each man sat in his saddle with an easy grace, hands not far from weapons.

"You see now, fellas?" Jesse's grin returned full force. "There ain't no reason for things to get ugly. Me an' my friends here, we're just passin' through. Thought we'd get us a drink and a little time in the shade before movin' on. Maybe chat you folks up over current events?" He took out the cigarillo and spit a fleck of tobacco off to the side.

"Current events?" The lead man was still suspicious. The two men behind him looked more confused than anything else.

"Well, fer starters, how're the mines playin' out? How's the crop lookin'? Seen any Injuns hereabouts?" His smile was fixed but his voice became chill. "Any Union soldiers been through lately?"

All three faces on the porch turned sour at the mention of the Union. The man in front spit over the railing and into the dirt. "Don't think much o' the Union 'round here, boys."

"They's like locusts, comin' through on their way west." One of the men in the back of the group snarled. "Take whatever they want: food, water, whatnot; rough up the hands, play lewd with the womenfolk."

"You're not goin' to find many folks carryin' water fer the Union in Moberly, stranger." The lead man's voice was low as he shifted his gaze back to Marcus. "But that don't make them the worst sorts there is, neither."

Jesse swung down off his 'Horse and took a casual turn around the street. The windows of the nearby buildings were filling up with curious onlookers. It was just about time to play to the gallery.

He looked back up at the man on the porch, hooking his thumbs behind his gun belt and pushing back his duster. "Well, that weren't too friendly."

The man on the porch shifted slightly, his own hand creeping toward his gun. The two men behind him moved off to either side, clearing their own firing lanes.

"Marcus!" Jesse pitched his voice to carry out over the street. "You offended by that last remark?"

The big black man nodded slowly. "Yeah, Jesse," he rumbled. "I was."

As Marcus stood up, his size became more apparent. Rather than swing his leg up and over to dismount, he just stood up and stepped over the saddle. He was a huge man, muscles bulging from his doeskin vest. Heavy lengths of chain were draped around his neck and under his arms: the same chains that had held him down in Camp Lincoln, now worn with defiant pride. With slow and easy movements he reached down to a boot behind his saddle and slid out a smooth wooden shaft wrapped in cured leather.

When Marcus turned back to the porch he was holding a massive hammer with a heavy stone head. His brows curled down toward each other as he looked directly into the eyes of the men on the porch. His voice was a low, subterranean growl. "I ain't liked the way you folks been lookin' at me since we rode up."

Jesse smiled even wider and patted the air with one down-turned hand. "Now, now, Marcus." He turned to the locals. "We don't need to resort to violence, do we boys?"

The lead man on the porch had rested his hand on the butt of his pistol. He moved forward and rested his other hand on the railing and sneered down at Jesse and his men. "We don't if you an' yer friend turn those hellish machines around an' get the hell outta town, flannel mouth."

The Fords eased themselves off their 'Horses, eyes watching the men on the porch, hands resting on their weapons. The last words fell into the silence like a lead weight into a stagnant pond. The six men paused as if waiting for the ripples to reach them.

The moment stretched on, the pressure of the silence building. The people of Moberly crept backward, as if afraid they would disturb the tableau. An almost-visible line of tension connected the speaker on the porch with Jesse standing calmly in the street.

When the outlaw chief finally spoke, his voice was light, belaying the tightness that had settled over the scene.

"He just call me a flannel mouth, Marcus?" The quirley shifted from one side of Jesse's mouth to the other with a flash of teeth.

"He did that, Jesse." The large man twisted his hands on the shaft of the massive hammer. The leather creaked with subtle menace.

"That's what I thought." Without warning, one of Jesse's Hyper-velocity pistols was in his hand with reassuring speed, metallic arm rigid as the bore of the weapon settled on the local man's face. "That just ain't gonna stand."

The man had just enough time to dodge to the side before the bolt from Jesse's gun flashed past him and slapped into the front of the saloon, blowing in a window and scorching a wide circle in the dry wood. Rather than snarling in anger at his inaccuracy, Jesse's smile grew wider, as if this had been his intention all along.

The two men who had come out onto the boardwalk with the pie eater crouched down in place, their hands raised momentarily in shock at the detonation. The Ford brothers, on the other hand, had been ready. Their weapons were in their hands and sending shot after shot into the shade of the overhang. Jesse fanned a stream of shots, straight and true, into the flickering shadows as well. His exultant Rebel yell echoed off the saloon's wall.

One of the locals was struck several times in the body and arm, spinning back against the wall in a spray of blood and cooked flesh as his clothing fluttered away from the stunning impacts. Another window shattered as the hapless man crashed through it to hang there, suspended on the broken glass, a sheet of blood cascading down from his torn belly.

The last man on the porch got several wild shots off as he dove for a rain barrel at the corner of the building. The bolts snapped past the outlaws and into the sunny street, hitting buildings across the way and setting several small fires. The Fords ran slant-wise along the railing, their weapons steady, to get a clean shot around the big wooden barrel.

The leader of the local men had hit the wooden planks and rolled on his shoulder to slam up against a thick support beam that held the sunshade steady overhead. His back to the polished wood, he had his weapon held tightly to his chest. He cocked his head to the side, trying to catch a glimpse of Jesse from the corner of his eye.

"Now, I did take exception to the unkind words you sent in my direction, sir." Jesse's tone was still light. He knew that any story spreading outward from Moberly would feature his attitude as an important element. He chose his next words with special care. "But it was the way you treated my friend, Marcus here, that really set me off."

"I'm sorry!" The man squeaked from behind the pillar. His eyes were now fixed on the body of his friend, leaking life down onto the worn wood of the boardwalk. "I din't mean nothin' by it!"

"I give up!" The man behind the rain barrel threw his gun out into the dust, his hands raised, shaking, over his head. He did not stand, but he was clearly out of the fight. The Fords came around and gestured for him to back away down the side of the building while Marcus and Jesse settled the true conflict.

"Marcus, you reckon our local yokel here is sorry?" Jesse sauntered to the side, his pistol pointed, unwavering, at the large post.

The big man stalked toward the porch, hammer hefted easily before him. "He ain't sorry enough."

The outlaw boss nodded, again pitching his voice for the general audience. "No, he ain't. Folks gotta learn, it's a new world, 'specially here in the borderlands. It can't be about color no more, if'n we wanna live to see another day. It's stand together against the savages, the Union, an' the nightmares comin' out o' the west, 'r their gonna drag us down, one lonely fool at a time."

Jesse could see the round eyes of the townsfolk as they heard his words. Most folks on the frontier were too busy surviving to hold too tightly to the old prejudices anyway, but he was glad to see that not many of these folks looked too outraged at his little speech.

"It's fools like this that are as much the enemy as any blue-belly, brave, or walkin' corpse." He gave a theatrical shrug, stretching both metal arms out wide and taking his gun off the cowering man on the porch for the first time since he fired. "An' there's folks who won't understand that 'till they see some blood on the street. Don't you think, Marcus?"

"True words, Jesse." Marcus had reached the pillar on feet far too quiet for a man his size. On the other side, the local man, having found the courage of his convictions, raised his pistol, a snarl wiping the fear from his face as he turned to jump back up into the fight. The muscles beneath Marcus's vest bunched and stretched as he brought the enormous stone hammer back with only a slight snarl of exertion, and then his entire body wrenched with the effort to swing it around.

The hammer head struck the solid wooden post at head height on the man rising up behind it. The wood shattered, sending splinters showering in all directions. The weapon did not slow at all in its arc of destruction. The broad stone struck the cowering man in the side of the head, preceded by a blast wave of sharp wooden shards. Gobbets of wet matter splattered across the opposite wall and windows, and the headless body cartwheeled limply into a still heap in front of the batwing doors.

"Whewee, doggie!" Jesse holstered his pistol with a casual flourish, flexing his metal fingers in surprised satisfaction, and stepped up onto the porch, looking down at the horrific mess. "Marcus, when you make a point, you really make a point!"

The Fords brought the last would-be attacker around the corner, still held at gunpoint. The man's face was as pale as death, his breathing ragged, and he could not take his eyes from the slumped and mangled body of his friend hanging from the window. The headless corpse on the ground in front of him, though, was too much. The man sagged into the dust, nearly losing consciousness.

Jesse grinned at the slumped form and then spun around to cast his gaze among the men and women standing in shocked silence on the street and in the surrounding windows.

"Ya'll saw how that went down, an' I don't want no one missin' the point!" He gestured to the body at his feet with a gentle push of one heel. "We just rode up into town. It was your boys here who decided they wanted a fight, casting unfriendly words at my friend." He jerked his chin at Marcus, standing calmly by his side. Blood dripped gently from the head of the hammer.

"What I said to your man here holds true." Jesse hooked his thumbs behind his gun belt again. "These are dark times we're livin' in, and good folks gotta stand together, regardless of the color of our skin, or we're all goin' down before our time."

Jesse gestured for Robert Ford to bring him the last local man. "An' we ain't here to keep old hate fires burnin', neither." He pulled the limp man roughly forward and draped one solid metal arm over his shoulders. "Grudges won't keep us alive, an' so we ain't lookin' to settle any scores with folks we ain't got no feud with." He patted the man heavily and then gave him a gentle push down the stairs and into the street.

"Now, me and my friends are gonna mosey on inside and get ourselves a drink." Jesse's grin widened again. "I'm hopin' ya'll are comin' around to my way of thinkin' on this, cuz this little dance here," he gestured around himself at the blood and destruction. "This was thirsty work. I'm not lookin' to repeat it, at least till I get around a slug o' whiskey 'r two."

Jesse backed up the stairs to The Pavilion's main doors. His grin was still in place, his thumbs resting easily on his gun belt. Before he could make a dramatic turn, duster swirling in the warm shadows, a voice stopped him cold.

"Jesse James, as I live and breathe."

Chapter 5

James Campbell awoke to the soft sound of rain on canvas. Diffuse light filtered through the tan fabric, confusing the time of day. With a sour grunt, he rolled over, pushed himself out of his bedroll, and snatched his uniform pants off the end of his cot. Dressing in his tent had been one of the earliest indications that his new post would not live up to expectations. Nowadays, it was barely a footnote in a growing list of disappointments and distractions.

Campbell pushed his way out of the low tent and stood up, arching his back to a chorus of grinding cracks. The camp was coming alive around him, so he must not have slept too late. Taut, buff tents stretched away in all directions. Trails of red-tinged smoke curled into the grey sky from hundreds of powered cooking units. The men moving around him were downcast, their uniforms and gear sodden in the early-morning rain.

"Bill!" Campbell raised his voice, knowing his batman could not be far away. "Blodgett, where the hell are you?"

The former sniper appeared without fanfare or ceremony, standing directly behind his commander. Campbell gave a startled jump before spinning around and giving the larger man a quick shove.

"What have I told you about doing that?" He knew his tone spoke more to his own lack of confidence than his aide's transgressions, but he could not help it. He had to be able to pick on someone in this damned camp, and God Himself knew that none of the other engineers or soldiers paid any more attention to him than protocol demanded.

Blodgett nodded, his face impassive. "Sorry, sir. It certainly was not my intention to startle you."

Campbell snarled, looking around the camp with his hands on his hips. "Right then. I would like some breakfast, Bill. Can we do something about that before going up to view the progress on the outer walls?"

"Hardtack and dried beef is the best I can offer, sir." Blodgett stood at attention and kept his eyes focused just off Campbell's left shoulder.

The commander scowled and gestured to the camp all around them. "I'd rather not suffer through another meal of camp biscuit and shoe leather, Blodgett. These men appear to be cooking their breakfast . . . What are they having?"

The adjutant scanned the clusters of men nearby and shrugged. "At a guess, sir, they are cooking hardtack and jerky with water to soften it up."

Campbell sighed. He was never going to accustom himself to working in the field. "Well, fix me up some of that, then." He looked south, where his command sat just out of sight on the other side of a rise. His face twisted into a disgruntled frown. "I suppose I should go survey the construction while you get to it." He started to move away and then stopped, turning with what he hoped was a forceful energy. "And Bill?" When the adjutant turned back to him with a quirked eyebrow, the commander continued. "See if you can't find something better than camp provisions for lunch, will you? I know this whole mission has been rushing headlong without proper logistics, but much more leather and I might just up and head back to Boston."

Campbell felt a little better as he spun on his heel and headed up the muddy track. As he walked, men tossed him perfunctory salutes, huddled beneath heavy, sodden capes or blankets. The rain had been near-continuous for almost a week, adding to his long list of challenges. He knew there must be a terribly pressing reason for his men to be toiling away like this, but no one had yet seen fit to tell him what it was.

Coming up over the rise, he stopped as the project came into view. A man-made mountain of stone and steel rose before him, glossy with rain. Wooden scaffolds surrounded the edifice, providing steady perches for the men and machines that were climbing up to their day's work in the downpour. Figures swarmed all over the structure, most of them far larger than the human men overseeing the work. UR-10s, mechanical workers from the Pipetown Works in Washington, were lumbering up the steep wooden ramps with heavy slabs of stone balanced on their backs, or fixing those blocks into place with massive metal arms. Fat red sparks scattered down into the puddles below.

Situated a few hundred yards from the construction site was an awning of the ubiquitous tan fabric. Several men and women in the blue uniforms of the Union stood around a drafting table, surveying one of the many large building plans Campbell had brought south with him. When he stepped into the dry space beneath the awning, the officers at the table all popped to attention. His second in command, Major Thomas Dalton, saluted for the detachment.

"Good morning, sir." Dalton's voice was deep and powerful, just the voice Campbell would have liked to possess.

"Carry on." Campbell gestured with his hand for the engineers to turn back to their work. "What are we looking at this morning?"

"Sir," Dalton stepped aside to make room for his commander while pointing with one gloved hand down at a section of the plan scrolled out on the table. Campbell could see that it was the layout of one of the lower levels. "We were discussing the nature of the inner chamber again, sir. There's still a lot of disagreement over its intent."

Campbell leaned over the sheet and looked more closely, although he knew what he was going to see. Within the thick walls of the fortress, honeycombed with fighting positions, rally points, and defenses, the center of the massive edifice was to be entirely hollow, housing a smaller keep in the center. Campbell had never voiced his doubts aloud, but to him, the entire thing reminded him of a vermin trap, with that smaller blockhouse sitting as the bait.

The commander flipped one hand dismissively over the plans. "I'm sure General Grant has his reasons. It might make guarding the lower levels easier should there be a breach, though, don't you think?"

A female officer shook her head. "It doesn't make any sense at all, sir. And then, there are these chambers built into the lower levels. They're just as baffling."

Campbell gave her a weary look and then peered down at the plans again. "Ah, yes. Those were specifically designed by that Euro chap, Tesla? I believe they were also worked to General Grant's specifications."

The officer cleared her throat. "Colonel, what would we need two prison cells in the middle of the armory level for?"

Campbell felt a familiar pressure building in him. He hated being questioned by his subordinates. He particularly hated being questioned by his subordinates when he did not know the answers himself. He felt his lip curl and gave in to the surge of frustration rather than fight the losing battle yet again.

"Captain Baine, where in these plans do you see the words prison?" He tapped the table with more force than he had intended and the thin paper bunched beneath the pressure, threatening to rip. "For that matter, do you see any designation for an armory anywhere here?"

She looked taken aback, but rallied gamely. "Sir, these reinforced bunkers only make sense if they were containing magazines for the fort, or other weapons and ordnance. These two rooms, with only single entryways, heavy locks, and no provision for storage? We've been assuming they were cells for days now."

"Looks more like a trap to me." One of the younger officers, a lieutenant from Maine with more experience in the back woods than on the front line, peered owlishly down at the map from behind thick glasses.

Campbell hid his shock at the younger man's guess and shook his head. "Or guards' barracks? Or communication centers? Or vaults for the storage of General Grant's personal tea set collection?" He was snarling now, and forced himself to bring his temper under control. "I do not know what function those two rooms will serve, captain, and I designed this enormous pile of bricks myself. The entire fortress will be riddled with rooms, passages, and other mysteries whose purposes I cannot even begin to guess at." His voice was rising again, the command staff shying away from his tirade, but he could not stop himself.

"We have been sent down here, deep into what all but the most optimistic fool would consider enemy territory, to construct the most formidable fortification built east of the Mississippi since the war ended. When we are finished, we will have placed a nearly-unassailable fortress on the very edge of

Rebellion territory, and we have no idea at all WHY we are doing it!"

"Sir, I thought we had been led to believe this was going to be an advanced base for –" Dalton's mouth snapped shut at the Colonel's sharp tone.

"Based on the plans, Thomas? This will be an advanced base. But it is also appears to be designed as a depository for something that has yet to be identified." He felt his shoulders slump and the men and women sheltering beneath the overhang relaxed slightly, moving forward again as the commander continued in a softer voice.

"They mean to bring something here, and I can't even tell you what it might be." He shook his head and pointed again at the wrinkled section of the plans. "These two rooms? I have referred to them, in my private notes, as the vaults. As you can see, everything around these two chambers is reinforced." He waved a hand with a defeated cast to his face. "Whatever they mean to put down there, it's got to be very important."

For several minutes the command staff stood quiet and still. Some were looking down at the plans, others were looking up at the growing structure before them. Already it was taking shape: long, high walls forming an enormous square, crenellations rising up around the edges. Behind the outer wall rose the beginnings of another, shorter level of wall with a fighting parapet between. When they were finished, if the damned Rebellion let them finish, this place was going to be one of the strongest points on the continent.

"Sir, if they're going through all this trouble to guard something," Baine gestured up at the fortress. "Why put it so close to the enemy?"

The other men around the table nodded or muttered agreement. Campbell could only wish he had an answer for them. Instead, he shrugged. "I don't know, captain. I know we had a small fort here during the war. We kept it garrisoned to stop raiders from striking up into our supply lines. But the site's been abandoned for years." He shook his head. "Now we're rushed down here, put to work with the worst supply situation I've ever seen, and worked under intolerable conditions in hostile territory. All with almost no warning. . ." He shrugged again. "I tell myself ours is not to reason why . . . but believe me, I share your frustration."

"Sir," Dalton's voice was more subdued than it had been. "Has there been any word yet as to what they're thinking of naming the fortress?"

Campbell shook his head. "The name was chosen before I was even brought in." He turned to look out at the pile of glossy stone and the men and machines swarming around it. "They're going to call it Fort Knox, after some artillerist friend of George Washington's."

"Artillerist?" Another of the officers spoke up. "Do you think, maybe, they're planning on putting in some big guns? Something big enough to reach Lee and his cronies?"

Campbell shook his head. "No. You've seen the plans. No big guns. Just the support weapons on the walls."

"But maybe there's some new tech that will give those weapons greater reach?" Baine lifted one of her narrow shoulders. "God knows, they've been coming up with all sorts of strangeness in recent years."

Campbell, his eyes fixed on the hulking form of the fort, shook his head. "I just can't see that. Most of the set defenses are Gatling cannons. Knox also orchestrated Washington's surprise attack over the Delaware River . . . I think the significance of the fort's name is more likely to be found there than in his specialty."

*****

The officers stood watching the construction. Blogdett arrived with Campbell's breakfast in a tin bowl, and the colonel ate absentmindedly. The front wall was nearly done, giant UR-10s hammering locking stones into place and buffing the surface into a single, seamless facade. Clouds of white rock billowed out around the machines smoothing the stone, only to be pounded into grey mud by the rain. Overhead, smaller metal constructs and human workers were moving over the scaffolding, finishing up the forward crenellations and working to extend the corner regions into watch towers. The central bastion, rising above the fortified core, was still little more than a steel framework with just a few courses of large stone laid down.

"Well, whatever it's for . . ." Campbell stood, a tin cup of coffee held tightly in his hands, and stared up at the flagpole rising over the tall framework. "It will be as strong as mortal man can make it."

"Colonel Campbell, a communication over the vocal reiterator." A signals corporal Campbell did not recognize was standing at rigid attention just outside the awning. "It's General Grant, sir."

The colonel exchanged quick glances with the rest of his staff. "Well, we might learn a thing or two sooner rather than later." He nodded for the corporal to proceed, and then followed him to the signals shack.

The small building set aside for the mission's vocal reiterator was one of the few semi-permanent structures on the site. Rough wood with a tarpaper roof, it protected the precious technology that allowed Campbell and his officers to communicate directly with Washington or other military commands. In the center of the shack's single room was a chair seated before a table. On the table was a dark, metallic box connected to other components by tubes and wires. A tall metal mast thrusting up out of the room and into the sky over the hut held aloft a glowing crimson orb.

Campbell swept into the room and the soldier vacated the seat. The commander sat down and crouched low over the table. The black box contained a dark pane of glass that swam with swirling black and red mist. He took up a wand resting beside the machine and pulled to release a length of coiled tubing from the box. Deep within the pane a series of letters floated, shimmering in and out of focus.

"THIS IS ARXXXXQ REQUEXXING IMMEXXXTE COMXXNICATION WITXXCOLONEL XAMPBELLXXTOP"

"Damn, I hate these things." Campbell puzzled out the meaning of the words and then brought the wand to his lips. Forcing himself to speak slowly and clearly, he began. "This is Colonel Campbell reporting, stop."

The machine gurgled and hissed, then the letters vanished, replaced with a new message.

"COLOXXL CAMPXELL THIS ISXXENERAL GRXXT STOX I NEXD A STXXUS REPORT XXMEDIATELY STXP"

Campbell forced down the chill rising in his stomach and straightened in the camp chair. He gripped the wand with both hands and leaned into it as he responded. "Sir, construction is on schedule, the first level should be finished within the week, stop."

Again the machine rumbled, the words disappeared, and new ones emerged from the fog.

"EXCELXXNT STOXXQUERY THX VXULTS WIXL BE COMXXETED ATXXHE SAME XIME ENXXQUERY"

Campbell nodded but then cursed himself for his foolishness. He coughed and then responded into the wand.

"Yessir. All subterranean levels will be completed with the core structure, including the vaults, stop." Campbell felt a slight twinge of guilt, as that was more reflective of his fondest wish than any realistic assessment. He would rather not get into a deep discussion over the questionable medium of this infernal machine.

"VERY GOOX STOP PREXXRE FOR THE AXRIVAL OXXXREEMINENT WARXMATERIAL XO BE IMXXDIATELY PLACEXXWITXIN VAUXT AXXXOON AS FXXT KNOXXXS COXPLETE AXX ACTIVX XTOP"

The cold in the colonel's gut churned into icy heat. Whatever those vaults were for, they would be needed immediately. Still, there was no clue forthcoming as to what they were intended to protect . . . or contain, if looked at from another point of view.

"Sir," Campbell bent back into the wand. "Query: please advise as to the nature of the material in route, end query."

This time there was a long pause as the black metal box shivered and buzzed. The words within fractured into a thousand vague splinters of light, but nothing rose up to replace them. The chill spread through the colonel's entire body and he was suffering visions of summary executions and familial disgrace before new words appeared.

"MATEXXAL ESSENXIAL TXXFINAX VICXXRY STXP"

Campbell stared at the words as they floated before him. Final victory? Before he could ask for any sort of clarification the words swam away and were replaced once more.

"CONTIXXE THE GXOD WOXX COXXNEL STOX PREXXRE YOXR CXXMAND FOXXTHE ARRXXAL OF MXTERIALXXT OUR EARXIEST CONVXXIENCE STOXXCARRXXON SXOP"

Campbell shook his head at the blunt dismissal. Of course, communicating over the vocal reiterator, conversations almost always ended in such a fashion. The complete lack of emotional context to the communications tended to shade every exchange to pass over the new technology with just a vague hint of mistrust. At least, it seemed that way to Campbell.

The colonel went back to the command pavilion in a foul mood. He was barely aware that the rain had stopped as he walked along the rutted, muddy path. The command staff waited patiently to hear what the general had had to say, but he was not at all sure he wanted to share his ominous forebodings with them.

"Well, we can just start calling those two rooms vaults, now, anyway." He began. He knew he lacked the ability he had witnessed in many other officers, including Major Dalton, to set subordinates at ease with a quick dose of humor. Whenever he tried, he met with just the blank stares he was receiving at that moment. He shook his head and continued before anyone could embarrass him further by asking for a clarification.

"General Grant refers to the two reinforced chambers being built in the center of the armory level as vaults, and informs me that as soon as the fort is complete, we will be in receipt of some extremely important war material that may well be central to final victory."

The other officers all frowned. Baine shook her head, her brows dipped in question. "Final victory against whom?"

Another of the officers shook his head as well. "Never mind that, what are they sending us that they needed to build a whole fort to keep safe?"

Campbell looked into the eyes of each officer before giving words to the fear that had gripped him in the communications shack. "You don't just build vaults to keep things safe inside. You might also build a vault to keep things from escaping."

Dalton's eyes were fixed on his commander's. "He didn't tell you what to expect."

Campbell shook his head again and sat heavily in a camp chair near one of the drafting tables. "No, major, he did not."

"So it could well be weapons of some kind." An adjutant said.

"Or some other tech from the big brains at the Pipetown Works?" Another young man added.

Campbell shrugged. "Or anything else, really. Could be prisoners that need to be isolated. Could be essential personnel needed for the war effort. Damnation, could very well be gold, or jewels, or bank notes. Can't win a war without money, now, can you?"

"I think Baine's point is still a good one." Dalton's voice was low. "Who is this fortress emplaced to win final victory over? The Rebellion? Lee's a cowering dog afraid to come out of his hovel. We're too far away to have much impact on the Warrior Nation, and Carpathian and his creatures are clear across on the other side of the country." He looked back down at Campbell. "Could we really be here just to finish off the Confederates?"

Campbell eased back in the rickety chair and stared up at the fort taking form in the distance. He shook his head again. "Damned if I know, major. I don't have any more information than you have, and damned less insight, I'd have to say."

Campbell would never know if it was a shared sense of helplessness, or the dejected tone of his voice, or the oppressive weather. He felt a loosening of the tension in the officers around him and was only mildly surprised when Captain Baine produced a small silver flask. "Sir, I think you might feel better after taking a quick nip of this."

Everyone became still beneath the awning. Campbell had always avoided fraternizing with subordinates. Of course, fraternization had hardly been a danger in the small office beneath the Capitol Building where he had spent the majority of his career, designing fortifications, supply lines, and the like. He had been the only Army officer present, and the promotions had rolled in regularly as rewards for good designs and innovative thinking rather than stellar leadership or selfless bravery.

The colonel stared at the offered flask as it flashed in the watery sunlight, held stiffly in the hand of a fellow officer. He took the vessel before he could change his mind and dashed a swig down his throat, despite the early hour. The liquid burned as it hit, and he tried valiantly, to no avail, to stop the resultant hacking cough.

Campbell was suddenly aware of someone pounding on his back. His breath came in shallow gasps. His vision was blurred by tears streaming from his eyes. The heat rising from the back of his throat threatened to start him coughing all over again. When he regained sufficient command of his faculties, he gestured for everyone to move away, looking up at the young captain.

"Thanks, Baine." He was barely able to choke the words out, but he managed. The officers standing around him smiled. "That's good stuff. I hardly think it's regulation, though."

She blushed and shook her head. "No, sir. It's shine one of the patrols in my sector took off some locals a couple nights ago."

Campbell nodded at Blaine's admission, and then grinned. "Well, it would be the height of hypocrisy for me to cite you for it now, wouldn't it?"

The other officers laughed, the tension ratcheting down yet again, and the flask was passed around the circle. Their commander carefully pushed himself back to his feet and moved to the edge of the awning, looking out over his command. After decades in that small office, he still found it hard to believe that he was here, in full command of such a major operation.

Campbell shook his head as he followed the smooth movements of an enormous construction automaton trundling from the supply depot to the fort in the distance. The UR-10s were alien, their blank metal heads housing a single eye that flared redly with RJ energy. Their metal bodies with their dark, shadowed interiors and coils of hose and tubing, were only nominally humanoid, many replacing standard arms or legs with purpose-built elements designed to better perform their construction responsibilities. Most of those arms and legs were interchangeable. It was quite an advancement, and coming to grips with it was quite a struggle for a man who had spent so many years alone in a basement.

So much had changed over the last twenty years, and when he was brutally honest with himself, Colonel James Campbell knew that it was these changes, many of which had occurred seemingly overnight, that made it so hard for him to function out of his little office. Hell and damnation, when even the man who signed your orders was a creature of this new world, where was a man of yesteryear to turn?

Campbell was aware of General Grant's troubles, of course. The tales were well known throughout the nation and beyond. The slaughter of his family by Confederate insurgents was a tale used to set the heart of every new recruit to burning. The injuries that the general himself had sustained in the attack were also legendary. Terrible, disfiguring burns condemned him to a grotesque iron mask that not only hid the nightmarish injuries, but also sustained his life. General Grant was a legend among the men he commanded.

Campbell sighed, knowing he would never be able to command the fear or respect men like Grant seemed to wield with such ease. His scowl deepened and he shook his head. No wonder he saw contempt in the eyes of so many of his men each day.

Another robot lurched past the command tent and the colonel watched as it carried tools toward the construction. This was a lighter model, almost a walking skeleton, and the sight of the machine brought his mind to the object of Grant's personal hatred and quest for vengeance: Doctor Carpathian. Hidden away in the War Department's basement, Campbell had never faced the resurrected constructs of the mad doctor, but he had heard stories and seen the evidence.

The colonel knew the basic theory behind RJ-1027 reanimation, and had even studied the invigorating properties of the substances for the Department. But he had yet to see the dead walk, rods of Crimson Gold jammed into their brains. Army scuttlebutt claimed that Carpathian was raising entire armies of the dead to enforce his will upon the Contested Territories. It was said they worked his factories and served his food, as well as bearing his banner into battle. The thought sent a shiver down Campbell's spine. Of the many changes that had shaken the world since he had emerged from his little warren, the dead rising from their slumber was one of the most shocking.

Campbell grinned sourly as he caught his train of thought. He was watching animated metal men do the work of thousands, at the order of a maimed, masked, mad genius, while thinking about walking corpses. The world had become entirely unhinged, and he was trying to account for each change as if it even mattered. The savage tribes of the west had united under a council of chiefs and elders for the first time in living memory. By all reports, they wielded weapons that burst into actinic blue flame in battle, rode twisted and metamorphosed parodies of horses to war, and some even said they could twist their own flesh into abhorrent, horrific shapes to practice violence upon their enemies.

The world was nothing like it had been when he had first been assigned to the War Department's Office of Planning and Logistics. It was as if he had awakened from a safe, boring dream into a waking nightmare; and there was no escape.

"Doesn't look real, does it, sir." The deep voice was making a statement, not asking a question. Dalton was a good man, Campbell knew. When the colonel was able to control his raging jealousy, he knew his second in command was a very good man indeed. Apparently, given this last statement, he was a mind-reader as well.

Campbell nodded. "Just what I was thinking, major. We spent so many years fighting the damned Secesh dogs; a generation of blood and treasure spent in a few short years trying to keep the Republic together. And now . . ." He turned and gestured down the southern slope of the hill. "Not only are we still fighting the grey-backs, we've got the Warrior Nation, the lawless vermin of the Territories, and Carpathian's nightmare constructs fighting over the scraps."

After a few minutes had passed, the colonel shrugged. "Well, of all our problems, at least the Confederacy's all but dead. With Lee fighting yesterday's war, they're not much threat at all compared to everything else we're dealing with."

"True, sir." Dalton agreed. "This fort'll be the last nail in their coffin, and then we can focus out west where the true fighting's going to be."

They watched as men and robots continued to raise the walls of Fort Knox, each confident in the security of their new construction.

Chapter 6

The lilting, Ohioan accent was eerily familiar. Jesse James turned slowly around, brows furrowed and left hand drifting toward the butt of a pistol.

Behind Jesse was an older gentleman in the clothing of a man of business. The duds were fine if worn, much like the man himself. The hair was graying, the once-smooth face wrinkled in lines of pain and care, but the broad mustache was still in place, and a twinkle that declared, as hard as the intervening years had been, there was a spirit there that had not been beaten yet.

Jesse staggered back. His usual, sardonic grin gave way to a wide, honest smile that took years off his own face. "I'll be damned! Colonel Bill!"

William Quantrill smiled in return and reached out to shake hands. Jesse stopped cold and stared down at the offered appendage. It was a mechanical replacement, far more crude than the outlaw chief's own. The dull iron structures of the hand and forearm were joined to a rounded stump, shiny with scar tissue, about halfway to his elbow. Iron support rods, with connecting bolts sunk into his flesh, continued up his arm, jointed at the elbow, and formed a thick cuff around his shoulder.

Quantrill shook his head and reached out to grab Jesse's sleek metal hand in his own. "It's been too long to get squeamish now, James." The older man's grin was fierce, and after a moment, Jesse's face smoothed, the smile returned, and he pumped the hand vigorously.

"Sir, is it good to see you!" The smile faltered slightly. "What're you doin' way out here? Were you comin' north to meet us?"

The older man tilted his head at the words and then smiled wider. "Not sure what you mean, Jesse, but I do think maybe we should head in and have that drink you were talkin' about?" He nodded his head toward the locals. "I'm not sure, given the weight of recent events, that we want to spend any more time out here in the sunshine than necessary at the moment."

The men and women in the street stood dumbly, staring at them. Jesse saw that many could not take their eyes off his arms, and he held them up again so everyone could get a good look. "Alrighty, then!" Jesse stepped back toward the door. "We'll see ya'll on our way back outta town!"

The Fords and Cunningham were waiting by the door when Jesse turned, and the four outlaws pushed their way past the louvered wood and into the darkness of the saloon, Colonel Quantrill preceding them at a measured gait. The outlaw chief saw that his old commander walked stiffly, an elegant cane grasped in his natural hand. The cane was of intricately-worked metal, with pipes and wires woven through its center. A red telltale pulsed slowly, deep in the thing's core, as if measuring out the beats of a heart.

Inside The Pavilion, small groups of men stood at the windows or sat at their tables; glasses, cards, and dice lay forgotten behind them. Jesse gave everyone a wide smile and fished out a single gold coin with nimble metal fingers. "I'd like to buy everyone a glass, if you don't mind."

Most folks loosened up a bit at the sight of the gold and the mention of a drink. Some stayed near the windows, more than a few staring at the head and torso of the man who had shattered the glass with his fatal entrance. Almost everyone was quick to take the glasses the bartender and his serving girls began to distribute, though. Soon enough, Jesse and the others were sitting at a corner table, sipping on half-decent whiskey.

Jesse poured Quantrill a generous drop, off-hand resting on the smooth wood of the table top. "Did Henderson get word to you? Are you here to meet us?"

Quantrill tossed the whiskey back with a single powerful motion of his metal hand and then looked across the table. "Who, now? No, I din't have any idea you were hereabouts. I'm heading back west after. . ." He gestured vaguely with the claw-like hand. "Headin' back west to recuperate."

Jesse shook his head, a glass forgotten in his hand. "Henderson din't get word to you?"

The older man leaned back in his chair and quirked an eyebrow at the outlaw. "Son, I don't know who you're talkin' about. Only Henderson I can recall was old Allen Henderson, but he got put down years and years ago, before the war even ended. Can't recall any other Henderson. Certainly there ain't no one I'm in constant communication with, by any name. Now, why don't you slow down and let's chat?" He smiled again. "I can't help but notice you got a sleeker set o' replacements than mine, eh?"

Jesse looked at the dark iron hand again, then down at his own shiny metallic limbs, and shrugged with a smile. "Well, they may be purty, but they seem to have a mind of their own at times, colonel. Seems, though, might be they're comin' around. But I got some good news for you, sir. Henderson ain't dead! He's with me! Well, out on the plains aways, with my folks."

A darkness crept into Quantrill's eyes, and he leaned over the table. "Son, I assure you, Allen Henderson's dead. He died in my arms over twenty years gone. Yer startin' to undo all the good yer kind offer o' whiskey had started inroads on."

Jesse shook his head again. "I'm sorry, colonel. But that can't be. I've been ridin' with Henderson for months now!"

"Jesse," Quantrill leaned into the words. "Allen Henderson died, cut down by blue-bellies out Virginia-way. I din't know you were anywhere around here, an' I don't know what the Sam Hill yer talkin' 'bout. That just about settle things on that score?"

The outlaw chief leaned back in his chair, his eyes dark. He could only shake his head.

Robert Ford leaned over his steepled fingers. "It don't fer me, Jesse. If Henderson's been callin' shots, playin' of this swell's name, but the real Henderson's been worm food since the war . . . what in the name of Hell does that mean?"

A dark suspicion kindled in the back of Jesse's mind as he recalled words Carpathian had spoken during their last encounter. *"Our red-eyed friends . . ."*

Jesse shook himself and forced a smile through the doubt and suspicion. There would be plenty of time to deal with Henderson, whoever he was, when they got back to camp. "Never you mind, Robert. We'll sort that out later. Boys, let me introduce you to a good friend from back in the war, Colonel William Quantrill."

Quantrill nodded to the men, his eyes settling for a moment longer on Marcus than on the others, before he looked back at Jesse with a sly grin of his own.

"You made quite an entrance into town just now, Jesse." He gestured with his empty glass at Marcus. "Folks here abouts'll be thinkin' twice afore they front yer buck, here. Least, 'till yer gone."

Marcus bridled at the term, and Jesse stiffened a bit as well. "Sir, I wasn't tryin' to make a mash. I meant ever' word I said—"

Quantrill laughed and eased back into his chair. "Son, don't try to teach your ole' grandma how to suck eggs, now, you hear?" He pointed with one iron finger back at the younger man. "Who was it, you reckon, first taught you how to lay a legend down? Couldn't o' been ole' Billy Quantrill, now, could it?"

Jesse started to respond, but was silenced by that wagging metal digit. "Now, son, don't try to bilk an ole' huckster, alright? I recognize speechifying when I hears it, and that was some fine talkin' you were doin' out on the porch."

Jesse opened his mouth again, but the older man rode over him. "Jesse, I'm not questionin' the strength of yer convictions. I don't doubt you an' this big man here is friends of the first water. But I remember a young little coot followed his big brother into my outfit when he was too young to piss straight, an' that young'un din't cotton too much to . . . dark complexions, if I remember well enough?"

"Folks change, colonel, an' that was a long time ago—" Jesse's face was clouded again as he leaned forward on crossed iron forearms.

"No doubt, son. I'm just sayin', time was, you woulda reacted the same way as ole Herschel Brown there, that you left bleedin' out of his neck hole on the porch." Quantrill shook his head slightly as if disappointed. "An' you din't give much thought to the local law, either, did you?"

Jesse sat up straighter at that, an annoyed look on his face. Before he could speak, Quantrill raised his metal hand in a reassuring gesture. "Don't worry, none. Moberly ain't got no law to speak of as yet. Folks here mostly take care o' their own troubles. 'Course, that din't help Herschel none, now did it . . ."

Jesse did not relax. "I ain't much afraid of some Podunk border law, neither way, colonel." But he forced himself back into his chair, sharing a sidelong glance with his men.

Quantrill continued, making a quick, calming gesture with his natural hand. "Way I reckon it, most folks here abouts have you pegged now, James. They're gonna know you're the celebrated outlaw with the famous arms and the imposing body count, and that'll give us a little time afore anyone decides to act on the umbrage they all must be feelin' right about now." He picked up his cane with his flesh-and-blood hand and tapped it absentmindedly against the rim of the table. "Now, where were you boys headin' next, after your fine display of street theatre?"

Jesse's men shared another guarded look and then watched their leader to see where he went with the question. The outlaw boss watched his old commander for a moment before speaking in a lower voice. "Well, funny you should ask that, sir, as we're currently at odds as to our exact next step."

Quantrill made a rolling gesture with his metal hand, indicating that the younger man should continue.

"Well, we're of a few minds, currently." Jesse looked at his men, then shrugged and continued. "Allen Henderson has been urging me to burn out all the border towns to send a message to the Union and the Rebellion alike."

The old colonel stared at Jesse in silence. When he spoke, his voice was dripping with contempt. "Burn out the border towns? You eager to kill everyone in the Contested Territories? And yourself crushed in the middle?"

The tone brought Jesse back more than twenty years and he sat up straighter in his chair. "No, sir. I was doubtful—"

"Doubtful that anyone suggesting such a strategy had half the brain God gave 'em?" Quantrill leaned forward, all tension and disbelief. "Leave off how this yahoo convinced you he was Allen Henderson, didn't that entire plan strike you as hare-brained? Attack in all directions, leave yourself no path of retreat or sanctuary?" He shook his head. "I thought I'd taught you better, James. What happened to Frank? Is he dead? He'd never let you keep something this ignorant in your head long enough to leave an impression!"

Jesse nodded, shook his head, and then nodded again so quickly it looked as if he had suffered some sort of apoplexy. "No, sir. I mean, yes sir. Frank's still alive. He was against that plan."

Quantrill nodded and leaned back a little. "Good. Then you're not completely lost yet. You said you were torn between courses. I hope the next isn't nearly as empty-headed?"

Jesse leaned back, his eyes drifting away and refusing to meet Quantrill's steady gaze. "I got a bunch of men with me, sir. We busted 'em out of Camp Lincoln a month or so back, and I was thinkin' I might head out west, past Carpathian, and the Nation, and all them, and maybe set up on our own. Someplace we can call our own, an' where folks can just leave us be."

Quantrill's brows came down slightly, and his eyes drifted to the table where he gingerly interlaced fleshly fingers with black iron. "You were goin' to found your own town."

Jesse forced his eyes up into his old mentor's, and sat up straighter. "Yessir."

The old man's eyes flattened. "And how were you goin' to live?"

The outlaw's face lost its proud strength as he cocked his head slightly to the side. "Sir?"

Quantrill shook his head, bowing down over his entangled fingers. "God bless you, Jesse. You got such a benighted mix of brains and confusion in that head of yours." He looked up again. "Were you gonna mine? Get your hands all dirty? Were you gonna farm? Herd cattle? Any of these old war hounds you got waitin' on you any good at blacksmithing? Carpentry? Any of the other hundred things you're gonna need, if you're gonna build your own town up from the dust?"

Jesse's eyes flared defensively. "No, but I figured—"

"And who's gonna lead this grand scheme, Jesse? You?" Quantrill leaned in toward the outlaw chief. "You gonna hang up your blasters, there? You gonna spend all day decidin' who owns what square foot o' dirt? Who which cow belongs to?"

Jesse sat back, eyes losing focus as all of his fears and insecurities came crashing in upon him.

"That ain't you, kid. Leastways, it weren't you twenty years ago." Quantrill nodded toward the broken window and the leaking corpse, the crowd still watching him from the corner of their fear-tinged eyes. "And your friend over there in the window, and his friend on the porch, would seem to agree with me."

Jesse stared at the body in the window frame. He could still remember the burning rush of his blood as the locals had sealed their fates with their own mouths. The outlaw chief's head shook slightly back and forth.

"No, that ain't you, Jesse. And I know, somewhere in that head of yours, you knew all along that weren't you." Quantrill tapped briskly on the table, setting all four of the other men jumping, and he smiled. "Now, knowin' you, you got another plan, and I'm willin' to bet it's the Jim Dandy of the lot."

"Yessir." A new, bright smile just touched Jesse's face. "At least, I think so." Jesse swallowed before continuing. "I were thinkin' of maybe headin' down toward the gulf." He sat up straighter, the conviction of this new course lending him strength before his old mentor's contempt. "The Union's goin' to crush the Rebellion as soon as it gets its house in order out west. There's nothin' the southern states can do to stop it, the way they're goin' now. Lee's fightin' a war that ended twenty years ago, and don't even realize that Grant and the rest changed the rules on him. He's goin' to lead the southern states to a defeat they won't ever come back from."

Quantrill settled back into his seat and nodded. "Can't argue with you there, son. Lee ain't the man we all thought he would be. That last runnin' defeat beat the sand out of him, an' he's been runnin' in his head ever since."

Jesse sat forward, fire igniting in his eyes. "Exactly! If we keep fightin' the old war, we're gonna keep losin'! But we don't have to! We got a huge advantage, if only we can take ahold of it while we can!"

Quantrill nodded again, then his eyes slowly shifted to Marcus' still face, and then back to Jesse. "I'll be damned. You're talkin' about black folks."

Jesse nodded. "Honest folks know all that hogwash 'bout black folks bein' less'n white folks is nothin' but tripe. Honest folks who know black folks, anyway. Folks is folks, with some of 'em dumb as a stump, an' others smart as cats. And there's thousands an' thousands of black folks down south, as eager to defend their homes as any white man."

Quantrill put up his metal hand again to stall Jesse's excited speech. "Son, you know, ain't many white men in the south'd be eager to hand a black man a gun, now, don't you?"

Jesse nodded, but the fire was still there. "There ain't, I know. But they gotta wake up. The Union don't care what color a man is if he's in their way. An' anyone who's faced 'em, black or white or brown or yella, knows it. We gotta convince the rest, before we're all crushed beneath Grant's boot."

Quantrill sat back again and stared at Jesse with calculating eyes. The Fords and Marcus stared back at the old commander while Jesse, having wound down, watched for any reaction at all.

The moment stretched on, and Jesse's men shot him glances to see if he was going to speak. But before he could continue, Quantrill cleared his throat, smiled a small, secret smile, and nodded.

"Jesse, you ever been to New Orleans?"

The question caught the outlaw chief by surprise, and he shook his head.

Quantrill's smile widened a little. "Well, I'm just comin' from down that way." He waved the metal hand. "Where I was bein' seen to by a most strange lady of a particularly . . . dusky visage. I think you would be very surprised to experience the difference in opinion most white folks down there have compared to many of the folks you're used to."

Jesse nodded slowly, but his face was a mask of confusion. "Okay . . . ?"

Quantrill settled back. "You see, New Orleans is at least as much a European city as it ever was American, and they've always had . . . a more lenient way with the black folks livin' there. Since the war ended, it's been a free city, not declarin' allegiance to either the north or the south. At the very edge of the Contested Territory, it was quite a bustlin' neutral port for years. Most folks there have been judgin' other folks on their actions an' their history more'n the color of their skin fer a long time, now." He pointed at Jesse with two joined iron fingers. "You gonna find anyone willin' to listen to your line of argument, you're gonna find 'em in New Orleans."

Jesse nodded. "That makes sense, I guess."

Quantrill tapped his cane against the table again. "While I was down there, I made some friends, Jesse. Friends that I think might be very interested to hear your ideas themselves. In fact, I might just turn around myself and head back down there with ya'll, if yer of a mind to go."

Jesse looked down at the dark iron hand and tapped the table with his own metal fingers. "You said they did . . . that . . . down there? Who was it? Last I heard, there's only one man can do that sort of work . . ." His eyes darkened slightly with memory, and he shook his head. "Well, two, I guess, if you're counting that butcher back in Camp Lincoln. But ain't neither of 'em in New Orleans that I heard."

Quantrill looked down at his own crude hand, flexing the thick fingers. "Well, remember, New Orleans ain't beholden to any of the folks been tearin' the country apart, but they all got people down there one way or 'nother. The Union Army's actually been swarmin' down there, fortifyin' the waterfront an' the harbor for months now, but they don't bother much with the rest of the city. An' there's one lovely lady, a special friend of YOUR friend the good doctor, I believe," he reached across and tapped his iron finger against Jesse's metal forearm. "An' that lady is the one who . . . healed me, so to speak." Again he looked down at the roughly formed hand.

"A lady done that to you?" Jesse's voice was low.

"Well, lady, now, that's a sort of fluid term, is what I learned." Quantrill looked down, the portrait of an embarrassed southern gentleman. "I got caught just outside of Louisville, an' one o' those damned blue-bellies winged me as I rode out. All but tore my fool hand clean off. I was dyin', James. I was bleedin' out an' nothin' the boys I had with me did was doin' any good. So, one of 'em, he'd heard about a black woman livin' in the swamps around New Orleans, could work miracles on folks were injured on farms and in factories and whatnot. Me, I was all but unconscious, so didn't have much say in the matter. The boys dragged me across the country down to New Orleans, and brought me to this medicine woman.

"Her name is Marie Laveau. An . . . older . . . lady." He shot a look at Marcus before continuing. "Dark of skin, with wild hair and burning dark eyes. The black folks of the bayou surrounding the city call her the Voodoo Queen, and say she is attended by a court of the dead. I never did see them, but I don't doubt, having spent so much time around her old mansion while she did this to me," he waved the metal hand listlessly in the air. "I don't doubt it could be true."

Robert Ford scoffed and kicked back in his chair, but Jesse held up one metal hand. "Now, hold on there, Robert. Ain't much to separate those old Voodoo zombie stories from Carpathian's creatures, now, is there? And the colonel did mention as they might be affiliated somehow . . . ?"

Quantrill nodded, looking up at Jesse again. "She's some sort o' ally, or apprentice, is what I come to understand. Their dead, in New Orleans, they hold a lot of sway over the livin'. An' from what I heard, that sort o' thing is just what might draw Carpathian's attention."

Jesse held his eyes for a moment and then gave a shallow nod of agreement. "It might, at that. Truth to tell, though, colonel, I ain't on great terms with Carpathian. Might be this Queen o' yers, she might not take a likin' to me."

Quantrill shook his head. "No, she ain't his creature. She's her own person, fer sure. But might be, she could help us. Also, she's the one we'd have to go through to get to the man I think you need to see."

Jesse's eyes sharpened a bit. "The man I need to see?"

Quantrill jerked his head sharply. "Colonel Warley; Alexander to his friends. Led a platoon of engineers from Louisiana during the war, and as things began to wind down, he returned home. Grew up on a big plantation right up against the bayou. A lot of his boys stayed with him after the war, working his land, his ships, and whatnot." A small smile crept back onto the old commander's face. "And I happen to know he shares your . . . soft spot for . . . well, let's say former slaves and leave it at that?"

Jesse sat back. "A commander from the war?"

"Yeah. And he's still got a lot of his boys with him, an' their families. Fiercely loyal. Had a lot to do with seein' the carpetbaggers off around thereabouts after the war. He's also got connections with the rebel bands still in the swamps and coastal regions that haven't taken to Lee's tender ministrations. If there's anyone can set you up with what you're lookin' fer, it's Colonel Warley."

Jesse stared down at his hands. Another Carpathian . . . ? Or, rather, someone who could do similar work, but was not entirely attached to the madman? That might be someone he needed to meet. This Warley, as well, struck him as a potentially useful person.

All thoughts of destroying Moberly were gone; all designs against the border towns forgotten. The last tattered shreds of an imaginary new town floated away on the rising tide of his chosen profession: violence. There would not be a better chance at raising the south effectively than an ally such as Quantrill described. And it sounded like there would never be a better place to begin than in the free port of New Orleans. It all gave solid form to the fantasies that had plagued his dreams since Billy the Kid had sat down at his table in Kansas City what seemed like a lifetime ago.

"Now, since your original plan was to destroy the entire border region . . ." Quantrill tilted his head toward Jesse's hands. "How big is this little band of yours, out on the plains?"

The responding shrug was eloquent. "A few hundred. And some Union armored vehicles, and the like."

For the first time since he had appeared behind Jesse, Quantrill seemed impressed. "Really? A small army already, and with the armor to support it? I imagine there's a tale worth the tellin' behind that brief comment?"

"Not one I'd care to tell at the moment, sir, no." Jesse was still haunted by the stink of bodies left behind in the rolling northern hills. A few hundred might impress his old commander, but it was a sad number when expressed as the remainder of the thousands who had followed him out of Camp Lincoln.

"No, well, I'm sure we both have our shadowed vales, Jesse." Quantrill lapsed into thought for a moment and then looked up again. "Well, I was going to suggest we head east and pick up a riverboat down to New Orleans, but I'm not sure we could sneak a few of those Rolling Thunders aboard even the biggest."

"Well, sir, the pace of the column I've got now, we won't see the coast for more'n a week. I have folks I can leave in charge of the rest, and we can head down by river with a few chosen hands. I've also got some folks with me, might be able to rustle up some more strength, out back west, in Robbers Roost, Diablo Canyon, an' like that."

Quantrill nodded with a smile. "That sounds fine, Jesse. Mighty fine." He stood up stiffly, bringing the cane back underneath him, and looked down at the younger man. "I would suggest, however, that we take to the trail soon, before someone in town decides to face the infamous Jesse James on behalf of the late, currently unlamented, Herschel Brown?"

Jesse stood up as well, followed by the Fords and Marcus. "Yeah. I do want to head back, and we'd love to have you, too, colonel. We'll just have to borrow that wagon outside, maybe. I can't wait to introduce you to Allen Henderson an' maybe have a little talk 'bout some things."

Jesse was not very surprised when, as they pulled up to the camp a couple hours later, Frank stumped out to tell him that Henderson was gone.

Chapter 7

The low growl of the Interceptor echoed from the surrounding pines, the long, sleek vehicle crawling over the packed dirt of the trail. The rider crouched low over the control bars, his duster fluttering out behind him, blending with the cloud of trail dirt stirred up by his passage. He had been alone on the trail for days, with no sign of other travelers ahead or behind. Well, save for a strange, freakishly tall man, half-glimpsed in the shadows of the pine forest, who had looked out at him from beneath a strange, tall hat. He had left the man behind over a day ago, and seen no one since. The rider still cast nervous glances to either side as he eased his machine along, however. The occasional furtive look cast over his shoulder revealed his fear of pursuit. Such emotion did not sit well with the rider.

Virgil Earp, brother of Over-marshal Wyatt Earp and renowned lawman in his own right, was not used to skulking through his business. Resentment burned behind his eyes, and he was not used to that either. The Interceptor swerved drunkenly, Virgil's control hampered by his injuries. His useless arm was secured tightly to his body with worn leather straps.

Through thick amber goggles, the old law dog could just make out a decrepit sign looming out of the shadows ahead, hanging askew on a dried old signpost.

Green Valley: Five Miles.

Virgil shook his head. He could not believe he was on this road again. This time, though, he was alone. No dying brother to spur him onward, obscuring doubts and fears in the focused light of immediate need. It seemed like forever since those thrice-damned Clantons had shattered his arm, leaving him worse than a hopeless cripple. The injury had not only robbed him of his confidence and his humor: it had taken away his sense of self.

He had been fighting ever since; fighting the Feds for medical help, fighting Wyatt when it became clear that the chiseling government was going to deny their responsibility.

Virgil knew that Carpathian was the only hope he had of regaining the use of his arm, but his brother refused to see the truth. And Wyatt had refused, over and over, to let him ride out after the doctor.

And then Wyatt had forged his unlikely alliance with that soaplock, Jesse James, to burn down the Clantons. It has all been to avenge Virgil, but he had been less than useless. It was that day that he had decided: Wyatt had no right to keep him from the help he needed. It was becoming more and more clear, even to the slowest deputy, that anyone working with the Crimson Gold was going to live a long, long time unless he got shot down. Virgil had no intention of living out such a span without the full use of both his arms.

Carpathian was Public Enemy Number One to any and all Federal Lawmen. It would be a dark day if anyone ever found Wyatt Earp's own brother dealing with the madman. Things were deteriorating quickly in the territories. In fact, even in official dispatches they were referring to the entire region west of Kansas City as the Contested Territories now. Although the Warrior Nation savages sweeping down off the plains had a lot to do with that, Carpathian was the man pushing most of the violence in the Union's direction. Very little occurred anywhere within the scorched deserts, rolling, rocky hills, or deep pine forests that did not have Carpathian's fingerprints all over it.

Virgil wobbled his Interceptor to a halt beside the battered sign. The wheels came to a crunching stop and the lawman dropped his feet into the dirt. He would not know when he passed the point of no return. Once Carpathian's guardians noticed him, they would never let him turn around. They would be somewhere nearby, and he knew that once he crossed that profound, invisible line, his life would never be the same. He would be a fugitive, even if only in his own heart.

The old lawman looked down at the twisted claw of his useless hand. The blast had charred flesh and shattered bones. One of the local sawbones had even spoken of amputation for fear of infection. Wyatt had backed his play on that, at least, and they had told the old butcher to walk away before Virgil decided to take HIS arm in trade. So the limb lay still, throbbing with dull pain, but otherwise dead meat hanging in a sling.

Virgil's eyes hardened behind the goggles. He would be damned before he would spend an hour more than necessary as a cripple, dependent upon the charity and assistance of others. He spit into the dust beside his machine and grasped the throttle tightly in his one good hand. There would be no more delays. He was going to do this thing. Further hesitation would not help anyone.

The Interceptor began to roll forward, he brought his boots up onto the footrests, and was about to flood the engine with power when a high-pitched voice snapped out of the silence behind him.

"Why don't you just stay right there, Virgil Earp, or I might satisfy myself with bringin' just yer head back for the law." A short, squat man moved out of the shadows of the forest in front of Virgil. An oversized blaster was clenched in both hands, the muzzle locked on Virgil's forehead. The old lawman let his vehicle's engine idle down to a quite gurgle, and then killed it completely. His eyes did not waver from the slick-haired youngster with the gun as he kicked the support prop down into the dirt, swinging his leg up and over the saddle.

"Provencher." Virgil nodded minutely, his face blank. Before the smaller deputy could reply, however, he continued. "You little pin prick."

The olive-skinned Provencher grunted a quick laugh and then shook the big pistol at Virgil. "Pin prick, is it, VIRG?" The older man's eyes tightened at the familiar nickname. "I'd rather be a pin prick than a dirty rotten traitor. Or a common criminal."

Virgil reached up to pull his goggles down off his face with slow movements. His expression was impassive as he stared at the kid with the gun. "Hmmm," he muttered. "Traitors and criminals, is it, now son? How you figure?"

Provencher grunted. "Don't think I don't know where you're goin', Virgil. Ain't no one left in Tombstone don't know where you're goin, if they had the sand to stop you!" He gestured with the pistol again, back down the road the way Virgil had come. "Now, I got me a little wagon back yonder, an' yer gonna get in it without kickin' up a fuss, an' yer gonna go with me back to Tombstone, an' yer gonna tell yer brother just what it is you were fixin' to do."

Virgil raised his good hand up to head height. "Well, kid, I'm not sure exactly what yer talkin' about. What is it you think I'm doin' up here?"

"You don't think I know where we are, old man?" The smirk gave way to a dark scowl as the bitter anger surged to the surface. "I've known where you had to be goin' fer days now! Last night, whiles you was sleepin', I left the wagon behind and crossed wide around to lay in wait ahead of you. You ain't nearly so clever as you think you are, Virgil Earp. You ain't so clever by half!"

Virgil nodded. "I was wonderin' how you'd a gotten in front of me." He smiled. "You know, just the information you got would be enough for quite a nice shiny medal from Washington if you left right now."

Provencher laughed again. "Yeah? An' just think how shiny the medal'll be when I bring you in, prove what a bunch o' lowlife four-flushers you an' yer whole family are, AND lead Grant right to Carpathian!"

Virgil's face lost all expression, his eyes flat and dark. "My family don't have nothin' to do with this."

The younger man barked again. "Oh, please! You take me fer a pale fish, Virg? With that metal nightmare of a brother, an' Wyatt supposedly watchin' over all the territories, you think they're gonna believe he had nuthin' to do with you showin' up sportin' a metal arm as well? When the whole Union's lookin' fer Carpathian's hideout?" He shook his head with fevered energy, a cruel grin spreading over his face. "No, this is gonna bring yer whole family down, Virgil. We'll see who's been wearin' a hat too big fer his head when they slip yers through a noose!"

Virgil stood still for a moment and then asked. "My hat?"

That brought Provencher up short. "What?"

"They gonna slip my hat through a noose?" The older man's face was as still as stone.

Provencher looked confused for a moment and then the anger boiled up again. "No, not yer hat, you daft cripple! Yer head!"

Virgil nodded, his good hand resting on his gun belt, just behind the pistol grip. "Din't think it made too much sense, but you did say we'd see who's hat was too big when they slip it through a noose . . . I guess I was just confused, is all."

Provencher stared at Virgil in disbelief. He shook his head, his voice low and menacing. "I got you dead to rights, Virgil Earp." He shook the heavy pistol. "I got you on point, an' yer still shovin' dust my way?"

Virgil shrugged. "It's always been a weakness o' mine. I see a little pisspot, I gotta piss."

The younger man's eyes went wide and round, all color draining from his face, and the massive blaster came back up, every muscle rigid with lethal intent.

The sharp detonation of a blaster shot echoed off the trees. Provencher's weapon lowered with a jerk, his mouth round in a startled 'O' of pain and confusion. He staggered back and looked down to see a dark stain spreading out from his side. The fabric of his shirt was smoldering, tendrils of smoke snaking up into his face. Before he could make any kind of response through the shock and pain, Virgil stepped forward and brought the butt of his own pistol down on the boy's forearms. The deputy made a harsh, clicking noise in the back of his throat as his heavy pistol fell into the dust.

"You think I ever needed both hands to deal with a shavetail Jonah like you?" Virgil gave a gentle push against the boy's chest and he fell over into the dirt of the trail. "Kid, you musta been born under one hell of an unlucky star to have run into me so early in life."

Virgil watched the reactions play out on the deputy's pale face. Pain and confusion were swiftly giving way to anger and frustration with a healthy leavening of fear. "You ain't no man o' the law, Virgil." He snarled from the dirt. "You ain't no good man, an' neither are your brothers. You're all goin' to burn before this is done!"

Virgil shrugged, a thoughtful expression settling over his face. "Well, I ain't sure you're wrong, kid. And that ain't no good thing, given that we're as good as the folks in the territories got. An' you may even be right 'bout us burnin'.

Plenty o' folks will, afore this is over. But I don't think that's anythin' you gotta worry yerself about now."

Provencher grunted, one hand clasped to his bleeding side. "I'm gonna see you all burn, you rat bastard! And that monster doctor as well!"

Virgil crouched down close to the deputy's sweating face. "Kid, I promise you, that doctor *is* gonna burn. But he ain't gonna burn afore I get what I need, an' you ain't gonna be there to see it."

Virgil pushed himself back up to his feet. "Now, I'm gonna continue on my way, son. I'm goin' to finish my business here, an' I'll be comin' back this way sometime soon. If you're here, I'll shoot you, an' this time I won't be aimin' to miss. If I find you back in Tombstone, I'll shoot you. If I ever run into you again, no matter where or when, I'll shoot you." He worked some of the dust in his mouth and then spat off to the side. "That clear enough for ya, big fella?"

Provencher stared up in disbelief, and then found his courage again, spitting weakly back at the tall lawman. "You don't scare me, old man! You an' me, we got a meetin' set, an' we're gonna have it afore too long!"

Virgil nodded as he turned to stride back to his Interceptor. "Whatever it takes to let you sleep at night, you little kit weasel."

In the dust of the trail, Provencher reached down with a blood-slick hand and drew a small hold-out pistol glowing with dull red energy. The gun snapped off two quick bursts of crimson fire, both passing directly through the space Virgil had occupied a moment before. The old lawman had spun to the side, his good hand coming up, and his pistol barked again, slapping several shots into the deputy's chest, sending fans of charred flesh flying into the surrounding forest. The body jerked a couple times before settling into a final stillness.

"Forgot to mention," Virgil holstered his weapon and swung awkwardly back into the saddle. "You draw on me, an' I'll shoot you."

The Interceptor roared back into life, swung wide around the smoking body, and headed off deeper into the trees.

*****

Virgil's mind was clouded as he emerged from the forest into the outskirts of Payson. He had never liked that kid, and he had never thought much of him . . . but he had never wanted to kill him. When Provencher had drawn the hold-out, something had snapped in the old lawman's mind, and that had been the end of the deputy. A quiet voice insisted that Virgil had not had a choice when that second weapon began to fire. But another, darker voice whispered that he had had a choice, and he had made it.

The dirt trail gave way to cobblestones at the edge of Payson, brick buildings rising up before him. Entering the quiet town presented him with more than enough to keep his mind off the dead boy miles behind. The last time he had visited this strange town, the streets had been empty, as if the people had been warned away. Once again, he was presented with an unnatural quiet. A familiar, sweet stink permeated the region, and had been causing his lip to curl in disgust long before he came out of the woods.

Virgil sent the Interceptor growling slowly forward in its uneven path, heading down toward the cliff- edge palace that was Carpathian's seat of power. The smell seemed to be getting stronger, the oppressive air pushing in around him. He slowed down and reached back to loosen his new blunderbuss, Justice, in its boot. The weapon had been a gift from his brothers after the bank heist that had seen him maimed. It was Wyatt who had named the gun. It could sweep a street clean with a single shot, and when it came time to pull the trigger, it was as blind, regarding friend and foe, as the old goddess Justice was said to have been.

Justice was still in the boot when some sense warned him of danger. Whether it was the smell, or a sound only partially heard, or something else entirely, he could not have said. Virgil sat up straight, whipping his head around, and was just in time to dodge aside as a rusty scythe blade swept at him from his left. Virgil felt a moment of startled fear before a lifetime's instincts took over. The thing that had stumbled out of an alleyway to attack him had been a man, once. It was a dried-out old corpse now, tattered rags hanging off in strips while a dirt-encrusted metal frame seemed to be all that held the rotten flesh upright.

Virgil slid off the back of his saddle and drew his pistol. As he lined the aiming blade up with the shambling corpse's forehead, he noticed several others coming up behind it. Their hands had all been replaced with vicious-looking, bladed weapons. Raw scars marked the point where metal and wood had been joined with the meat.

"Doctor, I'm here to trade!" The old marshal waited a moment, and then fired off three quick bursts. The three approaching animations each halted in their tracks, their heads disappearing in ghastly clouds of pink, red, and green. Each one staggered a step or two forward and then collapsed sideways onto the cobbles. Two more were behind them, and as Virgil raised his pistol again he noticed more coming in from the side. "I'd rather we negotiate over a whiskey or a bourbon, to be honest!"

He took several firm steps, punctuating each with a burst of crimson force that blew a body down the street. When he was back beside the Interceptor, he holstered the pistol and drew Justice from the boot. With a practiced, forceful spin, Virgil ratcheted an RJ cylinder into the firing chamber one-handed and turned to his left. A small mob of animations shuffled toward him, their rusty weapons raised listlessly over swaying heads.

Virgil braced his good arm, holding Justice out straight, and steadied his legs against what he knew was coming. With gritted teeth, he pulled the trigger. Justice gave a kick like a frightened mule and roared like an enraged dragon. An enormous cloud of crimson-tinted smoke bellowed out to engulf the unsteady mob. As the old lawman straightened up, he watched through the swirling smoke as shattered bodies collapsed onto the street. Some of them were scrambling limply with ragged stumps, trying to stand or reach out to him with their mangled weapons. Most, however, had suffered damage severe enough to put them down for good.

"Doctor Carpathian," Virgil cast a look around to assess his position. "This don't make much sense—"
Virgil turned Justice on the mob approaching from his right. Again he twirled the gun around his good hand, the mechanisms cracking a new cartridge into place.

"Hope you boys miss hell," Virgil brought Justice back up again, leveling the snout down the street. "Cuz you're headin' back."

Again, the bone-shaking detonation of the massive cannon echoed back off the surrounding buildings, and an entire street of animations was reduced to harmless scrap and putrefied meat.

Virgil impassively watched the feeble, aimless movements of the few corpses left capable of motion. The rest were pressing in, and he knew he would run out of ammo before long. He saw a raised brick landing in front of a building off to the left. He skipped and sidestepped through the shredded remnants of the first group and leapt up onto the platform. He nearly lost his balance as he landed, hindered by his useless arm. He felt himself going over, saw the street rushing up to meet him, and dropped Justice onto the bricks. He made a desperate grasp for the edge of the landing and just stopped himself from falling. Justice struck the street below and he cursed. Over his shoulder, he saw the animations, now joined into a single pressing crowd, moving toward him.

Virgil stood up, brushed off his knees, and drew his pistol. He checked the charge, dropped the current cartridge with a single flip of his thumb and then reloaded a fresh one with a grim glance at the oncoming horde. A fresh cartridge might be worth 30 or 40 shots, but never enough to stop the endless tide of lumbering corpses moving his way.

"Okay, doctor, I'll be here as long as I can!" Virgil pitched his voice as loudly as he could. "The next move's yours!"

Virgil snapped shot after shot down into the swarming mob. He lost count of the animations he had put down. His arm was aching and his body was growing stiff. His grin had slipped a while ago, his face a blank mask of concentration. He would last as long as he could.

The pistol barked in a slow, steady pace. The corpses were close enough, now, that he could see the rubbery texture of their skin and the clouded orbs of their eyes.

Virgil punched the blaster at a large animation staggering up the stairs. He pulled the trigger and the weapon coughed out a weak bolt of crimson that merely slapped the creature back. The thing lost its balance but was pushed back up by the animations pressing in behind it. It shook its head and then fixed its sightless gaze upon him, moving back up the stairs.

"Damnation . . ." He backed up, pressing against the locked door at the top of the landing and brandishing the pistol like a club. "If this is how you want it, doctor!" he shouted. He was startled to realize that his throat was dry, his voice hoarse. "I guess the consideration of the Federal Bureau of Marshals ain't worth what it once was!"

The corpses continued to lurch toward him, their blades glinting dully. The marshal's eyes tightened as he thought about the choices that had led him to that moment, when a shouted order brought the animations to a swaying halt.

"Back avay!" The voice was low and grumbling, but carried more than enough authority to force the nightmare constructs back down the stairs. There was no hostility or frustration on their slack faces, their eyes as wide and dead as ever. For some reason, this gave Virgil more of a pause than anything that he had seen since entering the little town.

"You are Virgil Earp, Marshal of zee United States?" The voice asked. Virgil could see the bodies in the back of the crowd being shoved out of the way as a large man wearing an archaic suit of heavy armor pushed his way through the putrescent crowd.

"You know I am, Ursul." The lawman moved to the edge of the landing and tried to stand easy.

The dark man stopped at the foot of the stairs. Peering from beneath bushy black eyebrows, Vladimir Ursul, majordomo of Doctor Burson Carpathian, regarded Virgil with a slight smile. "You made quite a showing of yourself, Marshal Earp. Vee ver most impressed."

Virgil spat into the crowd. "Hope you were." He gestured at the pile of stilled animations. "You're gonna need some more bodies."

Ursul laughed. "Zese? Zay are but verker drones, my friend. Tools near zee end of zere usefulness, sent here to test your mettle."

The lawman shrugged. "How'd I do?" He sauntered down the steps and retrieved Justice from the pile of dead.

It was Ursul's turn to lift his shoulders phlegmatically. "Vell enough. Come." He turned and started to walk away through the eerily-still crowd. "Zee Doctor eez vaiting."

Virgil watched Ursul push his way through the swaying corpses and then moved to catch up.

"I see you have injured yourself." The hairy man muttered through his tangle of beard. "Not serious, I hope."

The lawman could imagine the man's cruel smile. He decided not to take offense, yet. Carpathian did nothing without a reason. The countless dead scattered across the nearby streets was as nothing to him. Sending this offensive minion could only be another test.

"I've seen better days." It was the best he could come up with while managing his anger and frustration.

"Hmmm." Ursul grunted. "As has zees country of yours, I sink vee can agree? Perhaps a few more of you Union NELEGITIM lacking for better days, and vee vill all see our fortunes restored, no?"

Virgil decided to ignore the foreign insult. Even if he had understood correctly, that was not his fight.   "I'm not a Union soldier, Ursul. You know that, and so does your boss."

The majordomo frowned. "Perhaps, for zose of us from more civilized lands, zee difference is not so easy to discern, *pricepe*?"

"I'm a marshal. I'm only concerned with the law, not the politics of the government or the plots of Grant and his gang of mudsills." Virgil suddenly felt it was important to impress this upon the large man stalking along beside him. "My job is to keep as many folks safe as I can, so they can make their own way in this world."

Ursul grunted. "And yet, still so many die. It vould seem this eez just not a very safe country you have all made for yourselves, from my point of view."

"We do our best." The old lawman felt unsatisfied, unable to give a better answer. "We all do our best."

The stalky man stopped in his tracks and swung ominously toward him, the armor shining in the sunlight. "Your best was not good enough for my sister, though, Marshal Earp. And so vee seek out our own justice here, if you don't mind."

Ursul continued on again, leaving Virgil standing there alone for a moment before hurrying stiffly to catch up. "I'm sorry. I had no idea. How . . . ?"

The big man shook his head. "No, Marshal Earp. You do not deserve zee intimate details of my family tragedies. My sister eez gone; one among countless victims of zee corrupt military of a debased government. Zee price for zat death vill come due, in time. For now, leave your vehicle. An animation will follow along with it later. Vee are late to speak vis zee Doctor."

*****

Virgil had last been in Payson almost two years ago, bearing the broken and bleeding body of his brother Morgan. They had whisked his brother away and he had been summoned up to the tallest tower of the strange, gothic pile of bricks Carpathian called his manor house. He had been half-mad with grief and agitated at the abrupt separation, but even then he had known, once he had decided to come, he had to play the cards the doctor dealt.

And here he was again, playing with a marked deck. As Ursul led him through the big double doors and into the winding hallways of the main house, Virgil knew where they were going. The palace was not nearly as desolate as the city streets had been. There were servants moving quietly, both living and dead. In one salon he saw two sleek young men in black dusters talking quietly with two other young men wearing thin white coats over slick widow's tackle. He did not care for their fancy duds, but somehow their gear blended well with the castle around them.

Finally, Ursul led the marshal to the elevator chamber. One set of double doors slid open onto the tiny room beyond. Ursul urged the lawman inside. "I have too many duties zees time to accompany you. Just remember, go to your right, and you vill find your way." He held out one massive paw, a look bordering on regret crossing his face. "But first, I'm afraid you must surrender your sidearm."

Virgil knew it was coming. There was no way they were going to let him carry a gun into the great man's presence. He nodded, slipped the blaster pistol from the holster, and handed it over, butt-first.

Without a word, Ursul turned and clanked off down the hall, leaving Virgil alone. He went into the room, surveyed the buttons, and pushed one from memory. At once the doors slid shut, a series of clanks and grinding sounds emerged from the floor, and the room began to shake slightly. The marshal's head swam for a moment as if he was dizzy. He had hated this trip the first time he came to Payson, and it had not gotten any better this time around. As suddenly as it had begun, the sensation ended, the sounds ceased, and the doors opened on the familiar upper hallway.

Virgil moved to his right, along the hall, and came to the last, window-lined stretch leading to the heavy, ornate doors. He looked out the tall windows once again, down at the valley and the bustling activity of the mines and factories of Payson far below. He had not enjoyed the views on his first visit, and enjoyed them no better now. He shook the queasy feeling off and moved to the door, knocking sharply on the flat plane within one of the elaborately carved 'C's.

"Come in, please." The urbane voice from inside echoed slightly. Virgil pushed the panel and the door swung silently open. Doctor Carpathian stood nearby, speaking quietly to a tall, elegant woman who hid the lower half of her face behind a crimson fan. Cold, bright green eyes watched him from over the fan, and he felt an unnerving chill.

"Ah, Marshal Earp!" The Doctor smiled warmly without moving from the lady's side. His accent was not as thick as Ursul's; smoother and easier on the ears. "I'm just finishing up here, if you don't mind." He turned back to the woman and took her hand gently in both of his. "Miss Mimms, I think we can help each other a great deal, and I am so very glad we were able to come to this accommodation."

The woman nodded her head gracefully and then turned to go. She shifted the fan so that Virgil never got a glimpse of her face as she passed; only sparing him a last look before walking away. Carpathian followed her to the door and then closed it behind her. He smiled apologetically and gestured for Virgil to have a seat in one of the elegant, high-backed chairs.

As the lawman settled stiffly down, Carpathian sat himself, smiling behind steepled fingers, his elbows resting on the arms of the chair. "Now, marshal. To what do I owe the distinct pleasure?"

Virgil's eyes flitted around the room, only settling upon the doctor for a moment before moving away again. Nothing here offered him the slightest comfort. This man was a ruthless adversary to almost everything the Earps had fought for their entire lives. But with the Union unwilling to help him, there was nowhere else to turn.

Still, he was reluctant to speak of his needs and desires. Instead, he muttered, "You spent an awful lot of your fodder welcomin' me to town, doctor."

Carpathian shrugged, his arms wide. "Now, marshal." The warm smile grew even brighter. "You can hardly fault me measuring your resolve, no?"

Virgil's eyes settled at last on the doctor, and one eyebrow rose in question. "How'd I measure up?"
The doctor smiled. "Quite well! Now, please, marshal. To what do I owe the honor?"

The lawman stared into Carpathian's eyes for a moment more and then brought his shoulder forward, indicating the ravaged arm with a jerk of his chin. He muttered, "I've been wounded." He took a deep breath before continuing. "It's bad. Really bad. No one else can help."

Carpathian glanced down at the arm, his face a mask of sympathy. "Terrible." He leaned forward in the chair. "In the line of duty, I presume? And yet the beneficent Republic cannot help you?"

Virgil grunted. "Can't move it. Can't hardly feel it, except it burns all the time."

The doctor nodded and sat back in his chair. "And, as I said, your government cannot help you?"

The marshal squirmed in his chair as if trying to escape. "My requests were denied."

Again, Carpathian nodded. "Which is good for you, but you know that. You know that their so-called scientists are no match for what I have accomplished here." Before Virgil could respond, the doctor held up a hand. "Of course you do. You have seen the value of my work first hand. See it every day that you spend with that delightful younger brother of yours, in fact."

Virgil looked sharply at the smiling doctor and then away. He jerked a single nod but stared out one of the broad windows at the sky beyond.

"There is literally nothing I can not accomplish where the human body is concerned, Marshal Earp, let me assure you." Again the fingers steepled, the smile replaced with a look of supreme self-satisfaction. "I have worked at the tumblers of life's lock for over half a century, although you would not know it to look at me. There is very little I cannot do."

A light, friendly laugh brought Virgil's eyes snapping back to Carpathian's open face. "Now, President Johnson, General Grant and the rest, they push piles of money and resources toward Tesla and his ilk in the hopes of narrowing the gap before I crush them completely. It's hopeless, of course. I mean, Tesla and his electricity? It's to laugh!" The doctor chuckled again. "There is no way electricity will ever rival RJ-1027 in potency or cost. But you must appreciate their scrambling efforts in the depth of desperation."

Virgil said nothing, sinking further back in his chair and looking out the window. All Carpathian's talk about the Union was making him feel worse for being there at all.

"Have you nothing to say about these efforts, marshal?" The doctor's eyebrow quirked. "What of this Francis Tumblety, ostensible doctor and butcher of Camp Lincoln, as they say? He works for your allies, as I hear it."

The marshal shook his head. "I don't much care about any of that. I just want my arm back."

The contempt Carpathian displayed for the Union was painful. Even though the Earps were not fervent supporters of Grant and all he was doing in the western territories, they still very much viewed themselves as loyal sons of the Republic. Coming to this nightmare sawbones in the middle of this accursed valley of the dead was bad enough. Listening to him mock the very government Virgil upheld twisted the knife.

And the guilt was all the worse, most likely, because feeling abandoned by that same government, he could not help but doubt his own loyalties. Still, it made listening to Carpathian no easier to bear for all that.

"I just want my arm back." Virgil repeated, trying to hide the shame behind a firm voice and a steady gaze.

Carpthian nodded and pushed himself out of his chair with a grunt. "Of course you do, marshal. Of course you do." He moved across the room and kneeled down beside the lawman's chair to get a better look at the arm. "There is no movement at all? No sensation beyond the dull pain you have described?"

Virgil shook his head. "Can't do anythin' with it at all. And yeah, it just sorta hurts all the time."

"May I?" The doctor undid the straps that held the arm immobile and then proceeded to move the limb this way and that, peeling back the sleeve to look at the puckered, mottled flesh beneath. "Hmm." He rocked back on his heels. "The damage is catastrophic. Right through from the hand up into the biceps and beyond." He stood up, looking down at Virgil, and then moved back to his own chair.

Several moments passed as the two men locked gazes, and then with a slight smile, Carpathian looked away, shaking his head. "I'm afraid there is no saving your arm, Marshal Earp."

A cold sensation washed down the marshal's back at the same time a dangerous heat rose in reaction to the doctor's smirk. "You can't do anything?" His voice was heavy with disbelief. He had surrendered his personal honor coming here . . . all for nothing? He was working himself up into a rage when the doctor raised a calming hand.

"I did not say there was nothing I could do, marshal. There is quite a bit I can do, in fact." The smirk blossomed into a fully-grown smile. "You have heard of Jesse James, I believe?"

Hope and suspicion exploded into his chest together. "Heard of him. I met him once."

The smile grew even broader. "Excellent! Then you've seen those wonderful arms of his, yes?"

A greasy taste of dread slid down his throat as Virgil nodded. "I have."

The doctor answered with his own smile. "Very good. And would you be satisfied with just such an arm for yourself?"

Ever since he had been shot, Virgil had hoped that, somehow, his arm could be saved. Despite the constant pain, the total lack of recovery, he had wanted to believe his life could return to normal again.

But the doctor's words pushed him into a reality he knew he had been denying. There was no saving his arm. He would either be forever maimed, or he would be a monster creation, like his brother or that damned Jesse James.

"How much?" He forced himself to ask the question before he responded.

"Well, that is the question, is it not?" Carpathian's smile took on a predatory gleam. "Such technology, such opportunities as I alone in the world can offer. This cannot come cheaply. You agree?"

Virgil shook his head. "I don't have a lot of money—"

The doctor raised a single hand. "I do not require money, Marshal Earp." Now the smile was that of a wolf approaching its prey. "Certain considerations of the Federal Bureau, now . . . And from a brother of the Over-marshal himself, no less . . ."

The marshal shook his head. "It's bad enough me bein' here. I won't betray the law for—"

Carpathian shook his head and raised both hands in denial. "No, no, no, marshal! Perish the thought! I am not asking you to betray the law, or the good people you protect!" He leaned in closer. "No, all I will ask of you, from time to time, is information about the federal forces. I already know a great deal, so please do not believe you are the only person willing to work with me against the Union. For instance, I know all about what happened with the Clantons in Tombstone . . ."

Virgil's eyes tightened. "How –?"

Carpathian leaned back in his chair, smiling warmly again. "I have many sources, marshal. Some in the Bureau itself. Do not concern yourself, aside from knowing that you will not be alone. For the vast majority of your time, your life will continue as it has always been, except that instead of being a pathetic cripple, unable to hold your own in the struggle that slouches toward us all, you will be fit, and strong, and more than worthy of standing by your brother's side when the dark day dawns."

Virgil nodded slowly, unsure of what half of that meant, but desperately focused on the half that made sense. "Alright."

"Excellent!" Carpathian's smile glowed. "I do truly enjoy helping people, marshal. And the more people I assist, the more people will know they can come to me for assistance!"

The marshal shook his head at that. "I won't be spreading no Gospel Accordin' to Carpathian or anything like that . . ."

The doctor smiled more gently and shook his head. "Of course not. But everyone will know where it came from, nonetheless. And they will come to me in their own hour of need, and I will help them as well. For such bonds of goodwill are the only riches with real value in this world, marshal."

And those folks would owe the doctor just as Virgil owed him. And as his reach and his influence spread through these obligations, he would bring people from all walks of life into his control. For everyone is in danger of getting injured, or sick, or old. A chill gripped the marshal's gut as he realized that he was sinking deeper and deeper into a web that would someday spread all across the Contested Territories and beyond.

"Now, we'll need to get you down to my surgical assistant, Kyle. He will prepare you for the procedure. The soonest begun, the soonest done, as they say." The smile was again predatory with anticipation.

All Virgil could think about was what Wyatt would say when he found out.

Chapter 8

Jesse James rested his metal forearms against the railing of the NATCHEZ IX as the distant shores of the Mississippi drifted past. For five days they had been travelling aboard the enormous riverboat, and Jesse was still not accustomed to the daunting scale of the vessel. Aside from the colossal Heavy Rail terminal the Union had dropped into the middle of Kansas City, this boat was the largest man-made construction he had ever seen. The idea that such an enormous edifice was moving bothered him more than he would admit.

Watching the waves thrown up by the bow of the enormous ship slap at the shore reminded him of the Union packet boat he had taken down with Frank and the Youngers back on the old Missouri River. That little war-boat would have fit into the dining hall of the *Natchez IX* several times over, but back nearly a year ago, he remembered with a smile, it had been more than enough boat for him.

In fact, Jesse was more than a little suspicious that it was memories of that long-ago heist that had convinced Frank that he would be better off healing on the slow, steady journey south on land, rather than on the mighty steamboat. Remembering his past glories, however, reminded him of his more recent setbacks, and his face settled back into its brooding lines.

Leaving his tattered little army had not been easy, even with Frank and the Youngers in charge. Moberly had yielded up just enough food and RJ to keep the people and machines moving southward toward the planned rendezvous north of New Orleans. The plan, using one of Colonel Quantrill's river contacts to ferry the army across the river at Baton Rouge, would have been nerve-wracking even if Jesse had gone with them. Knowing that it would be up to Frank and the Youngers to pull it off was enough to give him the cold sweats each night.

He had sent Will Shaft and his Exodusters back west to Robbers Roost to collect any desperadoes that might be willing to assist in Jesse's grand new adventure. He had ultimately decided to tell them to avoid Diablo Canyon, where rumor said Billy the Kid had come to rest. No matter how daunting the thought of raising an entire army might be, there were just some bummers he was not ready to ride with again.

If there was one place designed to keep your mind off your worries, however, it was the *Natchez IX*. Quantrill had somehow finagled passage for himself, Jesse, Lucinda, and Marcus Cunningham, who Quantrill thought would be an invaluable asset once they reached the city. Lucy had spent the first day aboard in the enormous copper bathtub reserved for first class passengers. The Ford brothers had somehow wangled their way aboard as well, but with accommodations much more unassuming than the suites given to the old Confederate officer and his guests.

The river boat was easily the largest plying the wide Mississippi. Its enormous RJ engines drove a single huge paddle wheel, churning the muddy waters of the river into a tan froth that trailed along in the vessel's wake, shimmering with the glow of crimson power conduits and vents. The dining room was the largest chamber Jesse had ever seen. The gaming rooms were the poshest, most brightly lit he had ever lost a hand in. The suites themselves were a level of luxury and excess that he could not have even imagined before boarding the boat at Festus, a dinky little town south of St. Louis.

It had gotten to the point that Jesse had to forcefully remind himself each day that this was only a brief respite along the rough trail. Still . . . He tilted the brim of his hat back to catch the glowing sun. He might just be able to picture himself giving up the dust and the sand for one of these suites and a seat at those gaming tables each night. Maybe, if he could convince Lucy to join him –

"Quite a sight, ain't it?" A voice broke into his reverie. Jesse turned, ready to snap out a harsh response, when he recognized the sharp, rodent-like face of Charlie Ford. Although older by several years, Charlie was by far the tamer and more timid of the two brothers. He followed Robert's lead, staying in the background and letting him do all the talking. In fact, Jesse could not remember the last time Charlie Ford had spoken to him directly.

"Sorry?" Still clearing his head from its wanderings, he had missed what the quiet man had said.

"The shore. It's quite a sight. Ain't it?" It was obvious Charlie was making an enormous effort. His eyes, having established brief contact with Jesse's, flitted out over the glistening water.

Jesse smiled at the kid and went back to resting against the smooth wood. "Yeah, it's quite somethin', that's for sure. Robert still enjoyin' his run of the faro table?"

Charlie shuffled up to the railing and gripped it tightly in one hand, looking down at the water sluicing along the boat's side. "Yeah. The tiger ain't bucked 'im yet."

Jesse grunted and went back to watching the shoreline. He had no idea what Charlie wanted from him, and was in no mood to tease it out. If the kid wanted to talk, he would find the sand. Otherwise, it was too nice a day to waste holding his hand.

"Jesse, I got somethin' I wanna ask ya." Charlie was gripping the railing with both hands now, his eyes fixed fiercely on the rolling water.

The outlaw felt an itch between his shoulder blades. In his experience, there was no good conversation that had ever started with those words. He started to review all of his dealings with Charlie and his brother. Was there some way they might have bilked him? He kept his pose relaxed, his eyes focused on the distant shore, and muttered, "Yeah?"

The young man cringed a bit, but stayed where he was, eyes unmoving. He nodded quickly, and then said. "I ain't brave."

Jesse stared at the boy for a minute, trying to process what it was he had said and what it might mean. He had seen the kid in the thick of things several times. He was never a tomcat in battle, but he had never seemed shy, neither.

The outlaw chief waited for the kid to comment further, but when nothing else seemed forthcoming, he said, "That all?"

Charlie's head snapped around, his face a mixture of shame and anger. "Ain't that enough?" He spat over the railing, his eyes burning. "Hell, you're on the shoot to start a whole damned war, Jesse. You, and Frank, and the Youngers, and Robert, even; you're all of you right tartars in a fight." His shoulders slumped. "Me? It's all I can do not to piss myself when the first shot's fired."

Jesse nodded and rested one elbow back on the rail. He took his hat off with the other hand and let the river breeze cool his head for a moment before he responded. "Kid, that ain't nothin'. You *ain't* pissed yourself, right?"

Charlie shook his head so fast his hat almost went over the side. "'Course not! I'm just sayin! I . . ."

The silence hung there, heavy with whatever it was Charlie had been about to say. Jesse came to his rescue with a brisk pat on the back that almost cost him his hat all over again. "Charlie, you got not to worry so much. You seen the elephant, and you been fine. There ain't nobody can complain about your worth in a fight."

"But I ain't brave!" The pain in the man's voice was clear even to Jesse. "Robert's brave, he don't care none when the bullets start flyin'! And you don't, nor Frank, nor any of those others neither! Hell, that woman that follows you all over? She don't so much as flinch when the shootin' starts!"

Jesse looked at the pale face for a moment. When he spoke, he tried to inject every ounce of his life's experience into the words. "Kid, let me tell you somethin' about bein' brave."

Charlie turned slowly around at the tone in Jesse's voice, looking into his face with a pitiful hope in his eyes.

"Bein' brave ain't about not bein' scared, Charlie. Bein' brave's about bein' scared and doin' what needs doin' anyway." He shrugged. "Hell, ever'body's scared when the dust is flyin', kid."

The hope flared even brighter, and Charlie stood up a little straighter. "Everybody? Even you?"

Jesse tried to contain his reaction, but the laugh burst out anyway, echoing off the bulkhead behind them. "Hell no, kid! I'm Jesse James!" He saw the hope start to collapse in Charlie's eyes, but after a moment, the outlaw's laughter, rolling over the surrounding water, tipped the balance and he smiled in response.

Jesse slapped Charlie Ford on the back again and they both turned to watch the shoreline slide past, smiling as wide as the river.

*****

As the NATCHEZ IX churned its way through the outskirts of New Orleans, Jesse and his party stood along the railing, watching the city grow before them. Even this far out, the buildings were like nothing most of them had ever seen before. Colonel Quantrill watched their reactions with a wide grin, as if unveiling a masterpiece of his own creation to new eyes.

Most of the buildings were brick and stone with beautifully ornate facades. Most had elaborate gardens that stretched down toward the water in green spills dotted with vibrant color. Small private docks and boat houses held sleek, RJ-powered speedsters. As they approached the main waterfront on the east side of the river, men in the uniform of the riverboat company came running out onto the pale wood. They caught heavy ropes heaved to them by the crew and wrapped them around heavy metal bollards that shone dully in the sun.

Beneath Jesse's feet, the engines surged with a rumbling growl, forcing the vast paddles backward, slowing the boat and bringing it up against the pier.

The wharf was connected to the land by several high wooden bridges. On the shore, a parade of ornate street lamps marched off into the distance up and down the bank. Each had a small RJ generator built into the base, nearly hidden behind decorative ironwork. Jesse could see a broad walkway beneath the lights.

The city, beginning just on the other side of a cobblestone street, struck him once again with its ornate, decorative architecture. Off to the right he could see a broad square where even larger, more impressive stone buildings presided over several monuments and gazebos. There were trees everywhere, along the streets, in cultivated gardens along the public square, and rising up from behind low walls attached to many of the buildings. Crowds of men and women in fancy clothing meandered down the lanes and beneath the gently-drooping trees.

Jesse was about to say something about the beauty and strangeness of the city when the first hot whiff of this new world reached across the cool water and slapped him in the face. As the NATCHEZ IX came to a halt, bumping gently against the docks, the breeze of her passage died away, and the outlaws got their first hint of life in New Orleans.

The foul smell that hit them was accompanied by an oppressive heat, laden with all the moisture of the river. The combination of smells, heat, and humidity was like nothing the men from the western territories had experienced outside the hell of Camp Lincoln itself. Lucinda and Quantrill seemed entirely unaffected, and Marcus's face was as impassive as always behind his kerchief and hood. Jesse looked at Lucy and Quantrill suspiciously; as if there were some secret to their composure they were keeping from him.

In fact, Lucy was never looking better, bedecked in a glittering gown she had picked up in the riverboat's shop. Her shopping spree, and the enormous copper tub, had gone a long way toward washing the stink of Camp Lincoln and the subsequent flight out of her hair.

"Is it always like this?" Robert Ford gasped out. "I'm soaking through my coat! How do those Dapper Dans stand it?"

Quantrill smiled. "It's not always like this." The smile turned downright evil. "I mean, we're hitting the tail end of autumn. Sometimes it's hotter. As for those boys walking the waterfront? Most of them are wearin' linen, or somethin' similar. A man can still cut a fine figure and not drown in his own sweat."

"What's that smell!" Charlie's face was pale.

The Confederate officer smiled as if apologizing. "Well, that there's the smell of the big city, boys. A European city dropped into the middle of a New World swamp, at any rate."

Lucinda smiled and put her hand on Jesse's shoulder. "Don't worry. You'll get used to it."

"Not damned likely!" Jesse scowled out over the city, watching it change from an object of wonder and curiosity, to a foul test of endurance before his eyes.

As Jesse was glowering out over the rail, he saw a detachment of soldiers march past, blaster rifles sloped over their shoulders. Their familiar blue uniforms sent a chill down his back, despite the stifling heat.

"You didn't say nothin' 'bout no blue-bellies, sir." Jesse jerked his head carefully in the direction of the unit as it disappeared down a side street to the south.

Quantrill frowned at Jesse. "I sure did, son. Told you there was a big mess of 'em down by the naval yards off Lake Borgne. They bed down hereabouts in town, but don't kick up too much of a fuss. Like I said, most of 'em's down by the small lake." He reached over and pulled at the sleeve of Jesse's duster. "That's why you're wearing these, remember?"

Jesse jerked the fabric out of the grinning man's hands. "What are they doin' here? Ain't New Orleans supposed to be a free city, you said?"

Quantrill shrugged and rested his elbows against the railing, watching out over the city. "No one knows for sure. They don't much trouble the folks here, so that ain't it. They got the waterfront along the lake shore sewed up to a fare-thee-well, though, almost as if they're expectin' trouble to come in on 'em by sea."

"But if we're hundreds of miles from Union territory, what the hell do those mudsills care what happens to the city?" Robert Ford was annoyed. "Don't make no damned sense!"

Quantrill shook his head. "It don't, but they're here. They do march around like they own the place, but they don't usually get into local goings on too deep." He tilted his head a bit. "No more than they have to, to keep their forces down by the lake."

"It's also the closest port to the Contested Territories." Lucinda had not spoken much for the past day, and her voice was distracted even now. "If someone were to try to get a large force into the territories, they could find a worse way to do it than pushing it up the Mississippi from here."

Jesse watched the street that had swallowed up the Union detachment for a few minutes more. "Well, not much we can do about it. Colonel, you say they don't queer the deal, I guess we gotta believe you."

Most of the passengers were making their way off the boat, crowding onto the docks and moving into the city. A line of wagons rumbled idly nearby, taking up the more lavishly-dressed passengers and whisking them away in clouds of crimson smoke.

Quantrill stood up, hands on hips, and turned to the little group. "Well, shall we? I can speak to the purser, have the Iron Horses brought up?"

Jesse shook his head. "I ain't seen any 'Horses out there. Have they come this far south?"

The colonel shook his head. "To be honest, no. The blue-bellies have them, of course. But the only other source for them would be your good doctor, or those who steal them from the authorities." He smiled as he gestured at Jesse and his companions. "So no, you won't find many, if any, in the city."

Jesse looked back down at the wagons in the street. The sun was starting to set, casting a ghostly reddish hue over the scene. "What's the plan, colonel? I don't think we wanna catch any sort of official attention, but I'm not sure how much territory we gotta cover . . ."

Quantrill nodded. "Well, Colonel Warley's not the easiest man to get ahold of, to be honest. An' if we try to head out toward his plantation without an invitation, the chances of us makin' it aren't gold-plated."

The outlaw chief bridled at the challenge, but his old colonel silenced him with a raised hand. "You'd be goin' up against a small army, Jesse. Until we get yours out of the swamp, I'm thinkin' you don't wanna try those odds." He smiled up at his young friend. "Besides, that's an army you mean to sweet talk over to your side, so killin' 'em all might not be the best notion you've had."

"So what would you suggest?" Lucinda's full lips were quirked in skeptical regard. "We're going to have to get off the boat eventually, and the Iron Horses will be coming off at some point as well."

Quantrill nodded quickly. "Of course. Well, we can have the 'Horses placed in a holding warehouse downriver for a few days without too many questions. I would recommend we take up rooms at one of the local establishments and see if we can't find one of my contacts, or Mistress Laveau, who may also be able to extend to us an invitation to Warley's place."

"Laveau, Carpathian's friend? The one that fixed up your arm?" Jesse's brows came down suspiciously. "Like I said, sir, I ain't super keen on meetin' up with a friend o' Carpathian."

"And like *I* said, James," Quantrill's voice was firm. "Mistress Laveau uses Carpathian's technology and techniques, but she is very much her own creature."

"A creature that uses dead bodies. And ain't none of those type folks ain't sick." Robert Ford's voice was cold, and his brother grunted in agreement.

"An' that freak from Camp Lincoln that the Union was usin', too. That ain't no kinda shindy we need to be gettin' caught up in." His lips were thin and tight as he shot a sidelong glance at Jesse.

The outlaw boss nodded. "We'll try to find one o' these ol' grey-backs first, boys. See if we can't skip meetin' the local medicine woman, if it's all the same to you, colonel."

Quantrill shook his head. "I'm just interested in bringin' you and Warley together, James. You know that. Marie Laveau did well enough by me, but I don't feel the need to drop in an' say hi, neither."

The group disembarked from the *Natchez IX*, the last passengers to step onto the dock as the crewmen and dockworkers began to unload cargo through massive iron doors in the boat's flank. Quantrill led the group across the cobbled border street and into the tight confines of the French Quarter. The fancy brick and stone buildings, their wrought-iron detailing and elaborate balconies, were nothing that Jesse had ever seen before. Even the fanciest cathouses back in the territories were no match for the meanest building on the poorest street in this city.

Quantrill led them to a particularly fancy building painted a bright, warm pink with cream detailing. An impressive iron sign painted with delicate letters and the image of a woman's eyes proclaimed the building to house an establishment named *Hotel Ses Beaux Yeux*. Judging from the women lounging on the balconies overlooking the street, Jesse thought he recognized the kind of business they were running, alien architecture and jibber-jabber name or not.

"I'm as ready to take a filly for a ride as the next man, colonel." Jesse's grin was forced as he glanced around the group standing in front of the building. "But you think this is the best use of our time?"

He had expected Lucy to rise to the bait, but instead she was looking thoughtfully up at the ladies above them. He shook his head at the wasted opportunity.

"Josie's got some rooms out back she lets friends rent without the usual . . . adornments?" Quantrill took the marble stairs at a jaunty pace, leaving the rest of them to hurry after. Jesse was the last to enter the building, cursing the sodden heat once again.

Inside the hotel, everything was soft and pink, with ladies sauntering through a dimly-lit salon in costumes that would have seen them arrested in most places Jesse had ever frequented. He could hardly keep his eyes focused on the handsome older lady Quantrill was speaking with at a polished wooden desk in the back of the room. He felt exceedingly awkward with Lucy nearby; for some reason, he did not want her to catch him ogling the local talent. Even so, he could not restrain his customary grin, and he took his hat off, nodding to several lovely ladies as he stepped up beside Quantrill.

"We'd be very much obliged, Madamoiselle Reneu, thank you." Quantrill held his hat tight to his chest as he bowed to the lady. Jesse nodded as well, his grin wider still.

"It is my pleasure, monsieur." There was only the faintest hint of an exotic accent in her voice. She turned her gaze upon Jesse and he found himself suddenly uncomfortable, as if he might be unworthy. Her eyes were a disconcerting pale gold, only slightly lighter than the caramel shade of her hair. Although she was older, her face was easily the match of any woman in the room, with the possible exception of Lucinda, who was staring at her with open admiration.

"And this must be the famous Jesse James of the Wild West." Madamoiselle Reneu extended her delicate hand toward Jesse and in a panic he grabbed it, shaking it quickly and releasing it.

"It's a pleasure, ma'am." Suddenly, Jesse could not find a safe place to settle his eyes.

She smiled in warm satisfaction and turned back to the grinning Quantrill. "I assume you'll be out and about till the wee hours, as usual, William?"

Quantrill shrugged. "Well, now, miss, I don't know precisely *what* the evening holds."

"Well," the lady pouted. "If it does not hold at least a fleeting moment for me, I will be terribly disappointed."

He laughed and nodded. "Me too, mistress, me too." She smiled in answer and gestured for him to lead the group through a glittering beaded curtain and down a dark hall.

Jesse, walking beside Lucy, was increasingly aware of their elbows brushing. He was very happy when Quantrill led them down a narrow stair and into a small suite of rooms. These were not nearly so well-appointed as the upper level, but comfortable nevertheless.

"So, that was Madamoiselle Josie Reneu." Quantrill smiled broadly to the group. "A friend of the cause, let us say." He gestured for everyone to take a seat in the various chairs and sofas in the suite's common room. "I think things would go best if we split up at this point, each take a section of the Quarter, and seek out someone who might be able to make the appropriate introductions? I can give you the proper words and phrases that should open the doors we need opened."

Jesse settled back into the soft cushions of a faded pink loveseat and stretched out his legs. "Well, colonel, you know best. I figure we can make our way 'round here without too much trouble. But someone's gotta head out into the swamps and watch for Frank an' them. They should be crossin' the river in the next couple of days if they pressed things, and they'll get lost in the Mourepas without someone to guide 'em in. I'll wanna know if they're okay before I join us up with any new outfit."

Charlie raised a hand. "I can do that, Jesse. I'll rustle me up one o' those local wagons and head on out later tonight. Shouldn't be too hard."

Jesse nodded and turned to Robert. "You wanna go with yer brother?"

Robert shook his head with a smirk. "No, I'm gonna stick with you. This many blue-bellies runnin' around, don't want you gettin' frisky. Frank'd never forgive me."

"Lucy, you okay movin' about on yer own?" Jesse looked around to find Lucinda moving around the walls of the small room, scrutinizing the fading wallpaper and the shiny metal lighting fixtures. When she heard her name, she looked up, preoccupied.

"Hmm?" When his question registered, she looked at him coldly. "I have been taking care of myself all my life, Jesse. Just because I ride with you for a spell, don't think I'm a helpless maiden."

The outlaw chief raised his hands in mock defense. "No! 'Course not!" He grinned and turned back to his old commander. "So, divvy us up, colonel!"

Quantrill set Lucinda toward the waterfront district, while he went south toward the port. Jesse volunteered to go westward, deeper into the Quarter. There was a moment's trouble as Marcus refused to be separated from Jesse, but the outlaw waved it away.

"So, I'm tramping around with a couple o' thugs followin' me, one in a hood . . . I'm sure we'll blend right in!" He laughed it off, and the five of them moved out into the hall toward the stairs.

"Now, you remember you got a job to do, Charlie!" Robert yelled back to his brother before closing the door.

"Don't worry, little brother." Charlie came to the door and rested his back against the jam. "I don't tucker that easily." His smile would have done a tomcat proud.

*****

Jesse, Marcus, and Robert Ford started to doubt the plan after checking their tenth café. They had found plenty of saloons and taverns, but none of them felt remotely like the watering holes back west. Even at the lower establishments, the furnishings were nice, the folks well-dressed, and the lighting bright. There was plenty of gaming going on, but Jesse refused to indulge. They had a job to do, and they were not going to stop with it still before them.

The phrases they had learned from Quantrill earned them only vague looks, shaking heads, and closed mouths. Jesse was starting to think maybe this Warley was a phantom. That thought led to an image of Henderson floating up in his mind, and he snarled as he forced it down into the shadows.

He had expected to have more trouble with Marcus following him through the streets. Other than an occasional shouted proposal from a woman of the evening, it was as if there was nothing special about the hulking, dark-skinned man. Something about that made Jesse feel better about the place, say what you would about the smell.

Coming out of a café with the wildly improbable name of the *Café Joyau du Mississippi*, Jesse noticed the skyline drop off ahead of them, a void that seemed strange in a city so dense.

"What you reckon that is over there, boys?" Jesse pointed with a metal hand at the emptiness. He had taken the gloves off a while ago. He was stifling in his coat, despite the drop in temperature with sunset, and any relief, even the phantom sensation of fresh air moving across the feedback pads of his metal limbs, was welcome.

"Hang this for a lark." Jesse looked around at the street signs overhanging their current position. Toulouse and Rampart . . . He felt like he had left his entire world behind. "Let's check out what that might be over yonder, an' then maybe swing back around to sweep the northern streets to the waterfront."

The two other men nodded silently. They were tired, neither of them particularly eager to spend any more time in the oppressive heat and stink of the city.

Crossing the quiet Rampart Street, they swung around to the left and found themselves facing a long, high wall of old stone. It looked like a small fortress, and Jesse thought, for a moment, they had stumbled upon one of the Union garrisons. A small gate in the center of the wall was open, nothing but darkness within. If it had been an active fort, there would have been sentries and weapon emplacements. This place looked deserted and decrepit.

"What you reckon—" Jesse began, but the sharp, grinding sound of many boots slapping against the wet cobbles stopped him. He dragged Robert back into the shadows of a small clump of trees while Marcus disappeared on his own.

A detachment of Union soldiers marched briskly past, looking neither right nor left as they stalked by the wall and its gaping entrance.

"Damn chiselers!" Jesse growled. "Give me half a chance—"

"Jesse!" Robert clipped him on the shoulder. "Look!"

A small figure had broken off from the shadows further down the street and was crossing the road toward the shadowed entrance. It paused to look after the Union soldiers, then ducked into the darkness and disappeared.

"Well, that ain't half queer, eh boys?" Jesse moved to the corner of the building across the street and peered into the gate. He could see nothing. "I say we check this out, and then head back." His voice was light and unconcerned. "What do you say, fellas?"

Robert looked to Marcus, but the big man's eyes were flat, fixed on the gate across the street. Ford turned back to Jesse. "We're with you, boss."

Jesse grinned, nodded, and then gave a quick look back and forth across the street. The wall was not quite twice the height of a man, the stone a white, crumbling rock with dark, meandering cracks that looked diseased in the harsh light of their RJ hand lamps. The gate was an opening flanked by two plain, square pillars, and beyond they could only see a confusion of hard, solid shapes.

Somewhere in the distance, a soft sound scratched at the very edges of Jesse's mind; a clicking, slithering sound that he could not quite place.

Jesse drew a Hyper-velocity blaster, holding it high and leading with his hand-lamp as he walked sideways through the arch. The beam fell on a stone box directly behind the gate and forcing him to the left. He waved his companions after him with his pistol, eyes sweeping the dimly-lit avenue. He turned the first corner and saw what seemed to be a miniature city, small stone houses placed close beside each other, flanking a street that disappeared into the darkness.

The structures came in a dizzying array of shapes and sizes. Many were plain slabs of stone with flat roofs. Others were elaborately carved affairs that reached with towers and columns into the warm night air. Eerie statuary gazed down upon them with cold blank stares as they moved through the twisting streets.

"What in the Sam Hill is this?" Robert's voice was harsh as he clutched his massive blaster with one hand, a knife and his hand-lamp in the other. "Jesse, half these here statues is skeletons!" The clicking sound came again. "And what the hell is that?"

Jesse cocked his head, but the sound was gone. He looked more closely at one of the images hovering overhead. It was, in fact, a skeleton. Its empty eye sockets glared down at him, its skeletal smile unnerving in its welcome. "I don't know, Robert."

Marcus's eyes, reflecting the light from their lamps, burned brightly. "It's a liche yard." He shrugged. "I don't know what that sound was."

Jesse stood up at that, casting an incredulous look at the miniature buildings that now surrounded them. "Ain't no way . . ." He tapped on the side of one tomb with the butt of his pistol. It gave a hollow sound. "I'll be damned. This here's a New Orleans Boot Hill?"

Marcus nodded once. "Ground's too soft, can't bury their dead. They gotta put 'em in these crypts or they'll never stay down."

"You ain't sayin' . . ." Robert Ford's voice was quavering. He had not yet faced Carpathian's animations, but he had heard plenty of the stories from Jesse and the men who rode with him. "They come back?"

Marcus cast a withering gaze toward the smaller man but did not respond.

"Marcus, how the hell you know so much 'bout how they bury folks in New Orleans?" Jesse stood up from his worried crouch to confront the larger man.

"Because Marcus Cunningham has returned home." A soft, melodious voice said from somewhere overhead. "Welcome home, Marcus. We've been waiting for you."

Two enormous men, bigger even than Marcus, with skin the color of midnight, moved out from behind a large tomb directly across from the three outlaws. The tomb was marked with countless scrawled crosses scratched in sets of three into its marble surface. The newcomers moved with an unsteady gait, arms hanging limply at their sides. Upon each man's face had been painted the shape of a human skull in thick, cracking greasepaint. The effect was distracting enough that at first, Jesse did not notice the men's eyes. Eyes that were cold, blank, and clouded in death.

"Damn. Animations." Jesse's gun came up and pointed unerringly at the head of the corpse on the left.
"I would prefer if you would leave my GAD PALÈ intact, MSYE James." Again the voice came from directly overhead, and Jesse dropped his hand-lamp to draw his other pistol, waving it uncertainly at the roof line on either side of the street.

"Come on out, now, where we can see ya!" Jesse was trying very hard to control his annoyance. "I know animations when I see 'em, an' I'm not too worried 'bout takin' down these two rips right here, if'n you feel like staying hid!"

A slim figure rose up on the roof across the cramped street. Robert's lamp beam flashed up to illuminate a beautiful, coffee-colored face. Her dark brown hair floated about her head like a halo; bright white teeth shone down upon them in a wide, welcoming smile. At her feet, looking down from the edge of the roof, was what looked like an enormous half-rotted serpent, its eyes clouded and empty. A framework of articulated metal struts and joints was sunk into the creature's flesh to provide the support its dead muscles could no longer convey.

"There is nothing to fear here, my friends. We are fellow travelers upon the same road." She gestured gracefully at the two enormous animations. "Now, please lower your weapon, *Msye* James. Although I can make more gad palè, *finding the raw materials for such* specimens can often present its own . . . challenges."

The woman dropped lightly from the roof and landed with just the slightest of sounds upon the packed dirt of the street. At the same time, a small girl emerged from the shadows behind the tomb with unnerving grace: the figure they had followed into the graveyard. She moved to stand beside the giant animations with a queer smile on her lips. The dead snake stayed on the roof, its white-eyed head swaying back and forth, while the woman rose from her landing, nearly as tall as Jesse himself. Standing proud in an ornate white dress, she nodded calmly to the outlaw chief.

"Marie Laveau welcomes you to New Orleans, Jesse James." He nodded jerkily, not sure what else to do. She grinned and gestured with one graceful hand back up at the roof. "And please excuse my pet, Nzambi. He can be shy around newcomers." The snake stared down and opened its mouth in what probably would have been a hiss if it had had a tongue.

She continued, turning away from the serpent. "You are correct, of course. My guardian gad palè are, indeed animations of a sort." Her smile vanished, and her eyes burned cold. "However, do not, therefore, believe you understand what you see here. There are realities, truths, and powers far older than the clever Doctor Carpathian." She glided toward him, sweeping around the still outlaw as if she were floating on air. "You will meet others, if you sojourn long within the limits of my city."

Jesse's gaze was fixated upon the woman's tawny eyes. He nodded again and holstered a weapon. He used his free hand to tip his hat. "Ma'am."

She smiled at him and moved toward Marcus. He had been staring at her with eyes so wide they accentuated the darkness of his flesh. When she reached up to his hood he shied back, but she persisted, pulling the fabric away.

Jesse looked at the twisted horn, shining redly in Robert's lamplight, protruding from the center of the man's forehead and curling back along the side of his skull. Marie Laveau made a sympathetic sound and drew one finger down the length of the horn. "So, it is true, my Marcus."

The big man continued to stare. His expression was frozen between despair and rage.

The strange woman walked around him, looking at the horn from every angle.

"Marcus . . . it's alright . . ." Jesse patted the air with one hand. Nothing good could come from killing this strange woman before they learned more.

"Marcus was raised among the savage northern tribes . . . Were you not, Marcus?" The woman's tone was soothing, almost hypnotic. "You wanted only to belong. You wanted only to be one with the warriors whose fires you shared. But you lacked their control, their knowledge, their heritage." She reached out again and touched the horn. "And you were marked for your failure."

Marcus only nodded again, his eyes fixed on the shadows between the monuments. He was shaking slightly, as if from cold or exertion. When he swept his gaze back around to stare at the woman, however, his body had become fixed and rigid. "My momma told me stories. It was you who told them to go west. It was you who sent my pa up there to die, an' me to . . . to . . . this!" One big hand wrenched at the horn as if wishing he could pull it out. There were tears of rage in his eyes as he stopped and looked down at her again. "Why . . . ?"

"But, Marcus, that is hardly the right question to beg, certainly? I am the Voodoo Queen of New Orleans! What a creature of power such as myself will always ask herself is not why . . . but why not?" She laughed again.

The big man grasped the haft of his hammer with both hands and began to raise it. "You bitch!" He roared, the animal sound echoing off the surrounding stone structures. The two gigantic animations moved forward and the undead snake reared up to strike as Marie Laveau stepped back lightly, the smile never wavering from her face.

She pursed her lips in mock sadness and shook her head. "Oh, Marcus."

The big man heaved the hammer up over his head, roaring again. Before he could bring it down, however, a booming voice from the cemetery gate bellowed, "In the name of the rightful government of the Republic of the United States of America, come out of there now, with your hands over your heads!"

Jesse's head snapped around to glare in the direction of the gate, then back at Marcus and Robert. Marie Laveau was already gone, disappeared into the shadows with the little girl. Her hulking gad palè were lumbering into the darkness after them. The horrible clicking, slithering sound drifted into the distance, and the roof of the tomb opposite was bare. The last thing they saw of the Voodoo Queen of New Orleans was the dazzling smile disappearing into the shadows as a soft, "Oh, dear!" floated after her.

Marcus shook his head, looking all around, the hammer shaking as its weight bore down upon him.

Robert Ford held his pistol in the air, looking from the distant gate to Jesse and back again.

Jesse stared at the maze of narrow streets that had swallowed Marie Laveau and her entourage. He stood up, the tension leaving his body and his shoulders slumping.

"Damnit."

Chapter 9

"Covert's the third agent we've lost this month, sir." Robert Pinkerton rested his elbows on his knees and tossed the scrap of parchment onto the low camp table. All around them, tall dark trees rose into the general shadows overhead where a thick canopy blotted out the night sky.

"And we're no closer to the bastard than when we first came out." The voice was slow and measured, slightly higher in pitch than one might expect, but still possessing a great deal of power and authority.

Pinkerton shook his head sadly. "No, sir. Each time we believe an agent has infiltrated his supply chain, they disappear. These were all good men and women, sir. And Curt was one of our best. I wouldn't want to be throwing more of my people into the fire for no good reason."

Robert Pinkerton, as the master of the Federal Pinkerton Secret Service, was one of the most powerful men in the country. He preferred to be out in the field, working directly with his agents, than staying in the rat's nest of political intrigue and petty empire-building that Washington had become. This would have hurt the career of any regular civil servant. Pinkerton, however, had friends in very high places, and those friends wanted him right where he was; right where he could do the most good.

The shadowy figure on the other side of the fire leaned back against a chair and pushed his heavy boots out in front of him, stretching with a gusting sigh. "I know, Robert. I agree. I just don't understand how a man can be so successful spreading his influence over such a wide territory, and yet we can't slip a single agent in."

"Well, sir." One of Pinkerton's lead agents, Levenson Wade, shrugged noncommittally. "The truth is, the more territory Carpathian takes from us, the more he can arrange his defense in depth. Those folks that have gone over to him won't talk. Some for fear, yeah. But most know, if they talk to anyone in the other camp, Carpathian'll stop the flow of Crimson Gold and they'll be back to . . . well, back to crouching around fire pits in the cold of the night." He grinned somewhat cruelly as he tossed a stick into the fire.

"It's true, sir." Pinkerton hated to admit weakness. In the nearly twenty years he had been running the organization, very few solutions had eluded him for this long. "We keep trying to get into his supply line and failing. We haven't been able to shadow them, either. That Interceptor heading down his trail looked promising, but then that poor young deputy . . . Once they get into the Tonto, there's no following them. You've seen it. It would take an army to fight down that road."

The tall man across the fire sighed and nodded sadly. Their small team had tried to penetrate the depths of the Tonto Forests several times. Each time, they had been set upon by roving bands of animations, barely able to escape back out into the bordering deserts. The horrific guardians, the irregular terrain, and the thick pine conspired to protect the old European from any attempts to discover the whereabouts of his hidden city.

"Are we even sure it's Green Valley?" The tall man muttered. "Half the folks hereabouts, they claim they've never even heard of Green Valley."

Wade shook his head. "We're not sure of anything, sir. The maps we have, courtesy of Agent Loveless, can't penetrate the pine forests, so there are literally thousands of square miles for us to cover." His mouth quirked in a sour frown and he threw another stick into the fire. "If we could cover it at all."

The man nodded and then turned to Pinkerton, one long hand gesturing to another paper on the camp table. "Speaking of Agent Loveless, do we know yet how she was even able to procure these maps?" There was a smile in the voice now, but it was not a pleasant one. "They're better than anything I ever saw at the War Department, and that's got me feeling a mite bitter, I don't mind saying."

Pinkerton shook his head. "We don't. She drew them herself, we know that. But as to how she was able to put together such a complete picture of the region? No, sir. All we have is speculation."

The tall man nodded again and then turned to Henry Courtright, another of Pinkerton's top agents. He was standing nearby, braced against the thick trunk of a tree and looking out into the impenetrable darkness. "Agent Courtright, could you shed any insight into how Agent Loveless was able to provide us with such faithful reproductions of such forsaken territory?"

Courtright looked down at the man, over to Pinkerton, and then back out into the surrounding forest. "There's no telling, sir; could be anything with Luce. To be honest, I wouldn't be surprised if she flew up there on a bird and sketched them while she floated along."

The tall man's impressive height unfolded beneath him as he stood up with a grunt. He began to pace around the small encampment. There were two or three other agents within view of the campfire, keeping watch over the surrounding forest. They looked up quickly as the man stood, and then went back to their own vigils.

"We've been out here too long to have nothing to show for it but a series of funerals for empty coffins." His hands worked nervously into each other as his mind teased at their situation. "We've been away from things back east too long as well. The Almighty alone knows what they've all gotten themselves into while we've been away. The Republic was tearing itself apart when we abandoned the front with the Warrior Nation to come haring off into the western territories after Carpathian, and we're no closer to solving either situation."

"Sir, to be fair, the Carpathian issue seemed far more manageable when we left the savages to Grant." Pinkerton knew the dark self-doubt that hunched in the tall man's heart, unseen by all but his closest friends and advisors. He knew how that shadow could torture the man when things were not following their prescribed course, and he hated watching him suffer. "None of our information indicated he was as entrenched as he was."

"Indeed, Robert." There was no agreement in the tall man's voice, however. "And despite not knowing, he *was*, in fact, entrenched. And now the madman owns just about every town and village in the western-most territories. By God, the entire region between here and Kansas City is now being called the Contested Territories, even in the official dispatches!" The man stopped and turned his heel in the deep loam to stare at the agents around the fire. "And nothing we have done for over a year has penetrated his hiding place or given us the least ability to curtail his efforts in any way."

"Well," Courtright looked sour. "Who knows where the stinking corpse soldiers would have been sent if he didn't have to guard the entire Tonto from us?" He stood, looking to Pinkerton for some support. "I mean, even forcing the enemy to reallocate resources can be seen as a partial victory in war, if it wreaks havoc with his intentions."

Pinkerton nodded, eager for the slightest hint of success. "And we have come close several times, sir. I believe, with Agents Courtright and Wade applying their more . . . rigorous . . . questioning techniques to the right individuals, we may yet be able to find a way to track him, or his men, anyway, back to wherever it is he's hiding."

The tall man was less than satisfied. "Robert," his voice was flat. "Why would you think the idea of torturing my own people could POSSIBLY make me feel better about our current situation?"

Pinkerton cursed himself silently. After serving this man for so many years, he should have seen the trap he was setting for himself. He raised his hands in a placating gesture. "Sir, that's not what I meant to say. I meant—"

"You meant exactly what you said, Robert. We have been fighting a losing battle here while the rest of the Republic falls apart behind us. Carpathian will be coming out of this forest someday, and he will have an army behind him. The savages, united beneath that bloodthirsty animal, Sitting Bull, tears our people apart and terrifies them off their lands. And Grant continues to spin his ugly metal wheels, driving first at the Warrior Nation, and then into the south after Lee's pathetic remnants, and then out into the so-called Contested Territories, unable to unite his forces against one threat at a time." One big hand, balled into a tight fist, slapped into the flat palm of the other. "We are worse than Nero, playing the fiddle of vain pursuit while the Republic burns down around us."

Pinkerton knew the man's assessment of many of the threats was not entirely accurate. Early misfortunes with the Warrior Nation, for instance, had forever colored his perception of them and their leadership structure. However, now hardly seemed the time to push him on the subject. "Sir, do you wish to return east? There's no denying that there is plenty we could be doing back home. And I know I would be far more effective running the Service a little closer to civilization."

The tall man seemed to deflate, sinking back down in his seat against the tree. "And yet, if we leave here, what do we have to show for our comrades' deaths?" He shook his head, sadness darkening his deep eyes. "We've all given up so much, and yet things just continue to fall apart. I believe Grant's pet scientists and Carpathian would agree: entropy, not humanity, will win this battle in the end."

"Bullshit." They all looked up sharply to where Courtright stood in the shadows, hands on hips.

"Excuse me, agent?" Pinkerton stood, concerned that he was about to lose one of his best men.

"You heard me, sir." The agent tipped his hat to the tall man by the fire. "With all due respect, of course. But entropy, as you call it, can't win as long as good men are willing to fight for what they know is right." He flung one hand out at the darkness as he continued. "Sure, we're gonna lose some fights. Hell, don't think this doesn't irk me something fierce. I've been out here longer than any of you. But if leaving Carpathian is what we need to do to get our house in order back home, and to assure that we're ready for the sick puttock when he comes out of his hidey hole at last, then that's what we've got to do!"

The tall man stared at Courtright for several tense moments, and Pinkerton was almost sure he was going to have to arrest his own agent. The firelight soon gleamed off a small smile in the shadows, and the tall man nodded, once.

"You speak the truth, Agent Courtright. And you rightfully put me in my place. Hope truly springs eternal in the hearts of lovers, fools, and civil servants." The men around the fire grinned, but he continued. "I fear you are all correct. We must prepare ourselves for a swift journey back east, to set things to rights and see that the Republic is in a position to repulse Carpathian when he emerges from his lair."

A sense of relief swept around the fire, but was swiftly dispelled as another agent stepped up, standing at stiff attention and looking uncomfortable. "Sir, the vocal reiterator."

Pinkerton sighed and stood. "Alright, Billy. I'll-.

The agent shook his head. "No, sir. Sorry, sir. They want to speak with . . ." His eyes flicked to the tall man sitting against the tree. "They want to speak with you, sir."

"Well, tarnation." The man unfolded himself once again, a scowl on his face. "I hate that thrice-damned contraption."

The agent brought the man over to a small console on another low camp table on the other side of the camp. A rubber cord led from the back of a large box and up into a nearby tree. The cord was fixed to the bark by spikes, disappearing up into the shadows. At the very top of the tree, far out of sight, the cord ended in a large silvery sphere held in place by a rough scaffold of wood and metal.

The tall man took up a ball-tipped wand attached to the box with a thin wire and looked through the pane of dark glass at the letters that floated in the vermillion fog.

"PLEXXE   ADXISEXXXEN   REAXX FOXXGEXERAL XXANT STXP."

"This is ludicrous!" The man flung one long hand at the box. "Who can possibly understand this gibberish? It's bad enough with the full power backing it up. Out here in the boondocks? It's all but useless!"

"Sir," Pinkerton tried to sound reasonable. "It's the best way we have to communicate right now. And it's far more effective than anything you or my father had when you first started out. I think sometimes it's easy to lose sight of how far we've come, when we hit the limitations of these new techs."

The tall man shook his head. "No, Robert. It's not that. It's that I can't stand tryin' to communicate with a man if I can't see his face." He jerked his sharp, bearded chin at the vocal reiterator. "And this contrivance is the worst example of that there could possibly be. No artistry, no finely crafted verbiage, no eloquent facial expressions or revealing cast of body or eyes." He shook his head. "No, this machine is almost worse than not being able to communicate at all!"

"Sir," Pinkerton held his hands up in surrender. "I can't deny that everything you've just said is the Gospel truth. But

General Grant's on the other end of this line, nevertheless, and he's expecting to talk to you without delay."

The tall man grunted and turned back to the machine, holding the wand loosely as if still entertaining thoughts of flinging it away. "Go ahead, General."

Pinkerton stepped forward with one hand raised. The tall man glowered at him, raising a finger of his own. "Don't you so much as even mention the word 'protocol', Robert." The leader of the Secret Service backed away, shaking his head slightly.

Within the small window, the words had changed.
"SIXXREPOXXING   ON   XORT   KXXCKS SIXX SXXP."

The man shot back up to his full height, his eyes shining with indignant frustration. "Now what in the name of all that's holy is that supposed to mean?"

Pinkerton bent around the other man to look into the box and then stood up. "He's reporting on the Fort Knox site, sir. The machine heard him say 'knocks' . . . It's not too bright."

The tall man muttered under his breath before grasping the wand in an offended huff and nearly shouting into it. "Very well, general. What is your report?"

Pinkerton looked uncomfortable but said nothing.

"I swear, Robert. I'm still not even sure why he wanted this pile of rocks of his built in the first place!" A deep suspicion glittered in the man's eyes and he looked out at the woods, speaking as if to himself. "Not a single one of his briefings on the subject made the slightest bit of sense. And why we need heavy fortifications anywhere near where he's suggesting . . ?" He worked his mouth almost as if he were about to spit.

"Well, maybe that's what this report is about?" Levenson Wade sauntered out of the dark and crouched down next to the camp table. "Maybe we're about to hear just what the great man plans to do with his new castle."

"Remember," Courtright grumbled. "This is his second one in as many years. He had that God-forsaken pile built out in the wilds first. Fort Frederick, did he call it?"

The tall man nodded. "Yes. After his son. But at least I understood his excuses then!" Somehow, the tall man managed to convey an iron, echoing tone with his voice as he assumed a theatrical stance. "A fortress to guard the best scientific minds of the age, safely away from the conflicts of our time."

"The best scientific minds willing to take Republic coin, you mean." Courtright spat into the leaves in the darkness. "And tell all the good men who died during that last big Warrior Nation attack on the place that they were safely away from conflict." His sneer spoke volumes.

"Yes, well, perhaps not as safe as anyone would have wished," the tall man shrugged. "But I understood the concept. This new fort back east? I have not the first notion of what he intends to do with it."

"Well, here we go." Pinkerton indicated the window in the black box, and the men settled down to watch and read.

"SECXXCY REXXINS INTACXXSTOPX FACILIXY IS NXW IXXA STXTE XX XEADIXESS STOX."

"I'm going to assume he's reporting that secrecy is intact and that the fort is ready . . ." The tall man pursed his lips and turned to Pinkerton. "Ready for what, do you think?"

Pinkerton pointed to the box.

"THE OBJXXT MUXT BX BRXUGXT CLOXER TO THE FROXT STXXXI FULXX EXXECT TXE PRXXXDENT TO BX BXXIND TXXS DECISXXN XXOP."

The tall man stared incredulously into the swirling mists as the letters faded away. "Fully expect the president to be behind this decision? Why, that rat, scalawag bastard."

Pinkerton stepped away to stare up at the tall man. "Sir?"

Leaning over, the man had grabbed the low table with both hands, knuckles white with tension, and his voice shook as he spoke in low, coldly-measured tones. "Easier to beg forgiveness than to ask for permission, hmm, Lyss?"

"Sir," Wade moved beside Pinkerton and spoke in low tones. "What object?"

Courtright moved forward as well, his voice not nearly so low. "And come to that, what front?"

Pinkerton shook his head, staring into the eddying crimson mist. The letters had long since sunk from visibility. "I don't know, but if he's talking about Fort Knox, then he can only mean the Confederate Rebellion. There really isn't anyone else nearby to fight."

Courtright grunted in dark amusement. "You can't really call the border with Lee's pathetic little city state a battle front, though, can you?"

Pinkerton looked at him, his eyes hooded. "Apparently you can." He turned back to the vocal reiterator. "If you're trying to justify something."

"The bit about expecting the president's approval was a little heavy-handed, I thought." Wade folded his arms across his chest and rocked back on his heels. "I mean, no one really thinks he's talking about President Johnson, do they?"

The tall man, still crouched down before the console, spat the words over his shoulder. "That man never uttered a word without careful consideration in his life." He stood, the wand gripped tightly in one hand. He frowned out into the surrounding shadows and spoke slowly into the machine. "I want you to double garrison Fort Knox at once, and hold position until further notice. I swear to you, general, if you move out before you hear from me, you will be removed from command."

The agents standing to the side exchanged alarmed glances. Their leader's legal status was about as gray as you could get, but that threat had been spoken in ringing tones they had not heard in many, many years.

Words began to swirl and form within the window on the box console, but the tall man purposefully turned away. A sneer played across his lips as he spoke one final time into the wand. "All communication will cease until further notice." The sneer grew into a cruel smile. "Stop."

He reached behind him and flipped two metal switches. The red indicator lights and vent glow all died away at once. The words within the window were torn apart, half-formed, as the colors within the display dissolved.

"Well, that was not entirely well-thought out, but it certainly felt good." He dropped the wand behind him and moved back to the tree that had supported his back most of the night. "We need to prepare to break camp."

"Sir?" Pinkerton knew this was coming, but he wanted to make sure before he passed along any orders.

"We're heading back east. We can't do anything more here, obviously." The man threw an open hand out into the surrounding darkness. "As long as we're stumbling around in enemy territory, it's only a matter of time before Carpathian is hunting us instead of the other way around." He shook his head. "This was ill-conceived from the start. We should never have tried to sneak our way into the man's house like common footpads while the might of the Union Army was incapable of supporting us."

The man's long face was sad in the flickering firelight. "We have lost good men and women to no avail. Machinations are beginning to turn back in the Old States that, if left unchecked, could well spell the fall of the Republic. Carpathian and his cabal of characters out of a dark romantic horror novel are potential future threats, but no larger danger for the present."

"There's no denying, sometimes it seems things would be much easier if we could turn back the clock a couple decades." Pinkerton wiped one forearm across his face. "It'd be nice if we could dispense with all these scientists and their damn fool gadgets."

"All of them?" Wade's gave him a lopsided smile. "You want to get rid of Tesla and his crew as well?"

The tall man responded, "I see Nikola Tesla as just another side of the coin of progress represented by Carpathian." A wry grin twisted his face. "Hell, I don't trust anything I can't understand. And I sure as Hades do not understand anything that comes out of that man's mouth." His look darkened. "I have half a mind to stop the spread of his damned metal men now, before they get shipped all over the continent. Something itches in the back of my mind at the very thought."

Pinkerton nodded. "There's something about them that sets my teeth on edge as well."

"Ain't got eyes to look into." Courtright spat into the night. "When push comes to shove, I'm not going to trust anything with a gun, I can't look into its eyes."

The tall man speared Pinkerton with an intense gaze. "Regardless of Tesla and his machines, and even Carpathian and all his schemes, we must see to this Fort Knox, and we need to be there as soon as humanly possible."

Pinkerton nodded again. "Yes, sir."

Wade took the lead and began to snap out orders. The agents were well-trained and had been anticipating a swift departure, in one direction or another, for days. After a quick check with their leader, one of the men scrambled up the tree to dismantle the vocal reiterator and reel the cabling up while others packed weapons and the rest of the equipment.

"We will move out at first light." The tall man took a massive, ornate axe from a supple leather boot and checked some intricate mechanisms around the blade. "Make for the rendezvous at Diablo Canyon, hold tight there for a day, and then make for Kansas City." He turned toward Pinkerton as he returned the axe to its holder. "Make sure your men activate all the dead drops as we head east. I do not want anyone left behind unsupported."

"And who knows what we'll need when we get to where we're going." Wade's mouth was twisted in annoyance.

The tall man stared into the fire for a moment and then turned to Pinkerton with a sigh. "I think, given our current situation, I want to call in those two butchers, Sasha Tanner and the Wraith. If this turns as ugly as I think it might, men of such character might be a key ace in the hole."

Every man around the fire looked surprised at the words. Pinkerton looked at the others, then back to the tall man, his head down. "Sir, we don't need their kind. They're poison."

"They're worse than criminals, sir." Wade's voice was hard. "They're traitorous scum, not worth the bullet it would take to put them down."

The tall man nodded sadly. "And yet I stand by my statement. Grant knows something we do not. And his machinations focus upon this Fort Knox. Having two such men with us, unbeknownst to him, might be advantageous in the end. I want them summoned."

Pinkerton nodded, his arms crossed and his back stiff. He turned to Courtright and growled. "Speaking of needing every man, where the hell is Loveless?"

The agent shrugged. "I haven't seen her since we parted ways back in Texas. I saw the report from that Andersonville fiasco." He frowned. "If I had to guess, I'd say she's still back east."

Pinkerton shook his head. "Is she still shadowing that bastard, James?"

Courtright nodded. "As far as her reports have indicated, yes sir. But we have no idea where they went after Camp . . . Andersonville." For a moment he looked uncomfortable, then continued. "It got pretty ugly there, if you'll remember from the stories."

The tall man glanced over to them. "There have got to be ways to contact her, yes?"

Pinkerton nodded, frowning. "I can activate the deep cover network with a recall order. The army throws fits whenever we have to do that, but it usually works." He grinned. "But, knowing Agent Loveless, I wouldn't give that more than an even chance of working."

Courtright snorted, leaning against a tree without unfolding his arms. "I think an even chance might be giving her more credit than she deserves."

The tall man smiled. "Well, there's no denying the girl's got spirit, gentlemen. She certainly has her own means and methods. However, she cannot be off the table when we brace whatever we will be finding at General Grant's new castle."

"I'm sure she's fine, sir." Courtright 's voice was light. "No one can take care of themselves like our Luce."

Pinkerton nodded solemnly. "She's always been one of our best."

"When she's ours." Courtright's face had darkened.

"I'm not sure I know what you mean by that, son." The tall man raised a single eyebrow more eloquent than the loudest ultimatum.

Courtright met the tall man's eyes. "Nothin' much, sir. Just that Luce has always been her own person. His High and Mightiness, the Over-marshal, has filed several reports questioning her loyalty. The same reports in which he mentions that Ironclad lawdog, that's set up in Diablo Canyon. It's true, though, that Luce can sometimes disappear a bit deep into her cover when it brushes up against her past."

The tall man looked at the agent a moment longer before nodding and turning away. "Well, we all have our pasts, Agent Courtright, and that's the truth." He bent down to fetch the sheathed axe and hefted it in both hands. "And sometimes a fight with that is worse than a life or death struggle with a hundred dead men."

Chapter 10

For a handful of heartbeats, Marcus stood, hammer shaking over his head. Then he bellowed again, all restraint gone. "Noooooooooooooo!"

The echoes from the surrounding tombs were unholy. The large man brought the weapon down against his chest and ran into the darkness. He screamed an anguished animal cry as he disappeared.

Robert looked to Jesse, standing in sudden indecision. Then, with a flick of his eyes, he nodded once and gestured for the outlaw to follow after the big black man. As they skittered around the first corner, they came up against a solid stone wall. There was no sign anywhere of Marcus or the strange woman and her posse.

"If you do not come out immediately, we will come in after you, drag you from the shadows, and beat you until you bleed!" The voice from the gate sounded eager. Robert Ford looked from the direction of the gate back to Jesse again.

"Jesse," his voice was harsh as he attempted to whisper against the rush of adrenaline washing through his body. "What we gonna do?"

For a moment longer, the outlaw chief stood in the darkness, shoulders slumped and head bowed. Then, his teeth flashed in the lamplight as his old grin peeked out through the beard once again. "Well, Robert, it's like this. I never met me a stinkin' blue-belly I could stomach . . . I don't see no reason we gotta give these Billy Yanks a pass tonight . . . You?"

The strength in Jesse's voice calmed Robert's racing heart, and he returned the grin with a nod. "I reckon we ain't dead yet, Jesse, might as well kick up a ruckus while we got the breath."

Jesse grinned at him and then jerked his head deeper into the graveyard. Robert followed, and the two men were soon slipping through the shadows, majestic houses of the dead sliding past on either side. Near the center of the cemetery was an enormous tomb. It rose above them in tiers like a huge, waterless fountain, each adorned with ghastly statues of cavorting demons and weeping angels. A flagstone courtyard surrounded the gaudy monument, offering the perfect spot to stop during a casual stroll and reflect upon the tragedies of mortality . . . or at the very least, the questionable tastes of the sculptor. Also, however, it presented the perfect spot for dry gulching an ornery pack of four-flushing Union bastards.

Jesse waved Robert to the right of the giant pile of stone while he scooted toward the deep shadows on the left. They both spun in the darkness, waiting for the soldiers to come. It might have been that Jesse had been too long from an honest fight, or the Yanks he had faced recently had been of a particularly low caliber, but Jesse's little plot to add to the liche yard's body count went wrong almost immediately.

The outlaw chief was crouched in the shadows, wondering what was taking the northern galoots so long, when a flash of red flame erupted on the far side of the tall monument and he heard Robert grunt in surprise and pain. A series of blaster shots echoed off the surrounding tombs. A confusion of shouts, cries, and stomping boots burst from the shadows. Suddenly, the monolithically ugly statuary was lit in strobing red flares.

Jesse scuttled backward, around the monument, and swept up the other side. Both of his Hyper-velocity pistols were out and scenting for targets. They were not disappointed.

A surging mob of figures shuffled around in the dark where Robert had been hiding. Occasional blaster shots cracked out of the group in all directions. Some sailed harmlessly up in ruler-straight courses toward the lowering clouds. Others slapped into stone structures near at hand, sending ruby sparks flashing into the sky. Each illuminated the courtyard and the surrounding mausoleums in crimson-edged flares. The Union soldiers shouldered through the scene with jerky, stop-start movements as they searched for Robert. He was nowhere to be seen.

Jesse prepared to jump up on the first tier of the ugly monument to rain fire down upon the Yanks when a howled warning rang out from his left. He looked just in time to see Robert Ford, blaster streaming crimson flame, throw himself off the roof of a low tomb into the fringe of the crowded soldiers.

The bolts struck several of the blue-uniformed men, throwing them into their brothers where they swayed limply, unable to fall in death due to the close-packed bodies. A wavering pistol, its owner's head missing from the nose up, dropped away from its bead on Jesse's back.

Jesse wasted no time running back behind the big monument. Bolts flashed in among the statues, sending sparks, rock chips, and dust billowing out. The outlaw came around the other side, both pistols up and ready, and his robotic arms, shrouded in unfamiliar sleeves, began to whir and scream. The Hyper-velocity pistols spun up and began to fling a glowing double stream of red death into the close-packed Union soldiers. The bolts tore through the men's torsos. They tore arms off in sprays of gore. They splashed heads away into the crowd. Less than a third of the soldiers were killed by the attack, but the rest panicked, the scent of death and the tacky feeling of their comrades' blood warm on their faces. They ran, streaming through the narrow gaps in monuments and mausoleums, and soon Jesse was the only man standing.

Robert jumped down from his perch. He rose, wiping a splash of blood from his face, and grinned with wild-eyed abandon at his boss.

"Damn, Jesse!" He screamed, his ears still ringing from the concussive blasts. "Damn!"

Jesse grinned back at him and then nodded in the direction of the fleeing Union men. "They're gonna come back!" He shouted, knowing Robert would be hard of hearing after the terrific detonations, as well. "We gotta get goin' while the gettin's good!"

A voice rang out through the night. Jesse thought it was the same voice that had hailed them from the gate, but the echoes made it impossible to be sure. The words were unclear, but the panic seemed to subside, the shouts and screams from the retreating blue-bellies tapered off, and a cold tightness twisted in the outlaw's stomach.

"They're comin' back 'round." Jesse gestured with one pistol in the direction the enemy had run. "They ain't gonna all come back that way, neither. They'll surround us again, cut us off from the gate, an' make an end."

Robert nodded, his face set in a grim frown. "Gotcha, Jesse." He cast an overly-casual glance into the darkness. "Where you think Marcus got off to?"

Jesse shrugged, moving a little to place his back against a tall monument of smooth, polished marble. "The way he run off? He's probl'y still runnin' that witch down."

Robert gave a shudder. "I don't much like his chances, Jesse, if he catches her."

The outlaw boss gave the younger man a look and then patted him on the shoulder with a metal fist still wrapped around a pistol. "I wouldn't worry none 'bout Marcus, Robert." He pointed the pistol out into the now-silent cemetery. "You worry about these poor northern boys, ain't gonna see their mommas no more cuz they picked the wrong fight."

Robert smiled, nodded, and then squatted down beside Jesse. The outlaw stared out into the darkness. Robert had doused his lamp before the Union soldiers had come upon them, so the only illumination was the softly gleaming moss draping some of the oldest tombs, and the eerie crimson glow of the outlaw chief's powered arms. Jesse opened his eyes wide, trying to concentrate on his peripheral vision, sharper in the gloom than staring straight ahead. He was stock-still, tensed to catch any sound or hint of movement in the swimming darkness.

A sound that could have been the scrape of a boot off to the left had Jesse's head jerking that way. But a flash of light that might have been silver-sharp edged steel, glimpsed out of the corner of his right eye, sent him swinging his gaze back in the other direction. Both times, he saw nothing.

"Jesse, I don't know how much longer I can do this." Robert's voice shook with suppressed tension, and the outlaw chief knew just how he felt. Waiting was always the worst part. Once the guns started blasting, there was almost nothing he liked better. He could dance through the sprays of fire and death with seeming-impunity. He never feared for his safety, least of all in the heat of a firefight. But crouching down like this, waiting for the Union to come down on him? That was no fit way for a man to pass his time.

Jesse was standing tall before he even realized he had moved. If he was going to meet his fate, he was not about to meet it on his haunches. Whether it was the sudden appearance of the standing outlaw, or just luck, two Union soldiers appeared right on their left flank, their blasters rising.

"Robert!" Jesse's guns came up at the same time he heard the other outlaw shout in his ear.

"Jesse!" The voice was steady but harsh with surprise. There was no fear at all.

Union troopers had come up on either side of their marble shelter as the rest of their force pushed deeper into the cemetery. Jesse saw the pair coming up on their left, and in a moment of grim anger, slapped his two pistols together, flicking the thumb switches to free the power cells. The vapors of the ruddy brew lashed out, tangling together and binding the two weapons together with a bridge that quickly began to glow an intense crimson. When Jesse pulled the triggers in unison, a blast was unleashed that was so hot, it melted the torso of the man on his right, sending his arms flipping backward, his legs flopping onto the flags, and his head, eyes wide in horrified surprise, tumbling backward into the super-heated backwash. The man's companion flew sideways, hair and clothing ablaze, his mouth wrenched wide in a gasp of pain and surprise.

At the same time, hunkered down beside Jesse, Robert Ford unleashed a fusillade of shots in a steady two-handed grip. The bolts slapped into the chests of the two soldiers coming around from that side, knocking them back into the flagstones, dead before they struck the ground.

The outlaws took a moment to glance at the other's handiwork, nodded, and then began to move side-by-side toward the edge of the cemetery and the small gate. The tombs all around them blocked any view of the remaining soldiers. Both men felt like hunted animals as they eased their way toward escape.

The Union officer, clearly tiring of the cat and mouse game, sent four groups of his men toward the fugitives from four different directions. Jesse was the first to sense their danger as a dark shadow leapt overhead from one crypt to the next. He spun, his duster flaring out, and sent a stream of ruby blasts sleeting up into the sky. The bolts intercepted first one shadow and then another in mid-leap, igniting their uniforms, shattering their bodies, and tossing them down onto the crushed stone of the walkway.

Robert turned at the sound of gunfire, catching sight of two men approaching down a tight alley between two basalt structures, underlit by Jesse's pistol fire. Robert saw their eyes go wide as he registered their presence. Both men, rifles already raised into firing positions, shattered the night with the thunder of their shots. Solid bars of hellish energy flashed out, cracking the stone of the tomb Robert crouched beside. He ducked, shying away from the blast of dust and rock chips, and then placed two carefully-aimed shots back down the alley, taking each man neatly in the head. Their decapitated bodies continued to move forward in an eerie parody of a run until they slumped gracelessly to the ground.

Two more soldiers came pounding down their back trail. Jesse heard the crunching of boots on gravel and continued his spin, sliding down and firing beneath Robert's outstretched arms. Each Hyper-velocity pistol centered in on the chest of a different target, and when Jesse pulled the triggers, both men were stopped as if they had hit a brick wall. They looked like insects pinned in place with massive ruby spikes, then the ravening energy ate through their torsos and blasted out their backs, sending vivid crimson streaks off into the shadows. The tombs all around leapt and shivered in the shattering, irregular light.

The two soldiers fell backward, their hollowed bodies slapping into the gravel. Silence filled the cemetery again, and Jesse and Robert stood up, looking all around for the next threat. Robert had a long scratch down one side of his face where a sharp chip of stone had caught him during the last attack. They were both covered in dust, but otherwise seemed unharmed. Jesse's grin returned full-force, and he shrugged impishly at his young friend. "Ain't so tough, are they."

The remaining soldiers, taking advantage of the momentary lull, rushed the two outlaws from up and down the little street at the same time. Blaster rifles were raised as bludgeoning weapons in the heaving crowd; pistols cracked and spat crimson bolts more to keep the prey's head down than in the hope of doing serious damage in the chaos. Jesse's eyes widened as he watched the wall of blue uniforms storm over their fallen comrades toward him. Behind him, he could hear the other contingent. Robert uttered a single, stark blasphemy under his breath in response. There was no more time for thought.

The world resolved itself into a flaring nightmare sequence of images, targets, and puzzles. The heavy butt of a blaster rifle came sailing in from overhead, a snarling pale face behind it. Jesse could not swing his pistol up in time to shoot, so he simply jammed the entire weapon into the enraged mouth, pulling the trigger several times after it stove in the man's teeth. A knife flashed in from the side and glanced off his left arm, slashing up his sleeve and lodging in the workings of his elbow. Jesse reached across the lowered arm with his right, pressed the smoking muzzle of his pistol up against the man's chest where it sizzled against the sweat-soaked uniform, and pulled the trigger, blasting the man's heart out his back. The fat now sizzling across the barrel's vents might cause him trouble in the next few minutes, but no more trouble than that coot's knife would have caused in the here and now.

Behind Jesse, Robert had drawn a knife in one hand and flipped his depleted pistol over, catching it by the steaming barrel in one gloved hand. He was brandishing the weapon like a blunt tomahawk. He crushed the jaw of the first man to reach him, and then reached out and slashed his knife across the next man's face. The soldier fell back into the surging crowd, his agonized screams and flailing arms causing more disarray to the formation than a collapsing body. Bringing the knife back into a guard position, Robert immediately punched it out again, stabbing another soldier through the neck. Hot blood geysered out over the melee as the gurgling victim slumped against a cold stone tomb and sank into a limp pile at the base of the wall.

Jesse tried to bring his left arm up and across to shoot at another soldier closing in on him, but the limb was too slow, the metal finger spasming against the trigger and sending several ill-timed shots low into the threatening mob. Legs and kneecaps burst and shattered under the impact. The fight was knocked out of the men before him, but he cursed under his breath at the messy manner in which it had happened.

Robert's fight was going extremely well, a low rampart of bodies forming at his feet, when a heavy knife, nearly an Arkansas toothpick, was thrown from the back ranks. It flashed between the bobbing heads of his assailants and took him in the shoulder. It was not a clean hit, glancing off the armored shoulder pad sewn into his duster. The heavy blade bit as it past, sending a jolt of icy fire down his arm, tingling into the hand, and then burning back up again.

Jesse stepped back when he heard Robert's cry. His boot heel crunched down on a limp hand and he almost lost his footing. He cast a quick look over his shoulder, steadied himself, and then started to turn, reaching out with his one good arm.

If the Union soldier had been able to make his charge without screaming in triumph, Jesse may well have died there in that cemetery. But the man was overcome with anticipation of his own victory. Or perhaps his rage had gotten the better of him. Afterward, as he tried to reconstruct the events in his mind, Jesse was unable to shake the feeling that the man's eyes had flared a worryingly familiar shade of red before he had died.

The man wielded a cavalry saber with an RJ charging cell built into the hilt. Jesse had seen weapons like that before, but they were rare in the lower ranks. The blade was long, its metal infused with the shifting, smoky energy of Carpathian's Devil's Blood. It was cocked back, already slicing through the air toward his neck, ready to take his head. The face behind the blade was beyond madness, and its inhuman shriek echoed off the stone tombs around them.

Jesse ducked down. He reached out to steady himself with his left hand, only to have the arm buckle beneath his weight. He curled his body as he fell, losing his bead on his attacker. He hit hard, sooner than expected, and barely got his right arm up in time to block the descending blade.

Fat red sparks spat out into the night, bouncing off bodies, tombs, and the struggling combatants. The smell of hot metal shot through the air as the burning weapon scorched away the sleeve and ground against the mechanical limb beneath. The soldier leaned into his cut, trying to force the powered blade right through the arm and into the body behind. The madness faded from his eyes for just a moment and the soldier sneered, "Henderson sends his regards."

Jesse started at the name, then pushed his left arm up beneath the right. The limb responded slowly, and he was only able to pump two shots into the man's foot. The soldier's scream became a shriek as he fell over backward, the blade wrenching free.

Jesse surged to his feet, fear and anger tangling in his mind. He put three more bolts into the shrieking man, his mouth twisted in furious vindication, when he took a glancing blow to the back of his head that drove him back down to his knees.

Robert had been fending off the larger contingent of Union soldiers. However, he was being ground down by the sheer force of their numbers. Each man he killed was closer than the last, and a series of blows and kicks had been landed, each taking its toll. Dizzy with fatigue, each kill wore him down. The last soldier surged toward him, skittering over the smoking bodies of his comrades. If the man had meant to kill him, Robert Ford would have been dead. Instead, the soldier had seen Jesse James, sleeves torn, guns blazing, rising from the shadows over Robert's shoulder, and he had changed his target. He rushed past the stunned outlaw, blaster rifle raised, and had brought the weapon down in what should have been a crushing blow. But his ankle came down on the cold limb of a dead comrade, twisting and spoiling his aim. The solid wood of the weapon, when it struck, still came down with terrific force. It glanced across the side of the outlaw chief's head, sending him down into the gravel.

Robert was horrified as the man ran past, spinning to follow the movements, bringing up his pistol. It was reloaded and back in a proper grip again, and he stabbed the barrel at the soldier's back as he pulled the trigger. The bolts struck the man low, then walked up his spine and took off his head in a fountain of gory steam. The body collapsed, life's blood pumping from the smoking wreckage.

A silence settled over the cemetery, mocking the solemn tombs and their eternal guardians with mortal finality. Blue uniformed bodies, many mangled by close-quarters violence, were strewn about the narrow street. Blood was splashed across many of the surrounding crypts. Robert collapsed beside his boss. Jesse slid down against a crypt, gasping for breath and covered in blood.

"Damn!" He coughed, spitting blood into the pile of bodies that surrounded him. "Damn!"

Robert smiled through the grit and the bloody slime coating his own face. "Hot damn, Jesse! I thought, when that damned blue-belly rushed past me, you was a goner fer sure!"

"Damn!" Jesse glared around, wild eyed, at the scene around them. There was no way he could get a quick count of the bodies, but it sure looked like they had accounted for the remainder of the platoon. "We gotta get out'a here, Robert." Jesse shook his head, trying to clear it of the ringing and the glaring spots that haunted his vision. He looked up at the younger man and started again. "We both need a sawbones somethin' wicked."

Robert nodded, looking around as he helped Jesse to his feet. "I wish I knew where that damned Marcus went off to."

"Don't worry about him now, Robert." Jesse was standing on his own two feet, barely, but he was looking down at his arms. A steady flow of black fluid with glowing crimson rivulets within it was leaking down his forearms. The left arm was shaking slightly as if in the grips of a palsy. "We really need to get out o' here."

"Well, I hope he caught the damned witch, after this. She coulda warned us." Robert reached out and eased Jesse out of the pile of bodies and separated limbs. He was in little better shape himself. As they dragged themselves down the crunching gravel, a passerby would have been hard-pressed to say who was supporting whom.

The twin columns of the gate swam out of the darkness and Robert put on a surge of energy.

"Well, what have we here?"

The voice was cold. It chilled them to the bone, coming as it did from directly behind. Robert stopped in his tracks, Jesse swaying slightly at his side. Neither looked at the other, neither turned. Both stared out into the emptiness of Basin Street.

The outlaw chief did not turn around. "Some might say lettin' me go tonight'd be the smartest thing a man mighta done in his life." Keeping his voice even took all the energy that remained in his battered body.

A gust of nerve-tinged laughter echoed off the stone. When the man behind them spoke again, his tone was dripping with self-congratulation. "Reward notices have been pretty clear, James. Alive or dead. I reckon I'll be paying for my next big promotion with your head, hayseed."

There was no prearranged signal. They did not speak, sign, or make eye contact. They simply moved.

Jesse spun to his left, away from Robert, spinning to the right. Both men brought up their pistols. Neither of them had holstered their weapons.

A tall Union officer, a lieutenant by the gold bars on his epaulets, stood before them, an enormous blaster pistol in one hand and another glowing, smoking sword in the other. But as the two men before him turned in place, the cruel, gloating look slid into confusion, then concern, then fear. He brought his pistol up, but by then it was too late.

Each of the outlaws fired a single bolt. Both shots took the man in the center of his chest, blowing him back into the shadows. His spasming nerves caused his pistol to flare off once, sending a dart of crimson light flashing off into the tombs. Then he was still.

"That's a Yankee for ya." Jesse muttered, his breath coming in shallow gasps as he looked down at his arm. Even with the damage that had thrown off his earlier shots, both his mechanical limbs seemed to be operating smoother with each step he took down his new, chosen path. He turned back to take Robert's proffered arm. "Never know when they've won."

Robert murmured agreement, and the two men limped out of the cemetery, across the empty street, and back toward the French Quarter. Behind them settled over thirty dead bodies for someone else to answer for.

Robert remembered that Loveless had been sent to the waterfront, and so he made his way in that direction. His head was swimming, and he could barely marshal the focus to put one foot in front of the other, dragging Jesse along behind him. He knew he would never be able to find the damn whorehouse on his own. Jesse was barely conscious and would have been no help at all.

The streets were nearly deserted around the old cemetery, but the deeper the men moved into the French Quarter, the more folks they met, strolling along in their finery, taking the night air, or carousing from one hotel or café to the next. Eventually, several of the men, usually at the instigation of their fair companions, asked if they could be of any assistance. Robert just grunted at them, shook his head, and kept moving toward the river, his eyes fixed on the spires of the large cathedral in the distance.

Each step was torture. Robert started to wonder if he was going to reach the waterfront without help after all. Jesse was nearly unconscious, and the younger man's arm was going numb from supporting the steadily-growing weight. The glowing street lamps beckoned him on, and the cathedral grew larger in imperceptible stages, and he was soon too tired to acknowledge or care about the looks they were getting as they moved down the delicate, gilded avenue.

*****

Lucinda glanced nervously behind her, even though she knew no one had followed from the whorehouse. Her lip twitched at that. This city seemed so sophisticated on so many levels, and yet they avoided certain honest terms as if they were tainted by the touch of the devil himself. She shook her head, dusted her fingers with a delicate sweep of a linen napkin, and moved on down the thoroughfare of the waterfront. Saint Louis Cathedral loomed up behind her, dominating Jackson Square and giving ironic counterpoint to her last thought. Her mind was troubled, and could only dawdle on such trivial curiosities for so long before she found it curving back around to her chief concern.

From the moment the city had slid into view, Lucinda knew her little idyll with the outlaws was coming to an end. There had been a certain drape to the Union flag hanging from the guard station at the port. There were slight alterations in the order of the unit citations flown from the platoon guidons that marched through the city. There were even certain signs along the dock itself that screamed for urgent action . . . if a person knew the codes.

Something important was occurring, and the president was recalling all Pinkerton Agents. She knew she was being ordered to report to the new depot in Kansas City. Not her personally, of course, but every agent currently acting independent of central command. Something big was brewing out there somewhere.

Lucy knew Jesse's plans for the Confederacy would have easily justified such a drastic, universal response, had they been known. But she had not reported those plans. In fact, she was far from certain she *would* be reporting those plans. After everything that had happened at Fort Lincoln, her once-steadfast loyalties had been severely torn. She felt no certainty at all as to where her allegiance would fall when the dust settled.

As she saw the coded signs, she knew she was not yet ready to make that final decision, one way or the other. She would not high-tail it back to Kansas City just now, abandoning Jesse to his fate and returning to the indomitable will of the Union. Likewise, she was not ready to turn her back on the nation that had taken in her in, given her purpose, and sheltered her for all her adult life.

There were contingency procedures for field agents in the middle of sensitive operations when a recall order went out. When everyone had left the *Hotel Ses Beaux Yeux* on Quantrill's mysterious quest, she had taken a circuitous route to the waterfront, using all of her tradecraft to ensure she was not being followed. She had taken a small back table in the Café du Monde, ordered herself a plate of beignets and a thick café au lait, and had tried to enjoy the little pastries while carefully composing her response to the men who believed they pulled her strings.

The pastries were as delicious as she remembered, and the message as difficult to write as she had feared. She wrote of Jesse's plans in the broadest possible terms. She was vague where she could be, specific where she felt she had to be, and yet still knew she would be betraying Jesse by sending anything to her superiors.

She folded the brief note, putting it within a small pocket sewn into her sleeve, and then sat quietly, staring into the swirling colors of her coffee. She took the paper out, smoothed it down on the table, careful to avoid the powdered sugar, and read it again. Every word was a betrayal. But to ignore the coded signs and send nothing would have been a betrayal as well. She re-folded the note, returned it to its place, and left the café to walk the waterfront.

And so she found herself pacing the area around Jackson Square, making sure none of her current companions had wandered into her personal tragedy. When a command platoon marched into the square, she hurried toward them. Their guidon flapped limply on its staff, and by the order of the citations hanging beneath, she knew their commander would be able to see her report on its way. She skip-stepped, drawing up her skirts so she could move a little quicker, and made as if to trip just as the young-looking lieutenant, marching along beside his charges, came even with her.

Lucinda cast her arms wide as she fell, and the man's natural reaction to reach out to help her brought them into rough contact. She smiled apologetically up at him and muttered, "These Parisian heels . . ." She thought she heard a voice from around the cathedral call out her name.

At the code phrase the lieutenant's vaguely-concerned face sharpened and he replied, "They do seem high this season." But suspicion almost immediately descended as Lucinda, distracted by the call of her name, failed to give the correct final response. She was, in fact, whipping her eyes back and forth, trying not to look suspicious. She knew she had to complete the ritual.

"They're taller every season." She gave the boy a quick smile, palmed the note into his hand, and then pushed off, a look of indignant fury rising on her face. "How dare you, sir!" She shouted the question in a thick Creole accent, and at once the people wandering the waterfront, a substantial crowd even at that late hour, started to mutter, casting dark looks toward the Union soldiers.

A hard edge settled just behind the young officer's apologetic mask as he tipped his hat to her in a shallow bow.

"My apologies, ma'am." He muttered, and then shouted for his men to carry on.

Lucinda watched the unit march away, furtively watching the waterfront crowd. The soldiers were not very far at all when a figure staggered out of the shadows beside the cathedral, moving toward her.

Robert's eyes twitched uneasily between Lucinda and the Union column and back again, and she cursed whatever coincidence had brought him into Jackson Square at that moment. She pushed that down and assumed one of her more attractive expressions, intending to stun him with a frontal assault and then demand how he had come to such a bloody state, and—

"Where's Jesse?" An edge of panic entered her voice as she asked the question before even realizing she had lost her focus.

Robert cast one last look at the Union column, then turned back to her. There was an undeniable suspicion in his eyes, but suddenly she did not care. She grabbed him by his lapels and gave him a single, sharp, jolt.

"Where's Jesse?" She repeated, staring into his eyes. Robert shook himself, his eyes softening slightly. He jerked his head back in the direction he had come. "I sat him in a café back that way. I'm hopin' no one notices. He ain't much awake—"

"What?" Lucinda was moving in the indicated direction before Robert could even respond. He hurried after her, limping from his injuries.

"Hey!" He called. "What was all that with the blue-bellies?"

She stopped. She knew she needed to address it here, or it would fester in Robert's mind and cause untold trouble later on. She turned around, putting on a pretty but exasperated look, and shrugged. "That oaf of an officer tripped into me, and then had the nerve to proposition me in the middle of the public square!"

He looked into her face for a moment, suspicion struggling with fatigue, concern for Jesse, and the undeniable impact of her beauty. When he spoke, his voice was soft and vague, still floating between distrust and reserve. "Oh . . ." He started to soften. "The chiseling bastards."

She hid her relief, nodded, and asked in a slow, measured voice. "Now, Robert, please tell me where Jesse is and what happened?"

He shook his head. "Sorry. We got in a shindy with some blue-bellies. Didn't mean to, but they jumped us in a cemetery. And we lost Marcus. And there was this witch woman." Once he had started to talk, it flooded out of him. "Jesse and I, all on our lonesome, took on the whole platoon. We won, o'course, but we got beat up pretty bad. Jesse's real bad, but he'll be fine." Now Robert's face turned red and he dropped his gaze. "Truth to tell, Miss Lucinda, I knew I couldn't find that cathouse without you. I knew you was headin' to the riverfront, so's I thought I'd look for you here."

"Well, you did good, Robert." She patted his shoulder, noting with further relief the reaction that caused. "Now, we have to get you both back to the hotel. Do either of you need a doctor?"

He shrugged, suddenly bashful. "I don't think a sawbones would hurt, miss." She always found it oddly disconcerting when hardened killers like Robert Ford could be so easily manipulated by her most basic ploys.

She nodded again. "Alright, we'll have the madam send for one as soon as we get back to the hotel." She started to move back down the street, gesturing behind her for him to follow.

Robert did follow, but his eyes were fixated upon her as she moved away down the street. There was undeniably a stunned appreciation in his eyes. But there was also just a touch of unrelieved suspicion.

It sure had looked like Lucinda had been the one who tripped . . .

Chapter 11

As they entered the salon of the *Hotel Ses Beaux Yeux*, Madamoiselle Reneu rushed out from behind her small table and met them in the middle of the room.

"Get him to the back at once!" The woman's voice was brusque. She spun and preceded them across the carpeted floor, holding the beaded curtain open for them. "*Mon Dieu*! When will I ever learn that no good deed goes unpunished?"

Jesse was nearly unconscious, supported between Lucinda and a battered Robert Ford. In the soft light of the brothel's common room, their injuries appeared much worse. There were cuts, scratches, and bruises over every exposed surface. The fluids leaking from Jesse's mechanical arms had slowed to a trickle, but his duster was spattered with the black and crimson mess.

The salon was almost empty as they staggered through. Most of the girls were either working or had turned in for the night. However, a few night-owls were still lounging among the pillows and elaborate old furniture. They leapt up as they saw the condition of the newcomers. One offered to help, but the others just watched with mild curiosity. Madamoiselle Reneu ushered them all back to their places with a graceful flip of her hand.

As the trio moved past the madam and deeper into the house, she muttered to them. "Your guests are with Colonel Quantrill in your suite. Please keep things civil. I don't want any trouble."

Lucinda cast a confused glance at the madam, but the woman was already turning away, shooing her girls back to their places. Guests? She did not like the sound of that. Jesse was the only one here who really knew or trusted Quantrill. She was not at all sure she wanted to have to deal with the man herself.

The agent paused in the hallway. Could she turn around? Maybe find a cheap hotel on the outskirts of town, bring in a local doctor, and contact Quantrill after the boys were seen to? She looked down at the limp metal arm she held. Her dress was ruined with black and red stains. Jesse's face was pale beneath the dust and the blood. A local sawbones might be able to deal with the scratches and the bruising, but they would never be able to address Jesse's damaged arms. She shrugged. Quantrill would not be able to do much either, but given his own replacement limb, he would know better than she. Besides, she realized, how would she know who to trust, trying to find a doctor in this city? She cursed under her breath. Things were getting out of hand.

Lucinda guided the stunned men through the maze of textured wallpaper and dim light until they came to the short flight of stairs. Robert nearly tumbled over the edge. She had to reach across Jesse's bowed shoulders, grabbing the man and jerking him back to awareness by his collar.

"Uh . . . Sorry." Robert muttered, looking down at the stairs and then across at her. "Thanks."
She nodded. "Do you think you can help with the stairs? Or should I go fetch the colonel?"

Robert shook his head. "No, no. I can do it. Let me just . . ." He readjusted his grip on Jesse's arm and took a first, tentative step down the stairs. It took longer than it should have, but Jesse was safely at the bottom soon enough. The noise they had made, however, had aroused suspicion, and as they began the short trek down the hallway, the door to their suite opened and Quantrill's head appeared from around the door frame.
The old officer took one look at Jesse and Robert and then turned to put his heavy cane down. He rushed out to help, his limp pronounced. "Good God, what happened?" He swept in between Robert and Jesse and tried to support both of them at the same time.

Lucinda shook her head, her voice labored. "Robert said something about a Union patrol, but I didn't get much more out of him." She jerked her head at the outlaw boss. "Jesse had even less to say."

Quantrill guided them toward the door. After a bit of shuffling, they eased into the common room. Lucinda was focused on getting Jesse to one of the overstuffed chairs when she realized that the chamber felt far more crowded than it should have.

Charlie Ford rushed forward with a start. "Robert?" He took his brother from Quantrill and eased him into a chair. "Damn, what happened?"

Quantrill helped Lucinda set Jesse down in another chair as she looked up at the strangers before her. She fought hard not to go for one of her replacement blasters.

They were such a strange group, her mind did not know where to focus first. There was a man seated comfortably in one of the more formal chairs. He was dressed in the fashion of a local swell, his cream-colored suit offset by the deep burgundy of his cravat. The texturing of his rich waistcoat was a warm contrast to the light jacket. On one knee rested a pristine hat that matched the rest of the outfit. He smiled warmly at her as he gracefully rose to his feet with a nod.

In a chair near the man was seated an elegant woman whose café au lait complexion hinted at a mixed heritage that would have been a curse almost anywhere else on the continent. She was wearing an ornate white dress and sat like a queen ready to receive visitors. Her expression was painfully aloof.

In stark contrast to these sophisticated figures, however, were the dark-skinned, hulking brutes standing near the wall. Their black clothing was rough but serviceable. Their faces were decorated with elaborate skull masks painted right onto their flesh. A vaguely unpleasant smell lingered about the room, and Lucinda wrinkled her delicate nose. The smell triggered something in the back of her mind, and she looked more closely at their faces. She was not surprised when she realized that their eyes were cloudy and blank. Dead eyes.

Finishing up the tableau before her, Marcus Cunningham sat in a straight-backed cane chair against the wall between the two hulking animations. His eyes were open, but without expression. He sat loosely in the chair and took no notice of anything going on around him.

Lucinda stood up, one hand resting near her hidden pistol, and turned toward Quantrill. "It's not like you to be so remiss in your manners, colonel." She gracefully nodded her head toward the strangers, a wide, winsome smile professionally applied. "Are you not going to introduce us all?" Her eye flickered over to Marcus as well. Whatever was going on here, it could not be good.

Quantrill knelt down beside Jesse's chair, checking the outlaw's face and eyes. "Well, of course, miss. Sorry. I just thought maybe we'd like to see our boys looked after first?"

Lucinda smiled. She tried to mitigate her tone, but with only partial success. "They'll be fine for a few more minutes, colonel. They made it this far."

Quantrill stared at her for a moment, then looked back at the newcomers and shrugged. "Of course."

The old officer stood with a grunt of effort and indicated the gentleman with the hat. "Miss Loveless, may I introduce the inestimable Colonel Alexander F. Warley."

The man took her hand before she could avoid him. He brushed his lips quickly across her knuckles and then released the hand. "Please, miss, call me Alex, if you will do me the honor." His eyes wrinkled along lines familiar with an easy smile. "And if I may take the onerous duty from my old friend's hands?" He looked a question at Quantrill, who shrugged and leaned back down to Jesse.

"Miss Loveless, I have the unalloyed pleasure and honor of introducing you to one of the most eminent personages of our entire city." He held out one hand and the woman in the white dress nodded regally and stood in one fluid motion, taking the proffered hand. "This is the lovely Marie Laveau; a physician and student of the sciences, both natural and . . . otherwise. She has already made the acquaintance of the *messieurs* James and Ford." He indicated the wounded men with a tip of his head.

The woman nodded, taking Lucinda's hand in her own. "It is truly a pleasure to meet you at last, Miss Loveless." Her accent was refined, with just a hint of the bayou to give it spice. Her eyes bore directly into the agent's, and Lucinda was suddenly very concerned that Robert Ford might not be the most serious threat to her cover in this room.

"Well, it is a pleasure to meet you as well, Madam Laveau." Lucinda kept her voice even.

"Madamoiselle, actually." The woman smiled warmly, but the warmth never reached her eyes. "Now, let us look to these stalwart heroes, shall we?"

Marie Laveau joined Quantrill beside Jesse, reaching out gently to poke and prod his face and neck, noting the outlaw boss's sluggish reactions. She pushed his eyelids up to look at the unresponsive dark orbs behind, and then stood. "If you will please, I will have my gad palè take Mr. James into one of the side rooms?"

"Hey, what about my brother?" Charlie was indignant as he stood up from Robert's side.

Marie Laveau turned smoothly to regard the other wounded outlaw and then nodded. "He will be fine. Water with a little wine, I think. And clean his wounds." She turned away dismissively and Charlie was left sputtering behind her.

The giant animations moved forward, although the strange woman had not said anything. As they moved past Lucinda to ease Jesse from his chair, she could see the metal mechanisms on the backs of their heads that housed small, delicate-looking RJ cylinders. She could also just make out, beneath their clothing, the support frameworks that Carpathian seldom bothered to hide beneath his own creations' clothes.

She watched the animations take Jesse into one of the bedrooms, Marie Laveau following with a bag she had picked up from beside her chair. When they were gone, she turned back to Quantrill. "Well, I think you might owe us some words."

Quantrill eased himself into a chair and peered up at her. "What words might you be lookin' for, sweet thing?"

Lucinda breathed deeply through flaring nostrils. She sauntered across the room, putting a little extra effort into the sway of her hips, and grinned to herself as she noted the effect it had on both of the old Confederate war dogs. She settled herself into a settee a little apart from the central group and smiled.

"Well, colonel, while we're waiting to hear from the next room, why don't you tell me what's wrong with Marcus?" Her tone was light but her eyes were cold and lethal.

"I might be able to shed some light on that, Miss." Warley raised a finger. "The way I understand it, there was a little . . . misunderstanding, over in old Saint Louise Cemetery

Number One. The big man in the hood became distraught, and Madamoiselle Laveau gave him a little something to calm his nerves. Sadly, after being separated, it appears that Mister James and his compatriot were attacked by the Union patrol."

Lucinda turned in her chair, one arm resting against its back, and regarded the slack-faced Marcus. "He looks somewhat more than calmed."

Warley frowned. "As I hear tell, he was extremely distraught."

"Bullshite." The word snapped across the room and they all looked to where Charlie was administering to his brother with water from a shallow porcelain bowl. Robert's eyes were on fire as he glared at the man in the fancy suit. "She had words with Marcus, riled 'im all up, an' then laughed at 'im. He chased off after her at the same time those blue-bellies came rushin' in." He turned back to Lucinda, concern plain on his face. "That woman ain't natural, miss. She knows Carpathian, an' she's done somethin' with Marcus. An' now she's in there alone, with her two monsters, with Jesse." He was struggling to rise, but Charlie pushed him back into the chair.

"O'course she knows Doctor Carpathian." Quantrill muttered. "I told you that already, you silly corn-cracker. And I couldn't help but notice that his arms are all messed up too." The old officer sneered at Robert. "Who you think can fix those, if you don't want to travel all the way back to the Contested Territories?"

"Will Marcus be alright?" Lucinda felt a growing urge to rise and burst into the bedroom, to defend Jesse from God knew what. She forced herself into an unnatural stillness instead.

Warley nodded, one hand flipping up nonchalantly. "I have to assume so." He turned in his own seat, saving his hat from tipping onto the floor at the last minute. "He's a big strong galoot. I'm sure he's going to be fine."

Lucinda turned back to the room and looked first at Quantrill, then at Warley. She watched Charlie clean up his brother's face, Robert trying to push him weakly away, then turned back to the man in the white suit. "So, you're the man we've come to see. You dress pretty enough, at least." There was just a touch of acid in her voice, and she shot him a smile that artfully combined poison and allure in equal measure.

Her tone did not register with him at all, and from the smile he returned to her, he was either overcome with the allure or ignoring the poison. She suspected the latter. "I believe I am, Miss."

Lucinda nodded. "And you can help Jesse with this big plan of his?"

"Well, now, I'm not sure I can commit myself to anything just yet." He smiled broadly and continued. "But, I must admit I'm intrigued."

"So," the agent forced herself to sit back and give every evidence of relaxing. "What now?"

Quantrill leaned forward, his elbows on his knees. "We still need to get word to Frank and them. We can't move on without them knowin' where we're goin'."

Warley was arranging his hat on his knee, holding it in delicate fingers by the brim. He smiled. "My people can go fetch your boys, William. There isn't anywhere in the great bayou I can't reach."

"They ain't his boys, you flannel-mouth. They're Jesse James'." Robert spat. He was leaning around his brother to glare at Quantrill and Warley.

Quantrill grimaced and waved away the distinction. "They can't be left behind, is what I'm sayin'."

"And they won't be, is what I'm sayin'." Warley's voice was warm. "As soon as we head back to Belle Je, I'll send some of my best men out to fetch them."

"Bell what?" Robert snarled, Charlie trying to get him to settle back down.

"I have a small plantation buried in the bayou off to the east. Belle Je is my seat of power, if you will." He gestured at the closed door through which Jesse had disappeared. "If Mister James is willing to return with us to Belle Je, we can discuss his grand schemes and how they may be brought into line with my own."

Robert pushed his attentive brother aside and leaned forward. "We ain't interested in your schemes, chiseler. Jesse don't need—"

"If Jesse didn't need help, Robert, we'd never have come here in the first place." Lucinda tried to sound reasonable, but before she had finished speaking, the wounded outlaw was glaring at her as well.

Robert looked at Lucinda in a way he never had before. She thought back to the square, and the Union officer. How much had he seen? He spoke in a harsh tone. "We ain't goin' nowhere until Jesse—"

"We're goin'." The voice was weak but unmistakable. The door had opened, and Jesse was braced against the doorframe. Marie Laveau glided past him and moved to examine Marcus. Jesse was pale, with countless cuts and bruises marring his face and his bare chest. His left arm was caught up in a heavy sling tied behind his head, but his right arm seemed to be okay.

Lucinda began to surge to her feet but forced herself to stop. She settled back and turned slowly, her face schooled to calm detachment. "Nice to see you up and about." She kept her tone light.

He grinned at her, although the expression was a little strained. "Thanks. Same to you."

"We're what now?" Robert struggled to his feet, his brother offering unwanted support. "We're gonna rush off to this Zu-zu's fancy house just like that?"

Jesse nodded. "We need to get movin', Robert. If we stay here, we're just gonna keep runnin' into trouble, and we won't be movin' forward. We came here to talk to Colonel Warley, we're gonna talk to Colonel Warley."

"Besides," Marie Laveau stood up beside Marcus, her face still calm and superior. "I cannot fully repair Msye James' arm here. I will need the facilities of a full smithy. Which they have, at Belle Je."

The colonel rose to his feet and placed his hat back on his chair. Moving around the furniture, he approached Jesse with his arm extended. "It will surely be a pleasure, Mr. James, to have you and your people as my guests."

Jesse's face darkened slightly. He looked over to where Marcus sat, still and immobile. "We'll see, colonel."

BELLE JE was an hour's ride beyond the last buildings of New Orleans. They had made the journey in two powered wagons, both in Colonel Warley's white and burgundy colors. The final approach was a mile long causeway, the old trees reaching up into the darkness on all sides while cascades of pale green moss tumbled earthward from out of the shadows. The bayou lurked just outside the wagon lamps, the sounds of the creatures there a constant buzzing accentuated with occasional shrieks, hoots, and growls.

Jesse rested his head against the smooth glass of a side window and stared into the darkness. The pain of his injuries and the exhaustion of his running battle were still sharp, but he was already feeling better. Whatever that witch woman had done to him while he was out, it was having an effect. Beyond the wagon windows, ramshackle old buildings were just visible between the trees. Vines and grasses surrounded them, engulfing the rotten old shapes and dragging them back into the swamps. Jesse recognized slave quarters when he saw them, and he shook his head.

He had not spoken with Colonel Warley since Laveau had revived him. The old colonel rode with Quantrill, Mademoiselle Laveau, and her minions, in the lead wagon. Marcus, now sleeping comfortably, was with them. In the rear wagon, Lucy and Jesse sat facing the direction of travel while the Ford brothers slouched opposite them. Robert had been asleep since they had sat down, while Charlie was also staring out the windows at the passing view.

"They used to have slaves, anyway." Lucy kept her voice low to keep from waking Robert. She nodded out her own window. There were long, decaying buildings on that side as well.

"Every plantation used to have slaves, Lucy." He frowned. "These quarters haven't been used in a dog's age."

"Any slaves in his past might make this harder for you to do, Jesse." She stared into the darkness. She was exhausted. They all were. Charlie had caught a little sleep about an hour out of the French Quarter, and Jesse had been in and out of sleep for most of the trip, probably as a result of whatever the woman in the white dress had given him.

Above them, the driver of the wagon tapped twice on the roof and then leaned down to call through the window. "We're gettin' close, folks. You might want to start gatherin' your things."

Charlie turned to the open window and muttered their thanks while Jesse and Lucy sat up straighter, looking around for anything they might have left behind. Robert grunted as he came awake, looking around blearily at the worn decorations of the wagon's interior.

"Oh, hell. It weren't a dream." He groaned and worked his arms back and forth to drive the stiffness away.

Ahead of them, oozing out of the darkness, an enormous, ancient building appeared. Its columned front porch shadowed the first floor, where many windows were glowing brightly, despite the hour. The upper floor was easier to see in the dim moonlight. Windows were lit there, as well. Elaborate woodwork and decorative dormers of the upper windows made the large house seem more like a palace than a home.

There were several figures standing in the shadows of the porch. As the two wagons pulled up around the long looping drive, they came forward. All were men. None of them were wearing uniforms, but they all had the bearing of experienced veterans. Long-barreled blaster pistols rode on their hips, but none of them seemed concerned about security as they moved to greet the lead wagon. Jesse's nerves rose slightly as he realized all the men gathered around Warley's wagon were white.

Jesse reached over and opened the door to their vehicle with his right arm. His muscles rebelled at the movement, twinging in pain. As Lucy, Charlie, and Robert got out behind him, they all moved toward Warley, Quantrill, and the strange woman in white. The colonel turned at their approach and smiled wanly.

"Your friend is still sleeping, and I'd recommend we leave him that way. Madamoiselle Laveau's . . . guards, can bring him into the house and see that he's placed in one of the rooms upstairs."

Jesse frowned but nodded. "Alright. How about the rest of us?"

Warley made a show of looking his guests over. "Well, you all look like you've had a rough night, and that's the truth. If you'd rather, we can leave off talking over business until you've all had the night to rest?"

Jesse felt his chest tighten and his shoulders sag at the thought of making his case without rest or time to prepare. Then his old grin returned. "Well, I'll tell you what, colonel. You throw down a half-decent spread, and I say we bull right on through!"

Warley's soldiers moved off into the house while Marie Laveau's minions carried a still-sleeping Marcus up the wide stairs with worryingly little effort. Jesse, Lucy, and the Fords followed Warley and his other guests into a tall-ceilinged dining room. A long, polished table dominated the chamber, with ornately-carved chairs flanking the table, each sporting a lush cushion of deep burgundy. High overhead, a glittering crystal chandelier lit the room with sparkling, ruby-tinged light.

Jesse noticed that Quantrill stayed with Warley and the witch-woman. He tried not to let it bother him.

A series of platters had been placed upon the table's snowy central runner. Jesse saw sliced meats, heaps of steaming vegetables, and a tureen of thick gravy. Glasses of sweet tea sat beside each plate. His mouth began to water and he moved for the table, not waiting for an invitation. He threw himself into a chair about halfway down and began to shovel food onto a fine china plate. Before the rest were even sitting, he was pushing food into his mouth with his hands, utensils ignored on the table.

"Well, at least I can assume the food is satisfactory?" Warley smiled warmly as he pulled a chair out for Marie Laveau and then sat down beside her, across from Jesse. The outlaw grinned around a mouthful of meat.

The rest of the party gathered food with a little more patience and grace, and soon they were all eating to the silent accompaniment of metal tapping on china and the clink of glass. Warley and Quantrill ate sparingly, clearly only partaking to be social. Lucy placed a single helping of vegetables on her own plate, but was moving it around with her fork rather than eating. Marie Laveau's was the only empty plate at the table, and she drank from a small silver flask she had produced from somewhere within her dress. The tall glass remained untouched.

As Jesse and his companions finished their food, Warley smiled across at them and then raised his glass. "Shall we make a toast before we begin? Bewilderment to the foe!" Everyone raised their glasses to the sentiment except for Mademoiselle Laveau, who tilted her head with an uncaring curl to her full lips.

"Amen to that, colonel. Although this is the first time I've ever made a toast with anything this soft." Jesse downed the rest of his tea. Without asking, he reached across the table and took the Voodoo Queen's.

"Indeed." Warley's smile slipped just slightly at the breach of etiquette, but he continued. "Now, Mr. James. Why don't you tell me about this grand design I have been hearing so much about?" The smile took on a slight edge. "It sounds quite ambitious, for a man so far from home."

Jesse scowled, wiped his mouth with one ragged sleeve, and pushed his plate away.
"Right." He put his metal hand on the table, arm outstretched, and looked back up at Warley. "How much you know about Lee and his plans for the Rebellion?"

Warley's face was impassive, his hands folded on the table before him, and he gave a miniscule shrug. "I know that he is the rightfully elected leader of the Confederacy. Is there more to know?"

Jesse paused, his eyebrows raising at this apparent show of support for the Confederate president. "Well . . . How much you know about how he plans on fightin' the Union?"

Warley shook his head. "Do we need to be fightin' the Union? It appears to me, they have too much on their plate now to worry about us. A perfect time to shore up our position, lay low, and watch what happens next."

Jesse slapped the table with his mechanical hand. "Exactly! That's EXACTLY what Lee said! But that's ignorin' the fact that it's also the PERFECT time to take the fight back to them!"

"So, you would have us, in our shattered and diminished state, leap once more into the fires of open war?"

Warley's face was still blank, his voice calm. The words felt like stinging nettles to Jesse, and he wanted to shout at the man, to wake him up.

"Lee is still fightin' the old war. The world's changed! We're not fightin' for slavery, or state's rights, or any of that now. We're fightin' to defend ourselves from madmen, drunk on power, who want to crush us into the mud for no better reason now than they can!"

Quantrill smiled at Warley. "I told you the boy had fire. Could see that years ago durin' the war."

Warley did not return the smile. "The fact remains, however, that the south is a defeated nation. Has it ever occurred to you that President Lee might not still be fightin' the last war, but rather the only war he CAN fight, given our current situation?"

"That's hogwash, colonel, and you know it!" Jesse felt his anger rising, but he could not stop it. "Out in the territories, we've fought them almost to a standstill with stolen weapons an' clear heads. An' that's without numbers! If we had the numbers over them? They wouldn't be callin' those territories contested, now, they'd be callin' 'em Jesse James Country!"

That got a small smile out of the colonel. "Well, that might be true up in the deserts, but the Old States—"

"No!" Jesse slapped the table again, and this time his heavy hand left a cracked dent in the wood. Men ran in through several doors, but Warley held up a hand to stop them. The guards backed warily away, watching from a distance.

"Colonel, it has NOTHIN' to do with the terrain, or how far from their supplies they are out in the territories! The Union is surrounded by enemies! They're fightin' the Warrior Nation to the north, they've got Carpathian causin' problems off west, and they've got bands like mine wreakin' havoc all through the old western territories. To say nothin' of the Golden Army! The time is perfect, while they're distracted and off-balance, for the Confederate Rebellion to rise up an' push 'em back up north where they belong!"

"And yet," Warley's smile was gone again. "We keep comin' back to the same problem: with what do we fight? And with whom? We lost the cream of our fighting soldiery for a generation when that Devil's Blood swept through and changed the world forever. Our armies are diminished, defeated in spirit, and those that have not already joined Lee are unwilling to rise again."

"There are those who'd fight, if we gave them the chance." Jesse's face was hard, his eyes penetrating as he stared at Warley.

"Is there an army we may have overlooked, Mr. James?" The colonel's eyebrow rose in doubt.

Jesse's hand pressed against the table. "There is an entire nation, living within the borders of the Confederacy, that would fight beside us if we let them."

Warley's face was impassive, his eyes flat. And then a bit of warmth seeped in, and a slight tick erupted at the corner of his mouth. "You are, of course, referring to our former slaves?"

Jesse nodded, ignoring the possessive and waving the other word away with his hand. "That damned Emancipation Proclamation ended that, and you know it. The black folks have been kept down for decades since, on both sides of the border, but there ain't no one been keepin' slaves in all that time."

"And you think the word is what will make the difference?" Warley's eyebrow rose again, and Marie Laveau's face curled into an evil smile of her own. "You think, because they have not been called slaves, that they will rise up and join hands with us now, despite the way they have been treated?"

"No!" Jesse lowered his head, trying to organize his thoughts. "I mean—"

"Mr. James, the majority of black folks, through no fault of their own, lack any sort of training in the art of war." It was Warley, now, whose voice was intense. "Through no fault of their own, most lack education of any sophistication. They have been kept down, slavery or no, for longer than either of us would care to contemplate. And the fear with which many whites regard their black-skinned neighbors is inextricably entwined in that imbalance. Do you honestly believe that most of the white folks you know would agree to arm the colored folks? And furthermore, could you fault a man who had spent his entire life treated as an animal, for looking greedily at any chance he might have to redress that wrong, or generations of worse wrongs that had gone before?"

Jesse stared at Warley for so long the rest of the people in the room started to look toward each other, wondering what might be coming next. The colonel's speech summed up the fears that had been running around in his own head since the idea had first formed. He tried to remember the counter-arguments that Lucy, Frank, and the others had made to him in his moments of doubt.

With a shake of his head, Jesse changed his tack. "Colonel, do you think we're fightin' the same Union that held Fort Sumter all those years ago?"

The man in the white suit blinked at the change of course, his brow furrowed. "What do you mean?"

Jesse leaned forward, his good hand spread on the table. "The first three years of the war, if you can remember back that far, were brutal, weren't they?" He waited a moment for Warley to nod slowly, then continued. "Thousands upon thousands of men died on both sides, and there were some vicious acts of savagery by both north and south. Right?"

Warley sat back, his head shaking in denial. "Mr. James, I don't see how this—"

"There were, and you know it. I was even there for some of 'em." He sat up taller. "Now, do you remember Petersburg?"

The colonel nodded. "I sat out most of the war after New Orleans was taken, but I remember Petersburg."

"Both sides had set up for a major battle for the city. But the Union looked like it had lost its taste for savagery in favor of a long, drawn out siege. I remember. I was on the run down south with the colonel here." He gestured to Quantrill, who nodded, his face intense as he listened to Jesse put all of this together for the first time.

"And then somethin' happened to General Grant. He was up in Washington, and then we din't hear nothin' else for months." The outlaw chief's face looked gaunt by the light of the RJ lamps. "When he turned up at Petersburg, his head was wrapped in bandages, and he ordered the complete destruction of the city."

"He was tired of the war like everyone else." There was doubt in Warley's eyes now. "Except he had the power to end it, where no one else did."

"No." Jesse shook his head, his eyes never leaving the colonel's. "Somethin' happened to him. Everyone knows his entire family was killed, and he nearly died as well. And when he came back from that, he was a bloodthirsty madman, and he's been drivin' the Union war machine ever since."

Warley watched Jesse's face. "You're saying—"

"That the Union's army's bein' driven forward by a savage, murderous lunatic with no regard for human life? Yeah. The attack on Petersburg cost the Union more men than any other battle. They ran right at the city's fixed defenses, floodin' the streets with bodies until we just ran out o' bullets. And then, when Lee was forced to retreat, Grant pursued him, shootin' his men down wherever they were caught, until that bastard Lincoln, of all people, had to call him back."

"But that was war . . ." Warley did not sound convinced by his own argument.

"That was butchery, is what it was, colonel." Jesse leaned forward again. "And then he went on to smash Richmond, slaughtering men, women, and children to get to Jefferson Davis and any other Confederate politician he could find. And then Atlanta . . . The man was like a scourge from God, grinding every last Confederate stronghold into the bloody mud." He sat back, his dark eyes calm. "Now, I ask you, colonel . . . How many black folks died in those cities? How many have died in the years since, as Grant pursued his insane feuds?"

Warley's head slowly pivoted back and forth, his face pale. "I don't . . ."

"Hundreds of thousands, sir. Hundreds of thousands. And they know it. They ain't dumb. You give the black folks in this country an equal stake in their future, and they'll fight for it. Horrible things been done on this soil, an' that ain't gonna change. But you give a man, any man, a chance to fight for the future of his family? He's gonna take that chance, an' he ain't gonna be too worried 'bout the past. Havin' a wolf at yer door tends to make you forget what mudsills your neighbors are, sir."

He sat back, arm resting still on the table before him, and scanned the faces opposite. Warley looked thoughtful;

Quantrill's face was troubled. Marie Laveau's beautiful features were transformed by a righteous smile that was cruelly offset by the vengeful gleam in her eyes.

"Damn." Warley muttered to himself.

Jesse nodded. "Don't try to make sense of the actions of a drunk or a madman, colonel. They'll surprise you every time. And Grant's madder than a mountain lion on a hot griddle, and he's drunk on the power Johnson won't take away."

Warley's eyes refocused on Jesse and he nodded slowly. "Well, sir. It seems we had something to learn from you after all."

Lucy and the Fords shifted uncomfortably on his side of the table as Jesse sat back against the curved chair. "Sorry?"

Warley's expression softened. "Well, we hadn't seen the whole situation as nearly so dire as you've painted it, son, but we in New Orleans, at least, had reached the same general conclusion long ago."

Quantrill looked sideways at the colonel, eyebrows drawn down. Warley turned back to Jesse.

"Many folks in New Orleans have always had a . . . different view of race than elsewhere in the south. Some say it's because of our closer ties to Europe, others that things are just softer here. But either way, when we realized we didn't have the numbers to defend ourselves, when the Union started to funnel troops down here and to the navy yards, we knew we needed to do something." He looked at Marie Laveau out of the corner of his eye. "Making an alliance with our dark-skinned neighbors was the only choice we found that made any sense."

The witch nodded, her smile radiant. "My people have answered the call, *Msye* James. An' with the colonel's help, we've got quite a little army forming, back behind *Belle Je*."

Warley spread his hands as if in apology. "We don't have much, but we're trainin' anyone who comes to us with whatever we have, regardless of the color of their skin. We've found exactly what you've said, Mr. James. When their homes are bein' threatened, folks around here have answered the call, with no regard to skin color. We've had a few incidents among the men and women who've come, of course, but isolated, and far fewer than I would have expected."

Jesse looked at him with eyes that began to glow with anger. "You mean to tell me you agreed with me this whole time, an' made me jump through yer damned hoops . . ." Jesse knew that this was one of those times Frank or Cole would have tried to rein him in, but even that knowledge was not enough to impose any sort of self-control.

Warley nodded, but his head was cocked to one side, robbing the gesture of wholehearted agreement. "I did. And it worked . . . here. Will it work elsewhere in the Confederacy? I don't know. But I wanted to hear your case, to see if YOU believed, and if what you had to say might seem like it could sway folks more set in their ways than we are here."

Jesse tilted his head up, looking down his nose at the colonel. "And?"

Warley shook his head, his eyes tight. "You scared the hades right out of me, Mr. James. We here in New Orleans have always believed that true riches come from the spirit. And the strongest power obviously comes from the united spirit of a free and dedicated people. But can even that power answer for a madman commanding the most powerful weapons in the world?"

Jesse looked down at his decimated plate. He had not eaten this well in months and suddenly realized he had not tasted a bite. The fatigue of the battle and the drain from his injuries was starting to tell as well. He was not going to be able to stay awake much longer, end of the world or no.

"Well, there ain't anythin' else we can do, colonel." He looked up again, his exhausted face strong with conviction. "But we gotta do what we can. I believe that down to my very core."

Everyone was watching Jesse; the old Confederate officers across the table, the witch-woman, the men around the edges of the room. Lucy was watching him with eyes that looked suspiciously glassy, while the Fords were staring at him like he was the savior come again. He looked at each of them. The weight of their gazes drove him even further toward exhausted collapse.

At last, Warley nodded. "I do, too, Mr. James." He reached across the table, his open hand held firmly before the outlaw. After only a moment's hesitation, Jesse reached out and gripped the hand. "And despite the darkness of your message, you bring hope with you as well. You're not alone in believing that President Lee has grown too timid. In fact, there is a network of us throughout the south. Lee's advisors have been replaced by a new group of men. None of the old guard have even heard of them before. They're a fiery-eyed lot, making grand, blistering speeches, but always seeming to council for prudence and accommodation in the end. We have been agonizing over what to do for a long time now." He shrugged as he sat back. "We have contemplated everything from a vote of no confidence to assassination, but could agree on nothing."

Jesse shook his head. "You can't run a fight by committee, sir. When the bullets fly, the strongest lead, and the weak follow or fall away. I learned that from Colonel Quantrill."

Quantrill smiled vaguely, still lost in thought.

"I happen to agree with you, Mr. James. But until now, I feared there might not be enough of the strong, as you say, to keep the weak moving forward." His smile turned predatory. "I'm very much convinced now, that there may well be."

Jesse gave a single, sharp nod back. "Now, we've got the makings of an army, you and I. And I've got more folks comin' in from the territories, and even a troop of California Rangers, if they haven't run off yet. But what do we do with them all?"

Warley sat back, threw one arm across the back of his chair, and speared Jesse with his most intense look. "We have identified a possible target, but we didn't think we'd have enough power to give us a realistic chance, until now."

Jesse's look managed to mix suspicion and excitement in equal measure. "What?"

Warley waved a hand. "We've gotten reports that the Union is building a massive fortress along the stabilizing border between the north and the south. Somethin' huge, far larger than a border fort or even a forward base. Somethin' very nearly a castle in proportions and design."

Jesse shook his head. "What the hell'd they need a castle for? It's not Lee's been a threat to them in years."

Warley agreed. "No. And yet, there they are. Now, if we were able to attack this fortress, destroy it utterly and completely . . . Why, that might just be the perfect catalyst for getting all those fence-sitters throughout the Confederacy to fall down on our side."

"Prove we can take down something that big, and we prove that the Union can be beaten." Jesse nodded. "Makes sense. That was sort of my thinking behind burning down Camp Lincoln, but I ain't heard a peep. How many men you got hidden in the swamps back there? Even if Will Shaft and his boys bring all of Robbers Roost back, and Captain Ingram's boys stick close, I only got a few hundred, and a handful of Rolling Thunder wagons."

Warley shook his head ruefully. "Not enough, I'm afraid. But, with you going on ahead, giving your speech about madmen, and wolves at the door . . . I think you might be able to raise us an army large enough, by the time we get there. General Mosby may even—"

Jesse shook his head. "Mosby's not going to take a piss without Lee tellin' him he's gotta go."

Jesse's eyes took on a far-off look as his head moved back to rest against the chair back. He was a long way from the territories, leading a posse and looking forward to the next bank or train. There was a large part of him that yearned for the simplicity of those days, without all these people looking to him for answers.

Everyone sat completely still, waiting for what he would say next. He suddenly snapped his head back down and looked wide-eyed at Warley.

"I think you might be right . . . but right now, I think I need to sleep for about two days straight."

He got up and made his unsteady way back out into the entry hall. One of the soldiers there directed him up the stairs and to an empty bed chamber. A moment later he was gone.

The dining room was silent for quite some time after he left. Each person stared at the door, lost in their own thoughts.

Chapter 12

The camp, hidden beyond the fields and outbuildings of *Belle Je*, was extensive. It stretched away among the moss-hung trees. Gaps in the tents and lean-tos marked areas of black water where the bayou reached its oily fingers onto the property. Although warm and very humid, it was not nearly as scorching as the city had been. Colonel Warley led Jesse, his arms repaired after a day of extensive work by Madamoiselle Laveau, toward a large tent in the center of the camp. The outlaw chief was still sore from his escapades in the city. Glorious bruises and shallow cuts had made getting dressed that morning interesting.

The colonel waved a hand around them. "What we've done here would never have been possible without Captain Carney." The old officer nodded to several colored soldiers as they passed. "He fought under the Union in the War, but I don't want you to hold that against him, Mr. James. He'll be essential if this is to work."

Warley pushed the flap back on the dun-colored tent and peered into the shadows. "Captain Carney? A word, if you'd please?"

The tent was neat and tidy. A small table and chairs dominated the center. An old uniform coat, blue faded nearly to gray, was draped over one chair, accompanied by a torn and faded Union flag gathered up like a sash. Three men and a woman, all black, stood around the table, speaking in quiet tones. When the colonel spoke, they snapped to attention and turned, smiles on their dark faces. The oldest man, in white shirtsleeves and faded pants that matched the coat, grinned through a thick goatee and mustache.

"Colonel, sir. Always time for our gracious host." The man's voice carried the flat tones of the north, and Jesse had to tamp down his initial reaction. The man nodded to the other fighters, who left, saluting Warley with casual flips as they passed. "What can I do for you, sir?"

The colonel stepped into the tent with a friendly smile, gesturing Jesse to follow. "Someone I'd like you to meet, Bill."

Bill Carney sized Jesse up with a quick glance, his eyes lingering on the sleek mechanical arms. After a moment's hesitation, he reached out with an open hand. Jesse forced himself to take it without pause.

"Good to meet you, Cap'n." Jesse met the man's eyes levely. There was a terrible scar across his left temple. The puckered flesh disappeared into a curly widow's peak, a streak of white hair continuing the trajectory of the old wound. The man's grip was firm against the feedback pads of Jesse's hand.

"Good to meet you as well, Mister . . . James?" Carney's voice was deep, the question polite.

"Never try to slip one past Bill, Mr. James!" Warley slapped the black officer on the back. "So, captain, I was really hopin' you could fill Mr. James in on the local situation." His face took on a slightly sheepish cast. "I was also hopin' you might tell him a bit about your own story, at least as to how it relates. I think you two, workin' together, are goin' to be quite formidable."

Carney looked at Jesse for a moment and then stepped aside, gesturing toward the empty chairs. Jesse eased his aching body down, but Warley stepped back toward the entrance. "I've heard all this before." He smiled, holding up a placating hand. "You boys have fun." And he was gone.

The black northerner sat lightly down in a chair opposite and folded scarred hands on the table. "So. Jesse James."

Jesse nodded. "Yup."

The other man smiled a sad smile. "A stranger, far from home." He turned in his seat to reach for a metal canteen. He offered a drink to his guest before swigging down a quick slug of his own. "Very far from home."

Jesse nodded again. "Colonel Warley said as how you'd fought for the Union in the war."

Carney's smile faded. "I did, Mr. James. Is that going to be a problem between us?"

Jesse looked into the other man's eyes. They were dark, of course, but they burned with sincerity rare in a man of any color. And here, in the middle of this camp, the man could be no raging blue-belly. He shook his head. "I reckon it won't be."

Carney's smile returned. "Excellent." He leaned back, draping one arm across his chair's back, across the Union flag. "So that might as well be where we start."

The man splayed one dark hand over the table top. "I was one of the first black men to enlist in the Colored Regiments. Back then, the war seemed to make a lot more sense. I was born a slave, you see, in Virginia. My daddy escaped, worked up a stake up north, and bought us our freedom. Seemed like fighting was the only way I could really repay a debt like that, when the call came."

Jesse squirmed a little in his chair. The small wooden seat chafed at his injuries, just as this quiet man's story scraped at his conscience. Jesse's family had owned slaves of their own at one time. The pang of guilt that past reality caused now cast his memories of the war itself into an uncomfortable light.

"I fought through more than my share of battles, some big ones." Carney's eyes were distant as he continued his story. "Got winged a few times." One hand drifted over his chest. "I even won me some shiny medals. And then every man I called a friend, every officer I admired, was killed in a single day. I picked up the colors when the bearer fell." He absently patted the flag draped across the back of his chair. "Took more wounds returning the flag to our lines, and then I collapsed."

Carney's eyes were unfocused, lost in another time. "It took years for me to fully recover. And in that time, the world changed."

"RJ-1027." Jesse muttered under his breath.

The colored officer looked up and nodded. "RJ-1027. And the Confederacy crushed in the last bloody push of the war." He smiled sadly. "It seemed like everything I'd ever wanted was coming true. But things didn't change much. Grant turned the new weapons westward, against Carpathian and his walking dead, and ran straight into the Warrior Nation coming south. There was hardly a month of peace before the entire country was plunged back into war, even bloodier than before."

He shrugged. "The plight of my brothers and sisters in the remnants of the Confederacy was little better than before the Proclamation. But this time, the Union, with bigger fish to fry, had turned its back."

Carney's eyes were haunted. "I still had friends and relatives south of the line. I heard terrible stories. The south was in total chaos and disarray, and it took its toll on everyone. But my folks were the hardest hit. It didn't help that Grant wouldn't accept surrender under any circumstances. He wanted the old Confederacy to suffer, and so it let them rot on the vine. I knew I couldn't sit back and let it stand. I took my gear and some extra weapons from a quartermaster friend from the 54th, and I headed south."

Jesse leaned forward. "You were gonna keep the war goin' all on your lonesome?"

Carney shook his head. "No, I weren't gonna be fightin' no war. I came down to try to help my people, is all. I wandered around a bit, put down some dogs, collected a few more scars along the way." He sat back and gestured to the camp around them. "I ended up coming down toward New Orleans. Heard things were different here, and I was tired. I was very tired."

Jesse nodded. "And were they? Different, I mean?"

Carney's smile turned cold. "Not as different as I would have liked. The place was a mess. Different coalitions claimed to rule the city as the state of Louisiana dissolved around us into the lawless western territories and the chaotic Rebellion. One group was a hard-line pack of old-timers from the war. Tried to take control and push the colored folks back into the bayous. The locals wouldn't stand for it, but didn't have much in the way of weaponry themselves."

Carney rose slowly, wincing at a pain in his side, and moved to a low bench in the corner of the tent. He pulled a cloth back to reveal a massive Gatling blaster with a harness and support straps. He turned back to the outlaw chief with a savage grin. "My friend Joseph, the quartermaster? This was his last gift to me, after the war."

Jesse whistled and moved toward the weapon. It was a beautiful example of its type. Six hexagonal barrels were fit into the dull black body of the gun, crimson telltales winking brightly. "A man could do some serious damage with a gun like that." Jesse tapped the barrel with one metal finger.

"Yessir." The black officer nodded and moved back to his seat. "And I did. Worked with Colonel Warley and a few other locals, black and white, and we set those old bastards an' their carpetbagger friends a-runnin'. New Orleans' been one of the most integrated places on the continent ever since."

Jesse sat back, but he could not keep his eyes off the massive weapon. "So, you an' yer boys'll be fightin' fer the Rebellion now?" One eyebrow quirked upward. "How's that sit with you?"

Carney leaned forward, his dark eyes glittering in the dim light. "I've talked with Colonel Warley. I've heard your plan. My boys and girls won't be fightin' fer a Rebellion that don't recognize us as humans. But you wrench them in the right direction?" The smile was back, warmer than ever. "Then we'll fight next to anyone that'll have us. You just gotta go out there an' make 'em see that what we've done here in New Orleans, it's workin'. And it'll work for the rest of the country too."

Jesse met his gaze. "But what about the Union? Your loyalties must still be strongly inclined up north—"

Carney shook his head. "The Union I fought for, that sheltered my family and provided us with a home?" Once again he patted the flag behind him. "That don't exist no more. And it won't come back until Grant and his bloody-minded cronies fall."

Jesse sat back and nodded. "Well, we might just have more to talk about on the way north, captain, if this all works out. And I think you might just like to meet a friend of mine . . . name of Will Shaft."

*****

Jesse looked around the little hut, trying manfully to keep the disgust and disdain from his face. He could feel Frank standing behind him, his custom long rifle cradled in his arm, and knew that his brother was giving away nothing. Across the ratty little table, paint peeling and wood soft with rot, were three men that he needed to bring over to his cause before he could move out of the bayou and into the higher coastal reaches to the east.

Buford Nash, commander of the St. Tammany Parish Confederate Militia, sat in the center across the table. Bordering the north east shoreline of Lake Pontchartrain, St. Tammany was the gateway to the rest of the south. On the far side, in the true Confederacy, Jesse's real mission would begin.

Nash was a big man. His clothing was rough but clean. The lines on his face were deep, indicating a life far more familiar with frowns than laughter. A close-cropped gray mustache and small chin beard offset the smooth expanse of his scalp above. His watery-blue eyes stared at Jesse without emotion, but the men to either side had more than enough of that to spare.

Deacon Nash, the head man's son, was almost as big as his father. Flaming red hair matched the anger blazing in the young man's eyes as he flicked his attention from Jesse to Frank, and then, always, to Will Shaft standing silently beside Frank. Deacon Nash wore his facial hair wild. His chin had probably not made the acquaintance of a razor in years. His hand toyed with an old RJ power cell that looked like it might be older than he was.

On the other side of the commander sat Jeremiah Longway, by far the oldest person in the shack. The old man's skin was as parched and wrinkled as poorly-cured leather, but it still held the color of mixed parentage. That was something Jesse had become far more accustomed to as he moved through the area around New Orleans. There were more folks of mixed race down here than he had ever seen, and despite his current crusade, he found he still had a way to go to adapt himself.

Jeremiah Longway's beard put young Deacon's to shame. There was almost no way to tell what the color of the old man's vest was beneath the tangled white hair. Unlike Buford Nash, however, his head, too, was covered in an unruly white halo. He stared unblinkingly at Jesse with brown eyes flecked with gold that reflected the RJ lamps with a russet sparkle.

Jesse had finished his speachifying. He had quickly learned to pause here, watching the locals for any sign of which way he should jump next. This was the eighth local militia group he had approached since leaving Warley's estate nearly two weeks ago. His small army, following Warley's scouts through the bayous and the small towns, had managed to join him only a few days after his fight in the cemetery. Shaft and a fairly large contingent from the Territories had ridden into town a few days later, collected by some of Warley's boys, and brought back to *Belle Je*.

Frank had had no sympathy for Jesse's injuries, nothing but a disappointed look and a shaken head. Bob and Jim Younger had said nothing. Cole, some of his old humor perhaps returning, had made a comment about any man daft enough to go walking around a cemetery when he was hanging his hat in a brothel.

It had taken them a few more days to iron out exactly what the plan was going to be. Warley's sources said this mysterious fort Grant was establishing in old Tennessee would be up and running soon, but there was some wiggle room before the final troop deployments would see the place fully manned. Maps had been drawn, teams chosen, and Jesse, as the point man of the whole endeavor, had been heading east ever since. The further he got from New Orleans, the harder time he was having selling the idea of black folks and white folks standing together against the Union. Something told him Warley had planned it this way, easing him into the whole process.

Of course, now, sitting across from the Nashes and their old advisor, he was wishing he were back in Orleans Parish. He could not read these three for the life of him.

Jesse was about to ask if there was anything he could clarify for them, when old Jeremiah coughed, and then spoke. "I'm still not sure why 'tis ya'll want us heah to join yez, *Msye* James. What you t'ink Tammany Parish got to offer you an' you boys, when you takin' on bad *Msye* Grant? An why you t'ink we be wantin' to send our youngin's wit' you dere?"

The elder Nash gave no sign of hearing the comment, but Deacon nodded vigorously. "Yeah, now. Why's we want ta go runnin' after ya'll an' dyin' so far from our homes? We gots Union sojer-boys right heah we can be killin'!"

Jesse took a breath and turned slightly in his seat to look back at Frank. His brother gave the shortest of shrugs beneath his immobile face. Jesse felt his shoulders slumping and turned back to the locals with a sigh.

"Well," Jesse spread both of his hands out on the table in front of him. He had been hesitant to let Marie Laveau near him, knowing the crude work she had done on Quantrill, but the arms were working better than they had in months. Despite her haughty, aloof behavior, she had proven herself quite capable. He had not yet broached the subject of a possible alliance against Carpathian, but he was thinking that she might be just the person he needed by his side when the time came for a return engagement.

Jesse shook his head. He knew his mind was wandering in the face of this crew's blank response. Nonetheless, if he could not count on the militia of St. Tammany Parish, he was not going to get too far.

With another sigh, he replied. "You spend yer blood fightin' the Union troops they're sendin' around down this way, you're wastin' yer time *an'* yer blood." He jerked a metal thumb over his shoulder at his brother. "We've seen 'em in action up close. They ain't gonna be satisfied, crushin' Lee's little honor guard, when they finally get around to turnin' our way again. An' on some level, you folks know it. We gotta face them down, on their own land, an' show the rest of the south that we ain't beat yet. An' we can't do that, lessen' we dig deep and come together."

The three strangers across the table stared at him again in silence. The older and the younger looked angry. Buford did not move.

Jesse felt his own anger building in his gut. "They're gonna be comin' down here with enough force, they ain't gonna be happy 'till they've killed every man, woman, an' child who ever had a bad thought about 'em. They're gonna crush us, chew us up, an' spit us out lookin' just like 'em."

"An' you gonna stop all dat by rilin' up all the folks here 'bouts and drivin' 'em north?" Jeremiah's unsettling eyes bore into Jesse's. The old man turned to Buford, resting an old elbow on the table. "I say we see 'em on their way, Bue." He stabbed a large-jointed thumb at the thin, moss-covered door. "Let 'em go, an' happy be their goin'."

Buford Nash rested his hands on the table, fingers intertwined, and leaned back. The old chair creaked ominously beneath him. His shining head cocked to one side and his eyes squinted slightly. "You 'tink they's goin' ta be comin' down heah, by an' by?"

Jesse straightened. Buford had not spoken since they had all sat down together. He was getting ready to make his choice. It was up to the outlaw chief to convince him of the correct path. "I know they will. They won't stop until the damned Union flag is flyin' over every town and village from Atlanta to the Colorado and beyond."

Jesse took a deep breath and once again indicated Frank, standing behind him. "They took my brother. They threw him in a camp with thousands of others. The things they were doin' in that camp, sir?" He shuddered. "It don't bear thinkin' on. An' they're gonna be doin' that to everyone that don't bow down to 'em 'till they own it all." He pointed to Deacon, whose face had not relaxed as Jesse spoke. "Sure as sure, they're gonna do it to you an' yours, gatherin' here in the bayou, flyin' the old flags and singin' the old songs. Ain't no way your folks come out of this breathin', Buford."

Jeremiah sneered at this, obviously not convinced. "Ain't no way we can stand against 'em now, boy. Where you gettin' the rifles? Where you gettin' the hands to hold the rifles?"

Jesse stared at the old man, breathing deeply and focusing every ounce of effort on not jumping across the table and throttling him. "I tole' ya. Black folks and white folks, standin' together—"

"Ain't gonna happen." The old man sat back as if he had won the argument, his hands raised as if revealing the final piece of a magic trick. "Here in the bayou, things're different. But out there?" He waved one hand vaguely toward the east. "Out there, it's bad. Black folks is angrier. White folks is more set in their ways, more frightened. Ain't gonna happen. And without it happenin', this scheme o' your'n ain't never happenin' neither."

"It don't have to be that way." Will's voice was deep, almost like distant thunder or the rumble of artillery. "There's white folks and black folks get along fine, here, out west, an' other places. An' when it's a question o' standin' with a man you don't like, or dyin' alone . . . ain't most folks'd be takin' the second choice."

Deacon slammed his hand on the table. "But that ain't all, is it?" His face was twisted with anger and fear. "The Union freed 'em all, din't they! Black folks, they don't hate the Union, most of 'em. They'd ruther move up that way, many of 'em, if they had the chance!"

"That ain't so." Will Shaft spoke with a soft tone, but his dark eyes were intense as he stared at the young man. "Most folks, no matter their color, want to stay in their homes an' live their lives. And maybe the Union once freed my people, yeah. But that was a long time ago. Since then? Since Grant took over? They got nothin' but contempt for anyone livin' in the south, no matter the color of their skin. My folks? We went west after the Proclamation, tryin' to make a new life on the frontier. The same old hates and jibes followed us clear across the country, despite we was in Union Territory. Ain't no one up there cares any more for colored folks than the folks down this way."

"And they ain't gonna care none what color anyone is when they come rollin' down here, neither." Jesse nodded. "And that's the reality we gotta face, and that's why folks've gotta come together now. We come together, or we all die."

"But what is it you want, Jesse James?" The old man leaned forward now, his face intense. "Why're you, a famous villain o' the Wild West, down heah leadin' this chahge?" A fire seemed to light in his eyes as he finished, almost in a whisper. "What're YOU aftah, *Msye* James?"

Jesse shook his head. "I never made no secret of the way I feel fer the Union. They ain't never been nothin' but ugly to me an' mine. An' fer years now, they been gettin' worse. We gotta take 'em on here, when and where we choose, if we wanna stop 'em anywhere." He sat back with a slight shrug. "An' I can't do it alone. Folks who love their freedom, they gotta rise up with me, 'r it's all gonna burn away."

The old man seemed dissatisfied by the answer. "I don't believe you, *Msye* James. What you REALLY after?"

"Buford," Jesse's voice was tight with barely-controlled tension. "Your folks in or not? I don't wanna have to go the long way 'round east, an' we don't wanna go in without you. But we'll do both if we have to."

Jeremiah sat up sharply, his mouth open to protest, but Buford Nash stopped him with a single hand. Deacon looked like he was angry enough to spit, but he remained silent.

"You can move through St. Tammany Parish."

"But Daddy! You can't—" Deacon's voice was high with anger and surprise. He stuttered to a halt as his father slapped his calloused hand onto the table hard enough to buckle the old wood.

"Shut it, Deak!" He glared at his son. "I ain't led Tammany Parish fer as long as I done to get lip from my own son, right?" Deacon glowered back at him, but his eyes were tight with doubt. When he did not immediately respond, his father growled. "I ain't right?"

Deacon looked down into his lap, folding his hands there. "You's right, Daddy."

Buford turned to glare at the old man. "An' I get you, Jeremiah, but you livin' inna past. It gone, and we gotta look for'ard." He turned back to Jesse.

"You can move through St. Tammany Parish." He put up a hand to forestall Jesse's thanks. "But we ain't joinin' you till I see the quality of those that's already with you when you get here. I ain't sending none of my boys 'n girls off to die for some fancy talkin' flannel-mouth from out west, less'n I see there's other believes in you first."

Jesse nodded. Buford Nash was not the first man to make such a statement. Most of these folks remembered the crushing defeats at the end of the last war. Many of them had even been there at the very end, as everything burned behind them and the desperate flight became a thing of nightmare. The Union, little seen since then, was an object of legend more than anything else: a horror story used to terrify small children into obedience.

Jesse looked around the cabin. Hell, most of these folks barely had enough RJ tech to cook their food and keep themselves warm. He had even seen piles of wood stacked behind some of the cabins in the village. Most were not living in the past of twenty years ago; they were living in the past of a hundred years ago, and they did not much seem to care.

Jesse stood and reached out with one metal hand. Buford Nash stood but hesitated before taking the hand in his own firm grasp. "That seems more than fair, sir." Jesse nodded. "I'll have Colonel Warley and the rest of the local officers with me when we come through. I have no doubt they'll be able to give you every assurance."

Nash nodded. "I was surprised he sent you foreigners out without him, truth to tell. I woulda thought he'd of at least sent Captain Carney."

Jesse shrugged as he moved around the rickety old chair, holding onto the frail back with both hands. "He's smoothin' the way for those that're livin' closer to the city, so's they can sneak through without alertin' the Union outfit down near the navy docks."

The big bald man settled back in his chair. "Well, you best be on your way, son. You gotta lot o' work ahead of ya', before yer done."

Jesse nodded, spared Deacon and Jeremiah a sharp jerk of his chin, and turned to leave. Behind him, Frank was already holding the door while Will stared indifferently at the three men at the table. As he passed his brother, Jesse gave him a look. Frank only shrugged, but Jesse knew he would get more once they left the little huddle of huts.

Outside, in the center of the little town, Lucy waited with Robert Ford and their Iron Horses. Each machine sat in its own shallow puddle where it had pushed the soggy turf down into the water. The 'Horses were perfect for travelling through the bayous . . . until they grounded.

Lucy looked at him and he lifted one shoulder noncommittally. He swung his leg up and over the saddle on his machine and said, "No recruits to send back, but we can move through. They may join when they hear from some other locals."

Lucy rolled her eyes. "That's nearly half so far that won't commit without hearing from their neighbors. What do they think is going to happen? They're going to sink or swim together, they might as well get used to that idea."

"Right," Frank stepped up to his own vehicle and slid Sophie back into her boot along the saddle. "'Cept they don't see it that way. 'Till someone makes this real for 'em, it's just a game. Been a game to those that survived since Grant turned westward."

Robert shook his head. "I don't like it, havin' to toady up to these lowlife swamp-grubbers." He spoke softly, his eyes darting among the men and women in their worn clothing, standing around and watching the strangers prepare to depart.

"That old man had an evil in him," Will Shaft said as he slid onto his 'Horse.

Jesse nodded. "I got that. But he din't do much, other than try to get Buford to say 'no.'"

"He was mighty interested in you, though, brother." Frank fired up his 'Horse and the rumbling thunder of the engines rose up to blanket the little village. His brother shouted to finish his thought. "Diggin' after your where's and why-for's!"

Jesse pulled his red-tinged goggles up over his face and shrugged. "Let 'im stew!" He saw that the others had their own goggles on, and he waved a hand for Robert to lead the way. "Take us out, Robert! Get us across the Pearl and we'll make camp in good ole Dixie!"

Robert nodded, grinning, and gunned his machine around in a tight turn that scattered mud in a glistening crescent that sent him between two squat buildings and out over the inky waters of the bayou. A glittering curtain of mist flashed out in his wake. Will and Frank followed close behind, while Lucy waited, watching Jesse. He turned to look at the little village where they had just had their meeting. There was no sign of Buford or the others. Jesse waved to the people watching, and then jerked his chin after his brother. Lucy nodded and gunned her own 'Horse after them.

Jesse gave a grin and one last wave at the concerned villagers as he roared out of town.

*****

Lucinda sat as far from the fire as she could while still benefitting somewhat from its light. The heat had been oppressive since they'd arrived in New Orleans, and riding through the country rabble-rousing had not made things any cooler. Nearer to the fire, possibly more used to the blasting temperatures of the western deserts, the men sat discussing their latest victory, of sorts, and their next challenge.

Jesse stirred the fire with a stick. "So, we're lookin' fer some fella named Tinker Thane, head o' the militia for C.R. Georgia, or whatever Lee has taken to naming the place. Why they couldn't o' kept with the old names, I don' know."

Frank looked up from cleaning Sophie. The swamps had played merry hell with her delicate internal workings. "Defeat has a funny effect on folks, Jesse. Some folks, after they get beat, they wanna change everythin', as if that means it was someone else got beat that last time, an' wasn't them."

Jesse shrugged. "Anyway, this Thane is supposed to be the man to talk to if we wanna go 'round Lee's boys. We'll head toward his headquarters, some town called Kiln. Shouldn't be too far, no more'n a few days of hard riding. We can make a few more stops along the way, lay the ground work as we travel."

Lucy shook her head. They had been away from BELLE JE for too long. Her report, such as it was, would have been in the hands of people who knew what to do with it for at least a week. Somehow, however, she could not bring herself to care. Watching Jesse gather people around himself during these past weeks had been astounding. Listening to him make his case for equality among the people of the south had stirred something deep inside her.

Similar feelings had driven her into the bosom of the Union all those years ago. Back then, she truly believed that the Union was fighting for freedom and honor. As the battles dragged on, she had realized that only a small group of men and women still carried that particular flag. As more and more enemies rose out of the shadows, there was less and less time for the crusades of the past. Now, with Grant lashing out in all directions, and even the noblest of the Union's defenders fixated so strongly on the new enemies, it seemed as if those ideals had stopped mattering entirely.

Except to some, it appeared, among her old enemies. Jesse James was the most stalwart enemy of the Union that had ever existed. He had his reasons, of course, but his unrelieved hatred was irrefutable. And yet here he was, making the cases she herself had made when she was young, before she had been caught up in the new fights like everyone else. Watching Jesse convince these hidebound old rednecks to come around to this new, radical way of thinking had opened her eyes to how far she had fallen from her own ideals, and it hurt at the same time that it gave her hope.

"You think it's really goin' to be that much tougher here on out?" Robert's voice was soft as he whittled at a stick.

Frank nodded. "The folks we knew, out this way . . . a lot of 'em are gonna be deaf to yer words, Jesse."

The outlaw chief shrugged. "Well, that'd be true, years ago. But these folks are the ones who've seen what the Union is capable of. They've seen the meanness an' the violence up close, many of 'em. I'm countin' on that; they're farther from New Orleans, but they're closer to the Union." He shifted his back against his Iron Horse. "Way I figure it, should just about even the balance."

Frank spit a stream of tobacco juice into the fire where it sizzled and danced. "You gotta keep in mind, Jesse, old hates, they run deep on both sides."

Jesse nodded. "I know, Frank. But thanks for the lecture." He turned to Lucy. "Hey, Lucy, you're from the old south. We got a chance?"

She forced herself to smile at the men as they all looked at her with curious eyes. "Jesse, if anyone can do it, you can."

Robert laughed at that, and Will's teeth flashed in the dark. Frank's face was serious as he leaned toward her, resting on one splayed hand. "Seriously, Miss Lucy. They gonna listen? Or 'r they gonna run us out o' town on a rail?"

She looked at Frank for a long moment. There was real concern in his eyes, and it was not for himself. Frank, as always, was worried for his little brother. The ravages of Camp Lincoln were still evident in the gaunt lines of his face and the shadows of his eyes, and yet his first thoughts were still for Jesse. She realized in a flash that Frank would never admit to such emotions, despite the fact that his entire life, as far as she could see, was focused solely on keeping his brother alive. She owed him an honest answer.

"I don't know, Frank." She could not help a slight smile from twisting her lips. "But if anyone can do it, it's Jesse."

Chapter 13

The Drowsy Magnolia on old Delisle Road was once a proud tavern. Like most things in the battered town of Kiln, however, it had seen better days. Kiln was named after the massive charcoal kilns put in to accommodate much of the region's logging in the days before RJ-1027. It had fallen on hard times after the technology began to spread across the countryside, however. The nation was dotted with such places. Towns that had depended on logging, coal, or whale oil; natural resources that had fallen out of use with the power and versatility of Doctor Carpathian's miracle elixir, had withered away. In most of the country, folks had taken to calling the substance RJ. In places like Kiln they called it Devil's Blood; or death.

Tinker Thane, self-styled commander of the Greater-Southern Militias, met them in a small private room over the common area of the Drowsy Magnolia. The wallpaper was faded, the furniture worn, but the beer was good, or so Thane promised as Jesse and Will Shaft were ushered into his presence. Frank, Robert, and Lucy had stayed down in the common area, taking a table in full view of the stairs and as far from the obnoxious RJ-powered piano as they could.

None of them had been happy about being left behind. Lucy and Frank usually took turns accompanying Jesse on his visits, while Robert stayed behind to watch their vehicles and for any sudden change in the local temperament. Will, of course, was always with him, more to make a point than for anything else. This time around, Jesse had gotten an immediate sense that he needed to go this one alone, with just Will beside him. It had been a tense exchange, but at last Frank and Lucy, accompanied by a slightly more resigned Robert Ford, had settled down to taste the local brew and wince through the plinking musical accompaniment, while Jesse, Will, and the militia chief disappeared upstairs.

Thane was smiling warmly on the other side of the table. He had given Will Shaft a curious glance at first and then seemed to ignore him. With a casual wave of his hand, he gestured for Jesse to speak.

The outlaw chief cleared his throat, unsure of how to begin. He was used to having a chance to warm up to his subject, but everything had happened so quickly as they pulled up before the Drowsy Magnolia, his head was spinning.

"Well," Jesse muttered, marshaling his thoughts. "I'm here because—"

Thane's smile widened and he nodded. "I know why you're here, Mr. James." Jesse was getting used to hearing these easterners refer to him as 'mister', truth be told. However, sometimes he wondered if it might not be quite as sincere as he could hope. "You want those of us who are dissatisfied with President Lee's policies to join you in some act of defiance, to prove the vulnerability of our eternal foe in the north, as well as to establish that we of the Confederacy are capable of looking after our own interests." He tipped his head slightly toward Will, standing by the door, without actually looking at him. "And lest we forget, you are also in favor of arming the colored population in furtherance of your military goals. Is that about the size of it, Mr. James?"

Jesse swallowed the plug of acid that had risen from his belly while the smaller man was talking. The smile had not wavered, the eyes still glowed warmly, and yet, Jesse felt as if the past year of his life had just been summed up and dismissed.

"Well, sir, that *is* about the size of it. And yet—"

Thane nodded. "And yet it sounds so crass and unrealistic when I say it. Right?"

Jesse swallowed again. Even the man's accent seemed foreign; flatter and devoid of some essential element he could not name. "Well, sir, if you're goin' to be the one who says it." He shrugged.

Thane's smile widened. "Well, good. So you can take criticism. I was wondering, what with some of the stories that have been going around."

Jesse was feeling more and more out of his depth. "Do you wanna hear 'bout the plan?"

Thane flipped the question away with one casual hand. "Not necessary. You wish to raise the beleaguered forces of the old Confederacy, in spite of the entrenched passivity of our current leaders. You wish to do this, in part, by arming the most downtrodden and dispossessed among us. And you wish to use these forces to strike a blow for freedom and security for the independent Confederate States of America, long may the Stars and Bars wave."

Jesse sat back, his eyes flat. "I'm startin' to wonder why I'm here at all."

Thane leaned forward. "Why, you're here so I can look you in the eyes, Mr. James, and judge the depth of your conviction."

Jesse decided not to respond. The silence stretched on, however, and soon he gave in with a sigh. "And?"

Teeth gleamed behind a predatory smile. "I find you wanting, Mr. James."

Jesse was brought up short, his head cocked to one side. "Pardon?"

"I have looked into your eyes, into the windows to your soul, and I have found the depth of your conviction in this matter to be . . . wanting." The smile faded until only the flat eyes, gleaming with mild, suppressed mirth, remained.

Jesse was unsure what to do next. He was partly of a mind to draw iron on the croaking little pie eater, but he had come so far, and he had tried so hard not to resort to his pistols in a pinch. Besides, what did this little pissant really hold over him? With a deep breath, he shrugged.

"My faith's my own business, Thane. But I assure you, it's there."

The man laughed at him. Actually LAUGHED, out loud, at *him*! "I have no doubt, Mr. James. What does remain in doubt, however, is . . . in what do you hold that faith?"

His anger was building. He could feel his right arm, inner workings spinning and whirring, shaking with the desire to draw. He had a moment's fear that he would once again lose control of the arm, but with the thought, the limb immediately stilled. He looked back up at the militia commander with a dangerous glint in his eye. "Thane, we better come to a point mighty quick, 'r your little corner of the South's gonna be lookin' fer a new commander."

The man held up both hands as if to fend off an attack, but his smirk never wavered. "My apologies, Mr. James. Honestly, it's just been so long, stuck out here amongst the civilized as I am, that I have felt such primal surges of emotion. It is . . . invigorating, I must say." Jesse frowned, confused. Thane calmed himself, raising a hand. "I know wherein you hold your faith, Mr. James. Like most strong men, you hold faith in yourself. And so, as you push the world toward this mighty undertaking, you have faith in yourself if in no other part of it."

Jesse opened his mouth to disagree, but the raised hand, shaken once, stopped him. The anger, however, burned even brighter.

"I know you wish to disagree with me, but I implore you, do not. The truth of the matter is, you care no more for the plight of the coloreds, in the silence of your heart, than I do myself."

Jesse felt tension rising along his back and into his shoulders. His pistols were going to leap into his hands any moment. He could feel Will Shaft's presence at his back like the heat of a furnace. "They are, as most human beings are, a means to an end. However, I do happen to agree with your assessment of the Union. In fact, I support wholeheartedly your aims and designs upon the foe."

Jesse eased back into the chair. His vision was still hazed with anger, but now there was confusion in his eyes as well. "But—"

"But nothing, sir." Thane tapped his fingers on the table. "The Union will eventually turn south, and we must defend ourselves. There is little chance of our doing that unless we stand together. And by all, I mean the desirable and the . . ." His eyes flicked to Will. "I abhor that history has brought us to this pass, but I see no way to argue our way out of it without the piercing report of gunfire."

Jesse shook his head. "Then . . ."

"You have western C.R. Georgia, God bless its chimerical name, standing with you. In fact, I have been empowered to pledge to you the strength of all of C.R. Georgia, as well as the more strident militia units of C.R. Alabama. The Midlands, of course, is still rather firmly under the yoke of Robert the Meek and his tame general Mosby."

Jesse was shocked. "You're tellin' me . . ."

Thane nodded, but this time there was no sign of humor. "I am telling you that you will have the support you need to conduct your attack. Your move eastward, and your stops along the way, have impressed those of us with our hands on the levers of power, Mr. James. We would like nothing better than to prove to the world the supremacy of the white man . . . But history, and the thrice damned Doctor Carpathian, has taken that moment away from us." Again his eyes flicked to Will. "We will embrace the distasteful, that we shall live to taste another day."

Jesse stood up, the rising anger warring now with a sudden surge of wary victory. And yet at what cost? To ally himself with men such as Thane . . .

"Mr. James, let us know where we shall meet you, and we shall be there." Thane nodded a dismissal, but then raised his hand yet again to stall Jesse's departure. "But wait . . .You did not mention a target . ...?"

Jesse stood by his chair, unsure whether to leave or stay. And fairly certain he should not mention Warley's suggested target for their endeavor. "Well, Mr. Thane, sir, we have not yet—"

"You mean to attack the Union fort being built in old Tennessee, correct?" Jesse refused to squirm beneath those piercing eyes.

"I wouldn't know as of yet. And besides, I wouldn't—"

Thane threw one arm over the back of his chair, relaxing easily into a friendly pose. "Nonsense. Where else would you attack, raising such a force?" The eyes turned speculative. "And so we come to the crux of the matter, yes? What does Jesse James have faith in? What is in this fortress the hated enemy builds within a stone's throw of our own power?"

Jesse leaned over the table, his metal fingers digging furrows in the wood. "Look, chiseler. You best leave off—"

"It's the treasure you want, isn't it, Jesse?" Thane's entire body had stiffened, straightening out, arms outstretched to match Jesse's own. "A treasure being delivered to the fortress from the unassailable strength of Washington is what you truly hunger for."

Jesse leaned in even closer. "I don't know what you're talkin' about. My belly's rumblin' fer one thing, friend, an' that's takin' down the Union. Whatever's left after they fall and burn? Well, I figure we can all fight over that when the deed's done."

"Then you truly do not know about the riches?" The disbelief in Thane's face washed away all of the previous emotion.

Jesse ground his teeth together in an audible rasp. "I swear, I'm about done—"

Again the hand rose, and again Jesse found himself silent. The shaking was marked, now, and he knew that Thane was living on borrowed time. "Our sources tell us that treasures of incalculable value are being brought to that place. That, in fact, this was the purpose of its construction all along. There are those who believe, in fact, that controlling this treasure would be worth more than all the gold the Union has poured into the Contested Territories."

Jesse rolled back on his heels. The intensity of the man's speech was almost enough to make him forget his anger. "Bosh. That don't make no sense. If it's worth so much, why bring it so far south? Why not keep it up in the north? Ah, you don't know manure from a mint julep." He hooked his thumbs behind his gun belt, sure now that he was dealing with a madman.

Thane's intensity only deepened. He leaned over the table, his eyes boring into Jesse's. "You have heard no tales of powerful artifacts or relics, Jesse James? Never heard stories of ancient forces strong enough to tip the balance of power in the modern world? Such relics once decided the fates of nations, I assure you. Should the Union have one, or more than one? Not even your plan will save the Confederacy from annihilation."

Jesse sat back down at the table, Thane easing back into his own seat. Images slashed through the outlaw's mind: the underground chamber out past Diablo Canyon; Carpathian's interest in whatever had been kept there, and a mysterious wooden crate in a jouncing, fleeing Doomsday wagon. Then he got to thinking of the gold the Union poured into the western territories. An image flashed in his mind, crates of gold on a half-sunk war boat. Without that gold they would have lost control over the region decades ago. What could be more powerful than all that coin?

Thane allowed Jesse to mull his words over for a moment longer and then leaned forward to speak in low, conspiratorial tones. "Should you succeed in this quest, Mr. James, you could become the most powerful man on the continent."

Jesse's eyes flicked up to meet the stranger's. He looked closely at the man for the first time. The eyes were hazel, with flecks of light and dark swirling together. In the RJ lamps of the room, they seemed almost to mingle within their margins of green and brown, into a rosy blur.

"I'm not sure what you—" Jesse was lost in those swirling colors.

"Mr. James. I represent some very powerful people, people who wish to see these relics contained or controlled, if possible. They will pay handsomely, should you find them in the fortress and bring them to me."

Jesse shook his head, cocking it to one side and regarding Thane with a distrust growing to match his anger. "I ain't doin' this fer no treasure, and I sure as hell ain't doin' it fer you 'r anyone like you."

Thane sniffed and sat back. "Very well, Mr. James. It was only a thought. There will be plenty of time to speak further."

Jesse stood and stepped backward around the chair. He glanced out of the corner of his eye at Will and saw the man watching Thane with distaste. "We'll fight beside you, Thane. And we'll bring down the Union. After that, we'll see."

Thane nodded as if in satisfaction. "Excellent. And remember, please, Mr. James, that the folks of the true Confederacy do not embrace our darker brothers lightly. You should keep that in mind."

Jesse stopped at the door. His hand had slipped to the butt of his Hyper-velocity pistol. This man was his connection to the rest of the Confederacy. If he was going to take down the Union, it had to start here. He sneered, shook his head slightly, and then gestured for Will to proceed him. As he was leaving, however, he leaned back into the room, his own eyes glowing. "You ever show my friend, or any of his people, such open disrespect again, I will end you where you stand."

Thane's wide smile returned. "We understand each other thoroughly, Mr. James!"

Jesse slammed the door and stalked down the stairs. Will was waiting for him at the bottom, and he gestured for his brother and the others to join him as they headed toward the door.

"I'm real sorry you had to listen to that, Will. Thane's a mean-spirited blowhard, and no mistake." Jesse's frustrated anger was still at a high boil.

The dark man in the faded Confederate grays shook his head. "Ain't nothin' I ain't heard worse of, Jesse. 'S all right."

"Listen to what?" Frank's concern was plain on his face.

"Where we goin', boss?" Robert was hurrying to catch up.

"We got what we came for." Jesse grunted as he threw the door open. "The militias, for what they're worth, are behind us."

"Then what's got you so upset?" Lucy followed, but her voice sounded preoccupied.

"Nothin'," grunted Jesse. "We gotta get back to New Orleans. The militia commanders knew we were comin'. Thane spoke fer all of 'em. We need to go back and plan this thing fer real now."

"Not until you tell us what's got you so fired up." Frank reached out and grabbed Jesse's shoulder.

"Hey!" A rough voice called from across the street. "What ya'll doin' with one o' his kind in the middle o' the street like this?"

Jesse froze. Everyone else stopped also, offended or annoyed, looking to the tall man walking toward them, a scowl on his unshaven face. But Jesse, half way to his 'Horse, was as still as a statue.

"I said hey!" The man was closer now, pointing right at Will. The tall black man's hand tightened on the grip of a blaster, but he said nothing.

"What you thinkin', bringing that n—"

Jesse's metal fist lashed out as he passed the local, catching the man with a back-handed blow across the cheek. The crunching of broken bones underscored the slurred cry from pulped lips as the man spun heavily into the dirt. He lay there, moaning, as the outlaw chief stormed passed.

Jesse flexed the metal fingers of his imminently obedient hand and continued moving toward their Iron Horses.

With an extra spring in his step, he leapt into the saddle. Lighting up the engine, he looked over at Will with a wide grin. "Feelin' better already!"

*****

Lucinda walked slowly down Decatur Street and watched as a small ferry boat labored across the churning waters of the Mississippi. Light from the ornate street lamps reflected in red pools on the shifting river. There had been none of the coded signals she had feared when she returned to New Orleans. The flags were in no special order. The Union's guidons, although far more numerous, were all in standard positions. Regardless of her current fears, it appeared no further orders would be demanding her attention. The pressure was still there, of course – those orders *would* come – but for now, she felt more at ease than she had in weeks.

She had walked along the waterfront for over an hour. After borrowing a blackhoof from *Belle Je*, she had ridden into the city on her own. The outlaws and the rebels all had too much on their minds as they tried to train and arm every would-be soldier that flooded onto the plantation. She did not envy them their task, but she had concerns enough for her own mind.

Her stylish boots clicked along the cobbles. It was nice to be out of her trail gear and into something considerably more fashionable. The boots moved almost as if they had a mind of their own, bringing her, once again, to the *Café du Monde*. She smiled. There was no problem so dire that a beignet and a cup of café au lait could not stave it off, at least. She was thinking of Jesse again, as she often did.

Jesse had grown a great deal since their first meeting. There was a depth to him now, a vision of something larger than himself. The fact that this vision encompassed the destruction of the nation she had called her own for most of her life was something she usually forced from her mind. But in times of quiet reflection, she could see the crossroads coming.

It was at moments like this when visions of that horrible laboratory in Camp Lincoln would rear up in her mind. The madman, sanctioned and supported by the very government she had pledged her life to, leaning over her, leering down upon her helplessness, and describing in vivid detail his plans for her. The empty jars lined along the counters and shelves, waiting to be filled.

She did not know how long she could walk this fine line. Jesse was happier than she had ever known him to be, and her part in that happiness, however small, brought her more peace than she had known in a lifetime of service to the Union. Just being near him these past weeks and months had provided something she had never even known she was missing. She smiled again.

Lucinda shook her head and nodded as the waitress placed a linen napkin on her table beside the plate of pastries. The delicate china cup went down next, and the girl moved gracefully away. The agent looked down at the treats. Whenever her thoughts wandered down these paths, she found it best to focus on something else entirely. The future reared up before her like a monster, and she knew she could only ignore it for so long. Even though no orders had awaited her, there would come a day when they called, and she would have to decide whether to answer or not.

By the time Lucinda finished the beignets, she had calmed down enough to continue her walk with a placid mind. She swung around the slumping back wall of the café and up onto the river walk, looking out over the mighty Mississippi. She allowed her mind to drift along on its own course, free, for now, of those terrible choices.

"Lovely evening, isn't it?" The voice was amused, its tone light. She recognized it immediately.

She pivoted on one high heel and nodded as he came up even with her, as if they had intended to meet all along. "Henry. It's always charming to see you."

His smile widened. He was not looking at her, however, but out over the street to their right. "Really." He did not sound convinced. "Well, that sure is nice to hear."

Her mind was racing once again. Did they know how deeply she was entrenched with Jesse's forces? Did they know about the army or his contacts with the Confederates? She and Henry Courtright had been partners for years, but he could easily have been sent to eliminate her if Pinkerton deemed her a threat to the nation.

She kept the slight smile firmly in place and tilted her head dramatically to look at him out of the corner of her eye. She wore the mask of a coquette, but her eyes searched for any sign of violent intent. She was fairly sure she could best him as long as she kept her mind sharp and her eyes open. But she would rather not test the theory. He was nearly as good as she was, and when he meant to kill someone, they usually ended up cold.

"There are folks eager to hear from you." His tone was still even, but the humor was gone. She sensed no imminent threat, but there was only a thin veneer of the friendly banter that had been the foundation of their partnership. Learning what that veneer covered, she realized, could well mean the difference between life and death.

"I filed a report weeks ago. And before that, there was the report from Camp Lincoln." Her own tone was even. She was not defending herself; not yet, anyway. She was explaining her position. "It's been hard to get away. They're a tight-knit bunch."

He did look at her, then. His sardonic smile did not reassure her. "Yes, *they* certainly are, at that. I saw those reports. They were excellent examples of your usual . . . concise, work?"

She shrugged. The humidity of the river hung about them like a pall. She was almost certain the chill down her back was entirely in her mind.

"Conversation with you always grows tedious when you believe you're getting clever." The words would have made him laugh a year ago. Today, he had no response at all. Her patience reached its end. "Why did they send you?"

He grunted, and at least that sound was slightly amused. "Why do they send anyone anywhere? They want to know what's going on."

"With me?" She forced a light smile. "I'm doing wonderfully, thanks for asking. Have a safe trip north."

He stopped abruptly and grabbed her by one shoulder. He gently but firmly spun her around to face him. "They want to know what you're doing, Luce. You've been gone too long, with too little to show for it. And we've been wasting our time with Carpathian, so patience is wearing thin."

She looked into his eyes and was relieved to see no promise of violence there. So, there was still hope that she could escape this moment without making that last, definitive step one way or the other. She slouched slightly, throwing one hip out, and shrugged again. "You know what I'm doing. I'm close to James and his gang. They trust me now, they bring me with them when they go out on the trail. I've been watching every step they've made."

"And they have no idea you're an agent?" There was precious little faith in his eyes.

She looked over his shoulder, out over the roiling water. "I've convinced them I've left that all behind me."

He let her shoulder go and stepped back a pace. "Convinced them, or convinced yourself?" Now she could see the genuine concern in his eyes, and her heart hurt to think that she might disappoint Henry. Her choice was not between Jesse James and the heartless, violent Union. She would be leaving behind far more than that if she turned her back on it all now.

Lucinda forced the lines of her face into a disciplined frown, revealing nothing. "I am as loyal as you ever were, Henry." Her voice was clipped, although she kept it low. Despite the presence of the Union troops, or maybe even because of them, New Orleans was not a friendly city to the forces of the Republic. "Jesse James is possibly the greatest threat to the Union we have faced since the war ended. I'm the closest agent to him, and I will keep an eye on him and his friends and allies, for as long as I can. And when I have something concrete to report," she stepped into him, her eyes burning. "I will damn well report it."

He watched her silently for a moment. "He's a greater threat than Sitting Bull and his savages, or the European?"

She looked away before nodding. "He could very well be, yes." She was skirting the line again; flirting with the crossroads. She could feel herself balancing on a knife's edge.

Courtright's eyes were flat. "How could he be such a threat? When we ran into him in Kansas City, he was nothing but a washed up desperado playing to the gallery. Now, he's a threat to the nation?"

The heat in her chest was rising again, and Lucinda knew that she was going to have to give something away to justify her continued work with Jesse. If Courtright passed along an order to return with him, there would be no turning back. There was no way to know what his orders were, concerning her, if she refused.

"He's made contact with some Confederate rebels. He's developing a following down here and along the coast."

That made Courtright smile. "So? Lee's so damned concerned for his precious personal honor, he dances to Grant's tune with every note and trill. James could gather up every last rebel and the most he'd manage to get Lee to agree to would be a parade."

She did not want to give anything else up, but if she wanted to step away from this encounter alive, she was going to have to cleave to the middle of the road for a while longer.

"He's got his posse, and a large crew from the territories, as well as the men that he liberated from Camp Lincoln. They've got several Rolling Thunder wagons, and some civilian Ironhides." She wrapped her arms around herself against the chill in her heart. She was watching Courtright's face, trying to gauge when she had given him enough. Not yet. "There are elements among the rebellion that don't care much for Lee's methods. If there are enough of them, they could cause some serious trouble if he gets them all pointed in the same direction."

She could not give him more than that. It would have to be enough, or she was going to have to look for an escape route. Would she be able to swim the river, with that current? Her elaborate dress could well be the death of her, if she had to jump.

Henry watched her eyes for a moment, and Lucinda started to wonder what he was learning there. She knew he was almost as good as she was. She schooled her face to impassivity and smiled mildly once again.

Courtright shrugged and shook his head. "Don't matter. They'd need a lot more men than they'll ever raise to be a threat, no matter what they had with them or whose riding in front." He looked away, over the streets and the skyline of New Orleans. "I guess you can stay here a bit longer. Check it out, see if there really is a threat. But the president himself wants you to come back in. He wants you to report to this new fort Grant is putting in, up in old Tennessee, as soon as you can."

She kept her face completely blank. "A fort, in Tennessee? Isn't that a bit close to the Confederacy?"

He grinned. "On their doorstep, in their parlor, makes little difference when they can't really fight back." The grin slipped. "There's something big going down, Luce; bigger than any of us. They're calling everyone in. They've even put out a contract, bringing in renegades they haven't worked with in years." His eyes flicked back to her. "They're bringing in Tanner and the Wraith."

That stopped her. "Both of them? What could they possibly want with those butchers?" There was both fear and contempt in her voice.

He shrugged. "No one knows. Everyone's rendezvousing at this fort." He looked away. "You need to be there."

She nodded. "Big enough, I'll be able to find it, I assume?"

His smile widened. "They say it's huge, actually. More like a castle than anything else. So yeah, I think a gal with your skills shouldn't have trouble finding it."

"And the president is ordering me there? Not Pinkerton?" She dreaded clarifying this last bit of information, but knew it was important.

His smile vanished. "The president orders and requires you to report to Fort Knox in no less than one month's time. Failure to report will be seen as proof of high treason."

She nodded, looking out over the water. She tried one last ploy. "Which president?"

His smile returned, but this time it was cruel. "There's more than one?"

Chapter 14

The courtyard of Fort Frederick was a frozen mess, filled with a deafening cacophony of roars, grumbles, clashes of kit, and shouting troopers as the 7th Cavalry Regiment of the Union Army prepared to take the field, many bundled in wool cloaks and fur-lined hoods. Captains rallied their squadrons, sergeants exhorted their charges to greater efforts, and the command staff stood with their colonel on the wall above the main gate, looking down into the swirling chaos.

Colonel Custer stood with his arms folded over his chest and surveyed the scene. Nothing was being done to his satisfaction, but that was what he had come to expect since his exile into the middle of nowhere. His lip curled as the word occurred to him. He slowly pushed it through his mind and relished the aptness of its taste. Exile. He had been exiled to this northern outpost, slave to a madman, where his genius would be thwarted and he would find no outlet for his warlike spirit.

But the Powers That Be had not factored in Custer's gumption and his drive. Where there was a will, there was a way. He had always thought as much, and these last months had solidified the belief. The constant Warrior Nation attacks had grown steadily worse since his arrival. They taunted the sentries on the walls every night and fell upon isolated patrols out in the hills in attacks that followed no rhyme or reason. Morale in the fort had been plummeting, and his reports back to Washington and General Grant had barely received even cursory responses.

Custer snarled and turned to spit over the parapet into the churned mud below. He had been played for a fool, but the time for sitting back and accepting his lot was over. His men would not stand for this any longer, and he was not the commander to order them to do so. The entire 7th Cavalry was preparing to ride out and end this frontier menace once and for all. He would prove the error of his detractors and decriers upon the bodies of countless savage dead.

Reports had indicated that there was some sort of schism among the savages on the plains, with various bands clashing against each other despite the desperate fighting back east. Such childish actions could only weaken their hold on the hills, and had offered the perfect opportunity for a strike into their scattered holdings.

His patrols had carefully noted the patterns of movement among the Warrior Nation bands. There was only one possible explanation for everything they had found. A settlement had been established right under his nose, supplying warriors, weapons, and sanctuary to the war leaders who had harassed him since his arrival. Now, his scouts ranged across the plains seeking this new village, and the day of his revenge had arrived. His mouth twisted into a familiar sneer. Not a single one of the flannel-mouthed pikers back east would be able to find fault with his actions when he had soured the region of every last savage threat.

"Sir," Lieutenant Shaw coughed into her gloved hand and stepped close enough to speak behind the gesture. "Here they come."

Custer closed his eyes in frustration. The worst aspect of this entire nightmare assignment had been his forced interactions with the two men now approaching across the parapet. He could not remember the last time they had exchanged a civil word to each other, so the fact that they were both coming at him now, their faces matching visions of righteous indignation, did not bode well.

"Gentlemen," The colonel turned to meet them, seizing the initiative and hopefully pushing them onto their back feet. "What a pleasant surprise to see you both out and about on such a fine day!"

The day was not fine. Early winter snows had come swirling in over a week ago, the corners of the courtyard still sheltering glittering banks. It was brutally cold, and had been for weeks. Many of the troopers were bundled up in their winter gear, those that had it. Requisitions for enough of the equipment for the rest of his soldiers had seen no hope of immediate fulfillment, which was just another fly in his jelly.

Tumblety and Tesla were well-situated for winter gear, though. Tesla was now standing on the parapet in a sensible black wool coat that draped down to his knees, a fur hat crammed over his ears. But Tumblety was a vision in an elaborate crimson uniform long coat that would have done Napoleon's Chief Cook and Bottle Washer proud. The ridiculous mustachios swung out to either side of his bloated face, probably stiff with ice. Custer's casual glance at the self-proclaimed doctor's chest told him that today the man claimed to have been wounded in battle three times, shown conspicuous bravery in the face of the Mexicans, and served with honor at the Battle of Bunker Hill. It would have been more impressive if Custer had not known that the 'doctor' had never once suffered so much as a hang nail even near a battle, had never been to Mexico, and the Battle of Bunker Hill had not happened the better part of one hundred years ago.

"Colonel, this will not stand!" It was Tumblety, of course, who began the attack. Tesla was more even-tempered, although he could be quite violent when provoked. In situations like this, he was more likely to hang back and let his tempestuous colleague lead the charge, and coincidentally take the brunt of the resultant grapeshot. Tumblety was breathing heavily from his hurried climb to the parapet, his face beet red behind the wildly waving facial hair. "You must not embark upon this lunacy, sir!"

Custer took a deep breath, looked down at his boots for a moment, and then looked up again, a pleasantly-bland expression firmly affixed to his features. "What will not stand, doctor?"

The man's beady eyes flared. "Do not play the fool with ME, sir! We know full well what you intend! Riding off into the hinterlands with your full power, leaving our experiments and personnel without so much as a corporal's guard!" He was heaving, now, trying to stand upright while his anger conspired to keep him short of breath. "For shame, colonel! With a duty as clear as your own, to spend not a moment's thought or preparation for your primary charges! This is *not* why I had you put in charge here, as you well know!"

The colonel felt his gorge rise at that last accusation. Unfortunately, it held enough truth that he let it go for now. Custer's eyes flickered back to where Tesla stood hiding behind his chief rival. At the moment, however, he was nodding vigorously in support of Tumblety's case. The colonel shook his head and turned back to the primary target.

"Doctor, I assure you, I have nothing of the sort in mind for you or this installation while I am away." The words were as mild as he could make them, but his nerves were wearing thin. He was not sure how much longer he could maintain the facade of propriety.

Apparently, Nikola Tesla had had enough of playing second fiddle and so stepped forward to add his own grist to the mill. "Colonel Custer, we know you are mobilizing the entire 7th Regiment. The cream of our best efforts were wrenched away and thrown back east nearly a month ago. Our newest creations are not nearly ready to shoulder the burden of defending the fort. So with what forces do you propose to keep us safe from the savages while you are away?"

Custer was at the end of his rope. Explaining himself to uninitiated laymen had never been a skill at which he excelled. "Mr. Tesla, I assure you that I will not be leaving Fort Frederick undefended in my absence." He raised one gloved finger to forestall the coming objections from both men. "I am taking the 7th with me, that is true. And elements of the garrisoning units as well, riding along as mounted infantry in support. However, there will still be more than three quarters of the garrison soldiers left behind. More than enough to watch over the fort until we return."

Tumblety was not comforted, his head still pivoting back and forth in vicious denial. "No, no, no! You are taking the best of the soldiery with you, sir! You are leaving the dregs behind, and you know it!"

Custer was stepping toward the 'doctor' before he realized it, his hand rising as if to strike the man. He stopped himself, but did not drop his arm. They were very close, their noses almost touching, and the colonel sneered as he muttered, "If I ever hear you denigrate men under my command again, DOCTOR, we will see how well you fare beyond the walls without them."

Tesla stepped forward, his dapper face struggling to conjure up a smile. "Gentlemen, no need for a confrontation among friends!" He clapped both men on their shoulders, far more comfortable in the role of reconciler. "I'm sure we can come to some sort of agreement, colonel? A few squadrons to be left behind, just in case, maybe?"

Custer shook his head and stepped back himself, looking out over the courtyard as if dismissing the two men of science. "Firstly, two squadrons would be nearly half my force. And secondly, no, I can't. Our strategy has been very carefully planned out, and I intend to implement it without amendment or adjustment." He glared back at the two men. "I will be bringing with me enough force that the savages will be crushed in a single engagement. I'm going to split the regiment into three prongs, and we will be coming at their new settlement from entirely different vectors of attack. There will be no way they can defend against our numbers, our technology, and our spirit."

Tumblety shook his head, even more forcefully. "Colonel Custer, you cannot leave us without adequate defenses! Do you not understand that I am engendering the future of the nation here? Tomorrow's world is being born today, right here in this fort, and you threaten to abandon it to ignorant savages and barbarians!"

Custer grimaced as the words registered with the smaller scientist.

"YOU are engendering the future?" Tesla's anger boiled back to full burn in the blink of an eye. "You engender nothing but waste and fodder for circus side shows! The future of the Union is in metal hands, you charlatan!"

"Charlatan?" Tumblety's eyes were bulging from his head as he shook within the enormous confines of his uniform coat. "Who, pray tell, are you referring to as a charlatan, you quacksalver? You should superintend your words more closely, or I shall demand satisfaction!"

Custer watched the two men turn on each other, their arguments with him forgotten. Of their own accord, his eyes rolled. He looked over to his command staff. With barely-concealed contempt, they were being careful to look anywhere but at the two scientists whose shrill cries were rising higher and higher, bouncing off the tall tower and the surrounding cliffs.

To one side, Lieutenant Shaw was having words with a young runner, and the look on her face sent an alarming chill down Custer's back, despite the cold. She nodded to the young man, snapped off some quick orders of her own that sent him running back down the stairs, and turned to look at her commander. Her brown hair, kept in a tight bun beneath her uniform cap, had sent several escaping tendrils questing out into the cold air. They whipped against the side of her pale face as she approached.

"Sir, there's been a development." Her voice was pitched low.

Custer nodded, not taking his eyes off the howling spectacle before him. He knew he was not going to like what she had to say, and could probably guess where it was coming from as well.

"It's the general, sir." The title, said with heavy infliction, could only mean one man. Custer turned to stare at his adjutant. He could feel dismay settling over his face, but he gestured for her to continue.

"His eastern fortress is almost complete." She looked away, as if she could not bear to see his reaction. "Apparently, the actions against the savages back east are not going well, however. He cannot spare any of his own forces to man the fort. He orders you to take the 7th, depart without delay, and report to Fort Knox before the month is out."

He felt numb and knew it was more than the cold. "Within a month." He mumbled. There would be no time for his grand assault. "They would take even this away from me."

Shaw leaned closer, her eyes betraying her own anger. "Sir, they can't do this to you. There has got to be another way."

Custer turned his gaze back to the two grumbling men. Apparently, their energy was not equal to a sustained assault. He grunted at his adjutant and then moved toward the scientists. Tesla saw him first and cringed from his expression. The reaction warned Tumblety, who spun around as if he expected to find Sitting Bull himself had leapt atop the wall.

"Gentlemen." The colonel's eyes were intense as he regarded the two men. "How close to deployment are your respective projects?"

Tumblety and Tesla exchanged a wary glance, suddenly less than enthusiastic to compare the preparedness of their work. Tesla was the first to turn back to the colonel, straightening his shoulders and schooling his features to some semblance of calm confidence.

"Well, the shipment east that Washington demanded took all of my active units, including even my most experimental items. But I will be able to deploy a small, elite unit of combat automatons within the next few weeks." He shrugged. "I would have to retrofit weapons from existing stock, which will not be ideal. I would have liked a chance to field test my displacer gauntlets, but they took those as well. But I am confident that new combat units would be able to take the field within a few weeks' time."

Custer turned his gaze upon Tumblety. Pride wrestled with caution and fear across his face, and threw them down. "I am confident that I will be able to field at least a company of new Reconstructed in half the time!" As he continued to speak, his voice strengthened, his posture stiffened. Reality, in his own mind, changed before his eyes to conform to his growing conviction.

"I, too, was required to send subjects east, as you know. However, the Reconstructed that I can put into the field will be stronger, faster, and more resilient than the metal automata of my colleague, and more effective in battle as well." Tumblety finished his little speech with a flourish of his hands and then placed them firmly on his hips, mimicking a statue of a war hero he had once seen while vacationing in England.

Custer was still and silent for a moment while he measured his own reaction to their reports. He smiled for a moment, looked down at his boots again, and then over at Lieutenant Shaw. She was staring at the men with her mouth hanging partly open in naked horror.

"Sir," Shaw muttered, turning her back on the scientists. "You cannot leave the defense of the fortress to these men's creations. Since Washington stripped them of their active units, neither of them have anything remotely ready for the task. The Warrior Nation has been ramping up its attacks for months. With winter coming on, there will be almost no resupply for the foreseeable future. The chiefs have a burning hatred for us. If we leave things in the hands of those two . . . men . . . there will be nothing at all left when we return."

The colonel nodded slowly. He pivoted on his heel and moved to the outer wall, his gloved hands resting lightly on the cold stone. The rolling terrain of the Black Hills stretched out beneath the walls of the fort and into the distance. The jagged gray bones of the Earth were visible where the soil had been worn away by centuries of wind and rain. It was harsh country, and he had come to respect the land. He knew that even at that moment, the land concealed countless enemy scouts, watching his fortress with dark, hostile eyes.

There was no denying the truth of Shaw's words. Something about this complex had enraged the savages. Whether it was the experiments and technologies developed here, the placement of the fortress upon some sacred site, or perhaps even the mere presence of white folks within the ancient hills, they would stop at nothing until Fort Frederick was destroyed.

Custer turned back to his command staff and the two scientists. He began to walk down the parapet, jerking his head slightly as he passed Shaw, indicating that she should follow him. He knew from her expression that she did not like the glimmer in his eye. There had been a lot of quiet, respectful dissent from his command staff over his proposed attack into Warrior Nation territory. Shaw, although never one to question him before the rest of the troops, had expressed her own questions when they were alone. Everyone had lined up behind him when he'd put his boot down, and he knew they would do so again.

"Lieutenant, I would like to leave three companies behind." He tilted his head toward the scientists. "When these gentlemen are ready with their own forces, I think such a joint force will be sufficient to teach the savages a lesson they won't forget before we return." He stopped and turned to face her. "If I leave any of my commanders behind, however, they would most likely countermand my orders as soon as I was out of sight." He looked sourly back at the men and women of his command staff before turning back to her. "You're the only officer here with any real loyalty to me, personally. However, there is no way I could ever ask the seasoned captains beneath me to follow a lieutenant, even if I gave you a field promotion. They would all outrank you in seniority."

Shaw's face set in lines of dissent. Beneath them in the courtyard, the men and women of the 7th continued to prepare, unaware of their twisting fates. "However, if I give you a field promotion to captain, and then split off a small portion of each company's troopers, taking one lieutenant from each group for command –"

"Sir," Shaw's voice was low and sharp, but he silenced her with a gesture.

"I would be able to string together an ad-hoc squadron for you, I think. I could leave you the entire garrison, as well. None of this will look unusual, even in Washington." He looked back at his commanders and the two scientists. Both men strove for his attention. He ignored them. "It would be left to your judgment if the abominations of either gentlemen were worthy of inclusion. But you are correct: if someone does not go out and push back against the savages, there will be no stopping them."

Shaw looked at him for a long moment, then back to the rest of the command group. She lowered her head in resignation. "I understand, sir."

The colonel put his hand on her shoulder and squeezed once with a grimace of sympathy before moving back to the group huddled around the stairs. "Gentlemen, there has been a drastic change of plans."

The officers all stood taller. They were hoping, he knew, to hear that his proposed attack on the elusive village was being postponed. The scientists, however, looked as if they were balanced between hope and indignation. It was a natural state for men of science, if these two were an average representation of the breed.

"General Grant is ordering the 7th back east. Apparently, there's trouble with the Rebellion. The general has it in mind that we're the ones to teach them a sharp lesson." He ignored the slumping shoulders and looks of relief that passed among his officers. "I will be brevetting Shaw to Acting Captain and placing her in command of this fortress in my absence." He raised a gloved hand to stop the growing protests among the senior officers. "The general wishes the 7th to arrive on the border intact at the command level."

As the words sunk in, both Tesla and Tumblety were again fidgeting with agitation. "Colonel, once again I must protest." Tumblety, of course. "Leaving our safety in the hands of a feckless girl! It hardly bears thinking upon!"

Tesla's agreement was so emphatic he nearly nodded his head clear off. "With the future of the Union at stake, you cannot—"

"I agree." Custer's simple words brought both men stumbling to a halt.

"You . . . agree . . . ?" Tumblety could hardly believe his ears, clearly.

"I do. But gentlemen, the future of the Union is not only at stake here. It is at stake to the east, where General Grant contends with Sitting Bull and the united chiefs. It is at stake in Washington, where useless politicians daily debate the minutia of bureaucracy while around them the Republic burns. It is at stake in the contested territories, where madmen and bandits flout the law, strutting in their flagrant destruction of civilized convention." He looked gravely at the scientists, happy to see they were lapping his words up like kittens with cream. "Here and now, the future is at stake as well, I agree. But my men and I are called away. And so today, defending the future falls to you, gentlemen. It is you who must hold the line."

Custer could see his regimental commanders, beyond the grinning madmen, looking at each other in confusion. He almost smiled. Instead, he maintained his grave expression and continued. "Captain Shaw will have a solid force with her, as well as the entire Army garrison. And when your creations are ready . . . weeks, I believe you said?" Both men nodded, but there was a sheepish cast to their faces that did not bode well for the prediction. "Excellent, then. Let us say in four weeks' time, Captain Shaw will form an assault force of the most prudently spared forces. They will push the savages back from Fort Frederick with a lesson that will hold them over until my return."

The scientists watched him for a moment, their minds struggling with the dual impressions of abandonment and empowerment. Their egos won the day, as he knew they would, and both men swelled with pride, visions of victory rising in their heads. Perhaps Tumblety was even imagining a few new medals he could add to his collection.

It took several days to shave the numbers off each company and form them into temporary commands. When the 7th Cavalry Regiment prepared to ride east, Shaw, her lieutenants, and the two scientists were there to see them off. The roar of hundreds of Iron Horses and Locust support vehicles was nearly deafening, and the scorching, faintly-chemical smell of RJ-1027 filled the air.

Shaw had already said her goodbyes, and Custer had passed along all the wisdom and advice he could in the short time they had had. Tesla stood, tall and dark in his long coat, face grim with the reality of their situation. But Tumblety, as always, had one more thing to say as the Colonel gunned his engine and began to drift toward the gate.

"Good hunting, Colonel!" The 'doctor' shouted to be heard. Custer knew that was not all he would have to say, however. "I pray you are doing the right thing! History will not be kind to you if the Warrior Nation proves stronger in resolve than you believe, and our efforts here are lost."

Custer grinned despite himself. He was leaving all of this behind and taking the first steps to free himself from the chains Tumblety had forged at Camp Lincoln. And even though he felt bad for Shaw, the idea of commanding in the field once again, far from the puling demands of the scientists, had lifted his spirits amazingly. He tipped his hat to the 'doctor', and shouted in response, "Well and good, doctor. But I do not answer to history. I answer to General Grant. And of the two, he is by far the less forgiving!"

*****

The small balcony shot out from the hostel, leaning over the canyon that gave the town its name. He had paid extra, both for the view and for access to the canyon, in case he needed to lose something in a hurry. The fact that the Lonely Rose was also about as far from the center of town as you could get was a bonus. There had been a lot of law moving through Diablo Canyon recently, and he was not interested in tangling with them so soon after the . . .

unpleasantness that had cost him most of his posse out in the desert the last time.

William Bonney tossed back the cheap firewater and with a convulsive heave launched the cloudy glass out into the air. It tumbled erratically, catching the thin winter sun as it twirled, sending dazzling glimmers shooting off in all directions. It sank slowly, as if defying gravity, over the edge and into the jagged rocks below. He watched the glass drop out of sight and then settled against the makeshift railing, his hands tight on the rough wood.

Nothing had gone right for him since Jesse James had landed in the middle of his camp that day. Well, if he was going to be honest with himself, nothing had gone right for him since he had first broken into that damned chamber of horrors beneath the desert. Filled with Carpathian's castoff corpse-slaves and stinking to high heaven, standing in that room, staring at that empty stand, and then his meeting with Jesse afterward, had been the lowest point in his life. Not even losing the rest of his posse down in old Texas at the hands of Pat Garret and those Pinkerton agents had put him lower.

After that, he had had a tough row to hoe. Most of the hired hands were dead. Ringo and Smiley had gone their separate ways. Billy had had a small stash in Diablo Canyon, so he had returned, laid low, and brooded over lost opportunities. The Apache Kid was staying in a room down the hall, having refused to abandon his boss. But the renegade warrior was naturally silent and little help in lifting Billy out of his low spirits.

When those Union agents had come through about a month ago, he thought they were after him and he had hidden in the Lonely Rose for almost a week. He had ventured out finally, bored out of his skull, and convinced he would rather die than spend another day in the miserable little garret. He had run right into an agent, of course. He had been recognized, and prepared to go down fighting. The agent had not cared at all.

That was the second lowest point. There was a time, not so long ago, that Billy the Kid had been one of the most wanted men in the western territories. But there was so much going on right now, he had not rated a second glance even from the agents who had once chased him the length and breadth of the west. He spat out over the railing, but the bitter taste remained.

On the heels of the Washington muscle men, some new-fangled lawman, calling himself Mick Ironhide, had shown up in town, waving a government writ and declaring Diablo Canyon once more under federal protection. This guy claimed to be working independently of the Earps' Federal Bureau of Marshals, and he did not have any of the heavy firepower the Earps generally brought to bear. Turned out, though, that he had more than enough to make the town too hot for Billy's liking.

And now, local gossip-mongers were talking about a large cavalry force, maybe a whole regiment, roaring out of the north west; Warrior Nation territory. They had torn through the territories on their way back east. Hundreds of men and machines, riding hell-bent for leather. It was that thought which had really started to get his blood moving again.

Billy had been hearing the stories about Jesse, of course. How he had found his brother in a prisoner camp out east and pulled him out through some ridiculous heroics. He had been glad to hear that. Frank James was a gentleman of the first water, and Billy would not have wanted to hear that he had been lost. But the stories of Jesse coming out at the head of an army, riding up into Warrior Nation territory and disappearing? Those were stories he could have well done without.

Billy remembered talking to Jesse back in Kansas City about the damned artifact that had ended up in Carpathian's liver-spotted hands. They had talked about leading armies and raising the south against the Union. He could not have honestly said if he had been serious back then, but it seemed like Jesse had. There was even some talk that James had been seen heading back south, maybe even down the great river.

Whatever was going on, though, it was not happening in Diablo Canyon. The place had been a rip for a while, totally lawless without its old UR-30 to keep the peace, except when the big lawmen or their Union masters came through, of course. And now, with Mick Ironclad, the place had died right down again.

Billy turned on a boot heel and sank into a creaking chair, contemplating the canyon through slit eyes. Why would Jesse James be heading down the Mississippi? It skirted the border with the Confederacy. What had happened to the army he had apparently led out of Union territory? The young-looking outlaw could feel the stirring of ambition again. He wanted very much to be out of Diablo Canyon and back into the thick of things. Spending the entire winter here on the margins, away from all the excitement, did not sit well. Carpathian's agents were moving into all the local towns, offering cheap power, generators, and other tech in exchange for a simple promise of allegiance and support in the future. He did not want to be around when they came to Diablo Canyon and met Sheriff Mick.

If James was headed back into the Confederacy, why? How did he think he was going to convince them to listen? In Kansas City, Jesse and Billy had talked up big plans, but back then they were imagining themselves in possession of the mysterious artifact. They had no idea what it might be, but they had imagined it to be some talisman that could convey power and prestige before the cowering remnants of the old south.

Could Jesse have—

A harsh, raucous sound smashed into his thoughts as a heavy object crashed onto the railing beside him. With a muttered curse, Billy's battered pistol was in his hand. Two quick shots snapped off, the second bolt soaring out over the canyon and into the distance. The first bolt had done the trick.

Billy sidled toward the pile of meat, metal, and feathers that had flopped onto the balcony with a wet slap after his shot had done its work. With a little effort he located what must have been the head. A bird skull gave it shape, but most of the actual head had been reconstructed out of crude black metal. A slight red glow was fading fast from its eyes. It had been a large bird of some kind, probably a vulture, but heavily modified with bits of metal, rubber, and wires. The lower jaw was rattling, opening and closing spastically as if laughing at him. Judging by the smell, it had been dead for some time.

Billy nudged the corpse with his boot, moving aside a wing and spreading the pieces out along the floor of the balcony. A small ivory tube, covered in black, oily liquid, poked out from beneath a metal claw. He reached down and plucked it out of the stinking pile. It was a message tube. He wiped it against his pant leg and popped it open. Several small rolls of paper slid into his palm.

The first thing Billy noticed as he unrolled the note that was wrapped around the rest, was the intricate 'C' drawn across the bottom in an elegant hand. The short note was equally graceful, but the contents froze his heart.

"An artifact of your own?"

Billy shuffled through the other two papers. Each was a map; one of the Old States with several locations noted in red ink, the other some sort of underground complex. He stared at the sheaf of papers, at the dead, twitching bird, and then out over the shattered landscape of the canyon. His hand tightened into a fist without his conscious will, crushing the note.

"James." He spat.

Chapter 15

Frank James rested his forearms against the hatch cowling atop the Rolling Thunder wagon. Although his raider's spirit had at first balked at the thought of being trapped in a giant target, the firepower of the Rolling Thunder had brought him around. He had been riding in *Ole Bessie* the entire trip south, ever since Jesse had left for New Orleans. Frank did not much care for water or boats, and had had no interest in taking to the river himself.

The army of independent Confederate groups had gathered around a quiet little river town called Maycomb. By the time Jesse, Colonel Warley, and the New Orleans contingent had arrived, Tinker Thane and the other militia commanders were already ensconced in town. The commanders had taken the majestic courthouse, easily the largest and most impressive building in town, as their headquarters.

Jesse was still ill-at-ease with the big bugs of the rebellion, but he hid it well. Warley treated him with a great deal of respect, and that lent him a certain amount of implied respectability in the minds of the others. He knew the battle-hardened survivors of Camp Lincoln, the outlaws from Robbers Roost, and Ingram's Rangers, as well as their small contingent of Rolling Thunder wagons did not hurt, either.

The Army of New Orleans, marching with a swinging gait behind the impressive might of their stolen heavy armor, had crossed the border into the Confederacy without hindrance. Sure, there had been some hard looks at the number of dark-skinned soldiers marching with them, but he had been heartened when he saw the soldiers' reaction to these looks. After the first few days, the entire army began marching to the unmistakable cadences of melancholy spirituals. All of the soldiers sang together, loud as could be, with smiles that only got wider as the locals turned red. It was a start, but it was enough to reassure Frank that there was hope to their cause after all.

When they had arrived in Maycomb, Frank was a little saddened to see that most of the militia units were not nearly as integrated as their own. Each group did have its share of black folks, however. They might not have been sharing fires with the white folks often, but they were there all the same. They wore similar uniforms, those that had a uniform, and all were armed with similar weapons. Jesse had managed to save nearly all the weapons when they fled the Warrior Nation in the north, throwing them into the surviving wagons for the long, hungry trek south. Those weapons had first gone to arm the New Orleans forces. The rest were distributed as evenly as possible among the other militias. Frank noticed a funny thing, though: not many seemed to get to Thane's group.

They had not stayed in Maycomb long. Most of the army was already assembled when they arrived. They were only waiting for those few stragglers coming in late, mostly from the deep swamps of what had once been Florida, now part of C.S. Alabama. Frank was still not sure why all the old state names had been changed, or erased altogether, and the old lines redrawn. That was just another thing he could ask President Lee, if everything worked according to plan. There would be some changes when they finally confronted the old coward as the conquerors of Grant's mighty citadel.

If everything they had been able to find out about this Fort Knox was true, they were bringing more than enough men to bury the place several times over. Most reports said the fort was desperately undermanned. Riding in *Ole Bessie*, visions of swift victory were easy to come by.

The thought brought Frank back to the present. Maycomb was many days behind them now. He cast his eye over the men and women he had come to think of as his own. Most of Jesse's group, outlaws, freed prisoners, and militia, now had Iron Horses of their own, with only a small contingent riding in Ironhide wagons or marching alongside. Many of the best had been seconded to militia units from the towns around New Orleans as advisors.

Their other surviving Rolling Thunders crunched along on the narrow trail just behind *Ole Bessie*. Considering that the full strength of the independent rebels stretched out as far as he could see in nearly all directions, it was hard to imagine the pile of bricks at the end of their march posing too much of a problem.

The deep-throated roar of a band of Iron Horses rolled over the armored wagon. Frank looked down to see Jesse ride up with Robert and Charlie Ford, Marcus Cunningham under his customary hood, and the beautiful Lucinda. Frank's smile widened and he waved down. Damn, that was a fine looking woman. He knew she had run into a little difficulty the first night the Army of New Orleans had made camp. A couple of the men from an outlying town had taken an unhealthy interest, despite Jesse standing nearby. But Jesse had just smiled, stepped back, and let Lucy speak for herself. The many variations on the story he had heard differed only in the details of how long each man had been unconscious.

Jesse grinned up at Frank and then gestured straight ahead. He followed up with several other gestures they had shared since their time in the war. Jesse was bringing his command group forward to scout ahead. Several mounted squads were already out there, Frank knew, but Jesse always liked to be in the thick of things. He nodded and waved, watching as the five of them thundered away down the trail on columns of thickened air.

Frank looked around for the Ironhide carrying Quantrill, Warley, Captain Carney, and the other commanders of the New Orleans group. He stared hard at Quantrill, his mind returning to the mysterious Allen Henderson. Frank shook his head. The man had vanished months ago, and no apparent harm had come from his strange game. Cole, currently riding herd on the far right flank, had been urging him to forget the specter and focus on the work at hand. None of the big bugs seemed to think twice about it. He had tried to put it aside, but every now and then he was haunted by memories of the man's strange eyes . . .

A dilapidated old Ironhide rumbled up next to *Ole Bessie*. Frank looked over and grinned widely when he recognized Buford Nash standing in the rusty machine's flatbed. His son, Deacon, crouched next to him, polishing a Union blaster and staring daggers at the outlaw rifleman. Frank could not have given two squats over a full latrine. Buford, however, had become something very close to a friend during the journey north. It was good to know the St. Tammany militia was nearby. Frank did not have many friends among the Confederate fighters, but he knew Jesse trusted the New Orleans folks, and he had gotten to know many of the St. Tammany men himself. He would trust a mud-stained swamp trotter long before he trusted some flannel-mouthed city croaker from Atlanta or Charlotte.

Frank was about to shout a crude joke over to Nash's truck when a low rumbling echoed up somewhere off to the left. A column of smoke rose into the sky from their distant flank. Frank ducked down into the armored heat of the Rolling Thunder and shouted for his driver to pull up. The wagon rolled to a halt, and by the time he emerged, three more columns of smoke rose into the pale winter sky. The rumbling was nearly continuous, now.

"Something not too good goin' on over dere, I t'ink!" Buford shouted.

Frank hoisted Sophie out through the hatch and swung the long rifle around, pointing toward the disturbance. He sighted through the powered scope, searching through the colorful swirl of shifting images for the cause of the commotion. He found one of the churning smoke columns in the sky and followed it down to the base. A raging fire, erupting from the twisted wreckage of an overturned Ironhide, writhed at the bottom of the smoky pillar. The fighters around the vehicle were fleeing toward the main army, many throwing down their weapons as they ran. The entire scene was eerie in its silence.

Frank brought Sophie's gun sight back to the smoke and tried to see through to the other side. There was a hint of surging motion, but nothing more. Some of the militia, braver than most, had settled into cover around fences, tree stumps, or boulders. They were aiming off to the west where a fallow field and clumps of trees hid their targets. The weeds and small trees thrashed violently as Frank watched. It appeared as if something massive was moving toward the army's flank.

"Whatch'ou see?" Buford Nash shouted again. Whatever was happening, they could hear nothing but the distant thunder.

Frank lowered Sophie and looked over at the militia leader. "We're bein' hit!" He pointed toward the smoke.

"Somethin' took out three or four wagons. Most folks'r runnin', though some are standin' their ground!"

Buford craned his head off to the left. Around him on the flatbed, his men were all clutching weapons. Aside from ambushing an occasional hapless Union soldier, none of them had seen the elephant up close before. They had felt unassailable in the center of the huge army. The fact that someone was attacking them now was nearly unthinkable.

"We gonna head over, see what there is to see?" Buford was holding a massive blunderbuss that he called his gator stick.

Frank stared back toward the commotion in the distance. There were several wide fields separating them. He looked down at Buford's beat-up old wagon. He shook his head. "I don't think you're gonna make it, old man!" He smiled. "I'll let you know how it stands, though!"

Frank lowered himself back into *Ole Bessie's* rumbling hull and tapped the driver on the shoulder. The kid nodded. There really was no hope of being heard when the enormous engine filled the compartment with its thunder. The driver turned back to his vision slit, hands grasping the controls.

Ole Bessie lurched around, spinning on its enormous drive wheels, and started to push behind Buford's wagon, off into the field to their left. Two other Rolling Thunders followed suit, pivoting on the packed trail and bursting through a low stone wall. They churned over the turned earth, shaking themselves out into an arrowhead formation. Many of the small militia bands, lacking any real military doctrine to fall back on, ran to follow. They shouted with excitement and waved their new weapons in the air.

"I hope Jesse's turning back 'round." Frank muttered, knowing that his crew would never hear him. Aside from the driver, the small space was filled with three gunners who shared the duties of switching out exhausted power cells, aiming, and firing. The largest weapon, of course, was the enormous blaster cannon on the forward turret. The Gatling cannons that covered the front and sides were nothing to dismiss lightly. Frank was pretty sure that, no matter what had snuck up on their left verge, *Ole Bessie* and her sisters would be able to take care of it.

Frank was settling down in front of the commander's vision slit when he felt someone tap him on the back of the head. He turned, and one of the gunners pointed back toward the rear of the compartment, where a small vision slit provided a view of the vehicle's back trail. Frank maneuvered his way through men and machinery. He pressed his forehead against the leather brace pad above the viewport.

In the narrow field of vision, he could just make out Nash's old rust bucket lurching over the tumbled stones left behind by the Rolling Thunders. The old wagon was bucking and swaying wildly as it negotiated the rutted, uneven field, but it ground forward nevertheless.

Frank sat back, smirking, and shook his head at the gunner. The man returned the grin. There really was no telling with these swamp folks. Frank returned to the commander's position, but quickly changed his mind and pushed back up through the hatch. He turned and waved at the old Ironhide churning along in his wake. He saw a big arm wave in reply and knew that Buford had been watching for his reaction. Frank's grin widened and he turned back around.

There were men and women running past him now, folks that had been the first to flee from whatever had hit them. Their eyes were wide with panic, their faces pale. Their legs drove them forward, despite obvious exhaustion. They were muddy, battered, and bruised from their headlong flight through the fields. There was no sign that they planned on stopping any time soon, running right past the big wagons crawling across the fields toward the trouble.

Frank watched as one group of militia, moving with the wagons toward the fighting, tried to stop some of their fleeing comrades. The retreating men fought with insane strength to break away, pushing, punching, kicking, and shrieking, until they were released. The attempt took a lot of the excitement out of the fighters moving west. No one else tried to stop the bolting troops.

The Rolling Thunders had crossed about half the distance to the shindig, and Frank brought Sophie up again to look through her scope. There were now seven wagons burning, and an unbroken wave of return fire flashed like sleeting crimson rain off to the west. The weeds and grasses all along that line were burning, sending a pall of smoke in all directions. Within the smoke, Frank could see things moving. The distance, the swirl of smoke, and the play of light and shadow made it impossible to know exactly what he was seeing.

The Rolling Thunder wagons churned to a stop at another low, tumbled wall. Only one field lay between them and what now appeared to be a full-blown battle. The field was strewn with bodies, most of them smoldering or blasted into long streaks of tattered cloth and meat. The group of militia fighters holding the line was much thinner than it had been, with large holes blown into their defensive position. The smoke rising beyond their crouching forms was even thicker, obscuring everything on the other side in a thick haze.

Frank watched as red bolts came tearing out of the smoke. Lines of explosions stuttered in their wake and fighters were sent spinning away into still, crumpled heaps. He looked to either side. The militia who had followed the Rolling Thunders stood gaping, staring at the death and destruction before them. There were times when Frank felt that his brother's ambitions had taken them out of their depth. This quickly became one of them. All of his military training and experience, aside from being decades out of date, revolved around leading small bands of lightly-armed men in attacks against heavy, clumsy, ignorant enemies. He did not enjoy having the situation reversed.

"Get behind the wall!" He shouted at the men on either side of *Ole Bessie*. He repeated the order again, accompanying his cry with frantic gestures. A few of the quicker fighters caught on and dropped, dragging their slower fellows after them. They assumed defensive positions behind larger stones or old, overgrown tree stumps. Most continued to stand and gape, however, and Frank was ready to turn his guns on them out of frustration when Buford Nash's wagon rumbled up. The Tammany man leapt off the flatbed and began to harangue the men and women standing like tobacco shop Injuns in the mud.

Frank nodded to Buford and then looked back at the faltering line. Shapes swayed back and forth within the smoke, like giant figures emerging from the mists of ancient myth. There were only a few survivors of the initial defense, and while he watched, they all began to scramble backward. First, only one or two moved, but soon they were all clambering out of their cover. He could hear them shouting, thin across the wide field, but it was meaningless sound; carrying no sense.

The first large shape breached the smoke and a low moan passed over Frank's secondary line. The thing was taller than a man. It was hard to make out any detail, but it seemed to move with an unnatural, stiff gait, a single crimson eye peering balefully through the fog. Both of its arms ended in massive Gatling cannons, and it fired directly into the fleeing defenders, cutting them down in showers of red mud.

The militia fighters stood still and silent as several more of the giant shapes strode out of the smoke, their bolts slapping the last of the fleeing figures into the dirt. When the last man collapsed, only a hundred feet or so from Frank's position, the monsters paused. Under the rumble of his wagons, an eerie silence descended upon the battlefield.

He looked to either side. All of the fighters were staring at those enormous shapes. He shook his head and shouted down into his own wagon. "Get a bead on one o' them big galoots!"

A gunner shouted up, asking which one, and he rolled his eyes before yelling, "Any one!"

Buford was still moving among the men, pointing frantically toward the towering shapes. *Ole Bessie's* turret cranked around. When it fired, the lick of crimson flame reached almost twenty feet into the field. The blast took one of the tall shapes in its broad chest, and in a shower of sparks and deflected energy, tossed its shattered form back into the smoke.

That was enough to break the spell. Suddenly, the entire line erupted as the fighters unleashed their rage and fear on the distant targets. The Rolling Thunders to either side of *Ole Bessie* added their own cannons to the mix, and soon the line was on fire from end to end. Most of the giant shapes were down, the survivors moving forward with awkward, shambling steps.

Frank did not know what else he could do. He had his troops in good cover, they were firing in the right direction, and they seemed to be hitting their targets at least often enough to get them to think twice. Except they were not. The remaining brutes were firing again, and although their automatic fire was sleeting off the armor of the heavy wagons, they would eventually get lucky. Every few moments, one or two fighters from the line would leap into the air away from their cover, trailing arcs of blood.

More figures were emerging from the smoke, moving forward through the giant armored forms. These new attackers were about the height of a man, but far heavier than the average soldier. They slid forward in a loping run, moving much more smoothly than the larger enemies, long arms hitting the ground every few paces to propel them along.

The Gatling cannons of the three Rolling Thunders responded to the new threats. Streams of ruby destruction sprayed into the smoke, cutting the new targets down as they approached. But there were many of them, and the smoke made them nearly impossible to target. More and more were appearing, running past their towering partners and closing the distance on the secondary Confederate line.

Frank was struggling with an array of bad options when another wagon came rumbling up behind *Ole Bessie*. He looked back, relief washing over him as he saw Colonel Warley disembarking from the Ironhide. Quantrill, Captain Carney, and a few of the other commanders hopped down into the mud after the dapper colonel. They spread out through the line, stiffening resolve wherever they went. Warley nodded at Frank as he passed. The outlaw nodded back, choosing to take the signal as a sign of approval.

Carney had an enormous weapon attached to his arm, a frame of ornate metal and leather straps holding it in place. He braced himself visibly and leaned into the cannon, letting forth with a radiant burst of crimson fire that sleeted across the field and into the oncoming mob. Around him, heartened by the devastation the dark-skinned officer wrought, the soldiers renewed their own attacks, standing firm and firing into the enemy.

The redoubled power of the rebel fusillade staggered their attackers' charge. For a moment, Frank thought they had turned the tide. Then a ridiculously thick beam of coherent crimson force lashed out of the smoke, striking the Rolling Thunder to the right, full on its front armor. The vehicle flashed like a paper lantern. Illuminated from within, it disappeared in a shattering blast. Infantry all around were scythed down with screaming shrapnel which rattled off the nearby wagons. Frank grunted as he took a jagged bit of metal in the shoulder. With a gasp, he fell back into *Ole Bessie's* guts. He could tell at once it was only a superficial wound, but it was more than enough to prove to his mother's smartest son that he needed to keep his head down.

By the time Frank got to his vision slit, however, the battle had changed completely. Whatever was firing the heavy beams from the smoke had claimed another victim, this time one of the wagons behind the line. The low, running shapes were emerging from the fog. As he saw them clearly for the first time, all rational thought fled his mind.

In a moment he was catapulted back to that laboratory within Camp Lincoln. There was no doubt in his mind: he was looking at Reconstructed. They were only roughly shaped like men, having been surgically altered to be bigger and stronger. They were also faster. The hide of each creature was varicolored, a patchwork of black and white and tan, but mostly the unmistakable burnished gold of the Warrior Nation. Thick black stitching held the various pieces together. Their faces looked truly alien, as if animal skulls or artificial implants had been combined with their human features to provide enormous biting mouths, wild eyes, and other unnatural features. Hands ended in vicious claws, with the stitching to show where they had been added to the nightmarish whole. Each wore tattered rags, in some cases sewn right into the flesh itself, providing only the barest argument against indecency.

The Reconsctructed made short work of the men and women on the defensive line. Bodies were tossed into the sky, others struck down with sweeping claws slashing through flesh and bone. In at least two cases that Frank could see, rebel fighters were being eaten. The monsters were among them now, and he had no idea what he could do to help from inside the heavy wagon.

Frank tapped one of the gunners. They were all paralyzed, staring in disbelief through their own vision slits. "Keep firing on the big ones in back!" He shouted, and the gunner, shaken out of his daze, nodded. The men began to move with a purpose again, and soon the Rolling Thunder's main gun was lashing out into the smoke once more.

A shape, larger than the others, could now be seen approaching through the haze. It crawled forward on four legs, an enormous cannon on its heaving back. The thing stopped while Frank watched, the legs adjusting themselves as if seeking a comfortable position, and the barrel of its cannon began to swing toward *Ole Bessie*. Frank's eyes went wide as he realized what was about to happen. He fell down to the floor plate next to the gunners. "Take it down! Take it DOWN!" His voice was hoarse with sudden desperation. There was no way *Ole Bessie's* main gun turret was going to come around in time.

Chapter 16

Frank was disappointed as his life failed to flash before his eyes. A sudden blast from another Rolling Thunder struck the central body of the figure in the smoke, splitting armor and igniting crimson power cells. A titanic ball of red-tinged flame flashed out, catching some of the smaller shapes in its convulsive destruction and knocking them into the mud.

Frank pressed his head painfully against the leather pad of the vision slit, trying to slow his breathing. A corner of his brain wondered at fear that could cause a man to break out in a cold sweat within the oven of a heavy wagon. He glanced up at the hatch and decided that he needed to see more than he could from inside *Ole Bessie's* belly.

Working against the primordial fear rising in his throat, he emerged into a swirling confusion of bodies. The commanders had fallen back to their wagon, an elite group of veterans forming a ring of blaster pistols and rifles blazing to keep the nightmare creatures at bay. Captain Carney held the left flank alone, fans of ruby bolts churning up the ground before him. A group of swampers fought from the back of Nash's wagon as a violent melee swirled around it. The vehicle rocked alarmingly as the men on the back shifted from one side to another. Long gaff poles pushed away any beast-man Reconstructed that came too close.

Buford Nash and his son stood back to back on the flatbed, firing calm bursts into the churning mess. Frank felt the tightness in his chest ease to see the old mud-farmer still standing. Before he could turn away, a blurred form leapt from the confusion and sailed toward the pair. He followed the thing's flight in disbelief. It arced over the surrounding combat, unnatural claws slashing downward as it fell. landed on Buford's back, pushing him down into the truck and knocking his son into the surrounding chaos. Frank struggled to bring Sophie to bear, but as he watched, his eyes wide with horror, the thing dug repeatedly into Buford's back, tossing heavy gobbets of flesh in all directions. The old man had stopped struggling at once, but the monster kept tearing at him until one of the Tammany men, turning at the sound, blasted it in the head from point blank range.

Frank roared his anger, Sophie swinging over the armored top of the Rolling Thunder, looking for victims. This was fighting as Frank understood it, and his lip lifted in a cruel sneer as he sighted on his first target.

The thing's musculature was massive, like boulders shifting clumsily beneath the patchwork quilt of its skin. It was drenched in blood and its face, more human than many of the others, was twisted in a madness that would have been terrifying if Frank had not been staring through Sophie's sights. His eye lost its focus for a moment, a vision of John Younger flashing before him. Then he shook his head and leaned in to his shot.

The custom long rifle bucked against Frank's shoulder. The thing's enormous head folded in upon itself, showering the field behind with beads of red and gray. He was sweeping around for his next victim when a high-pitched roaring erupted from his right. Five Iron Horses, followed by countless more, swung in from the army's direction of advance.

Jesse was in the lead, hunched over the controls of his machine and pouring Gatling fire into the monsters all around. Lucinda rode beside him, followed by the Fords and Marcus Cunningham. One of the 'Horses screaming up behind them bucked as twin contrails of rocket exhaust lifted off and spiraled into one of the hulking shapes still holding back in the smoke. It was blown off its wide feet by the twinned detonations.

The Iron Horses roared closer to the attacking monsters. The beasts turned to meet them, many charging past more vulnerable fighters, as if eager for the new challenge. Jesse swerved to miss the tumbling corpse of one construct only to side-swipe the next. His 'Horse tumbled over the screaming beast, crushing it into the mud. Jesse was thrown high into the air.

The outlaw chief rolled to his feet, duster flaring wide and metal hands full of gun. He sent a steady stream of crimson bolts into the approaching monsters. Soon, however, the Iron Horses were surrounded. Robert Ford abandoned his steed to stand beside Jesse, massive hand cannon in one hand and his ridiculously long knife in the other. The rest of them were struggling to join the pair, and the smoke soon swirled up and around the mess, blotting it from view.

Frank realized what was happening as Jesse disappeared behind the scudding curtain. They had been after his brother all along.

Frank dropped back into his wagon and started to shout before he hit bottom. "Go, go, go! Straight at my brother!"

The machine was moving before Frank stopped shouting. As he rose again into the cold air, he saw that the other Rolling Thunder was following. A surge of fighters was also breaking in that direction, released from the pressure of the assault when the flesh-constructs had turned to attack Jesse's group.

Bessie's Gatling guns chattered away, scattering bolts up and down the mob that surged over Jesse's position. Beasts were blown into the dirt all around. None of them showed the slightest interest in self-preservation. Instead, they tore at each other to get at their target; they were all trying to kill his brother.

Sophie barked, blasting one after another, shattering skulls and blowing holes in torsos. There was no need to aim, the press was so tight. Even firing from the pitching deck of the wagon, every shot killed at least one target. As they pulled up, however, it looked like Jesse had everything under control.

The outlaw chief was standing, legs wide, in the center of a circle of blasted, malformed bodies. His Hyper-velocity pistols smoked in his metal hands. Behind him, Robert Ford had taken a knee in exhaustion, but they were both alive. A little further away were the three tumbled 'Horses of his other companions.

Frank scrambled out of the wagon and leapt down into the mud, but as he scanned the area to make sure everyone was okay, he came up short. There were only four figures standing there. Marcus, his hammer clenched cross-wise and dripping black blood, was casting around as if looking for someone. Charlie Ford, crouched beside the wreckage of his vehicle and holding a shotgun in both hands, was also frantically looking all around.

There was no sign of Lucinda.

*****

"She's gone, Jesse." Frank crouched down beside his brother, wrists resting on his knees. "We've combed every inch of the field. She's not there. That has to be good news, right?"

Jesse's back rested against the cold steel of his brother's wagon. He shook his head weakly. "Not many of those things ran, Frank. They weren't thinkin' like that. They didn't take no prisoners."

Frank stood up and looked out over the field. "I don't know, Jesse. I'm just sayin' she ain't here. There's bodies everywhere, but hers ain't one of 'em."

Jesse stared back down at the churned mud between his boots. "I don't get it, Frank. What the hell *were* those things? What did they want?"

"They wanted you, Jesse." The new voice brought them both around. It was Quantrill, natural arm in a sling and resting on a splintered length of stick instead of his fancy cane. "As for *what* they were? I don't think any of us know."

"The ones out in the field were metal, like the robot marshals, only bigger." Frank gestured out across the churned mud with one hand. The smoke from the original clash still hung in the air as a haze that burned the eyes and caught in the throat. Salvage parties were moving within the murk, gathering around each downed metal brute. There were not many of them, but they had been more than enough to cover for the approach of the true nightmares.

The man-beast constructs had, indeed, been Reconstructed. They had been living, breathing creations sewn together from the parts of countless men and beasts, with metal enhancements to add to their horror. They had required no RJ-1027 to function. There was no way, Jesse knew, that the drastic surgeries and modifications that the poor souls had undergone would have been possible without the foul Devil's Blood somewhere in the mix. There had been no engines, batteries, or other powered elements in their design; just the twisted energy of life. Doctor Tumblety's perverse creations, rather than Carpathian's.

Jesse pushed himself up and away from the Rolling Thunder and looked at Quantrill. "Why'd they want me? Why'm I so important?"

Quantrill's smile was cutting. "Didn't you want to be? Isn't that what all this is about?" He gestured with his makeshift cane at the enormous force of rebels and militia fighters that surrounded them.

Jesse frowned, his eyes hard. "I just want to kick the Union where they'll feel it for the next hun'erd years, colonel. I ain't got nothin' in my head past that." He turned and moved off into the field.

Robert Ford was crouched down by his brother, disconsolate beside his overturned 'Horse. Runnels of clean, pink flesh had been carved in the dirt and grime that caked Charlie's face. He had been crying.

"What the hell's his problem?" Jesse moved up, his frustration, grief, and guilt settling on a target at last.

Robert stood up, trying to smile as he stepped in front of his brother. "He's worked up over Loveless, is all." Robert's words were quick and thin. "Blamin' himself, as usual."

Jesse sidestepped him and stared down at Charlie. The man refused to meet his eyes. "What's your beef, Ford?" Charlie cringed at his name. He looked off over the blasted field, not seeing anything. "Told you I wasn't brave."

"What the hell's he talkin' about?" Jesse looked around. Marcus was nearby, elbow-deep in the guts of his own 'Horse. Frank and Quantrill, who had followed Jesse out into the field, shook their heads. Robert chewed on his lower lip but said nothing. Jesse looked down at Charlie again. "What the hell are you talkin' about, Charlie?"

The man was shaking. He looked away. "When they came at us, I froze." His head darted up with the speed of a rabbit, staring at Robert, then Marcus, then the other men. "You saw 'em! They were straight out of a nightmare! I froze!"

Jesse reached down with one metal hand and cupped Charlie's jaw, forcing him to look up. When their eyes met, Jesse leaned in and whispered. "What is it yer sayin', Ford?"

Charlie collapsed in on himself, sobbing. "She was watchin' my back, Jesse! I froze, and Lucy was watchin' my back. I din't see what took her, but all of a sudden-like, she was just gone!"

Jesse stared down, dumbfounded. Then, faster than any of the men watching could see, he hauled off and cracked Ford across the face with the back of his metal hand. Charlie was thrown into the mud. The outlaw chief followed almost as fast, his duster billowing out behind him, and came to rest crouching down beside the sobbing man. Jesse leaned in close and whispered into the dirt-filled ear.

"You are now livin' on borrowed time, Ford." Each word was ground out between gnashing teeth. "There's gonna come a day when I'm feelin' tetchy, and I'm gonna end you. 'Till that day comes, you man up, you little worm, and you walk tall, or that day'll come all the quicker." He stood, spitting into the mud beside Charlie's head. "Now you know. If you're gonna be scared o' somethin' on this earth, Charlie Ford, you be scared o' me."

Jesse shook his head and stalked off, leaving the Fords behind to deal with their own mess. Quantrill followed after as quickly as his new cane would allow. Frank took a couple quick steps to catch up. "Jesse, we got a lot we gotta consider, an' not a lot o' time for considerin'."

Jesse stopped and turned around. "What, Frank? What is there to consider?"

"You got an army you have to deal with, James. This is no time for you to retreat into that brooding head of yours." Quantrill's face was stern.

Jesse just looked at him. "Now what the hell are YOU talkin' about?"

"The joint commanders were in the thick of this, Jesse." Quantrill gestured over his wounded shoulder. "There have been casualties at the very top of the chain. They want to talk to you."

Jesse looked to Frank, who shrugged. The outlaw chief cursed under his breath, kicking at an offending clod of dirt. His head came back up and he looked around them. "Where the Youngers at, Frank? I ain't seen 'em since before this started."

Frank looked awkward, his eyes shifting to the distant trees off to the east. "They were on the right flank as we marched, Jesse. Them and the California Rangers. I ain't seen any of them, neither."

Jesse shook his head again, with even more conviction. "Well, who'd we lose, colonel?"

Quantrill turned and gestured for him to follow. "Warley's down. He might be okay, but he's done for the season. Carney's okay, but you know we lost Buford." His eyes would not meet Jesse's as he muttered. "And Tinker Thane's in a bad way. Several of the other commanders from out east are goners. Thane, though, he's holdin' on. Wants to talk to you, he said."

Jesse snorted and started to move toward the battered command Ironhide. A makeshift infirmary had been established in the bed of the wagon, with several of the commanders lying on low pallets. Warley was laid out toward the rear. Carney, standing nearby, nodded to the outlaw chief as he passed. Jesse started as he recognized the figure standing over the colonel: Marie Laveau. The woman looked at Jesse with the regal bearing he had come to expect and nodded a fraction of an inch in recognition.

Jesse tipped his hat to her. "Ma'am, I didn't know you were with us."

"Thank God Almighty she came, Jesse." Warley's voice was soft. Jesse saw that a bandage covered most of his chest. "None of these old army sawbones would have been able to drag me back, that's for sure."

The woman's full lips curved in a slight smile. "I have enough gad palè *for now, colonel. No need for more."*

He smiled wanly and then turned back to Jesse. The outlaw had to lean in close to hear his words. "Jesse, you have to lead the Army of New Orleans, now. And you listen to Captain Carney. He won't steer you wrong." Jesse started to protest, but a sharp shake of the colonel's head stopped him. "The men know you. Black and white, you brought many of them together. We lost too many in this foolish skirmish. The army has to go on, and you have to lead them."

Jesse stood up, looking to Frank with raised eyebrows. Frank gave a grave nod. "He's right, Jesse. We come this far. Ain't nothin' that brought us out in the first place been changed by what happened here today."

Jesse looked between his brother and the wounded colonel. "But, I'm not a—"

"It's worse than that." The voice that spoke now came from farther down the wagon bed. Jesse searched the wounded until he found the man speaking. His face was swathed in bandages black with blood. One hand was gone at the wrist, and more bandages covered him from the waist to the neck. A garden of red blossoms spread across the snowy white. Jesse had to look hard before he realized it was Tinker Thane leaking out his last moments on the dirty pallet. The outlaw's lip curled just a little.

"What d'you mean, worse?" Jesse spat the words across the wagon's bed.

It was impossible to tell beneath the bandages, but it sounded as if Thane was smiling. "Too many of us are gone, James . . . Too many of the regional commanders are dead, or dying, or too wounded to continue . . . You're the man with the vision, James. You're the man who brought all this together . . . You have to finish it."

Jesse shook his head. "No way, Thane. Did they tell you how hard we got hit? We lost nearly a quarter of our fighters to those things. And more'n that went runnin' so fast, they ain't gonna stop 'till they hit the Gulf."

Warley grabbed Jesse's metal arm. The feedback pads told him the wounded man was applying considerable pressure. "Jesse, everything that drove us this far is still true. The Union can't keep that fort where it is. And whatever they built it to hold? If we can take that, then the South may yet have a role to play in the future of this continent."

Jesse looked down at the man in pity. "Colonel, I'm right touched you think I can do this, but—"

"It's not a question of *can*, James." Thane spat from where he lay. "It's a question of *must* . . . You can't leave this where it stands or you'll rob the Confederacy of the . . . last reserves of bravery it possesses. This army is scared now . . . You don't walk away from a battering like this without scars that last a lifetime."

"We won, din't we?" Jesse's voice was sour as he spoke the words. His mouth worked with an intense desire to spit.

Warley stretched his pale, thin lips into a smile. "A win like this is almost worse than a drubbing, Jesse. You know that."

"He knows." Quantrill muttered.

Jesse stood where he was, his head tilted back and his eyes focused on the scudding clouds overhead. He looked down at his boots, his eyes haunted. "This ain't what I wanted."

Thane's voice rose again, sharp as one of Bob Younger's knives. "You gotta go through this valley before you . . . get what you want."

Jesse's head snapped up, his eyes now hard again. He jumped up onto the bed of the wagon and stalked across the wounded men until he was crouching down beside Thane. A single eye watched him from within the entombing bandages. The eye was very calm.

"I'll do it." Jesse muttered, then he whispered. "But there's something I want you to know, Thane. I walked the line of casualties after the battle. More than half the boys lying there? They were darker than you 'n me. The colored folks held, Thane. And the rest of the boys know it. You take that down with you into Hell when you go."

The wounded man's head slid back and forth, his chest heaving. Jesse thought for a moment he was coughing out his last, but then realized that Thane was convulsing in laughter.

"What's so funny, you squirrelly bastard?" Jesse spat.

"You really think that matters to us, James?" The man's eye was cruel. While Jesse watched, the blood from a broken vessel invaded the yellowed white, turning the orb a gruesome burgundy. "You're all animals, you fool. The death of any of you makes this world a better place." The chest convulsed again.

"You filthy, fen-sucking maggot," Jesse reached down and grabbed the man by his stained lapels. As he stared down into the man's eye, however, he felt as if his mind suddenly opened up. Light crashed in around him. An impression of vast distances, enormous spaces, and immense stretches of time washed over him. He saw a blur of faces snap by; some he knew, most he had never seen before. He recognized Ty, the young kid from Kansas City, among them. Then he saw Allen Henderson's smiling face, clear as day, and he fell back against the wagon's sidewall.

"Why you—" Jesse did not know what he had just witnessed, but the feeling of heavy evil it had left in his mind rattled him. His metal hand fell to his holster, pulling at a pistol of its own volition. Even as one orderly tried to stop him, another leaned quickly over Thane's quivering body. The shaking stopped, the tension eased from the limbs, and Jesse did not need to be told that the commander had escaped his wrath for good.

*****

Jesse stood with his brother near the wreckage of Lucy's 'Horse. The earth was a churned, muddy mess, dark with blood and swarming with flies.

"What the hell we doin' here, Frank?" Jesse's voice was pleading. He stood in the mud, his feet wide and his mechanical thumbs hooked behind his gun belt. He stared down at his boots, head shaking back and forth. "How the hell'd we get so far from home?"

Frank watched his brother, not sure how to help. "We're fightin' the battles neither of us wanted to give up on all those years ago, Jesse. We're gonna hand the Union their heads with this, an' the old Confederacy, she's gonna come back stronger than before because of it. That's gotta mean somethin'."

Jesse nodded and then looked up at his brother from beneath the broad brim of his hat. "Don't you miss bein' back in the territories, takin' down banks and holdin' up trains? Back where Billy was the closest thing to competition we had to worry about?"

Frank smiled. "Part o' me does, sure. I was always happier closer to home. But you, you've always been driven faster, farther, an' I just got in the habit o' followin' you."

Jesse nodded again, back to staring at his boots. "There's somethin' goin' on here that don't even start to make sense, Frank. Thane – there was somethin' in him. Somethin' evil."

Frank snorted. "You hated that polecat the moment you first laid eyes on him. There don't need to be no deeper thinkin' on it than that."

Jesse shook his head. "It wasn't just what he said. When I looked into his eye there at the end, it was like I was seein' for the first time." He put one metal hand to his head. "I can't really put words to it, Frank, but it was mighty queer." He looked up from beneath his hat brim. "And it felt . . . heavy . . . somehow."

Frank watched his brother and then shook his head. "I don't know from heavy, Jesse. An' I don't know from evil. Seems to me, every man or woman makes their own way in the world, and those that get jealous, they get to shoutin' words like 'evil'. All I know is what we got here an' now. An' what we got here an' now is a machine you helped to build, runnin' headlong into disaster without no one sittin' at the controls."

Jesse gave him a sour look and turned away. For a long moment there was only silence and then he muttered, softly. "She's gone, Frank."

Frank looked at his brother with concern in his eyes. There was no comfort he could offer. "The Fords have gone over every body, Jesse. She ain't here."

Jesse barked a bitter laugh. "So she got taken by those things? That's supposed to make me feel better? You remember that cracked Union doctor even better than I do, Frank. Her bein' taken ain't a better scenario."

Frank sighed, looking off at the surrounding fields. The dead had been buried in mass graves, all except the most prominent men and women who had fallen. Buford Nash, for instance, got his own plot. Frank's chest tightened at the thought. Small bonfires smoldered some ways away where other fighters had piled up the abominations and set them ablaze. The destroyed wagons had been scoured for anything that might be salvaged and now stood empty like stripped carcasses.

"Jesse, she's a tough woman. If anyone'd be okay, it'll be her." He searched for anything else he could say. His brother's practical nature made such comfort hard to find.

"They'd have taken her for a reason. And that reason'll keep her alive. She'll find a way to escape, and she'll be back."

His breath gusted again, this time even harder. "Thing is, little brother, that it don't even matter."

Jesse gave his brother a sharp look, and Frank forced himself to meet the glare with a hard face of his own. "You gotta lead this circus north, and you gotta take that fort, and it wouldn't matter if Lucy was dead in front of you or draped all over you, kissin' yer ugly mug. You gotta lead."

Jesse's shoulders slumped. He looked one last time at the devastation around them and then turned away with a nod.

"Well, then, best start leadin'." They walked back toward the band of suspicious commanders together. Behind them, the shattered wreckage of Lucy's Iron Horse leaked smoke into a grey, leaden sky.

Chapter 17

They said nothing, staring at her in a silence that stretched far beyond mere social discomfort. She sat, spine straight, with hands resting lightly on her thighs. The fabric of the utilitarian dress they had provided to replace her worn riding gear was rough beneath her hands. The desire to avert her eyes, to look down at the dusty floor or at the scattered papers on the table before her, was nearly overwhelming. It took every trick she had ever learned to keep those eyes steady, to keep her hands firm. The only visible sign of discomfort, whether fear, frustration, or anger, was a slight tightening of her jaw. Unfortunately, the men staring at her were among the few in the world that she could not fool.

"And they're coming here." Robert Pinkerton sat loosely in front of her. His legs were crossed, his hands clasped in his lap, and his eyes mild. But she knew him. He had been her mentor for the entirety of her career. He was angry, suspicious, and very, very tired. She knew, no matter how relaxed and calm he seemed, her freedom, and perhaps her very life, hung in the balance.

"They are." She kept her face cool, but beneath the facade her soul was boiling. Slipping away in the middle of a battle was not her way, and a part of her could still not believe she had left that poor boy, Charlie Ford, quailing beside his Iron Horse. She thought she had timed her departure well, while there was still enough chaos to hide her leaving, but late enough that the rebels' victory was a foregone conclusion. Still, leaving a fight before it was finished – she could not remember ever having done that.

Henry Courtright stood behind Pinkerton, one elbow resting against the sill of a long window. His face was cold and empty as he stared at her and then turned slightly to gaze out. She had been unable to gauge his position on her return since she arrived the night before. She did not know if the anger she sensed radiating from his enigmatic mask was real or if it was in her imagination. She did know that if she had lost his trust, there was no hope of her leaving this fortress alive.

"I'm not sure why we're taking care of this up here, and not down in a dungeon somewhere." Levenson Wade was a young agent. He had joined the Pinkerton Secret Service after she had left Washington for her first assignment in the western territories. She had heard of his recent exploits, of course. He was one of the most successful agents Pinkerton had put into the field in recent years. He also had a ruthless reputation. From his voice, she knew he was serious.

Pinkerton's mouth quirked into a slight smile and he looked down, shaking his head. "Well, Lev, that'd be great if this pile of rock even *had* a dungeon."

Henry grunted and spat on the floor. "This is crazy. If she was a traitor, why'd she come back?"

Wade's lip curled in contempt and he shifted his eyes to the other agent. "If she wasn't a traitor, why'd it take this long?"

Pinkerton stood up with a huff and swept his hands apart in a separating gesture. "Gentleman, if Agent Loveless had not stayed with James and his mob of ruffians for as long as she did, we would still be guessing at his true target. The military would be forced to spread its assets all across the border. When they struck, we would be in a much weaker position. Let's not forget that."

Wade snorted and looked at his chief in disbelief. "I think you're not giving any of us much credit if you honestly think there was a doubt in anyone's mind that they were heading straight here, sir."

Courtright took a step toward the other agent and only stopped when Pinkerton's rigid hand shifted to point a warning at him. Her old partner nodded to the chief, but then glared back at Wade. "When you can give me one good reason why she would have come back here, if she's a traitor, I'll start to listen."

"One reason?" Wade did not move, but his body was stiff, ready for a fight. "Maybe she's going to open the gates in the heat of battle. Maybe she's going to note our dispositions within the walls and then scamper off to her boyfriend." His eyes flicked to Pinkerton and then back to Courtright. "Maybe she's here to assassinate some of our top-level commanders, decapitate our forces, and then open the gates."

"You Copperhead bastard—" Henry started toward Wade despite Pinkerton's outstretched arms. The commander jumped in front of him, grabbing the lapels of his coat to get his attention.

"Courtright, stand down!" Pinkerton was shouting, flecks of spit striking the agent in the face. "This gets us nowhere, and only helps that flea-ridden mob riding hell-bent for leather right at us!" He pushed the younger man back. Courtright nodded curtly, his face tight.

"Now, Wade, you don't know Agent Loveless, and your head's in the right place." He looked over his shoulder at Lucy, still sitting in her chair. "But you've gotta stand down too. I have trusted her, implicitly. If she says Jesse James is headed this way, then we damn well better get ready to greet him."

Lucinda felt a distant rush of heat behind her cheeks. It was almost as if she were watching the humiliation of a stranger as her mentor defended the indefensible.

Wade looked at her for a moment, then back up at the chief, then across to where Henry was glaring at him. He nodded, but there was still heat in his eyes. "Okay, you're right. I don't know Agent Loveless. If you trust her, sir, I'll give her the benefit of the doubt."

Pinkerton watched him for a moment, looking for any sign of dissent or insincerity. There was none, but then, these were the best liars the country had ever produced. He shrugged and nodded.

"Alright, then. We move forward, and we bring this information to Colonel Campbell and his merry band of shovel pushers." He held up one warning finger. "And we do not air our dirty laundry in public. Agency problems are handled entirely within the Agency, and this one's been dealt with. Is that clear?"

Pinkerton looked to each of his agents in turn, not moving to the next until each had nodded in assent. When they had all agreed, he nodded himself and gestured toward the low, narrow door.

"Now, shall we go see the colonel and let him know his day is about to get worse?" The old agent's face was sour.

"Sir, if you don't mind, I'd like to bring Agent Loveless up to speed on our situation here." Henry did not look at her as he spoke.

Pinkerton looked from Henry to Lucinda and back again, then nodded, his face blank. "Of course. Wade?"

Wade was staring at her as he moved to the door. He went through with only a slight hesitation. The chief nodded once more and then closed the door softly behind him.

Henry stood by the window for a few moments, looking out over the scoured plain. When he spoke, he did not turn around. "So, you decided to come back after all."

Lucinda did not know what to make of the flat voice, the rigid back. She looked down at her hands, clasped on the table before her. Her mind began to scan the papers there out of habit. They were technical drawings, and the surest proof, if she had needed any, that Pinkerton had trusted her all along. She wondered what Wade would have made of it, if he had noticed them laying there.

She forced herself to look back up and was surprised to see that Henry had turned back to face her. His expression was bland, and she was frustrated, once again, that she could read nothing there.

"I was always coming back, Henry." She thought she did a pretty good job of keeping her voice level.

He nodded, sighed, and slouched into a chair opposite her. "Yeah, I know. I just wish you hadn't been so dramatic about it, is all."

His trust in her should have been reassuring, but instead it just added weight to her guilt. "I left them as soon as I could sneak away without suspicion."

He smiled, but it was a tired, thin expression. "Well, that won't matter much if you run into him at the little party we'll be having here shortly. Or at any time in the future, either, I guess." He sat back, tilting his head to stare unseeing at the ceiling. "But I've got a choice here, and I'd rather live in a world where I still trust you, no matter how loony you're acting, than in a world where you're every bit as guilty of treason as you sometimes appear."

She stared at him for a long moment, then shook her head and looked back down at the papers. "What's all this, now?"

Henry looked back down and pulled a paper toward him. He glanced at it for a moment and then flipped it back onto the pile. "The inventory and specifications on the cargo sent back from Fort Frederick. Tesla and –" He shot a look at her deepening frown. "Well, you know."

Lucinda had tried not to think of Tumblety and his madness since she had escaped with Jesse from Camp Lincoln. Whenever she did, it made reconciling her loyalty to the Union that much harder. She shook her head and lifted up a sheet of flimsy paper.

A heavy, ancient-looking glove was sketched there. It seemed to be attached to an ungainly-looking pack by cords and wires, paragraphs of cramped writing filling most of the blank space.

"What's this?" She asked as she scanned the writing.

Henry craned his neck to look at the paper and then sniffed. "That's Tesla's latest. He claims it can open a hole in the fabric of the world or some-such nonsense." His voice was flat, and he shook his head. "It's supposed to be able to transport objects through thin air. Might prove very useful in a battle, or even in our line of work, if it operates as he claims." He shrugged. "I haven't heard anyone mention it, so I doubt it does. I know it didn't go south with his heavy automatons and the other – things." He trailed off.

Lucinda continued to work through the close writing.

"Well, shall we head up?" Henry stood, adjusting his heavy pistol. "I thought you could use a moment to settle down. We wouldn't want you to be prying the young Master Wade's head off in front of the brass, now."

She marshaled a smile she did not feel, let the paper drop to the table, and stood. "I would have waited until they were looking elsewhere."

Together they left the room and made their way up toward the battlements.

*****

Jesse moved forward on his belly, his elbows and knees driving him through the cold mud. The difference in sensation, as the mud soaked through his trousers and registered against the feedback pads of his arms, was enough to trigger one of those rare moments when his world seemed to spin, as if in a dream. The weight of his metal limbs bore more heavily upon him. He shook the sensation off and pushed himself slowly to the crest of the hill.

On either side, Frank and Cole Younger scrambled through the undergrowth, coming up even with him as he stopped. Jesse pulled his monocular from its pouch on his belt. He flipped a switch and the crimson telltales of RJ power cells began to glow. The fading stain of sunset was little more than a memory. He would need the tricks of the new tech to see his target.

Cole was holding a similar device to his face, his grin peeking out from beneath its boxy structure. Frank sighted down Sophie's length, her enormous scope providing even more amplification, if not quite as much of the light-enhancement as the monoculars.

"Anything?" Frank muttered to his brother as he settled the long gun into a firing crouch.

Jesse shook his head. "Nah. See some sentries along the top of the wall, maybe. And looks like some gun emplacements. Heavy stuff." He looked over at his brother. "But nothin' that'd make me think they know we're comin'."

"They'd have to be pretty damned dumb not to know we're out here somewhere." Cole's voice was light, his grin unfazed. Even though the Youngers had been on the far flank during the attack, away from the action, he had seemed like his old self since the battle. For some reason, though, Jesse was still uncomfortable around Bob and Jim. And he was not entirely sure he could trust any of them. Sadly, he still trusted them more than he trusted the rusty old pie-eaters that he was serving with.

Jesse nodded, despite his misgivings. "Yeah, we're not goin' to be surprisin' anyone, and it's best we not fool ourselves into thinkin' we can."

Frank's head rose up from behind his scope. "There's some serious firepower up there, brother." He shrugged his shoulder toward the fort brooding on the horizon. "And no cover for those heavy wagons. My poor *Ole Besse*'ll be nothin' but target practice for those blue-bellies, we come straight at 'em."

Jesse looked again through his monocular. The image was hazy and gritty, as if seen through a piece of heavy red burlap. Figures skulked along the ramparts of the double walls, manning watch posts and weapon stations. Each time they swept their own monoculars in his direction, he felt a crawling between his shoulder blades, despite knowing that the tech could never differentiate three prone men among all the foliage of the forest's edge.

He could identify several heavy cannon emplacements along the wall, the massive barrels thrusting out into the night. At one corner, a guard tower rose away from the rest of the squat structure. Figures huddled in the compartment on top, peering from behind large Gatling cannons that could tear a squadron of 'Horses to shreds. Far below, the gate was a uniform cold gray, metal or stone. It was massive.

Jesse shook his head and then gestured for the others to follow him. He shrugged his way backward, down the back slope of the hill. When they had cleared the crest, they stood and moved back into the tall trees. Jim and Bob Younger came forward to meet them, with Marcus and the Ford brothers not far behind. Farther back in the woods, their faces hidden by the shadows of their caps and hats, stood the other commanders of the allied Confederate army. Postures stiff, these were the men who had relinquished, some under protest, command of their own units to this outlaw from the western territories.

Jesse nodded a quick greeting to his friends and allies while raising a metal hand to the others, holding up one finger to forestall any questions. He turned to address Frank and Cole as they came out of the trees.

"So, what d'you boys think? Ain't much tougher than some o' the banks we taken down over the years." His grin was wide, and the only people in the world who would have recognized it as forced, were the men he was speaking with at that moment.

Cole grunted, his own grin still firmly in place. "Even if they're crammed in there cheek-to-jowl, we got 'em outnumbered. An' you KNOW they ain't packed in there nearly so tight."

Frank watched Jesse and Cole, then shook his head. "We ain't got nothin' near so big as the heavies they're packin' on top of those walls, Jesse. Even the Rolling Thunders ain't close."

Jesse nodded again, acknowledging the point. "Yeah, I know. How many hits you think a Thunder could take from somethin' that big, afore it's knocked to flinders?"

Frank shrugged, looking off into the dark woods as he tried to imagine *Bessie* getting knocked about by the enormous weapons. "Not more'n two or three hits, I'm thinkin'."

Jesse rubbed his jaw with one metal hand, the bristles of his unshaven cheeks rough against the feedback pads. "An' how many times you reckon they can fire, afore a Thunder would reach the wall, startin' far enough, they can't hit us?"

Bob Younger barked a harsh laugh, shaking his head at Jesse. "That's a fort, you corn cracker. They got as much power as they want. They'll be blastin' us the minute they see us, an' they won't stop 'till they run outta targets."

His brother Jim nodded while grimacing slightly at the insult. "There ain't nowhere to hide up there. We go in, we go in with all the world seein' us swingin'."

Jesse lowered his hand and hooked his thumbs behind his belt. "Yeah, there's that." He looked around at the forest, only starting to dampen from the winter rains. When the idea struck, he felt his eyes light up. He knew Frank had noticed when his older brother's face tightened in suspicion.

"What?" Frank snapped, distrust heavy in his voice.

Jesse's grin widened, not forced at all now, and he slapped his brother on the back as he moved past him toward the waiting Confederate commanders.   "Come on, Frank. We gotta talk to these boys who keep callin' me 'mister.'"

"You like that too much, Jesse." Cole's tone was light, but his gaze was flat. The outlaw chief's steps faltered slightly as their eyes met. The force of Jesse's grin did not waver, and he nodded to Cole as if nothing had passed between them.

"Gentlemen," Jesse's voice was robust as he moved into the center of the ring of officers and commanders. "I'm going to need you to divide your forces into three equal groups. My riders will assemble up front, forming a spearhead. Once we have everyone reshuffled and we've loaded the deck, our real work begins." He rubbed his mechanical hands together in a gesture of unmistakable excitement.

"It's goin' to be a long, hot night!" His grin, even in the dark, was bright enough for all of the men around him to see.

*****

They stood atop the wall above the massive gate, looking out over the blasted, rolling plains that surrounded Fort Knox. For nearly a mile in any direction, there was nothing but tangles of trampled grass, torn down trees, and rutted mud. Colonel Campbell panned his monocular along the distant horizon, unable to distinguish any threats among the tangled life-aura of the far-off forest. Major Dalton stood nearby, his attention evenly divided between his commander and the strange contingent of Washington agents conversing nearby.

Dalton moved up beside the commander's adjutant, Blogdett, and leaned in close. "William, what do you make of the tall one in the old hat?"

William Blogdett lowered his massive sniper rifle. He had made a point of keeping in practice ever since leaving the marksmen during the war, and was looking forward to putting the old girl back into action. He glanced over his shoulder at the agents. "The one who always keeps to the shadows? The one with the hood under his topper?" The old sniper shrugged. "They're agents from the president, sir. I don't make anything of them at all. Way above my pay-grade." The man turned back to the parapet and braced his long rifle against the stone surface of one raised merlon. "I'll tell you what, though, sir. I'm thinkin' it's a bad night comin' our way."

Dalton nodded, shifting his eyes slowly from the agents to the blackness out beyond the wall.

"What are the two of you muttering about?" Campbell's voice shook slightly, and Dalton knew he was holding himself together more through fear of losing face before the men from Washington than through any form of natural courage. As the fort had taken shape on its low hill, Campbell had really started to come into his own, and the soldiers had responded.

When the UR-10s had been sent back to Washington, however, things started to get strange again. And then, when the special deliveries began, and first the nightmare strike force from Fort Frederick had arrived, and then the UR-30 Enforcers with their secret cargo, the old, awkward Campbell had started to show through. The sense of impending attack, coupled with the arrival of the mysterious agents, had nearly undone him.

"Just our guests, sir." Dalton jerked his head back at the small group huddled around the tall stranger. "Since they sent those abominations of Tumblety's and Tesla's down south, and the Enforcers disappeared into the vaults, they're the only decent topic of conversation we've got left."

A shiver gripped the colonel and Dalton cursed himself. His superior had come a long way, but the man was still a bundle of nerves where any of the current intrigue was concerned.

"Colonel, if I might have a word?" Agent Pinkerton, the director of the president's Secret Service, beckoned Campbell to him. "I believe your lookouts should be seeing some movement on the road soon."

Colonel Campbell gave a quick start and turned a little faster than Dalton would have liked. "Yes?"

The old agent jerked a thumb up at the main tower. "Your boys up there should see two men approaching. I need you to let them come forward."

Major Dalton watched conflicting reactions twist his commander's face before resignation barely won out over fear and indignation. He nodded. "Just two?" Dalton was proud of the hint of sarcasm, anyway.

Pinkerton nodded, resting his hands upon the stone of the battlement. "Yes. We're bringing in a couple of contractors."

A bubble of resentment rose in Dalton's throat. "Contractors?" He had not spoken more than a few words to any of the agents, but he could not stop himself.

The old man nodded. "Yes. They've worked with us in the past. I was hoping they would arrive earlier, to be more fully-integrated into your defenses, but I only got word this evening that they were near. Thankfully, before the Rebs attack, but too late to get the best use out of them, I'm afraid."

As if the mention of the two men had conjured them out of the night, a sentry far above called out. Dalton looked up to see the soldier point out onto the plain. All along the battlements, monoculars were raised. Dalton quickly jerked his up as well.

Two men approached the fortress, walking calmly as if without a care in the world. One bore an enormous sniper rifle casually slung over his shoulder. The shadows beneath his hat brim were impenetrable, even to the advanced tech of the monocular. There was something subtly but fundamentally wrong with the figure that walked beside the first. The arms were too long, jointed in the wrong places and in the wrong directions. But as Dalton watched, he saw that the man's arms were perfectly proportioned. He bore two massive blades affixed to his forearms, their serrated edges arcing out past his clenched fists.

A cold sweat curled down Dalton's spine. He recognized those weapons. And if the killer with the blades was who he appeared to be, then the sniper strolling along beside him could only be one man.

"Not Tanner and the Wraith!" The major muttered the words under his breath, but the colonel heard him. His head snapped around at the note of disbelief.

"You know these gentlemen, major?" Campbell's voice was tense.

Dalton almost laughed, but he knew it would come out as a sick croak, so held it in. "Mercenaries, of no good reputation. Certainly not gentlemen, sir."

The colonel turned to the older agent. "You vouch for these men, sir? My second in command seems to have some reservations."

"He ain't the only one." William Blodgett nodded toward the two figures now emerging from the darkness, visible to the naked eye. "The Wraith, he's got a mean name even amongst sharpshooters."

"I will admit to a growing alarm, sir." The colonel's voice was firm, but Dalton could hear the ever-present shaking just beneath the surface. "It appears these two contractors of yours are known to my men, and—"

"You will allow them into the fortress, colonel." The tall man, his face still shrouded in darkness, said in a voice higher-pitched than Campbell would have expected. "We will see that they behave."

Colonel Campbell stared at the gaunt, mysterious figure. Something moved deep in his eyes before he gave a slight, jerky nod. He muttered an order that the gate be opened and watched as the group of Washington men, each nodding their thanks, moved past him and through a door on the inner wall.

"This just got uglier." Blodgett's voice was bleak as he turned to watch Tanner and The Wraith disappear beneath the wall, the clanking of the opening gate echoing into the night.

*****

The construction of Fort Knox was far less conventional within than without. The fort consisted of a squat main building with a second, slightly smaller structure above, and presented only these two-leveled walls to the outside world. The parapet, rising thick and crenelated before the fighting platforms of each level, gave the fortress the appearance of an ancient castle, its tall outer wall guarding a keep within.

However, the true keep of Fort Knox was not the second-story defenses, but an independent structure built within the fortress itself. The main gate opened out into a large open chamber featuring several defensible redoubts that led, like a maze, inward toward the center. A low stone keep crouched there, dwarfed by the massive, cathedral-like space around it. Another heavy gate, iron studded with RJ-1027-enriched bolts that glowed a sullen red, was sunk into the smooth surface of the keep; the entrance to the vaults below.

Lucinda rested against the keep, the cold stone leaching the warmth of her body through her clothing and the heavy cloak draped over her shoulders. Henry was with the others on the main wall, surveying the defenses and making whatever contingency plans they deemed necessary. They had left her here, guarding the entrance to the keep like a common soldier. At least Pinkerton had had the decency to look embarrassed when he had given her the orders.

The design of the entire fortress confused her. Despite the formidable appearance of Fort Knox from the outside, the high inner walls contained even more fighting positions, directed into the massive chamber at the heart of the structure. Perhaps the intention of the architect was for the defenders to hold the outer wall as long as possible, and then to fall back to the redoubts, and rain fire down upon the attackers as they fought their way through the main gate. The tall walls of the central chamber were riddled with firing ports and fighting positions that would serve that purpose well. Anyone who had forced their way through the main gate was in for a very hot time.

She knew her understanding of defensive architecture was rudimentary at best, but she could not shake the feeling that the entire building seemed more like a trap than a fortress. Lure someone here, allow them to break through the main gates, and then destroy them, inside, in detail. Having watched the garrison prepare, she had seen no sign that this was their plan. They meant to conduct a standard defensive action, with no intention of allowing Jesse and his forces to gain entrance. She knew, also, that Pinkerton and his crew were thinking along the same lines.

They did not know the true size of the army Jesse was bringing down upon them. She had downplayed their strength, and exaggerated their losses at the hands of the horrors that had struck at them from the twisted minds of Tesla and Tumblety. Her mind was being painfully dragged in too many directions, with no escape in sight, and she knew, with a chill that was worse than the piled betrayals themselves, that her mind was fracturing under the tension.

But it kept coming back to one nerve-jarring thought: if Fort Knox truly was the trap that it seemed, who was it intended for, and who had set it?

A commotion around the enormous gate caught the agent's attention and she pushed herself away from the wall.

One gate swung open, its thickness surprising, given how smooth it seemed to move. Soldiers rose from their positions on either side, blaster rifles raised, as two men walked through the narrow gap. Behind them, the gate reversed its motion and quickly sank back into place with a dull, heavy sound.

A large door to one of the primary stairways was pushed open and the men who had been her comrades for years came out, moving toward the gate. Courtright was the only one who looked her way, one eyebrow raised in a sardonic question. The impulse to join them was nearly overwhelming, but she knew that the ice beneath her feet was too thin for even the appearance of disobedience. She held her ground, hands on hips, and kept her distance, waiting to be brought into whatever was happening.

The agents moved to greet the two newcomers. There were hands shaken and heads nodding as one would expect, but there was little warmth in any of the faces as they turned and approached the keep. The two new arrivals wore no uniforms, but had the look of hard-bitten men of violence. She had never met them in person, but knew them by reputation. One man was just removing a pair of massive blades that had been strapped to his forearms. The other cradled a truly impressive sniper rifle in the crook of one arm.

Courtright and Levenson Wade moved toward Lucinda while Pinkerton and the two men held back, their heads bent together as the chief agent spoke to them with an earnest, somber expression. The two men, their own faces impassive, nodded. Their eyes flicked toward her for a moment and then back to Pinkerton. It happened so quickly she wondered if she had imagined it.

"So, I'd say that means we're in it up to our necks, Luce." Courtright stopped beside her and tilted his head toward their chief. "If Robert's called in *their* marker, I don't much like our odds."

Wade, standing beside her old partner, looked back at the two strangers, shook his head, and looked away. "Tanner and the damned Wraith. They've each themselves done nearly as much damage as Jesse James ever did."

Lucinda's eyes narrowed. "How could Pinkerton have possibly gotten them to agree to come here? Never mind fight for the Union, for God's sake! I'm chained to this stone relic," she slapped the keep. "But he brings them in?"

Wade looked away, his eyes scanning the interior defensive positions. "He wouldn't tell any of us why they're here or how he got them to come. They must owe him for something, at some time. One thing's for sure: as long as they're here, I'll be watching my back."

Henry nodded. "And you better, too, Luce. I don't like the feel of this."

They quieted down as Pinkerton approached, gesturing toward the two mercenaries with one hand. "Lucy, you've heard of Sasha Tanner and the Wraith?"
She nodded, first to him and then to the two strangers. They each gave a single, shallow nod in return.

"They're going to be keeping an eye on the keep with you. A little extra insurance outside the chain of command, if you will." Pinkerton's face was grave, but there were things going on behind his eyes that she could not decipher.

"What would General Grant think, sir?" She kept her tone even. She had never much liked the general, and lately those feelings had deepened. Whether it was Jesse's opinions rubbing off on her, or a rising awareness of the world at large, she had not examined too closely.

Pinkerton's face was sour. "From what I've been able to gather, Lucy, Grant's been pulling the strings on this from the beginning. But I'm sure the general wouldn't mind my having brought in a little extra muscle."

"You think you're going to need them?" She kept her voice calm despite the frustration and guilt roiling in her gut. "Those doors look pretty thick, and the walls are high. If the Rebels can overcome all that, two more men probably won't make a difference."

Pinkerton turned to look at the main gates and shrugged. "We have our orders, Lucinda. The general has something in the works, and he knows that we're all here. I'd like to have a little ace up my sleeve, just in case. I'd suggest you get acquainted with your new compatriots. You've got a little time. The grey-backs aren't at the door yet."

"Of course, sir." She stood straighter, her eyes fixed on a blank space of wall across the inner chamber.

Pinkerton nodded again and then jerked his head toward the side of the keep. He moved off in that direction and after a confused moment, she followed him. When they were around the corner, he turned to stare into her eyes. "Lucinda, General Grant's got a little secret somewhere within the vaults beneath our feet, along with whatever Tesla sent east that didn't get chewed up by the rebels. I get the feeling he thinks the stakes are very high indeed. I can't trust those grasping mercenaries near the entrance to the vaults alone. If this whole action gets knocked into a cocked hat, I'm going to need someone I trust watching that door."

She nodded, but could not meet his eye. "Sir, if there's something down there that powerful, why can't you just go down there, drag it up onto the wall, and point it at Jesse James? For that matter, why not go through whatever Tesla sent? See if it might help?"

Pinkerton chewed on his bottom lip and shook his head. "Lucinda, for all I know, it's a ton of used dynamite and a pansy patch." He snorted. "And from everything I've seen, it's more than a man's worth to go poking around in Tesla's wardrobe without him standing beside you." He patted his gun. "We'll stick to what we know and, God help us, trust that the general's not too far gone."

The chief agent moved back toward the others and they made their way to the stairway door. She watched them disappear, Henry's quirked eyebrow the last thing she saw.

"So." The man was strapping long blades to his arms and gave what he probably thought was a charming smile. "What did you do to deserve being left in the basement with the hired help?"

She looked at him wordlessly for a moment. There was nothing she wanted less than to spend any time with these two animals.

The Wraith, lights glinting off various skulls secreted among his clothes, chuckled a low, evil laugh. "I'm not sure how I feel, not being the least-trusted wolf in the henhouse."

She sniffed and turned away, eyes fixed on the heavy door. Somewhere below them were the last items Tesla had sent east. Anything that had not been deployed against Jesse and the rebels . . .

"Fire!" The cry echoed across the massive space of the inner chamber. Lucinda's head whipped from side to side as she tried to see where it was coming from. Concern and confusion rippled through the defenders.

"The plains are burning!" Something about the echoing sound of the voice made her look up. She saw, from a concealed firing position high on the wall, a soldier standing, shouting down to the soldiers below.

"They've set the plains on fire! The fields are burning!"

Chapter 18

Jesse crouched low behind the control console of his Iron Horse, his cheek pressed to the cool metal. Against the inferno swirling all around, the temperature was soothing. Directly in front of him, one of their big Ironhide wagons had logs, rags, and bags of sawdust jammed into every possible nook and cranny. It raced straight for the big fort, burning like the fires of Hell. An elaborate rig of chains, leather straps, and metal struts kept the thing barreling forward at its top speed without a driver.

Jesse gritted his teeth as a curl of bright yellow flame flashed past over his head. He gave out a Rebel yell as he felt the burn, despite his hat. He heard several answering calls through the roaring fires, the RJ engines, and the blood in his ears. He knew that Frank, the Youngers, the Fords, and many of his other men were hugging their own machines around him, tucked in behind the racing furnace. He squinted, even behind his thick goggles, and could only hope the drivers had been on target when they'd bailed out of their vehicles a few moments before.

There were nearly twenty wagons tearing across the fields toward the fort. Most of them were the ragtag rattle boxes that passed for command transport. Hidden among them, however, were their four surviving Rolling Thunder wagons. Jesse cringed to think of what the crews of those wagons were going through at the moment. The wood and fabric bonfires attached to all the wagons obscured their outlines and would hopefully hide the heavies in a shell-game any huckster would be proud of. But in order for his surprise to work, those heavies needed to stay hidden until their weapons were in range.

Each Rolling Thunder was filled with casks of water and sodden sheets and blankets. The crews had been doused just before igniting their vehicles. So far, they had covered over a hundred yards, and there had been no fire from the fort. He grinned, his dry lips cracking. If there was no cover to be had, you made cover or you died. So he had made some serious cover.

The burning wagons bore down on the fort at considerable speed, despite the terrain. The flames confused the sentries' tech, blinding their vision enhancement and hiding the number of infantry rushing along behind. Three walls of flame were tearing across the dry fields, from the south, east, and west; each aligned with a tall, forbidding wall. His two Rolling Thunders were nearby, aimed directly at the main gate. Each of the flanking forces had one of the beasts, prepared to take advantage of targets of opportunity or weak points that might become clear during the fighting.

Jesse slid his 'Horse to the side, peeking past the burning flank of the wagon. He caught a glimpse of the massive fort in silhouette just as a terrible rending crash erupted off to his right. He cringed, ducking back behind cover. He surged past the wreckage of a burning Ironhide canted into a smoking crater. Fiery debris was scattered all around the ruin, the grass beginning to smolder in a widening ring.

He shook his head at the luck. He knew he should be happy it took this long, considering how many unmanned vehicles were dashing across the broken ground. He knew he should also be happy that the fort still seemed too confused to—

A wall of horrendous noise crashed down upon the racing Confederate line. The massive guns all fired in disciplined unison with the sound of an avalanche. Between the difficulties of hitting moving targets in the dark, the dazzle of the blazing light, and the interference of the boiling flames on targeting tech, no more of the initial shots struck their targets. Most fell short, blasting huge holes in the fields and sending blooms of crimson fire high into the night sky. Two shots went long, however, and blasted matching holes in the charging infantry. More than a hundred men went down, torn to shreds, pounded into the mud by the pressure wave, or burned beyond recognition by the rising fireballs. Jesse crouched lower, silently urging the wagons to greater speed.

The cannons began to put down a steady, rolling pattern of fire. The crews were adapting to the situation quickly, and first one wagon, then several more, were reduced to twisted shards of metal and billowing flame, cutting down the infantry around them. One chassis, the body of the wagon ripped entirely off, continued to roll forward with the inertia of its mad drive. A second bolt from the wall threw it onto its side where it rolled once and then rocked to a gentle stop.

There was no way to pass orders now. Jesse and the other commanders had known that once they crested the low rise, they were going to be committed to the assault. Thousands of men and women were charging across the field, the bulk hidden by large wagons and roaring flames. As the wagons were torn apart, the flames were slowly spreading into the high grass as the infantry ran past. Soon, their retreat could be cut off by a wall of fire rising in their wake.

Jesse swerved aside for another look ahead and was heartened to see that the fort was only a few hundred yards away. More than half the wagons had been hit now, most of them torn apart to scatter their flames into the grass and surrounding troopers. Through a minor miracle, neither of the Rolling Thunders in the frontal assault had been destroyed. He had seen one take a direct hit, blasting the wood and fabric away from its armored hide, but having little further effect. They were approaching their own maximum range, so their charmed existence would not last much longer.

As the Rolling Thunders crossed the invisible line that freed their weapons, both vehicles staggered in their forward progress by the bellowing roar of their own main armament. One crew had opted to fire directly at the strong main gate, barely visible through the swirling smoke and flame. The shot scored a glowing line of molten rock and metal that cut into the door and then dragged along the main wall. The gate, however, was still standing. The other wagon, struck by the earlier enemy blast, had opted for a more personal target. Their shot blasted home into one of the armored turrets along the wall. The shot was either lucky or masterful, as the turret peeled open like a prairie flower, sending several men arcing to the ground far below and lighting up that entire section with ruby-tinged flames.

As the Rolling Thunders began their fire, rebels armed with heavy weapons decided their time had come as well. Jesse cursed them. He had known, however, that despite the repeated warnings of the experienced fighters in the group, there would be no stopping men and women with so little training from wanting to strike back in the savage chaos of battle. Fighters dropped to their knees, hoisting rocket pods, missile launchers, and even heavy blaster cannons to their shoulders. Streaks of crimson flame lashed out from the infantry all along the line. Most of the shots struck the impervious stone of the main wall, but several arced over to explode upon the parapet or against the secondary wall behind. More blue-bellies tumbled to a fiery death.

Jesse knew something most of these new fish had never been given the chance to learn: if you can shoot them, they can shoot at you. Heavy Gatling blasters, snipers' long rifles, and medium cannons lit up all along the wall. They were not aimed at the still-charging vehicles, but at the dark, crawling mass of infantry behind; the tightly-packed mass that had illuminated itself with the premature fire from its leading elements.

The heavy fire from the fort was devastating as it fell among the ill-equipped and under-trained militia. Men and women were cut down where they stood. Bodies were torn apart by heavy Gatling rounds. Heads fountained gore all around as snipers took their toll. All across the line, the rebel fighters were blasted back into the dirt. Any shot fired into the mob could not help but hit. Most shots were blasting through several victims before their fury was spent. Under the withering punishment, the entire contingent of infantry working toward the gates began to falter.

Jesse pulled his Iron Horse up short, riding in a sharp turn back toward the infantry. He pulled one of his Hyper-velocity pistols and fired it into the air, trying to get their attention. He saw his entire plan crumbling before his eyes as the militia fighters began to shrink away from the incoming fire, some turning toward the blazing flames rising up behind them.

Jesse was about to throttle for the back of the mob, expecting to get a Union round through the spine at any moment. A shape flashed past, first on his left, then another on his right. He recognized Bob and Jim Younger, waving their hats at him to return to the attack. Looking back, Jesse saw Frank, the Fords, and Cole had pulled up, waiting for him.

Jesse nodded, waved to Cole's brothers, and then tore back around again, throttling hard to regain his position behind the massive wagon. He roared through his posse as they leaned into their own machines to keep up, when the wagon that had sheltered them disappeared in a blinding flash of red and white light. Jesse raised a hand to shield his eyes from the blast, despite his goggles. Even as he swerved to avoid the wreckage, he grinned, however. By the strobing light of the Ironhide's destruction, he saw that the rebel fire had taken a toll on the fort. Several of the heavy turrets had been reduced to burning wreckage, and the gates, although still standing, had been pounded and lashed into slag.

Jesse swerved past the burning hulk of the wagon and lined up on the gate. He passed the torn hulk of one of his Rolling Thunders, smoke pouring from the vision slits and a massive hole blasted into the driver's station. As he looked for the hull markings of Frank's *Ole Bessie*, he was distracted by a flash of movement ahead. His head came up just in time to see a disciplined line of Iron Horse cavalry rounding the corner of the fortress and aligning for a vicious charge. The riders wore the blue and yellow of the Union army, and the guidons that flapped in the hurricane wind of their charge bore crossed sabers beneath a bold '7'.

Jesse's flanking forces erupted in chaos as the Union cavalry tore past them. The enemy could have devastated both detachments if the cavalry had crashed into their unprotected flanks. But the cavalry commander knew his business. The roaring Union vanguard dashed down the walls on either side, ignoring the flanking rebel forces and driving straight for the main assault on the front gates. Behind these lead elements, following companies wheeled to face the flanking units, confronting the Rebel assault all along their line of advance.

Twice in as many minutes, Jesse saw his entire plan crumbling. Who the hell was the 7th, and where had they come from? It soon became clear that there were not enough of the cavalry to stop a determined push on the gates. Even with the presence of several Union Locusts, those heavily-armored bastards he had first seen outside of Diablo Canyon, the cavalry were too late. The sheer volume of fire the untrained militia poured into the newly-arrived enemy shattered their counterattack. Jesse shook his head and gunned his own machine forward to meet the charge. He crouched low once again, and the Gatling cannons beneath the faring of his 'Horse spat ruby bolts into the oncoming 'Horses.

The lines crashed against each other, and the disciplined formations of the Union cavalry were shattered, devolving into ugly individual fights for survival beneath the towering walls of Fort Knox. Jesse watched as Cole whipped out his stubby shotgun, leveling it at a junior officer in a blue shell coat, and blasting his face back through his head. Another trooper rose high from his saddle, energized saber raised high for a killing blow against the back of Charlie Ford's neck, when his brother brought his own 'Horse crashing down on the tail of the trooper's machine, putting four bolts into the man's back as he tumbled from the saddle.

The Union commander came straight for Jesse, face wild behind sweeping blonde mustaches. With a grimace, the outlaw chief drew one of his pistols. At this range, it would be impossible to aim the 'Horse's own weaponry. Jesse sent a stream of bolts at the man's torso, but they tore into his mount instead. A blast of sparks and crimson flames flared up, obscuring him, and when the 'Horse canted off to one side, dragging itself to a stop, the Union officer was gone.

Jesse took advantage of a lull in the fighting to bring his Iron Horse around to face the steaming, slumping gate. A rising tide of militia fighters was pressing the Union cavalry back to either side. Rebel yells echoed off the cold Republican stone, and Jesse smiled grimly before adding his own voice to the chorus. He could tell the enemy cavalry were not beaten. They were retreating back along the side walls, still keeping those flanking columns back long enough to make a decent retreat. They would return, he knew. The rebels would need to secure the fort before that happened or they would be crushed between the defenders and the cavalry coming back with blood in their eye.

Jesse stood before the massive front gates of Fort Knox and regarded their daunting, metallic solidity. Frank pulled up beside him and jumped down into the dirt. They were soon joined by the three Younger brothers, and Robert and Charlie Ford, both grinning far more than was seemly. Jesse

looked around at the surging Confederate infantry pressing
toward the walls, firing up into the blue-bellies on the parapet.
Above them, the fighting positions and mounted weapons
above the front gates had all been reduced to crimson smoke
belching wreckage and slumped, still bodies.

Jesse searched the mob for Marcus and Quantrill, uneasy at
their apparent absence, when he saw them moving together
through the press.

Colonel Quantrill had been with the bayou fighters,
accompanying the surviving New Orleans commanders.
Marcus had decided to stand with the bayou fighters as well.
The big black man was impassive as always as he strode
across the bloody and burning field of death. Quantrill,
however, was much the worse for wear. He clutched a new
ornate cane in his crude metal hand, but it sank too deeply into
the mud to offer much support. Jesse had begged him to stay
in the rear, but the old man was determined to be in on the kill.
Captain Carney stalked along beside the two men, his
enormous cannon seeking further targets. Behind the captain
stood Will Shaft and his Exodusters, their white teeth flashing
in cruel grins.

"Well, I don't know who they were, but they don't
seem to have put a damper on your little shindig, James!"
Quantrill's smile was wide as he moved up beside the outlaw
chief. "This is not really our sort of battle, son, but it seems to
be goin' okay."

Frank barked a dark, disbelieving laugh. "We've lost
thousands of men, sir! We're not even inside yet! How can
you—"

"Well, the greater allied army has lost thousands,"
Captain Carney smiled. "But by far the most casualties have
been sustained by the groups from the eastern states. So WE
have not lost nearly so much." The smile was predatory, his
teeth flashing in the dancing flames.

Frank looked away, shaking his head. Quantrill turned
to Jesse. "Nevertheless, we do need to secure entrance, or all
of this vigorous activity will have been for naught."

Jesse nodded and looked back up at the massive slabs of
melted steel. He cocked his head to one side, and then,

without a word, gestured for his men to move away. Those who knew him moved quickly, pulling any laggards with them as the outlaw chief drew both of his pistols and regarded the slumping metal slabs.

Jesse brought the two pistols up, his metal arms at full extension. The guns came together and arcs of intense red light reached out, linking the two weapons with a blazing energy bridge. Both pistols began to hum violently, their RJ cells flared like tiny red suns, and with a rushing roar, a wave of furnace heat blasted out before him. The concussion struck the gates with a deafening clang. The thick metal slabs withstood the pressure, sloughing off sheets of melted armor that scorched the ground where they struck. Even through the thick, rippling, tortured air, the men could see that the doors remained closed.

Jesse leaned forward, his shoulders hunched as they drove his metal arms at the gates like spears. The humming rose to a painful level and the heat shimmer emerging from the guns rippled out in visible waves of destruction. The gates groaned, showers of metal pouring down their canted faces, and then with a deep, visceral concussion, they shattered, metal fragments and droplets of molten armor blasting back into the fortress.

Jesse grinned at his friends over his shoulder. "We're in."

*****

"Damn, Jesse, what've you gone and done now?" Through the monocular, the scene across the plain looked to Billy like something out of some Gospel-sharp's Sunday morning harangue. The fields all around were burning, sending curls of flame high into the air. Above, columns of thick, churning smoke drifted over the spectacle, under-lit by the flames. The fires illuminated a squat fortress surrounded by an enormous, surging mob.

Crimson bolts rose out of the rising tide of attackers to splash against the high outer wall. Occasionally, something heavier would fire, momentarily revealing a section of the scene in lurid red highlights. There were still defenders on the walls, firing down into the surging crowd, but they seemed almost halfhearted as a response to the enormous wash of fire coming up at them.

"Looks like we got a bunch of blue-belly cav forming up behind there, Billy." Johnny Ringo pointed with one gloved hand off to where a large group of men on Iron Horses was gathering together. The outlaws riding with The Kid were all exhausted and covered in trail dust after riding hell-bent for leather for over a week. Billy had been hounded by a sharp sense of urgency ever since reading Carpathian's note.

Down on the fields behind the fortress, flags and pennons flapped in the fitful winds coming off the prairie fires. William Bonney slid his monocular off to his right until he saw them. They looked like they had been battered; some rode pillion, obviously having lost their mounts.

Billy grunted. "They got kicked in the fork, but they're goin' to be goin' back fer more. Hope Jesse's ready for 'em."

Billy was not entirely sure if he really did hope that. As he watched the surging attackers flood toward the front gate, he knew that he was watching Jesse realize the dream they had shared in the Arcadia Saloon back in Kansas City. Somewhere over there, Jesse James was leading a damned army against the Union . . . The army that should have been his.

"What do we do?" The Apache Kid looked across at the battle, the flames reflecting in his flat black eyes.

Billy eased back in his saddle, one hand resting on his knee, and twisted his face into a parody of deep thought. "Well, boys, it looks like this to me." He pointed to the forces flooding through the front gate. "We got a nice chance to kick up a little row against those blue-shirted chiselers over there. Kick 'em when they're down, maybe grab us some plunder as we run through." He cocked his head over to the side to address the savage renegade. "But this ain't our fight. We copper our bets. We look for the main chance, but we keep our eyes clear in case we gotta skedaddle fast."

The outlaws gathered around their boss nodded, eager to get in on what looked like a clean Union kill. "Now, boys, if we get in there, you keep together. I don't wanna lose anyone cuz they went off on their own. If the opportunity arises, I've got the doctor's little map. If I make my guess, what I'm lookin' fer'll be in the basement. I'll try to go down there, a couple of you can follow, if you want. If we do, we'll be leavin' by the doc's back door, though, so don't wait fer us. We've got a few more 'Horses laid in at the exit in case we need to head out that way."

Again, the men nodded. They loosened their weapons and stared across the plains with eyes glowing with greed.

Billy's smile turned sharp. "An' if any of ya'll see James, you leave 'im to me. That boy got me in the neck but good last time, an' I'm keen to get a little o' my own back."

*****

Jesse's throat was raw from the smoke and continuous shouting. His Rebel yell echoed constantly off the high walls as the militia fighters streamed past him, rushing through the broken gates and into Fort Knox. There would be no stopping them now. There was fighting within the fort, of course. No one ever accused the bastard Union troopers of being bad at their jobs. But there was just no way they could stop the flood of Confederate militia with what they had left.

As the rising tide of rebel soldiers pressed through, Jesse watched them pass with a growing smile on his face. The uniforms were patchwork and haphazard, the weapons mismatched. The faces, though, were what struck Jesse at that moment. Black faces and white faces, sharing expressions of triumph. Every face was grinning with the fierce rush of victory. Success here was going to redefine the world, not just the Confederacy. And no one would ever forget that he was at the head of this army as it charged to triumph.

He had been nervous when the Union cavalry made their appearance, but the weight of fire seemed to have seen them off. His brain was flying high with the heady rush of victory within his grasp. All around him were the people he trusted the most, and they would walk into the most formidable Union stronghold south of Washington beside him.

His grin slipped a tick at the thought. There was one person he had come to trust nearly as much who was not with him. The grueling march and furious preparations for the assault had not left him much time to brood over Lucy's disappearance. His heart refused to believe she was dead, but his head knew how easily it was for a man to fool himself in a situation like this.

"Jesse, did ya see Charlie?" Robert Ford thumped his brother on the back, his smile stretching his black-smudged face. "Did ya see him, when those Billy Yank bastards came ridin' 'round the corner? He got right in there, Jesse! Right in there!" His eyes glowed like a child who had potted his first tin can with daddy's rifle.

Jesse leaned toward the weasel-faced young men, trying to suppress his own smile. "Stay focused, boys! We got a long way to go afore we're hoistin' a whiskey in Charlie's honor!"

Despite his sour response, he did not know if he had ever seen a man as happy as Charlie Ford at that moment. With the burning thrill of victory rushing through his veins, he had a hard time stifling his own grin.

"Let's go, boys, before they string up all the blue-bellies and there ain't no more for us!" Jesse's metal arm rose up to urge his posse through the press of men at the gates and into the fortress.

Chapter 19

As Jesse pushed through the roaring crowd of fighters and into Fort Knox, he was brought up short by the immensity of the inner chamber. The room was huge, clearly taking up most of the fortress within the high walls. Across the hall were carefully positioned defensive emplacements that his people had paid dearly to silence. There were bodies strewn everywhere around the bunkers and barricades, in both the blue uniforms of the defenders and the motley array of clothing worn by his own folks.

The walls above them were broken up by firing positions and balconies clearly designed to give the defenders on the walls easy access to the giant chamber within. Brilliant slashes of crimson fire were snapping all around as rebel forces fired upon the soldiers overhead and were fired upon in return. There were several unprotected stairways up the thick walls leading to the upper levels. Many doors along the ground floor clearly gave access to larger stairways within. His people had pushed out toward them, and fierce battles were raging across the floor.

In the center of the huge room, looking strangely out of place beneath the high ceiling overhead, was another, smaller structure. A thin haze of smoke hung in the air, but it looked to Jesse as if another castle, with another armored door, had been built within the bulk of Fort Knox. A shoal of sprawled bodies was stretched out in front of the smaller fort, a testament to how far his men had pushed into the hall before they turned back toward the high walls. They were now attacking the doors and stairways, leaving the small fortress alone.

"Damn, it's hot in here!" Charlie Ford's grin was still huge. "Come on, boys, afore there ain't none left fer us!"

Jesse could not help but smile at the young man. There was still an edge of anxiety in his eyes, and his words shook just enough to hint at the bluster that was meant to hide it. He was on the shoot, a curly wolf in his own mind, and Jesse was glad the kid had come around. He nodded to the boy, turning to wave the rest of his posse through the press of fighters. Charlie pushed in front of Jesse and then jerked backward slightly, the fear and boasting draining from his eyes, replaced with confusion and pain.

Jesse watched Charlie fall. The gaping hole in the young man's chest, shirt slick with blood, barely registered. Robert Ford lunged down to catch his brother. The younger man's face was twisted with horror and rage, his pistol forgotten on the stone beside him. Charlie, blood bubbling from his mouth and nose, looked up into his brother's eyes. He looked like a frightened little boy, eyes wide with shocked confusion. Robert was shaking, trying to hold the dying man steady.

The sharp report of a heavy rifle sounded in the distance, loud enough to be heard over the general clangor of battle. Jesse looked up, tracking the course the killing bolt had to have followed. He saw a man in dark clothing ratcheting the recharge lever of a heavy sniper rifle just around the corner of the strange little castle. He wore ornate personalized armor beneath his duster, a leering metal skull flashing on his chest as he raised his rifle to fire again. At Jesse's feet, Robert howled as the light left his brother's eyes.

Jesse roared with his own anger and frustration as he brought both of his pistols up. He sent a torrent of fire flashing at the little fort. The sniper ducked behind the stone as the bolts shattered the corner in a detonation of powdered rock. The outlaw chief lowered his weapons, breathing heavily with grief and anger, and saw another man, decked out in fancy but nondescript black, running toward him.

The new assailant wore long glittering blades strapped to his forearms. They would be vicious in both attack and defense, and Jesse decided that he would rather not find out. He raised his pistols again to end the man. His shot was spoiled, however, as Marcus Cunningham, his usually impassive face knotted in rage, rushed past, heavy hammer held high over his head.

Jesse lowered his pistols as he watched the enormous black man bring his hammer down toward their attacker. The man raised one bladed forearm and dodged to the side, guiding the hammer past his head and leaping across to slash at Marcus's side. The big man threw himself away, the haft of his hammer coming up to block the cut. The strange attacker's other arm came up in a swift jab that punched the tip of his serrated blade up into the big man's side. The blade slid out his back, dark with blood, and Marcus staggered backward, the blade pulling free. He shook himself, gripped his hammer tighter, and hunched his broad shoulders. The blade-wielder's eyes widened in mild surprise.

The two men circled each other warily as the battle raged on around them. Jesse felt the near-overwhelming urge to blast the bladed man where he stood, but the stranger and Marcus were once again engaged, swirling around with weapons flashing in the dim red light. A shout from above caught his attention and he turned to look up the high wall behind him.

A broad balcony stretched across the length of the fortress's front wall, above the shattered gates, where the defense of the fortress could best be coordinated. A knot of men and women in blue uniforms heavy with gold braid were gathered at one end of the balcony with a smaller group of men in dark civilian clothing. Jesse felt his eyes tighten: Pinkertons. And where those agents were, the commanders of this damned blue-belly shindig would undoubtedly be as well. That had to be the command group for the entire fortress, cornered up on that balcony like rats.

Even as Jesse glared up, Frank grabbed him by one shoulder and shouted into his ear. "Jesse! Those riders are goin' to come back soon! If we take out the commanders, these boys'll drop their weapons, an' we'll be able to get ready for the next dance!"

Jesse looked at his brother, uncomprehending, torn between grief and rage. Then his eyes widened as he remembered the cavalry. Frank thought the troopers would be returning for another hand. Jesse started to shake his head and then stopped himself. If Frank was right, then he was also right about decapitating the defense of the fort. Even if Frank was wrong, they would still have to take out the officers. He nodded.

"Okay, boys!" Anger and sadness clashed within him as Jesse looked one last time at Charlie's collapsed body, his brother crumpled beside him. He pointed with one of his pistols at a doorway that had been cleared by militia fighters. "Up those stairs and at the big bugs! Let's show these folks who are in charge, and then we'll see what's what!"

Carney stepped away from the posse, hoisting up the massive Gatling blaster. With a gleaming grin, he engaged the enormous weapon and sprayed a fan of ruby death toward a knot of Union troopers holding out by a shattered defensive position. The soldiers were caught in the flashing red light, many blasted from their feet or diving for cover as the stone of the bunker detonated in a cloud of gray dust. Under the cover of that howling torrent, Jesse and his followers ran toward the stairway, their faces set in a mask of grim determination.

Robert Ford, tears still streaming down his dirty face, gently dragged his brother's body forward and rested it in a sitting position against a barricade. He reached down with one gloved hand and slowly pressed the eyelids down over the flat, glassy orbs. Wiping his face with an angry gesture, he trotted toward the doorway after Jesse James.

*****

Lucy paused on the stair landing to catch her breath. The box was heavier than it had first seemed when she'd dragged it from the vault. She hoped she had grabbed the right one. As her world came crashing down around her, and every pathway crumbled beneath her feet, she had given in to desperation and ran for the vaults and the treasures she thought she might find there. If this was, in fact, a trap, then there was only one possibility that might let her take a hand. The chest, she felt, would be her best hope.

But it was so damned heavy. It would probably have been easier to empty the chest and carry the contents loose, but there was no telling if anyone she encountered would have recognized it for what it was and stopped her with awkward questions.

She took a deep breath and hefted the thing up in both hands just as a commotion broke out around a bend in the stairs above her. Running footsteps could just be heard over the shouting. It was not the disciplined advanced of trained soldiers moving down to clear the vaults, however, but the sounds of a riotous mob. She had not met a single soul since abandoning her position by the small keep's door. With a cold, distant curiosity, she drew one of her powerful derringer holdouts. She wondered how this would play itself out.

Had Tanner and The Wraith been killed? From what she knew of them, that was not likely. Far more likely, they had abandoned their assigned posts, the filthy mercenaries . . . Her full lips quirked into a sad grin as the irony of the thought struck her.

The men who came trotting down the stairs were dressed in a mismatched array of clothing and armor that owed nothing to the Union Army Uniform Code. They bore a hodgepodge of various weapons ranging from old RJ hunting rifles to the latest military-issue blasters. As they saw her, their weapons all came up as one. Her pitiful pistol rose slowly in response, but then the lead man's cruel face split into a surprised smile.

"It's Jesse's girl! Boys, put yer shootin' irons up! it's Lucy! She's alive!"

The crew of outlaws all lowered their weapons, grinning foolishly at her. With open, honest faces they asked how she got into the fortress, if she was alright, and if she needed help.

Lucinda's hand was rigid, but the men did not seem to notice the gun still bearing on them. She tried to formulate some rational response when the shattering stutter of blaster fire echoed down the stairs. She cringed back, pressing against the cold stone of the wall, but no one was firing on her. A group of soldiers must have entered the keep and taken the small mob of rebels from the rear.

The militia fighters cried out, spinning around and firing their weapons blindly back up the stairway. One of the older weapons fired an ear-splitting spray of red light up around the corner, and a scream rose above the shouts and gunshots.

The rebels began to press their way up the stairs, return fire snapping all around them and crashing into the stone. "Come on, Lucy!" One of the men waved her forward. "Let's light a shuck!"

Lucinda looked around her, realizing that she might well be committed for good. She noticed a side door just a few steps down. With one last look at the rebels, now hard pressed by the invisible Union forces above, she hefted the box into her arms and shouldered the door open. The last thing she saw was one of the rebels looking back at her, a strange smile playing about his lips as his eyes caught the red light from an overhead bulb.

Lucy followed the small hallway through a series of storage rooms and chambers until she found another flight of stairs leading up. Much narrower than the main course, the crate was nearly impossible to muscle through in the confined space, but she managed, step by step. She could just hear the sounds of battle continuing to rage in the stairway behind her.

At the top of the stairs, a door opened out into the little keep, the main stairway off to her left. Distant sounds of battle could still be heard down there, but obviously the Union boys had pushed the rebels deeper into the vaults. She hoped none of them returned any time soon.

She put the crate down just inside the small keep's door and spun around to push her back against the opposite wall. She glanced carefully outside, her derringer once more in hand. There was no sign of Tanner or The Wraith, but that was no surprise. The bodies scattered all across the hall of the main chamber *were* a surprise, however. The battle had been fierce, and she could see that, although the rebels had obviously pushed on into the fort itself, they had paid a terrible price.

She took another glance, trying to gauge the flow of the battle. The fighting had moved into the upper regions of the fortress, with streaks of crimson flame crisscrossing through the air overhead as Union and rebel soldiers traded fire from the defensive positions scattered across all four walls. Many of the balconies and firing emplacements were blasted and scorched; rockets and missiles screeched across the vast space to detonate with deafening explosions against the walls.

It was hard to discern who had the upper hand with most of the combat going on in the walls and out of sight, but it seemed like most of the men she saw fighting were in the mismatched clothing of the rebels. The conflicting emotions that sank into her belly at the thought were enough to force her to one knee. She was in a nightmare born into the real world, as her conflicted loyalties played out all around her.

Lucinda sat within the keep, back pressed again against the hard cold stone. A new sound began to rumble beneath the general chaos of the battle. A sound she would never forget from her time with Jesse after Camp Lincoln. A large number of Iron Horses were approaching. Her head came up. The 7th Cavalry was returning.

Lucy peered around the corner again, twisting to get a good look at the command balcony over the twisted remains of the gates. She could see the command group, their blue and yellow uniforms indistinct in the scudding haze of battle. With them were the dark forms of her fellow agents, an unmistakably tall figure rising above them all. They were defending against a haphazard push by some rebels, but seemed to be focusing primarily on rallying troops on the fighting parapet for the main wall, behind their current position. As she watched, however, fear threatened to choke her as her throat tightened. A new force of rebels burst from a stairway on the far right end of the balcony and pressed toward the Union commanders. She recognized the men even as they pushed into the press of soldiers.

Cole and one of his brothers were firing their pistols into the defenders from the back of the mob, while another Younger, it had to be Bob, was thrashing at nearby Union soldiers with a knife glittering in either hand. Robert Ford seemed to be using his blaster to bludgeon anyone who rushed at them rather than firing it, a knife sparkling in his other hand. Frank James was near the back, his massive rifle raised as he kept watch on the main chamber, as if fearing a sniper's bolt might hit them from the flank; the Wraith, most likely. There was no sign of Charlie Ford, Bill Carney, or Marcus Cunningham.

At the head of the small formation, both pistols blazing away, strode Jesse James.

Lucinda watched with a growing sense of dread as the man she was terribly afraid she loved rushed toward the man who had saved her from her own past. Like a scene from a nightmare, she watched as they rushed toward each other.

Her heart began to hammer at her ribs. There was no way this could end but in heartbreak.

The trap had sprung.

*****

Jesse forced his way onto the balcony over the body of the doorway's last defender. He saw a sea of blue before him. The caps of the officers and the array of civilian hats worn by the agents were clearly visible at the other end. He knew this would boil down to time. Without waiting for the rest of his posse, he waded into the press of bodies. His Hyper-velocity pistols blazed away, their muzzle flashes charring the flesh of his targets; he was so close. Shattered bodies were tossed into their friends, onto the stone floor, and over the parapet to the left.

At first, the blue-bellies could not have known what was happening. The stairway had been a secure flank only a moment before, all of their attention on the doors to the outer wall and over the parapet into the cavernous inner chamber. They adapted quickly, though. These were the elite soldiers of the garrison unit, the best the Union had to offer. They had been sent to guard their most precious outpost in enemy territory. Soon, return fire was snapping past his head and charged saber blades flashed on all sides. He raised his pistols and pumped bolt after bolt into the seething mass of enemy soldiers, ducking and weaving to avoid their attempts to cut him down. The customary grin swept across his grimy face as the old sense of invincibility rose up within him. Crimson bolts flew past close enough to warm his flesh. Blades whistled by and he could feel the wind of their passage. He wove through it all without a scratch.

A sword blade caught him on the wrist with a blow that would have sheared his natural hand away. It clanged off the metal but scraped along his mechanical thumb, stripping the pistol from his grasp and sending it tumbling to the paving stones. Jesse growled as he realized he had lost one of his precious weapons, bringing the other around to punch two bolts through the offending swordsman's face. He relished the look of disgust and horror on the men behind as they were showered in droplets of their friend's head. If they thought taking a pistol away from him would stop his rampage, they had not paid close enough attention to his legend. He would just as easily kill them with his bare metal hands as with his storied weapons.

As he moved across the balcony, Jesse was aware of his friends fighting alongside him, finally removing some of the pressure of the Union men's growing desperation. Bob and Jim Younger were to either side, Jim's pistol barking defiance while Bob's long knives flashed in the dim light, sending arcs of crimson fluid into the air with every slash.

Robert Ford's eyes were wild as he leapt over the slumped bodies at the doorway. He was not even firing his pistol, but using it like a club in his crazed rage, a knife slick with blood in his off hand. He knocked two Union soldiers back into their companions. A third jumped at him with a flashing knife and he fell to the floor in a tangle of limbs.

Frank and Cole were the last out of the stairwell. Frank caught sight of something off in the main chamber, but Jesse had neither the time nor inclination to scrutinize the blaster-torn walls. His brother moved toward the parapet, dashing one blue-clad soldier into the ground with the butt of his sniper rifle. He took up a position at the railing, scanning the chamber for threats, his eyes tight. Cole's shotgun would have been murder in the confined space on friend and coot alike. He held it across his body, looking for a clear shot at the commanders gathered on the far side.

Jesse focused back on the fighting ahead and saw that a tall man in a strange hat seemed to be the center of the Union effort. Even the other commanders were defending the man from the fresh rebel assault. He wielded a long-handled axe with a broad, ornate head, brandishing the weapon in the air as his eyes searched for a likely target. They settled on Jesse with the weight of a coffin lid.

Before the tall man in the hat could move toward Jesse, Jim Younger rushed past with a howl of crazed, animal rage. The outlaw chief had no idea what had so enraged Cole's brother, but he knew the boy would probably follow their brother John's fate if he was left to his own devices. Jesse charged in after him.

Jim obscured the tall man as he charged, blocking any clear view Jesse might have had. He saw the axe swing up and then spin, as if the man was going to meet Jim's charge with the butt of the handle. There was a sharp report, a flash of crimson, and Jim was flying back toward Jesse, his body spinning as he came.

Jesse dodged to one side and watched as Jim Younger, his eyes wide with confusion and pain, landed on the ground beside him. The boy's face was shattered, nothing but glistening meat and shards of bone from the nose down. Blood poured from the wound to pool around his head, his eyes glazing over while Jesse watched.

As he saw the light fade from Jim's eyes, John Younger's face flashed before him again. Outrage rose up in Jesse's chest, made even more powerful by the surge of guilt. Of the three remaining Younger brothers, Jim had been the most even-tempered, the most willing to forgive him for what had happened to John. Jesse howled at the boy's killer standing before him, and raised his remaining pistol as his vision darkened. Soldiers tried to shield the tall man with their bodies and he cut them down as he charged, his only thought fixated upon blowing the bearded stranger's head into the far wall.

Cole and Bob Younger, shouting their own horrified cries for vengeance, rushed forward at his side. Bob began to match blows with a man that Jesse thought he remembered from Kansas City. The man was fighting with a pistol and a knife, an enormous Gatling rifling slung over his back. He matched Bob's speed with brutal strength. Cole blew four soldiers crouched by the parapet away with a single shot that took most of the low wall with it. Even as the stone and dust cascaded down into the chamber below, he turned back to square off against a tall, dashing-looking agent and an older man in a bowler hat. A glancing blow with the butt of the shotgun took the old man in the face, and he was going down as Jesse rushed past them.

Jesse paid no further attention to the combat around him, the tall man filling his vision. The man's axe was back in a cross-body guard position, ready to receive his charge. Jesse's pistol came up to fire into the man's gut, but the axe spun around fast as lightning, knocking the weapon aside. Jesse lashed out with his empty metal fist, crashing off a concealed chest plate. They settled down into a rhythm of attempted destruction, each trying to find a way past the other's guard.

As Jesse slowed his own combat to take stock of his enemy's abilities, he saw Robert Ford take a sword strike across the abdomen, just below his battered chest armor. His self-professed bodyguard hollowed out his attacker's head with a return shot, having finally remembered the primary utility of his pistol, but sank to his knees right after, lost in the surging melee.

Frank was still at the parapet trading shots with another sniper across the hall. With a cold certainty, Jesse realized it must be that damned Wraith again. He hoped Frank was as good as he always claimed.

The axe-man reversed his grip without warning, and Jesse lurched to the side as the broad head swept past, close enough for him to hear the whistle. He caught the return stroke on his metal forearm and then, with the long weapon bound away, brought his remaining pistol up toward the man's face. There was something about the face, seen from barely a foot away now, that nagged at his mind despite the desperation of the situation. He shook off the distracting fancy. Plenty of time to study what was left of the face after he had killed the bastard. Even as he thought it, the man's eyes widened as he realized his danger. The tall, familiar-seeming stranger fell backward, surrendering his solid stance in favor of getting his head out of the line of fire.

Jesse growled. This old man was harder to kill than he should have been. Nearly blind with frustration and finally-released rage, the outlaw chief began to rain blows down on the old man's head, lashing in from either side with metal fist or pistol butt. The pistol, rebounding from a solid block with the axe, snapped up and crushed the man's tall, peculiar-looking hat. The hood fell away with the topper, revealing the man's face to the dim light.
Jesse froze.

The face was completely familiar to him: the object of his hatred for over two decades. The jaw-framing beard, the beady eyes, the sharp nose; they had been etched into his mind with the force of ultimate, eternal hatred. That face that always robbed him of any reservation or control. Even on a mourning pin, that face was enough to drive him to acts of madness.

Abraham Lincoln.

Jesse staggered back, his mouth hanging wide. He stuttered, a sense of deep betrayal washing away much of his anger and guilt. This man, the man he had blamed for nearly every bad thing that had happened to him since he was a boy, was supposed to be nearly twenty years in his grave.

"You . . . You're dead!" Jesse stammered out, his mind desperately grasping for a certainty that eluded him.

The man's cold eyes tightened at the confusion and the disordered hatred he saw in Jesse's face.

"Son, I don't know you." The voice was completely devoid of emotion. With a grunt, the axe rose into the air.

Jesse's mind was still struggling with a reality that could not be, when he realized the axe was hurtling toward him, driven with all the strength his enemy's tall frame could muster.

The outlaw chief tried to launch himself to the side, bringing up his pistol in a desperate attempt to blast the revenant before the axe could land. He knew, even as he threw himself down, that he was too late. The invulnerability that had seen him through countless shootouts and battles had deserted him in the face of his most hated enemy, seemingly risen from the grave.

The heavy blade came crashing down into his shoulder, just where the metal of his artificial arm merged with the flesh of his body. The blade bit deep, tearing at metallic components and gouging through vulnerable flesh. A grunting whimper sounded in his ears and he was horrified to realize that it had come from him.

Jesse was dashed to the ground with the force of the blow, spinning as he fell. He landed on his remaining arm, the damaged limb falling free, dragging pieces of bone, wire, and tubing with it. Blood, glowing RJ-1027, and a viscous black fluid began to spread. His vision started to dim as his heart pumped furiously, widening the pool beneath him.

Chapter 20

A large chunk of the balcony's parapet detonated, sending a shower of crimson sparks and gray dust out into the chamber and over the struggling forces below. Lucy cringed from the blast, trying to follow what was happening through the haze and the smoke. She thought she had seen Robert Pinkerton fall, Henry pressed back against the forward wall beneath a vicious onslaught. Her killer's instinct faltered as she watched the two halves of her life collide before her eyes. As the parapet blasted away, the balcony opened up. Her heart froze.

Jesse and President Lincoln were locked in vicious combat. The president's axe, William's Wrath, spun and whirled, coming at the shorter outlaw from too many directions at once. But Jesse's arms were flashing with incredible speed, his iron forearms clashing against the axe handle, stopping the head inches from his flesh at every blow.

Even from this distance, through the swirling grit and smoke, she could tell that Jesse was faltering. His shoulders were slumped, his arms slower with each shattering fall of the axe. Most of the world had thought Abraham Lincoln dead these past two decades and more. Even within the Union government and military, only a tiny fraction had been privy to the layered deception of the faked assassination. Cries of disbelief, horror, and jubilation rang through the hall as realization of his identity swept through the fighting. The presidents eyes were impassive, his face calm, as the axe blurred around him, cutting away at the outlaw's last reserves of strength.

Lucinda spun around and dragged the heavy crate toward her. With desperate fingers she pried the top off and stared in growing frustration at the contents. Grabbing a nest of belts and webbing, she pulled a heavy pack out and slung the tangle over one shoulder. Forehead wrinkled in concentration, she then began to assemble the primary components. Although designed by the mad genius, Tesla, it had been built with battlefield utility in mind. The pieces fit together cleanly and quickly.

As her hands worked to tighten the connections on the power lead, she peeked around the corner again to check on the progress of the battle. She froze.

Jesse was off balance. Something had gone wrong, and he was falling. Whether he was purposely dodging or collapsing in defeat, she could not tell. The axe arced through the air, falling toward the fallen outlaw. Jesse's gun was rising to meet the blow, but somehow, she knew he would be too late.

Even from across the cavernous chamber, she saw the axe land. The President's shoulders shook with the impact, Jesse's body collapsed beneath the blow. When he rolled away, he left a piece of himself behind.

Lucinda shrieked a single syllable, slumping against the keep's doorway, her eyes wide with shock and horror. Tesla's creation lay forgotten in her lap.

The President stood over Jesse, the axe held loosely in both hands, and he said something to the prostrate outlaw. The axe came up again, swung with a workman's skill, no anger or hostility behind it: just a job needing to be done.

But Jesse was not finished yet. As the axe rose, so did the legendary outlaw. Pushing off the floor of the balcony with his remaining arm, Jesse stood like some ancient god rising from the underworld. He was off-balance, one mechanical arm lying at his feet; but his other arm snapped up, still gripping his custom pistol, and the barrel rose like a serpent ready to strike.

The gauntlet was on her hand, although she had no memory of how it had gotten there. She wanted nothing more in the world than to separate the two men rushing toward their final confrontation. She reached out, as if grasping for Jesse's distant form.

The power pack surged, flaring with bright light and flooding the inner keep with ruby illumination. Her back, where the pack rested against it, burned with a seething, gut-wrenching pain. Lucy felt as if her arm was being ripped off. There was a thunderous crack, her nose filled with a heavy metallic scent, and something heavy crashed into her at high speed. She was knocked back against the wall of the keep, the breath dashed from her burning lungs. She collapsed to the cold flagstone floor. A heavy weight draped atop her. Something warm began to wash over her arm and side.

*****

Frank screamed, reaching out with one hand as the axe fell toward his brother's head. There was no way Jesse would survive, even if his pistol came up in time to destroy his killer. Already suffering from the brutal injury, all of the infamous speed and artistry was gone. The old nightmare had finally come to pass: his brother was going to die in front of him, and there was nothing he could do to stop it.

When Jesse disappeared in a blinding flash of ruby light, Frank fell back against the parapet, his hand rising to shield his eyes. His brother's attacker, face eerily familiar now that the hat and hood were gone, cast about in stunned confusion. The agents and officers around him were dazed as well, blinking away purple afterimages that plagued their vision.

There was a sudden lull in the combat. Faintly, through the passages out to the main parapet, Frank heard a sound he had been dreading since entering the fortress. Massed Iron Horses were approaching, and that could only mean one thing. He had known the cavalry had not been routed, that they would return before the battle was finished. He had hoped to secure the fort before their arrival. Safe behind the high walls, Jesse would have had more than enough men to hold the fortress against a single regiment of cavalry.

But they were nowhere near securing the fort, and now Jesse had disappeared, literally. If they did not make a push for the gate soon, they were going to be trapped inside and slaughtered like cattle.

Frank turned to look out over the vast chamber, looking for someone to marshal the rebels and organize a fighting retreat for the door. As he scanned the floor of the central chamber, however, his eyes fell upon two figures slumped against the door of the small inner keep. One of them, lying on top of the other, had only one arm. The other, struggling to rise from beneath the first, was the last person he had expected to see.

Lucinda Loveless looked up at him, her beautiful face a mask of fear and concern. Frank looked around, the two were alone. He began to wave her toward the front gate when the parapet in front of him exploded, chips of rock stabbing into his face as he ducked beneath the stone.

That damned Wraith again. Frank swore he was going to execute that dark bastard before the day was done.

*****

Lucinda gave a sharp gasp as Frank James fell, a cloud of powder and crimson sparks erupting from his position. She watched for a moment, hoping to see him rise again, but there was nothing more than swirling smoke and glittering dust. She realized she could not wait for Frank, and looked around for anyone who could take Jesse to safety.

Jesse barely clung to consciousness. Blood continued to pour from the horrible wound at his shoulder, mingling with a black, foul-smelling liquid, and dribbles of RJ-1027. His eyes rolled in his head and his mouth worked desperately, but the sounds carried no meaning.

There were no rebels nearby. Most were fighting on the walls or running for the entrance. Lucinda gathered herself to lift Jesse up, planning to move him toward the gate, when a new flood of men came rushing into the fortress. The redoubts and barricades obscured the newcomers as they scrambled for cover against the desperately retreating rebels, but their insignia was clear. The 7th had recovered from whatever debacle they had suffered outside the fort and were back for revenge.

Lucinda looked around, but there was nowhere to hide. Only the keep, rising behind her, offered any sort of shelter. Her heart sank. Running now would be futile, she knew. She refused to lay there for Custer to find, with Jesse at her feet. With a grunt, she shoved the door wide and dragged the outlaw chief's limp body after her.

She pushed the heavy gate closed with her gauntleted hand and slid down against it, her breath coming in ragged gasps. Jesse's chest rose and fell with a fluttering motion that reminded her of an old hunting dog breathing his last. Blood was seeping from the corner of the outlaw's mouth, staining the short beard a deep black in the gloomy half-light. His eyes were heavy-lidded, pupils darting feverishly as if following a will-o-the-wisp that only he could see.

Lucinda scrambled to Jesse's side and hauled him back up so that he was resting against her leg, rocking him gently. For the first time in her life, she did not know what to do.

Jesse's mouth moved slowly, as if in a dream, and the shallow breaths came in a pattern barely recognizable as speech. She urged him to rest as she took off his hat, leather thongs clutching the scorched remnant of an owl feather. She brushed the hair away from his sallow face. As a single coherent word forced its way through his muttering, Lucinda felt her throat tighten painfully.

". . . home . . ."

Her resolve stiffened beneath the ringing of the single word. She hoisted him roughly to his feet.

"Come on, Jesse. On your feet, bastard! We can't go out, and we can't go up, so we're going to go down." Her voice was hoarse as she whispered the words, draping his remaining arm over her shoulders and bracing him as best she could. She flexed the fingers within the gauntlet, hoping the little machine would be able to produce another miracle down in the vaults.

The stairs were brutal as she maneuvered downward, the heavy power pack hanging from its tangled straps over her other shoulder. Every few steps she had to stop to catch her breath, resting Jesse against the cool stone of the wall for a moment before gathering him up once again with a grunt and dragging him a few more steps deeper down.

Lucinda's memory was betraying her, she knew, but she thought they were only a few steps from the bottom when the sound of a single pair of running feet broke into her concentration. Someone was running up, from the vaults, straight at them.

The agent settled Jesse into a sitting position against the wall and then drew one of her derringers. At this point, there was no telling who they were going to run into, but she would be damned if they were going to take him away from her.

She had never met the man who came stumping around the corner, but she recognized his face from a hundred wanted posters and a thousand fireside conversations with Jesse James and his posse. William Bonney had a distinctive face, and even without his signature arrogant smirk, she knew him.

The derringer came up just as Billy the Kid's own battered pistols drew a bead on her. His eyes widened as he saw that she was a woman.

Billy's arms froze, slowly drifting wide. The weapons' barrels pointed at the high ceiling in a show of peaceful intent. A ghost of the smirk emerged from the mask of dirt, grime, and disappointment.

"Well, I'll be damned." He nodded politely. "You must be Jesse's new girl, eh?" His face quirked slightly, his head cocking to one side. "What the hell you wearin', sweet thing?"

Lucinda lowered her own pistol but kept her arm stiff, ready to bring it up in a moment. She nodded back, despite her annoyance with the label. "William Bonney."

The smirk widened. "Call me Billy, please." His eyes glittered with amusement, and for a moment she wondered what he thought was so funny. Then, his eyes darted down and past her, to where Jesse lay, all but unconscious, against the stone. "Oh, damn –"

The derringer rose again as Lucinda stepped in front of Jesse. "You might want to step back a pace or two, Mr. Bonney." She kept her voice calm, but there was an edge that could not be missed.

Billy's pistols rose a bit higher and he bowed his head to show he understood. He gestured with his guns, then looked down at his holsters and up again with a single quirked eyebrow. She nodded, but kept her derringer on him until his own were secured.

"Can I look at him?" Billy gestured vaguely at his fallen rival. She nodded reluctantly and stepped aside, lowering her pistol.

"I was trying to get him out of the fort, but—" She did everything she could to control her voice, but she could hear an edge slipping in. Any moment now, and she was either going to break down into inconsolable sobs or tear back up the stairs and kill everything in sight.

Billy nodded even as he cursed. "Those Billy Yank trotters're back, eh?" He was kneeling beside Jesse's broken body, shaking his head at the other outlaw chief's condition.

Lucinda went to one knee beside him, also looking into Jesse's pain-twisted face. "I don't know what else to do." She made a gesture with the gauntleted hand. "I think this could be used to dig a tunnel, but I'm not sure how to make it do that." Her face tightened with frustration and concern. "And I'm not sure about Jesse. His arm . . ."

The outlaw gave her a grin she supposed was meant to be comforting. "Nah, miss. He's a tough ol' road agent. This ain't the first time this has happened to him, remember."

Her eyes did not move. "There's no way out, Billy. Once the cavalry have secured the fort, they'll come down here."

His smirk returned with full force. "Well, that ain't entirely so, miss. What would you say if I told you someone had . . . passed along a little consideration to some of the workers here, to build in a little tunnel, a little hidden back door, in anticipation of future need?"

Her eyes snapped up to Billy's grinning face. He nodded before she could speak, and continued. "I got a map. If we can't go up, like you say, we can always go down."

Her eyes narrowed. "You're offering to take Jesse away from here? After what he did to you out in the desert?"

The smirk faded, and the outlaw shrugged. "Well, yeah, that stung, a bit. But . . ." He nodded down at Jesse. "This ain't the way I wanna take the gold ring, miss. I don't want the story of the greatest rivalry of the Wild West to be settled by some blue-belly chiselers hundreds of miles from anyone who cares." The smirk returned. "Asides, I know a man who'll pay good money for the tech, if Jesse comes a cropper."

Lucinda rose to her feet, the pistol once again coming up, and Billy scrambled away a bit, his smirk still in place despite his raised hands. "Just havin' a bit o' fun, miss. I'll see him back to the doc, get him all fixed up. I swear it by my sainted father." A gleam arose in his eyes to match the smirk, but she let it pass.

She looked down at Jesse and then back up at Billy, her resolve once again wavering. When she moved, however, it was with the quick, sure motion of a striking rattler. Before he was even aware he was in danger, a derringer was pressed against his forehead.

"You're going to take him, and you're going to get him to safety." Her words were cold, her eyes flat. "And if anything happens to him before he is fully restored, and I mean ANYTHING at all, there is nowhere on earth you will be able to hide from me."

Billy nodded quickly, his hands held just a little higher. "I promise, miss. He'll get back to Payson safe."

She nodded in return, her pistol lowering slowly, and then she gestured with it, back down the stairway. "I hope you don't mind, but I think maybe I'll accompany you to the back door?"

Billy's frown deepened. "You ain't comin' with us, miss? I was thinkin', him in the shape he's in, you wouldn't be wantin' to stick around with those that nearly done for him."

Lucinda shook her head, looking back up the stairway. "I've got unfinished business up there, but I'll see you two safe away," she nodded toward Jesse. "I'll make sure you've gotten him out, but then I have to go back up." Her face turned grim. "There are a couple people who owe me some answers."

Billy looked at her for a moment and then nodded. "Well, suit yourself, lil' lady." He reached down, hoisted Jesse's body up with a grunt, and began to drag him back down the steps. He looked over his shoulder to pick his way down the stairs and then turned back to her with a smirk. "You think you wanna take the lead here, sweetheart?"

*****

Abraham Lincoln stood upon the broken wall of Fort Knox and looked out over the still-burning plain and the columns of smoke disappearing into the unrelieved darkness of the night sky. The last of the rebels had been ridden down by the cavalry or escaped into the broken land beyond, but the shattered walls and the scorched earth was a stark reminder of the battle. The massive holes in their ranks would be a harsher reminder still.

Robert Pinkerton was in the fortress's infirmary along with a score of other officers. Major Dalton had fallen protecting Colonel Campbell from the worst of the rebel's final assault, but even the Colonel had waded into the battle at the end, picking up several wounds of his own. Courtright had been cut savagely across his abdomen and arms, but had returned to duty as soon as the bandages had been applied. Despite the direst warnings of the infirmary's doctors, he would not be pulled from the president's side, and haunted the parapet like a silent shadow.

"Sir," the voice was hesitant. The rank and file within the fortress were all struggling with the problem of how to address him. Some, he knew, whispered that he was some vile replacement cooked up in a lab in Washington. Others were firmly convinced he was some sort of ghost, or a tool of Carpathian. Even those who believed he was who he said he was did not really understand. And every one of them would have to be sworn to secrecy, if there was to be any hope of rebuilding his anonymity.

He turned slowly to look at the young soldier addressing him. "Yes, son?"

The boy swallowed and nodded with a jerk. "Sir, Colonel Custer wishes to return to Fort Frederick. We've just received a report regarding some sort of attack his forces back west were conducting. It seems something's gone wrong up there. He's afraid for the security of the base."

The tall man bowed his head. Below the wall in front of him, and within the fortress itself, his dead and wounded were still being dug from the wreckage. Was this not tragedy enough for one night?

He nodded without looking up. "Certainly. Give him our thanks, and make sure he takes sufficient resupply for the return journey." The tall man's lip twisted slightly, "General Grant's reinforcements should be here before the sun rises." He looked up at the distant, dark horizon. "I doubt the rebels will have even stopped running by then."

The boy gave a sharp salute and pivoted on his heel. "Sir, yes sir."

The old man looked back out over the smoldering plain. After a moment, he tilted his head to speak to the shadow behind him. "Any word on prisoners, Henry?"

The agent shook his head. "No, sir." His voice was a whispered ruin. "The fighting was fierce around the gate, but a lot of the dogs escaped. We've got prisoners, of course, too many to count, really. Wade's begun interrogations, but he hasn't discovered anything of account yet."

There was a moment's silence, and then the agent continued. "Sir, that was a close-run thing." He looked out over the smoking plains, refusing to meet the president's eyes. "That damned outlaw almost had you. When he recognized you, I thought you were lost for sure. There isn't anyone on the continent that bears a hatred that hot for anyone."

The president nodded and continued his silent vigil. Behind him, in the shadows of the secondary wall, Henry Courtright's eyes were fixed on the hellish prairie fires. Lucy was still missing, and he hoped she would turn up soon. It was going to be a long night.

*****

Billy dragged the unconscious weight of his rival down the echoing hall, sweat stinging his eyes and weakening his grip. The clicking of the woman's heels echoed off the cold stone all around them, working its way into his head and making his brain itch. He had not really bargained on carrying Jesse James, all but a corpse and incapable of standing on his own, all the way back to the Contested Territories.

"We need to be careful moving through here." Her voice, a voice he would have loved to listen to under other circumstances, was just another annoyance as his back burned and sweat beaded down his forehead.

"Why?" He grunted out.

"The UR-30 Enforcers that were sent here were never deployed up in the fortress." She was probing ahead of them with a small hand light, a derringer in her other fist. "I'm thinking they were probably put down here. I know there are at least ten of them, and I haven't seen them since I arrived last night."

With a shrug, he continued on.

The tattered map he had crammed into his pocket was barely legible at this point. He was already deeper into the vaults than he had been during his brief search for treasure. All he had found in his initial exploration had been empty vaults, solid metal doors swinging loosely on their hinges. The last several doors they had passed had been closed tight. He was fairly sure he had stumbled upon the part of the place Carpathian had meant him to find all along.

Billy was brought up short as he realized that the woman agent had stopped at the next corner. She was making a patting gesture with her gauntleted hand as she peered around in the gloomy red half-light on the other side. The outlaw dropped his burden beside the wall, just a little less gentle than he could have been, and moved up beside the woman, his own pistol drawn again.

The hall continued on for about thirty feet before it reached an intersection, branching off to the right and left. In the center of the wall straight ahead was another vault door, this one closed tight. At the intersection, standing as still as statues, were four UR-30 Enforcers, their weapons holstered and their eyes burning a dull crimson.

Billy ducked back behind the corner, his spine to the wall, and smiled. The agent stooped beside him, her face dark. "What's so funny?" Her harsh whisper was not quite enough to overcome the appeal of her soft lips, and his smile widened.

"I'm just thinkin'," he shrugged. "I come a long way, miss. I'd like to have a little somethin' to show for the journey afore I hightail it back to the territories." He nodded his head toward the guarded passage. "I'm thinkin', they got so many metal marshals standing guard just there, might be that's a door I'd want to open on my way out."

She snarled at him. "We're trying to get the two of you out, not indulge in petty thievery."

He shrugged. "The size of that door? I'm not sure 'petty' would be the right word for it." His eyes hardened slightly. "Either way, not sure I was givin' you a choice in the matter."

She looked down at him with a sneer and then closed her eyes, huffing in exasperation. "What are you thinking?"

The grin brightened even more, and he scrambled around to gesture to the gauntlet and its power pack. "You said that thing can put a hole in anything, right?"

She nodded with a frown. "I was thinking maybe I'd try to dig out, before we met up with you. But yes, that's what I read."

He smiled. "Well, then, fancy givin' a lad a chance?" He held out his hands, and after a moment she stripped the gauntlet off and shrugged out of the power pack's nest of straps and harness clamps.

Billy untangled the harness and then hoisted the pack into position, putting both arms through the straps and tightening it over his chest. He looked up at the woman with eager eyes. "You reckon you can help me make a hole, say, about this big?" He held his hands about a foot apart.

"I think so." Her brow furrowed as she tried to remember the papers she had seen. With hesitant fingers, she fiddled with some knobs and sliders on the gauntlet's wrist. When she was done, some numbers in a little window, glowing red with RJ-1027, seemed to have changed. "That should to do it."

Billy nodded again and then gave her a questioning look, raising the gauntlet in a shrug. "And so I . . . ?"

The lovely mouth quirked in a smile that he thought showed some promise, then the agent reached out and turned the gauntlet palm up. "You reach toward whatever you want to open up, and you just grab at it, with a twist." She tapped on the thumb. "There's a button in there, against the nail?" He nodded when he felt the button. "As you reach out, flick that. It'll do the trick."

He felt a rush of excitement. He had always wanted to get a leg up on Jesse and his damned arms. This was the first time he had gotten the chance to play with some of this new tech himself. If his idea worked, this was going to be a legend he could put up against anything Jesse had ever done.

"Ready?" Without waiting for a response, he wheeled around the corner, racing for the intersection. He heard the agent swear under her breath as she charged out after him.

Billy laid down a solid stream of fire with his off-hand, the crimson bolts zapping down the corridor, illuminating everything in shifting, tottering highlights. The bolts slapped into the wall all around the metal men, some sleeting off their armored hides. The figures were still while he took his first full strides down the hall, then suddenly leapt into motion, as if triggered by some unseen puppeteer. All four drew their massive pistols, and the air filled with their humming, vibrating shots. Answering bolts flashed down the hall toward him, and he knew the time had come.

Billy dodged to the side and reached up with the heavy gauntlet. He made as if to snatch at the head of the robot on the far left of the line and flicked the button with a backward nudge of his thumb closing the hand and bringing it quickly back toward his shoulder. There was a red flash from the pack on his back, his arm wrenched painfully, and an awful, mechanical smell filled his nostrils. Something flashed into the air by his head and he threw himself down onto the stone floor. He was just able to make out the head and shoulders of a robot sailing over him, trailing wires, tubes, chunks of glowing metal, and crimson sparks.

Billy howled in uncontrolled glee as he rolled over onto his back to watch the bits of metal marshal bounce down the corridor. A massive detonation caused him to spin around again, and he whooped even louder. Glowing red traced where the head and chest sections had once been attached. The robot flailed wildly, its enormous pistol firing shots into the walls and ceiling. One of the shots, at point blank range, took the next Enforcer in line in the chest, blowing metallic components out its back and down the side passage. In a blinding flash of ruby light, both robots collapsed into a loose jumble of twitching metal scrap.

A cloud of dust and smoke, lit from within by flickering crimson lightning, spread out from the downed figures, obscuring their partners. The agent's bolts snapped into the cloud as she ran past Billy, dropping to slide across the stone floor beneath the erratic spray of fire, her skirts flaring in a very intriguing way. For a moment, there was only stunned silence as Billy lay on his back, staring at the spreading cloud, while Loveless crouched by the far wall, her derringers at the ready. The shooting within the churning dust had stopped.

With more dignity than they probably deserved, the two remaining UR-30s toppled out of the arid fog, a glowing hole in each of their burnished chests.

Billy sprang up with a whoop and snatched his hat off his head, slapping his knee. Rock dust puffed into the air. The agent rose more slowly, her guns trained on the thinning mist. It took a moment for either of them to realize that the cloud seemed to be glowing a rich golden color, getting brighter by the moment.

Billy slid the gauntlet off his hand, shrugged out of the straps, and let the power pack drop to the floor. He pulled his second pistol, finding comfort in the familiar grips of his regular weapons, and stalked toward the crumpled shapes of the metal men. As the dust and smoke continued to drift away, he approached the warm glow, one hand outstretched. The glow was shining out of the open vault door. Somehow, as the gauntlet had pulled the robot's head off, it had also grabbed a chunk out of the door behind. And as unlikely as it seemed, it appeared that he had pulled out parts of the locking mechanism.

He heard the agent step up beside him, and looked over with his customary smirk. "Pretty good for a first shot, if I do say so myself."

She looked at him with an arched eyebrow, her gaze flickering up over his head. "Yes, well, you did. You're also very lucky you're so short."

He had always been sensitive about his height, but this comment was so brutally random, coming at him from out of nowhere, that he forgot to get ornery. "What?"

She nodded to his hat. He took it off and looked at it. Two neat holes, their edges still smoldering, had been punched through the felt. He did not know whether to laugh or curse. He finally decided on a sarcastic little chuckle and then turned back toward the open door.

The chamber beyond was an exact duplicate of the room buried in the desert sands beyond Diablo Canyon. It lacked the piled dust of centuries, of course, and the horrid stink of Carpathian's abandoned creations, but other than that, he could very well have been back again. Except for one alarming difference; the pedestal in the center of the chamber beneath Fort Knox was not empty.

A fragment of stone, one surface polished and intricately-carved, hung suspended in the air above the column. It was longer than his forearm, thick and heavy. Swirled engravings swept along its full length, a silvery sheath curling around a portion of the stone. The radiance, however, was shining out from the buttery-golden rock itself. It was as if he were looking at a chunk of heaven fallen to earth, and its light flooded through him, overwhelming him with a sense of safety and warmth such as he had not known since before his mother had coughed her last breath.

"Holy mother of God . . ." A hoarse voice spooked Billy and he jumped, turning with one hand on a pistol, to see Jesse holding himself up by the door frame. "What the hell—"

Billy smiled widely. "This, I think, is what we been fightin' over for more'n a year, James."

The older outlaw chief could not take his bruised and hollow eyes off the floating piece of stone. "What is. . ." His words drifted off, his eyes rolled up into his skull, and he slumped back to the stone floor.

Billy's smile widened. "It's mine, is what it is." He turned to approach the object as the reverberating sound of metal feet echoed off the walls.

"The other Enforcers." The woman was beside Jesse, looking up at Billy. "You have to get him out of here. Is your tunnel nearby?"

Billy took a moment to recall what she was talking about and then nodded. "Yeah. We're almost there."

The beautiful woman nodded, her eyes cold. "Alright, then. You both go that way. I'll lead the rest of the robots off, then make my way back up to the fortress."

Billy's smile slipped a bit. He looked around her at the smoking robots in the hall. "You're still not comin' with us? Even after all that?"

The dark eyes hardened even further. "Especially after all that. These units wouldn't answer to any of the commanders upstairs. This whole thing has been a trap, designed to bring two implacable enemies face to face, and I'm not sure who was bait and who was prey. There's a deeper game going on here, and I'm going to dig up some answers before I move on."

Billy's smile disappeared for good. His head snapped from the artifact, to Jesse, to the agent, and back. With a snarl he lurched toward the stone, reaching out with both gloved hands.

"You idiot!" The Union woman lashed out with one hand to stop him, but missed.

The heat radiating off the stone became more uncomfortable with each step. The glow seemed to grow more and more intense, and he had to shield his eyes with one raised forearm.

"You don't even know what that thing is, you moron!" She was calling out to him, still standing at the door. "Trust me, it takes more than you've got here to make off with something like that! We need to get out of here now!"

Billy stopped beside the pedestal, looking up at the hovering chunk of ancient stone. With a tentative hand he reached up, thinking to topple it off its stand. The stone would not budge. He grunted and put both hands on the warm, smooth rock, pushing with all his might. It did not move.

With a roar of frustration, Billy backed away from the object, again shielding his eyes. When he stood once more beside the woman, he glanced at her through his pained squint. With a vicious twist he turned around, grabbed Jesse none-too-gently beneath his shoulders, and dragged him down the hall, away from the approaching metal footsteps.

"Don't matter none." He spat over his shoulder. "Someday, one of those rocks is gonna be mine."

Her smile, out of the corner of his eyes, held no amusement. "Whatever you say, you curly wolf, you." Before he could summon up a response, she was gone, running in the direction of the pounding metal feet.

The two outlaw bosses were far down the corridor by the time they heard the high, sharp reports of the derringers. The clang of falling metal bodies was followed soon after by the quick tapping of the agent's high-heeled boots moving off into the distance. No sounds of further pursuit spurred them to greater speed. Billy dropped Jesse in exhaustion and disgust, shaking his head and gasping for breath.

The rest of the way to the secret tunnel was quiet and dark as they moved through rough and unfinished corridors. The door itself was concealed behind a pile of wood and canvas tarps. Billy pushed his way through and then dragged Jesse out behind him. The tunnel was long, dark, and narrow. By the time they emerged, the young outlaw chief was panting again from the exertion.

The cold night air welcomed them to the surface, jerking Jesse awake with a painful snort. His eyes rolled wildly as he tried to fix his position, but his face was slack and confused. Billy squatted down beside him, looking into those wild, uncomprehending eyes, and thought seriously about leaving Jesse there in the abandoned gully to die.

But there had been the heat of truth in the lady agent's threats. Billy knew he would do everything he could to get Jesse back to Carpathian. They would both owe him, then, and that suited William Bonney just fine.

Although, thinking of debts, something occurred to Billy as he crouched there beside his dazed old foe.

The young outlaw chief took out his pistol slowly, feeling the heavy weight of the blaster, the heat of the RJ power packs glowing from the vents and indicators. Then, with a savage lurch of his shoulder, he brought the butt of the pistol across Jesse' jaw. With a grunt, the older man slumped into the wet grass, his breath releasing in a long, heavy sigh.

"Now I reckon we're startin' from even, Jesse me boy." The smirk was back as Billy stood, looking around for the Iron Horses they had hidden away earlier that day.

Epilogue

"Have no fear. You will be compensated for your losses and for your good service here today."
Something about the voice was familiar. There was an echo of a foreign accent. No name immediately came to mind, only a vague sense of pain, loss, confusion, and danger.

"Damn straight I will!" That was a voice more easily recognized, with the curves and burrs of the western territories. "Your pretty boy here'd be dead if it weren't fer me! An' if I hadn't been draggin' his sorry ass all over God's creation, I coulda walked away with a shiny little prize, too: a nice shiny rock just the match of your'n over there."

The voice's petulance was jarring, discomforting. It made his cheek throb with phantom pain. Something in the voice was uncomfortable and irritating, even through the cool shadows.

"So you said." The first voice spoke again. "And believe me, we will discuss that more at a later time. For now, I have work to do."

The phrase sent a shock of cold through the darkness, jerking him toward consciousness. A sudden, deep-seated fear stabbed through him.

"Yeah, I guess you do." The harshness of the second voice was colored with amusement now. The tone instantly shifted the fear to anger. "You gonna make 'im a new one, 'r leave 'im as is?"

Jesse James was catapulted back to full awareness with these final words ringing in his ears. Bloodshot eyes snapped open and his neck surged from side to side as he tried to take stock of his situation. His entire body ached as if he had been dropped off a cliff. His left arm burned, and a particularly deep ache throbbed throughout the left side of his face. His vision was blurry, as if he had just emerged from deep water. He peered through the pulsing distortion, and could just make out a figure leaning over him. A shock of white hair hovered over the half-formed features of a blurred face.

"Ah, James! Welcome back to the land of the living!" The voice clicked into place in his memory, and Jesse lurched forward again.

He was on a hard bed, rough sheets draped over his body. He surged upward, reached back to push himself off the bed, and pitched to the left as his arm failed to support him. He nearly fell, flailing wildly with the right arm and barely catching the edge of the bedframe before he slid onto the floor.

Carpathian was hovering over him, but as Jesse burst upward, the doctor backed quickly away. The outlaw chief steadied himself on the bed and sat up straighter, raising his left arm to inspect it. He did not have a left arm. The twisted metal wreckage that had remained jutting from his wound had been removed, and the insertion points covered over in rough bandages spotted with old, brown blood.

"Wha—" Jesse's head whipped around. His vision was clearing, and his frantic motion settled upon Carpathian. A self-satisfied smirk twisted behind the doctor's beard. Jesse snarled, his brows drawing down heavily over his eyes. "You bastard . . ."

Carpathian's smile widened and he put one hand out in a calming gesture. "Now, James, no need for base mockery."

Jesse's scowl deepened. He gestured with the shattered, cloth-wrapped stump of his left arm. "Then you best be callin' me *Mister* James, then, yeah? You left me out in that desert to die, you scrofulous dust gnat! You turned 'em off, dumped me into the sand, an' left me to die!"

Carpathian's face took on a calm, fatherly cast and he shook his head. "No, James. I left you there to continue your education." The doctor moved around the table, his eyes taking in the ruin of the outlaw's arm. The smile returned, although a little more subdued. "And it looks to me as if you're off to a fine start!"

Jesse looked down at the throbbing stump and then back up at the old man. "What happened at the fort . . . Where's Frank?"

Carpathian's eyes turned sad for a moment. "Oh, I'm afraid the assault on Fort Knox was unsuccessful, James. I'm not certain of the disposition of your compatriots, however—"

Jesse tensed, trying to sit up. "I failed, then. I lost everything that mattered in that damned fort." His eyes hardened. "But if you think that's broken me down, you go ahead and shut off the other arm, doc. I'll jump off this bed and kick you to death, and tear your heart out with my teeth!"

He lurched forward, planning on lunging at the doctor, trying to catch him unprepared, but he was brought up short by a leather strap around his waist. The outlaw chief was thrown back against the bed. Jesse growled low in his throat. It was a dangerous, cornered-animal sound, and it deepened as Carpathian's smile widened in response.

"Now, James. What makes you think you failed?" The man's eyes were almost kindly as he looked down on the wounded outlaw. If Jesse had been less familiar with the man, he would have almost believed him. "You have accomplished great things, my boy. *Great* things!"

The words scratched like tiny claws across tender flesh, and Jesse fell back against the bed with a heavy, desolate sigh. "I doomed the Confederacy. I sold them a hope, then got it burned away. I shamed 'em into standin' up, an' they got slapped down. Those folks won't be lookin' up from their yokes again."

Carpathian eyes now burned with sincerity as he firmly shook his head. Jesse felt a twist in his gut, shocked with the direct, honest power of the European's gaze. "No, James. You proved to them that they *can* stand up! You showed them the way, and they know they can do it now. You placed the sons and daughters of slaves on an even footing with the children of the old masters, and there won't be any closing *that* Pandora's box! The army you led against the Union was barely a fraction of the fighting strength of the new generation, James. And now they have martyrs to worship, and they *know* they can fight. They will rise again when the time is right." His smile was now almost predatory, and Jesse looked quickly away, a feeling of wrongness skittering down his spine.

"Well, they ain't gonna be fightin' any time soon." The voice behind his head spoke again, and for some reason, the pain in his left cheek gave a sickening lurch. "Leastways, not the ones *I* saw runnin'."

Jesse turned awkwardly around to stare at Billy the Kid with hard, cold eyes. The younger outlaw chief smirked at him and waved a jaunty hand. "Howdy, Jesse!"

"What the hell're you doin' here?" Jesse's voice was dangerous beneath its hoarse roughness.

Billy gave a pained expression with all the sincerity of a five cent whore. "Why, Jesse, who d'you think dragged you outta that mess? Why, without me, you woulda bled out on that floor!"

Fragmented impressions of his flight through the dungeons beneath Fort Knox came back to him in a rush. One image rose above the others, his heart racing with equal parts fear and hope. "Lucy?"

Billy looked at him with a blank face for a moment, and Jesse could see that he was weighing options in his mind. When the Kid shrugged, he knew he was going to get the truth. "Yeah, she was okay. Last time I saw her, anyway. She was headin' back into the fort. You reckon she's Union through an' through, Jesse?" The jab cut deep.

Jesse ignored the question and posed his own. "You know what happened to Frank? The Youngers?"

Billy nodded. "Yeah, most of 'em got out. Jimmy Younger came up a cropper, I heard, an' that Ford galoot, Charlie, was it?" He shrugged. "The rest of 'em made it out, much as I can tell. They's scattered all over hell's half acre, though, makin' their way back to the territories by a dozen different trails."

Jesse nodded, relief at his brother's survival outweighing his current distaste for the source of the news. His face turned bleak. "What about Lincoln?"

Billy's face paled slightly. "You heard that, eh? No one seems to know fer sure. Lots o' rumors, but that's it. He weren't seen after the battle by any o' my boys, so who knows?" He shrugged. "Maybe you can ask Frank when you see 'im next."

"And you will have plenty of time and opportunity to gather the old gang back together." Carpathian turned and began to work on something lying on a table behind him. "We need to get you back in fighting trim, James." The doctor tapped on his remaining metal arm. "I'm sure you will wish to have a working complement when you gather your friends again. And I'm sure William has someplace he needs to be."

Billy's smirk widened, the cruel light in his eyes flaring high. "Sure do. There ain't but room for one curly wolf in the woods." He nodded down at Jesse's mangled shoulder. "And it sure ain't gonna be no old Algerine down a paw, neither."

"Keep talkin', Billy." Jesse sneered at The Kid. "When I get outta this bed—"

The doctor waved a free hand at Billy. "Now, Mr. Bonney. If you could see your way out?"

Billy sneered for a moment, then straightened to his full height, tugged his vest down, and nodded once to them. "Well, I'll see you boys out on the trail, no doubt." He tipped his hat to the doctor and then Jesse. "And I trust we'll all remember today."

A door behind Jesse's head closed with a dull thud. He shook his head and muttered. "I ain't likely to forget that soaplock, no matter how far he carried me."

"You will have plenty to occupy your mind, James." Carpathian spoke over his shoulder, still working on the table. "I did not let you loose into the great wide world so you could damage my costly gifts, boy. The world has big plans for you, but it will all be for naught if you go and get yourself killed with carelessness."

Jesse turned back to look at the doctor. "I don't carry your water, doc."

Carpathian paused for a moment in his work, his shoulders tensing. Jesse would never have admitted to the sudden concern he felt as the seconds ticked away, nor the relief that came over him as the old man shrugged, obviously deciding to ignore the slight, and went back to his work.

"James, there are wheels within wheels churning just beneath the surface of our world. There are forces at work that none of us can even begin to comprehend." He turned slowly, placing his tools gently back on the table behind him. "There will come a day when we must all band together or we will all die alone." His eyes grew more intense as he leaned toward the bed. "It is not a question of carrying water, James, but of survival."

Jesse shook his head. "I ain't followin' you, doc." It felt good to push his luck further. "An' we ain't so situated that I'm takin' a lot on faith just now."

Carpathian ignored the belittling title completely, reaching back to pull a stool closer to the bedside. "You have noticed them moving through our lives, James. I know you have. The fiery-eyed avatars of a power that we are only beginning to perceive?"

Jesse's eyes tightened. "Fiery-eyed? You mean . . . folks with red eyes . . ."

The doctor shook his head. "Sometimes, James, but not always. Often there is no way to detect their presence until after their infernal work is done, or they are ready to move on." His eyes lost their focus as he shifted on the stool, his head lowering, voice growing distant. "They may appear as normal men for days, weeks, even years. But when their job is done, when they are ready to depart, you will realize that their advice has been poison." The doctor's eyes were bleak. "Everything they have offered you has turned to ash."

Jesse sank back against the rough sack beneath his head. In his mind he was seeing young Ty, who had died so strangely outside of Diablo Canyon, and Henderson, the false emissary of Captain Quantrill. He remembered the croaking last words of Tinker Thane as blood flooded the whites of his eye in the back of an Ironhide wagon.

"Who . . . what are they . . . ?" Jesse's voice was a whisper. He could not forget the eerie smile on Ty's face just before he was obliterated by Union fire.

Carpathian shook his head, looking back down at the outlaw chief. "Who are they? What are they? I don't know, James. And they have plagued my life longer than anyone else I have ever encountered." He gestured with a wave of his hand at the apparatus that surrounded them. "I have them to thank for all of this, ironically. They have haunted my every step since I was a young man, whispering dark words into my egomaniacal ears."

Jesse knew the confusion bubbling up in his mind was clear on his face. "You have them to thank for all of *this*?"

The doctor sighed, his shoulders sagging as he slouched down on the stool. "I believe so, yes. At several points in my career, when the world seemed ready to reject me or my discoveries, they would find me. They would assist me, point me in the right direction, offer me inspiration or insight."

His eyes were unfocused again. "I never considered the cost until it was too late."

Jesse struggled back up, resting on his one metal elbow. "Wait a minute, doc. Does this mean you ain't fixin' to end Grant no more?"

Carpathian's eyes hardened. "Oh, no, James. The existence of this dark cabal of mysterious strangers has no bearing upon the debts I owe *that* butcher. There will be a reckoning before long, never fear."

He stood up and began to pace beside the bed, Jesse watching him with confusion. "Throughout history, I believe, these dark strangers have plagued mankind. I do not know who or what they are. Yet. They seem to exist outside the normal order of nature's laws. I do not know what their motives might be." He turned to look directly into Jesse's eyes, and the wounded man knew he was hearing the truth. "But I am close, James. I am so close. And when I understand it fully, I will wrestle with that power, and I will bend it to my will."

The doctor stood up tall again, looking down his regal nose at Jesse's wasted body. "When that time comes, I will need allies, and I will not stand with a man like Grant. I will need those who understand the enemy, and the stakes. I will need allies like you, James."

Jesse shook his head. "I still don't cotton to your meanin', doc. I ain't gonna march to your tune any more than I was woulda marched to Lee's or Grant's, or anyone else's."

Carpathian sat back down, a slight smile now playing around his mouth. "Of course not, James. But when these dark days finally dawn, we will all be fighting for our lives, our friends, and perhaps even our very souls. In a battle such as that, one has no chance of winning without wealth. We will need gold to arm and equip our friends. We will need the strength of men and women willing to fight for a cause they believe in. And we will need experience to show us the way."

Jesse sat up straighter, looking at the doctor in disbelief. "You wanted this all to happen. You set this all up." His voice sounded flat, even in his own ears. When the doctor nodded, he felt a sour surge rise to the back of his throat.

"Yes, James. Yes, I did. Well, most of it. The trap itself was devised by others, meant, I believe, to provide both you and your resurrected arch nemesis an irresistible lure that would bring you together. I assume the intent was for you to kill each other, or at the very least, for one of you to die. That's all speculation, you understand. But I was more than happy to utilize the trap, insofar as I could assure your survival and extraction, when the time was right."

Jesse stared up at the doctor with leery eyes. "How could you o' known there'd be those who coulda gotten me out? You couldn't a'—"

Carpathian smiled kindly and shook his head. "Please, James. Don't think our enemies are the only ones capable of manipulation. I needed you there, and then I needed you taken away." He gestured around them. "And now here you are. It was a gamble, of course. You are not the only horse I laid money on. You were just the favorite to win."

Jesse shook his head, but could not marshal a more coherent denial.

"You needed experience, you see. And I needed to know that the Confederacy was still capable of rising from the ashes." The lecturing tone nearly drove Jesse out of the bed despite the restraining belt. "The men who rule there now are pale shadows of their former selves, and, I believe, completely in thrall to our real enemies. I have not even begun to disentangle the purposes of this Dark Council. They seem to instigate violence more often than anything else, but they have counseled caution and docility as well, when it suits them. I have been able to come to only one conclusion as to their deeper motives."

The doctor leaned down to look directly into Jesse's eyes. "They seek to weaken us all."

"Why?" Jesse struggled with the complex web of possibilities the doctor wove. "They ain't workin' fer Grant?" Carpathian waved that away. "No, no more than he is working for them. Each of us retains our free will, James. Each of us makes our own choices. That is why I will hound Grant to the ends of the Earth for his crimes. But no, these beings do not work for him, or any other power I have been able to discover. They work for themselves, undermining our every effort."

Jesse thought about it for a second. "They're going to attack us."

Carpathian nodded, his eyes dark. "Weaken us, play us against each other, and then strike when we are at our most vulnerable."

Jesse eased back on the bed again. A thought occurred to him that made something in his conscience itch. "What about the Warrior Nation?"

The doctor shrugged. "One would think they would be ideal allies. They seem impervious to the influence of this Dark Council. But they reserve a very special hatred for the advances these beings have made possible." His eyes turned cold. "I do not intend to surrender my technologies to join the savages in their tents in the forest, James. I will defeat these creatures, seize from them their knowledge and their power, and then . . . Well, then we shall see who rules this continent."

Carpathian stood once again, stared at Jesse for a moment, and then turned back to his table of instruments. "I do not expect you to carry water for me, Jesse. You will do no man's bidding, I know. And yet, now, with the abundant riches of experience earned in the bitter crucible of a lost cause, you will serve my purposes, and the purposes of mankind, quite well." He looked over his shoulder, his eyes carrying a heavy weight. "And you will do it with joy in your heart Mister . . . President?"

Jesse was caught off guard, confused, and his frustration was mounting. "What're you shovin', doc?"

Carpathian turned back to a bright replacement arm on the table behind him, shrugging. "When the Confederacy rises again, it will be fighting these new enemies and a depleted Union. The continent will need a new leader. A position I do not covet, despite what you may think of me." He held up a syringe and flicked its thick needle with a graceful finger. "The possibility bears thinking on, I believe?"

Carpathian turned while Jesse was still trying to make sense of the words. The quick sting of the needle sinking into his neck was a nasty surprise, and he squawked out a curse as he tried to shy away. Almost immediately, the light in the room grew hazy and the bed began to sway gently beneath him. His suspicions and convictions began to melt away.

"Wha—" Jesse tried to form words, but the effort seemed too much in the pleasant haze descending upon him.

A door opened behind the outlaw chief and a massive man in dark leathers, strange metal serpents swaying behind his broad shoulders, loomed up into his vision. Jesse felt a welcoming smile wash over his face.

"Kyle . . ." Jesse could not remember what he wanted to tell Carpathian's surgical assistant.

"Rest now, Mister James." Carpathian leaned down over Jesse, his face cold. "We all have a lot of work to do, and time is growing short."

The words made no sense at all as he felt himself sinking deeper into a foggy world of warm thoughts and soft edges.

"Lucy—" He tried to say as he felt a vague but persistent tugging on his left shoulder.

The End

About the Author

Craig Gallant spends his hours teaching, gaming, podasting, being a family man and father. In his spare time he writes outlandish fiction to entertain and amaze people .

In addition to his position as co-host of the internationally not too shabby podcast – The D6 Generation, he has written for several gaming companies including Fantasy Flight, Spartan Games and of course Outlaw Minatures.

You can follow Craig's writing experience and other fun things at:

www.Mcnerdiganspub.com

Zmok Books – Action, Adventure and Imagination

Zmok Books offers science fiction and fantasy books in the classic tradition as well as the new and different takes on the genre.

Winged Hussar Publishing, LLC is the parent company of Zmok Publishing, focused on military history from ancient times to the modern day.

Follow all the latest news on Winged Hussar and Zmok Books at

www.wingedhussarpublishing.com

Look for the other books in this series

For all your fantasy, science fiction or history needs look
at the latest from Winged Hussar Publishing